NOVELS BY
MAUREEN McCOY

Walking after Midnight
Summertime

Summertime

A NOVEL BY

MAUREEN McCOY

POSEIDON PRESS
New York

Copyright © 1987 by Maureen McCoy
All rights reserved
including the right of reproduction
in whole or in part in any form

Published by Poseidon Press,
A Division of Simon & Schuster, Inc.
Simon & Schuster Building
Rockefeller Center
1230 Avenue of the Americas
New York, New York 10020

POSEIDON PRESS is a registered trademark of Simon & Schuster, Inc.

Designed by Irving Perkins Associates
Manufactured in the United States of America
1   3   5   7   9   10   8   6   4   2
Library of Congress Cataloging-in-Publication Data
McCoy, Maureen.
Summertime.

I. Title.
PS3563.C352S8   1987   813'.54   86-30314
ISBN: 0-671-62187-4

Excerpts from Summertime *appeared in* Shankpainter *25 and 26. The author gratefully acknowledges the support of The Fine Arts Work Center in Provincetown.*

ACKNOWLEDGMENTS

I would like to thank Patricia Capon for her buoyant spirit shared, her support, and her commitment to this book. I would also like to thank Stacy Schiff for the high bright energy she has brought to this book.

For Lula McCoy Love

CHAPTER 1

For the second time in a week the couple stood in church asking to be married. Now on Friday the Reverend Thomas Lyton could comply, praise be to Jesus. On Monday there had been a legal snag. "You need blood tests," he had said. "I'm sorry." The woman was quick to declare, "We're in perfect health." She tapped her wrist, pulse side up, with two long white fingers. And the minister, a usually unflappable counselor to his congregation, could have kicked himself for going tongue-tied and evasive. He fumbled in his pocket for a breath mint and peeled back the paper with care, offering the little roll to his visitors, who declined. He wished that the venereal exam could be waived for the prospective bride and groom, in their eighties. "It's for the record," he had said neutrally. "A law for quite some time." Mr. Hazen Batten and his future wife predated Social Security cards, world wars and mandatory drivers' licenses. The minister knew that Jessamine Morrow (having been Mrs. Lawrence Mitchell Morrow for sixty-three years) had attended the Methodist Church forever, first in rural Iowa back in the days when Methodists disapproved of dancing and the movies, and for decades here in Des Moines. Let a gum-chewing official, not her church, bring her up to date. "The courthouse will issue a license," he told her.

Now, for the second marriage attempt, the future Mrs. Hazen Batten withdrew the certificates from a stiff black pocketbook. The ceremony proceeded; the three people clustered in a side chapel which smelled of summer morning, slightly dewy. The future Mrs. Batten was trim in pink shirtwaist and complementary rouged cheeks. She arched an eyebrow and gazed beyond the minister, out of the church, far away from the present, he felt, but whether to past or future Reverend Lyton could not guess. He did not suggest that the couple remain standing for his blessing; they seemed to accept being seated as part of the luxury inherent in a late-life marriage. The bride-to-be fitted her pocketbook on her lap like a shield and looked neither left nor right. The old groom's body sloped to one side. Silver hair was slicked back over the ears. His eyes, made childishly round by his glasses, would not leave the minister's face. He could be deaf, reading lips, Reverend Lyton thought as he turned to the marriage litany. He began by invoking God's grace for a prosperous marriage. He cut out the word "long" rather than cause distress. He sounded the "till death do us part" with ringing finality. For once as he stood before a couple taking vows he knew the intent and outcome of the union, the truthfulness of a marriage. He swore that a bristled back scratcher was going haywire up his spine, attacking his scalp.

Afterward he followed the couple outside.

"We thank you," Mrs. Batten said.

"I thank *you*."

Mrs. Batten linked arms with her husband and pulled away from the minister. She was sure-footed and tastefully bejeweled. You would not expect her to be so old, the minister thought. Eighty-five. You would not want to imagine her wedding night, and he quickly invoked God's guidance lest he do so.

The two approached a boat of a car and Mrs. Batten waited, smiling now at that distant point again, while her husband opened the door for her. Then Hazen Batten made his way back to the driver's side. He gunned the engine alarmingly and jerked into gear, but immediately became a very slow driver inching from the curb. Mrs. Batten seemed to remember something. She turned to the minister and waved a white-gloved hand. She smiled and looked girlish, mischievous, daring. Marriage at her age, she knew, was a scandal no matter how you did it.

"Are you turning around, Hazen?" The car seemed to be nosing, then hesitating at an angle toward a pancake-house parking lot, not entirely in the drive, but off the road.

"Just trying to get her out of town, Jessamine. Now, don't you worry. We're going to get ourselves south."

Jessamine looked around to find the sun and south. The plastic covering of Hazen's car seat creaked when she shifted her weight. By design, there were specks of glitter embedded under the plastic. She expected that Hazen knew where they were going, all right. Hazen laughed and the car bucked itself back onto the road. Jessamine liked Hazen's laugh—deep and generous, with a wheeze at the end. At Hillcrest Retirement Center he had played a practical joke on her to get her attention: he plugged in a tree ornament that made bird-chirping sounds. When Jessamine cried, "There's a sparrow loose in here!" Hazen had laughed forever. Lawrence Mitchell Morrow had laughed for decades, Jessamine recalled. Bless his soul.

Hazen drove, and Jessamine held the map as if she were navigating, but this too she left to Hazen. Some late suburban and ramshackle acreages, a final (horrid) furniture warehouse fell away and they were traveling in the sweet July countryside. After the Hillcrest reception and presentation (his-and-hers towel set), after changing reluctantly out of the pink shirtwaist into her good pantsuit, Jessamine was Mrs. Hazen Batten, settled alongside her husband, who was gallantly driving to the southernmost tip of the state to fulfill her dream: returning to her girlhood home, finally, at leisure. They would have to drive for hours and hours, she expected.

The original Walnut Grove had been nothing more than a farm crossroads even in her day. Landmarks would be scarce; even the trees would have grown to unfamiliarity, but home would consist of a fragrance in the air and an understanding of the lay of the land, no matter what they had growing on it, Jessamine was convinced. She had spent a few girlhood years in LeRoy, a little town near Walnut Grove. She and Hazen would make LeRoy their destination, register at the good hotel and venture out by day. She was used to traveling only as far south as Minneola, twenty miles from Des Moines, her present home. She and Lawrence had begun their lives together in Minneola years ago. James Lawrence was born and raised there. But post-Depression hardship forced them to move to the city, to Des Moines. Then it had never seemed right to ask Lawrence to take her all the way down to Walnut Grove and LeRoy just for a look around. And after a time he hadn't known leisure at all. One evening five years ago he had lain down with no more than a sniffle, and died. He had not lived to see their own James Lawrence taken from this earth in midlife. But the trip with Hazen now made for the perfect event. Here he sat, driving her south. "Heck, Jessamine," he had said, "I know Iowa like the back of my hand. We're off!"

Row after row, fields and fields of corn reached golden to the sun and waved happily, just for Jessamine's inspection. She expected they waved due south and guided her home. The superhighway could not hold her attention. The bleatings of big trucks, and the sudden sound of gravel spraying the car as Hazen swerved on and off the shoulder, were minor obstacles to the glory of the ride. Jessamine compared her marriage to the road: it reached in both directions, for the moment taking her straight back to childhood, and, she hoped, leading onward until her death. Jessamine watched Hazen drive and imagined him as a dairy farmer commandeering milk wagons, hoisting heavy cans. He had put up his own home, too, and claimed never to have taken sick. He swore he had never swallowed a pill. She had her hunches: Hazen would be with her until the end.

Now Hazen was off the road on purpose, slowed, winding down a narrow ramp where bright-purple ditch weed grew along the shoulder.

"Got to wet the whistle," he said, pulling into a gasoline-and-quick-store combination affair, the name of which was frankly distasteful to her. "Buy, and Bye-Bye!" said the big red letters printed at a slant with streaks out the left side to show just how fast would be the buying. This was not the case with Hazen, though. Jessamine could see him walking up and down the three aisles many times, an amiable look put to the magazines and whatnot.

She rolled down her window. The wind must have shifted. A fragrance that made her feel she was burying her face in the sweetest green-pea patch engulfed her. Her mouth watered and she swallowed several times. She stretched her head clear out the window. Alfalfa. It had to be. In late afternoon, all sensation deepened and thickened in the simmering day. Sun would be sinking by the time they reached Walnut Grove, but to Jessamine it seemed they had all the time in the world. They were not of the "Buy, and Bye-Bye!" era or philosophy, and she looked with pride upon her new husband, who was still ambling within the store, now passing some huge refrigerator cases. Jessamine smelled the alfalfa and used the outside rearview mirror instead of her compact to repair herself. Mrs. Hazen Batten, she said, adjusting one red button earring.

"I got this kiddie drink, Jessamine," Hazen said, getting into the car. He smiled behind a large bottle of grape soda pop. "They're out of the real juice, I guess."

Hazen drank and then handed the bottle to Jessamine. "Fella says go east over to Weldon and you're straight on to LeRoy."

Hazen followed the instructions, and when he turned off the superhighway for good Jessamine felt a sense of homecoming stronger than ever. The sun was turning to fire and she had trouble staying put on the creaking seat. The spangles became luminous in the intense low light. For Hazen, the wide flatlands of the north would have the feel of home to them, but this was Jessamine's turf—these rolling hills and the much smaller farms. In her day, the folks around Walnut

Grove believed that any farm exceeding one hundred acres was a sign of greed.

The road curled around on itself, sometimes fooling Hazen, who barreled along ditches and fenceposts, getting the feel of this new surface. The sun dropped behind a high hill, making the outline of corn on sky a spiky stylized sort of picture. The horizon glowed pink. Way up to the heavens it spread, the color of a baby's cheek.

"Down here we say 'roasting ears,' " Jessamine remembered emphatically. "Not sweet corn or corn on the cob, Hazen."

She chuckled and Hazen chuckled, too. He could not help but drive in a randy sort of way. Years dropped like the sun behind the hills: Hazen Batten was honeymooning, escorting his bride on adventure.

They pulled into LeRoy, a town of few streetlights. Jessamine waved Hazen toward the Bancroft Hotel, a massive front of red brick and gargoyles, with a great tearoom which all travelers used to visit, right across from her uncle's old livery stable. And there was one of the terrible Buy, and Bye-Bye! stores instead.

"Gracious," Jessamine exclaimed. "The hotel is missing."

Hazen could have predicted this. Through the years he had continued to cruise the countryside, returning to remote and lovely spots he had known on milk routes and pleasure runs, yearly watching progress obliterate his past. He had hoped for Jessamine's sake that the old hotel would be there in its glory for their honeymoon, but he loved her perplexity and his own calm.

"Don't you worry," he told Jessamine. He took her hand in his and squeezed, feeling authority in the new wedding band and the moisture from the grape-soda bottle. The world was a vast, dark shape and he and Jessamine were alone together in this one patch of blazing electrical light. And, despite his high notions, Hazen's head drooped.

Jessamine could see that, though Hazen was trying to protect her from the harshness of change, they had to get settled quickly: he snored before she fully understood he had dozed off.

"Wait here, dear," she told her sleepy husband, and with her light walk, pantsuit jacket open casually, Jessamine entered a quick shop for the first time in her life. She gasped as the doorbell sang out, announcing the occasion.

"Oh," she said, and clasped her throat. A man stooped over paper coffee cup and loud magazine eyed her.

"We're looking for the hotel. LeRoy's hotel," she said.

He shook his head. "No hotel."

"No? There must be a hotel." She looked down the aisle. Not a thing in the store was sold unboxed, it seemed.

"Motel," the man said. "Go two mile on down the country road. Two mile, hang right at the sign. Magnolia Court."

Jessamine rehearsed the directions carefully. Outside, the cicadas had begun poking a thousand tiny screams into the night. Gently Jessamine woke Hazen to explain.

The Magnolia Court woman could have been the sister of the quick-store man, the way she gave Jessamine and Hazen the once-over with disgust: they were intrinsically dull newcomers. At one time everyone in these parts was related, of course, but Jessamine did not feel like inquiring after family trees for these two. Even if they were related, they *felt* like people she didn't want to know lived in LeRoy or Walnut Grove.

She was contemplating the family ties and economic connections of the old days (her grandfather Stanley's orchard thrown open to charity cases for a day of apple-picking, the aroma of fruit in the air) when the woman stepped back from unlocking the door. Hazen's arm slipped around Jessamine's waist and propelled her into the motel room. The rush of motion and a glimpse of the room's turquoise motif frightened Jessamine back to the present.

The honeymoon. A motel room.

Though she loved this man Hazen dearly, it was the hand of a stranger holding hers now as he helped her to a sitting position on the bed. A strange bed. She had never slept in a strange bed. She had taken a family bed to her marriage. Her *first* marriage, she had to say now.

The mottled pudginess of Hazen's fingers reminded Jessamine of good pork links on the countertop, thawing. His were gentle hands and though Hazen had nodded to sleep moments earlier, he was wide awake now, ceremonious; and without words exchanged he understood her sudden fluster. The sausage fingers worked to comfort her.

"You may use the bathroom, dear," he said. He stood back, holding Jessamine's hands, urging her to rise. She stood and nodded.

Jessamine did not look at herself once as she carefully stepped out of her pantsuit. She wondered instead if the aqua shower curtain with gold-thread glitter running through it was supposed to represent a water scene or modern art. There were no hangers in the bathroom and she couldn't go back out now. She wouldn't call to Hazen, so she folded the clothes (underthings tucked inside the jacket) on the back of the toilet. Now. She had never worn much green, but she next removed from her bag a light-green summer gown the color of spring and mint. Beige lace bordered the bodice. Jessamine tied the string belt securely through the waist. She looked down at the gown and her feet, still in knee-high fleshtone hosiery. She rolled the stockings down and off quickly and stuffed them into her jacket pocket. Once the matching bed jacket was draped over her shoulders, she acknowledged the mirror. Jessamine looked back at herself the same way as always, with the secret expression that apparently eluded the rest of the world. No matter how often she compared, say, the portrait done of her at age eight by the traveling Jewish photographer with her fiftieth-anniversary photo or with her look right this minute, she saw the same person, beyond hairstyle and the rest: the ageless spirit, she guessed; a young, unchanging Jessamine.

Yesterday she had dropped a letter to Alice Morrow through the "local" slot there in the post office foyer. Across town today her daughter-in-law would be sitting at her desk reading the wedding announcement, stopped in her work, the nature of which Jessamine could not satisfactorily explain to herself, knowing only that since the death of dear James Lawrence, Allie's job had seemed to take on career proportions. And the letter to granddaughter Carla that must travel many miles, past fields and towns, clear over to the Mississippi and deep into a woodland known to her only through tale-telling and photographs—this letter she had double-stamped and marked "Airmail" over the postal clerk's objection. She knew the letters would arrive simultaneously, as she wished.

"Mrs. Hazen Batten," she told the mirror and her family. She touched up her lipstick, then blotted it carefully. This might not be the right thing to do, but what was? Hazen— the man—should know best, she assured herself, and that imparted some confidence to her hesitant glance at the doorknob.

And Hazen did know. Quickly he had changed out of his traveling clothes. It wouldn't do to be caught, well, with his pants down. Generally women took their sweet time with fussing, but Jessamine was swift and sure in other ways and might suddenly burst from the bathroom. He couldn't hear much going on in there. He hurried into sky-blue cotton pajamas, still creased where the cardboard had wrapped them. He tied on a thin robe. What else? He moved quickly to see that the lamp with gold flowers on the shade worked. This meant he could turn off the overhead. He pulled back the spread and covers clumsily, then tried to smooth down the sheets. He sat on the bed, then stood up. He should be standing when she came through that door. There was no basin in this room, so he looked in the mirror and tried to press his hair to his head; he had forgotten about the existence of combs altogether. He pressed and pressed. And, doing this, he heard the bathroom door open. He nearly fell. He caught himself on the back of the one chair in the place, some sort of canvas slingback jobbie. His legs were goners. Could a heart attack start in the knees? Lopsidedly, holding the chair, he turned and saw Jessamine shrouded in beautiful, soothing light green. She shimmered in the low light he had arranged. Knowing that he had helped create this flattery, Hazen swelled with pride.

"You're a beauty," he said. "Why, yessir, Jessamine."

And Hazen's laugh, as quick and uneven-sounding as the gravel hitting the car whenever he had veered a bit on the shoulder, broke tension. There was no question at all but to glide straight into Hazen's big dairyman's arms. Soft robes and wishes cast the spell. In bed Hazen hugged Jessamine to him tightly. She could not distinguish between their heartbeats, and she took this as a sign that they had all the time in the world to think up and down their bodies and marvel in the sensation of feeling as one.

C H A P T E R   2

Alice Morrow opened her top drawer and pushed a pin into the little voodoo creature she'd fashioned from a peach look-alike sachet and a dented outsized dollhead. She willed it to absorb with grace emotions which might otherwise be spent on life beyond reason. She buttoned on her suit jacket, picked up her lunch bag and walked to the break room with surpassing dignity, but confession attacked her:

"My mother-in-law has eloped. She's eighty-five years old, gone. A honeymooner."

The news flew from her and burst upon the Craftique employees placidly munching away. All of them—mail clerks and secretary, the errand boy with his woodpecker hair who had flipped the wedding announcement onto her desk, and her assistant Gloria whose date last night had been one more disappointment—all of these people consumed by Friday potluck (a giant soda bottle at every station) suddenly stopped chewing.

Alice unbuttoned her jacket. Her nails tore at the lunch bag; now her free hand pressed at her hair, in a bun—a perfect doughnut, this chestnut bun, thanks to a tucked ornament resembling in kind and springiness a new sink scrubber.

She looked at Gloria—mouth agape, poised over finger food. Alice had meant to endure the day, then after work call Carla. She had meant to speak of calamity only to her daughter, for heaven's sake.

"How racy," Gloria decided. She appeared to hold her heart in place as she sighed the down-elevator sigh of women who hunt men. "There's hope for me!"

A cheer went up for a perfect Friday, the free-floating office malaise relieved by sexual innuendo.

"I would think," Alice said rather louder than usual, "that a person so far past the compulsory age of marriage would rejoice in the company of a good book, period. I certainly do."

"Shame on you, Alice," said Gloria. She was all puffed sleeves, thirty-nine and divorced, and would forever wear suntan hosiery. Alice suspected that Gloria disavowed books altogether in favor of endless happy-hour schemes. One time she had tricked Alice into meeting men by driving her to the new liquidation warehouse: after an hour at the grand opening Gloria declared herself famished and swore that the bar next door was practically a coffee shop.

Alice unwrapped her peanut-butter sandwich. Brown bread looked like sawdust. And why, these days, must seeds stud a person's bread? She popped a chewable calcium tablet, untwisted from waxed paper, into her mouth. At fifty-six she was determined to outfox osteoporosis.

Across the table Alice spied a young receptionist with a paperback winged across her chest. The book cover showed a mauve display of cleavage and ruffles, and the girl's bared teeth testified to the rigor of her romantic notions.

"That's a dismal book," Alice warned, leaning forward. "If you want to learn something go to Alfred Hitchcock. Count on good horror tales and humor. I credit the Charles Addams cartoon characters with educating my daughter."

"I watch *The Addams Family* reruns on Channel Eight, too, Mrs. Morrow. They're funny."

"Ha! His cartoon books came before TV."

The girl turned an earnest red. She removed the offending paperback.

Alice had held the title of buyer for years, since Craftique's early days. Dr. Alan Rand began it all by bagging sachets and hooking potholders in his basement as a relief from his dental patients, who with alarming frequency had taken to transforming themselves into snapping turtles and trick dogs. During a sensitive plaque-scraping operation a woman became a Venus'-flytrap, and thereafter Dr. Rand devoted himself full time to Craftique. Selling door to door, he was amazed to learn of the housewife's strength of fantasy and isolation. Mail order made him a mint. Dr. Rand eventually turned the business over to son-in-law Smith in favor of travel. Smith hired more family: the girls with paperbacks, the Glorias. Now Dr. Rand was considered a wealthy old flake who sent postcards from paradises that no one, save Alice, bothered about on the map.

Smoking instead of eating, Alice wished to take her own advice: prop the feet high and read something amusing in the Hitchcock spirit, a story about a wifely disappearance and the sudden enrichment of the farmer husband's chicken feed, rather than look down to her knee as she was doing right now —a small moon of self-containment, that knee. She might know how Jessamine could marry, for Pete's sake.

Opening that perfumed stationery at her desk, reading "He is your stepfather-in-law," had called to mind the most abrasive foreignness: a hillbilly family—a fractious bunch of loud peaked children with jam on their faces, quarreling strangers, blackguard cacophony. The ache she had denied every night on coming home from work, for years, unbuttoning jacket and swearing that the house itself was shrinking from James's illness, was torpedoing within her, launching upward. Volcanoes, Alice had read in the latest *Geographic*, are evidence of the earth's vital signs, deep mineral deposits a person is pleased to read about but has no desire to see.

She felt done with the man-woman thing, truly deep, deep bone-weary done. Widowed fifteen months earlier, she was content with cheese-sandwich dinners and she contemplated getting a dog. It riled her to see mauve books at work and desktops bordered in cheap studio photos. (No one had such cherry lips.) But blurting family business made her as public as all that. Jessamine! The chomping faces remained turned toward Alice even as the hands reached for pickles and marsh-mallow salad. She had spilled the beans in the break room; henceforth, women might come to her for chiropractic advice or to complain of husbands who snore.

Jessamine was no longer a Morrow! She had attached her-self to a Hazen Batten, two words which might just as easily signify a thistle as a husband.

A crockpot lid resumed clanging, a hurdy-gurdy drone.

"Married," Alice repeated, despite herself.

Gloria said, "I've read where love combats senility."

"Pooh!"

Let the world know that she, Alice Morrow, had no reason, desire or need to rush out her door lipsticked for, of all things, finding a man.

I have stocked every last successful dowel, sequin and spool of yarn, Alice reminded herself, once back in her cubicle of office. The beige punchboard walls were properly bare. From memory she recited: sequins, ten thousand to the pound; chif-fon, a hundred yards per bolt.

She flung her suit jacket over the back of her chair and mentally rolled her sleeves. As if by a supremely orchestrated conspiracy of printing presses and mail carriers, the first week of July had delivered just about every catalog in the country to Craftique, and here they were, a treasure hunt stacked on her desk and visitor's chair, swaybacked in her mail baskets too. The wedding announcement had momentarily obscured her delight.

Amass these catalogs, Alice believed, and distribute them

around the world to friends and enemies, to developing nations and dying monarchies and small oil empires, and everyone could get the clearest idea of what a day in America might
hold. Newspapers were not up to this job. The catalogs had
an archeological significance begging to be studied and preserved, a Vesuvian importance that no history book or magazine could render. Catalogs of all sizes, colors and themes
covered her desk. Alice proceeded willy-nilly, quickly flipping through the poor-taste newsprint one: "Breast buzzer,
ring 'nipple' for service." For Pete's sake! Then to something
glossy and fragrant; she enjoyed reading the fine print describing Hammacher Schlemmer's monstrous inflatable pool.
A fresh pack of cigarettes and black coffee would accompany
the mission to track and revolutionize beyond recognition—
meaning scale down to the Craftique customer's budget—
anything at all, save the HS pool ($4,000 plus) and even then
who could say but that, once alerted, Design might miniatur-
ize that very pool, create a replica conversation piece with
floating plastic flowers?

Gloria stopped by to pick up monthly receipts. Was there
no limit to the size of a plastic Coke bottle? Crooked in Gloria's elbow, this one resembled an explosive. Nothing bottled
in plastic could taste right. Half the population of America
had no memory of glass milk bottles, a grievousness a person
could do nothing about except smoke another cigarette.

The phone line lit up. Next door Gloria confided, "He was
a steak-and-mushroom man, no more, no less. But guess what
I've just heard? . . ." She would be lowering her plum-
smudged eyelids along with her voice to tell the story of an
octogenarian's wedding.

Alice could disconnect her or at least shout through the
wall, but a dazzling misstatement caught her eye. Beneath a
woven napkin holder shaped like a duck she read: "Napkin
Boat Centerpiece." She circled in red "Napkin" and "Boat."
Why no mention of duck? Why shape the thing like a duck,
then? "A duck is a duck," Alice said aloud, with surging
heart. Craftique customers supported the company on blind

faith; for a few dollars a year they received a monthly surprise knickknack to be assembled, and they ordered prodigiously from the catalog. They deserved clarity, and Alice would guarantee it.

Smith had joined Gloria. "I can't read this scrawl, honey. I've asked you to type your memos. Now, please." His voice blammed at the wall; it was one of those flat monotone voices, manufactured rather than inhabited, something perfected but dull; and suddenly Alice feared that the tortilla-making device she'd slotted for the next catalog would flop.

"Ha, Bill. You've been practicing your golf swing all morning."

"Oh, now, Gloria."

"T.G.I.F., Bill."

Fondue sets—the worst! A company might lose money simply printing the tired word "fondue." Alice thought of the time Jessamine had gathered them all to dip silly long forks speared with strawberries into hot chocolate. Jack Benny was on TV. Immediately thereafter, the gift set—forks and pot and recipe booklet—was put away, quickly forgotten. One could abandon fondue. A person should. Jessamine, hike the Grand Canyon or join up with charismatics, but remarry? Such headstrong action was the French Foreign Legion of Morrowness, a drastic remove. A person might mistake Jessamine for one of those Arizona transplants who go in for lizardy tans and culottes and ludicrous three-wheeled bicycles that simulate youth.

A person was much better off working instead of thinking along this line. Alice smoked.

Would Craftique customers go for a cacti terrarium with colored strata of sand? A crocheted Christmas tissue holder and matching toilet-seat cover? Padded sateen clothes hangers?

Just last year Craftique had finally offered Alice a business trip to California during which she was treated to more fish and fruit platters than she would care to remember; she was given a ticket to Disneyland and a day ride clear down to

Tijuana, where she purchased five leather bags helplessly. And a machete. Two months after James's death, at the huge buyers' fair in Orange County she had walked acres of indoor displays and sales. (So many battery-powered demonstrations!) An astonishingly large world of craft believers out there had welcomed her with pins and badges and slogans incorporating every conceivable kind of material. (*"Touché, plissé!"*) There she met the man who had grown rich off the poodle skirt, and a woman with a line of blouses devised by sewing dime-store strips of lace into gorgeousness. Smiling people spoke in exact terms: "raffia yarn," "decoupage" and "handwoven blond willow" defied the language of disease, panic, loneliness, hospital. The talk here was a kind of short-hand, an Esperanto that demystified the heart. She realized that even the well-dressed people from New York ran small loner operations; their poodle skirts and what-all had sprung from an eccentric, loner dream. Here were people like her who understood without having to speak of it that adulthood was a crucial fashioning from the materials at hand, and thank God for a touch of glitter and paste.

Was she to think now that there had been—was still, yet—some other way to be but poised, good-humored, alertly waiting?

She composed a firm list: spool tree (easy and colorful way to keep track of your thread, no tangling), marble-look sundial, and on a hunch she wrote "Mosaics."

"You're home sick from school?" Gloria's phone voice came across as stern now. "Open a can of soup and keep the burner low. Don't look away for a second, kiddo, not even if the phone rings. No! Absolutely no cookie-baking, do you hear?" Then, directed through the porous walls: "My luck, a sick kid."

When the woodpecker boy returned—"Camera work, Mrs. Morrow, the X-mass catalog, you know"—Alice seized upon the immediacy of task. She set to checking color layovers, running her fingers along the surface, finding the sharp edges of the floppy plastic. She poked a corner under her nail and let the whole operation beat there in her thumb.

Alice left work carting a three-legged stool and a box of spice jars, sample items sent to her which would otherwise be stashed in the company back room, forgotten. At five-four, she swung her legs from hips with an elasticity that gave her a taller person's stride; she possessed the ability to glide past even a six-footer if he was the type who put unfortunate knee-lifting or elbow work into his walk. The good-soled wedgies were guaranteed to get her to the early bus, home to fling off suit and collapse in bermudas.

She walked east along Locust Street with the stool steadily ripping at the bag; one leg, then two, poked through. The spice jars were shaking and she tried to knee them up toward a better grip. Stopping to adjust, she caught the tang of metal and grease coming from the automotive repair shops along this block. Doors were open on the day; tools pinged onto concrete, echoing, and men's voices sounded excited and far away as if they called from tunnels. They urged forth James, a very young James who had stood right on the spot where Alice now stopped and inhaled deeply the racket and memory.

She had been walking along here when James called, "Alice, come over here. Take a look!" Full-skirted, she had whirled about to find her husband completely absorbed, a slim sort of angel in his parachute-light clothing, watching mechanics. She was downtown on errands, a red envelope pocketbook in hand. She'd thought James was job-hunting, and seeing him at the automotive garage tripped her heart funny. An adjustment on the beetle-blue Dodge was required, he explained. She told him, "I'm ordering percale sheets," and hurried away. Sears' Catalog was just around the corner. A week later she came for the sheets and there he was again, so wondrously lured to what could be repaired that, she thought now, he might have known, deep down unconsciously, despite his flame hair and a merry laugh, that his blood was giving out, he was shattered. He stood as if apprenticing for magicianhood, in a gritty, coded kind of darkness beneath cars raised high on silver poles, and Alice had taken his hand. There at his side she wavered between doubt and a firm belief that war heroes must be granted the wide allowance Jessamine conferred on her son. He loved cars. She thought James wanted her to believe these cars would fly. Cars, housewifery, what mysteries!

Now the sky rose blue-violet behind her; ahead it lay still creamy with low rays firing the reflecting windows of the newer buildings—nuisance windows turned festive for this moment. How had it been arranged that such clashing, dramatic, celestial celebration commenced exactly as a person left work? Alice leaned back and looked high to see arced across the heavens a long flaking fish-cloud.

She jackknifed, elbow to hipbone, in order to grab the unruly bag. Now her lowered gaze met but could not comprehend nor deflect the onset of a fat runaway tire, a solid black careering amputee followed by a man in green who hunched like an ape, arms open still on what had escaped him. The tire charged from shop to sidewalk and paused to perform, as if on pointe, some fancy wobbles; it skidded and nearly fell flat, then bounced on the pavement one high free determined moment and gained a force and path straight on for her; it ran up her legs lightly, like a mouse—"Scoot!"—and trounced her feet, and with a spanking puppy-sound flopped on its side before her. It had jogged her bag, and here came the spice jars slipping, one, two, three, splintering glass at her feet. She stumbled, a foot forward into the tire's doughnut hole; the other lay under the thing. Her skirt was stretched to its limit and had ridden above her knees.

"Crazy thing drops clean off a car I've got jacked up," the man cried. He wiped his arm across his brow. "Here, cripes." He snatched the tire, dead nonchalant weight now, and bounced and bounced and bounced it as if punishing that tire.

"It's a tire possessed," Alice declared in order to think no such thing. She swatted at her skirt. Shaking his head, the man began wheeling the tire back to captivity.

"Hold on a sec, Alice," a voice called from nowhere. The man with the tire had vanished. Some knee-buckling trick echo insisted familiarly, "Alice, Alice, look over here."

Alice threw a narrow hexing glance into lavender space. Her heart did twosies. A long white car was drawing curbside. The loud voice was attached to that car.

"It's me. Mel from out at printing, Alice. Wait!"

Her shoulders relaxed, her legs straightened, though she felt jangled and white-knuckled as a person does after catching a child falling from a tree. In a fit of relief, a person is fleetingly tempted to break every bone in the child's body.

"I see you, Mel," she called. Recognizing a driver was never an easy task, though drivers imagined instant celebrity, as if a person could actually see through sun reflections and identify visor-sheared heads at traveling speed. But you *would* know them, or hurt their feelings. Here was Mel Gifford, recognizable now because his grinning face was thrust through open window, a man Alice knew mainly as a booming telephone voice from out at the printing plant: they called back and forth during catalog seasons, and twice a year, when proofs needed checking, Alice visited. Though Mel was grinning like old home week, he was not a person she would go out of her way to greet if she were to see him at the mall, sitting at the fountain the way men do.

Now he was busy with signals and steering. Some flick of switch transformed the car into a blinking oasis, and here he came, grinning. Her bag had been torn away and, as Mel approached, Alice found she was holding the stool, a little ringmaster's stool, with its three legs pointed at him.

"I've just been attacked by a tire."

"Quick. We'd better get you home."

Mel tossed the stool into his car without asking where she lived, or anything else. Already he was holding the passenger door, fending off traffic with a raised burly arm and a frown.

Hi-diddly-dee, then, Alice thought. She wrapped her skirt tight and got in. The perfect antidote to multiple upset was a ride home with a man suggestive of a nursery rhyme: Humpty-Dumpty. Mel was an upright Humpty, as were so many men her age.

It could be refreshing, a car ride, though acceptance of a ride entailed so much more than the bus: a person must be agreeable, even entertaining, should issues arise; she must not lead the conversation too boldly; it was doubtful she'd be encouraged to smoke; don't sing to a stranger's radio, for heaven's sake; and in the company of this man be sure to eagle-eye the street signs.

The strap across the chest was too severe, of course (whatever happened to all that air-bag talk?), but sitting in the deep velour seats could pass for recreation. Alice lifted her heels out of shoes and felt a tickle of air on her soles. Surely the Mels of the world drove this kind of car for the sheer pleasure of piloting and intruding themselves anywhere, anywhere they wished. A type of person had the urge to do this. Satisfied that Mel knew she was not of this type, Alice looked out from an extraordinarily cool, floaty place to the pedestrians and just this once allowed she championed a car ride.

"I live south. Over the bridges."

"South Side, right-o. You've got all the good Italian restaurants over there, half of them hidden away, aren't they?"

Having had to think so strenuously about men and women earlier left Alice with a lingering keenness of perception. She understood that Mel was not married.

"They don't have atmosphere." She looked straight ahead.

Mel eased up the first viaduct—it was only a short stretch over the warehouse district—then took a dip down. Maybe he would stop for gasoline there at the station between bridges. Milk? No, they were climbing again, now onto the second bridge. They crossed the river, high and chocolate brown, wild along the banks with weeds that grew to tree size, unchecked. Almost home. Railroad tracks ran alongside the river, and once in a great while, looking down from her hilly outpost to that darkness at night, Alice spied what she knew had to be a hobo camp, a pinpoint of light on the far riverbank that made her want to cheer.

"Say, Alice, you know that guy Tompkins who runs the four-color press by me? One day a few years back he takes a bus to the plant, steps right in front of it—plenty of witnesses

—and got a car bumper. Clipped him good and wrecked the
one leg. Well, it's funny. I thought of him when I saw that
tire rolling at you. There wasn't a thing you could do but
watch. From out of nowhere this tire comes on. You were
stuck like an animal caught in the glare, a rabbit or a doe on
the highway."

Alice fitted her feet to shoes. Sudden intimate speculation
was not to be encouraged. Humpty-Dumpty jolliness had
masked calculation. A person might have known. And it
seemed that the protection of a lifetime, of a married woman's
lifetime, had suddenly fallen away. Doe. No one had ever
offered her a ride home and compared her to a doe. It was
cruel, she thought, to be suddenly living "The Emperor's
New Clothes," feeling cloaked when the world apparently
sees wild game. I am recently widowed, she would tell anyone. Like a whip, she would tell them.

Just when the startled silence between them had nearly
bricked the air solid, Mel's little winged window sputtered
forth a warbling soprano. The man's hearty chuckle caused
Alice to turn quickly, and she laughed, too, at the amazing
fact of his hair. An even streak of light collected along the top
of Mel's head. The man was fifty at least, surely the last man
on earth to wear a flattop, a real old-fashioned, silvery flattop.
By wiggling the triangle window like an itchy nose, he stilled
the soprano. He held a lazy sun-in-the-eyes smile all the way
across the bridge, and Alice kept marveling at that hair. His
barber understood: no fuss. She touched her bun and smiled,
too.

Mel's arm was draping rather than gripping the steering
wheel when Alice advised, "Up this hill. Wakonda. I'm on
the right."

"Must be a heck of a roller-coaster ride in winter. I've got
to see this." Mel gunned the car and drove past Alice's to the
top of the hill. He managed to bob his head on a rather thick
neck, looking every which way while maneuvering the car.
He pointed it downhill and braked. "What a view. All we
need is the Italian restaurant, ha, ha."

"My husband loved this hill on sight," Alice said against Mel's slangy discovery of it. She felt she was calling above a roaring waterfall in order to be heard, in order to be Alice Morrow. *Recently* widowed. Down below, past six Monopoly houses, was the thirty years' view of a river so still and brown these days it scarcely burbled. It looked like earth, a path winding away to the left. Traffic ran both ways, following the river's curve, as did railroad tracks down along the water's edge; and though a steep embankment of foliage and saplings lay between the busy street and the river, from the top of Wakonda Hill it appeared that a car without brakes would have no choice but to plunge straight down to the river. Opossums and hoboes and rich after-rain aromas rose up from this river. Growth on the far bank gentled the light industry behind it, and the downtown skyline just beyond was a perfect cardboard cutout.

"In Sioux, 'Wakonda' means uncanny or sacred," Alice said. And proprietorship resides in knowledge, she thought, continuing, "A tornado will never touch down here, thanks to the river and a confluence upstream."

"Say," Mel said. "But don't you hate the way that cortan steel tower sticks out? I call it Big Rusty."

So, Mel recognized abomination. "Big Rusty" was a sheer reddish eyesore filled with insurance employees, towering over downtown horridly. Now that fish-cloud feathered above the rust monolith in gentle dissolution.

"I've imagined skiing down this hill," Alice said. "I'm originally from Minnesota."

"A daredevil," Mel boomed. He raised his eyebrows as a motorcycle blasted up the street and turned in across from her house.

"What have we here?"

"New neighbors. Motorcycle worshipers," Alice explained. "They're very quiet over there until it comes to the motorcycle." She considered a moment. "They'd want to be called bikers."

Dear Wakonda! Her throat closed right up on the thrill of

being home. Look at the show: Big Rusty, the eternal river, and a ribbon of bright cars winding at the foot of Wakonda; now spangled helmets orbited on a girl's arm. Wakonda was thick with oak, hidden away, secreting an extravagant view and mum elegance. Dogcatchers had never discovered Wakonda, and taxi drivers searched in vain. Overhead, clouds frilled the sky, and here sat a man with a flattop. Dear Wakonda, dear cartoon panorama.

"Yes," Alice exclaimed, froggy in the throat. We need ice-cream cones, she thought; but when she turned to Mel her body made a jumping-bean motion and she gasped back an "Excuse me." A cigarette was what she needed. A cigarette and peace.

Mel coasted down Wakonda, feet off the pedals until the last moment, then he braked and ground into her drive; all the while Alice stared peripherally at his feet. Driving was an odd, incapacitated action she could not match up with the turn of key and roar of engine. She swung her legs free of the car.

Mel was already out, twirling the stool. "I'll give you a hand."

How silly, she meant for him to read in her smile, but he had turned from her, was taking the steps up into her yard two at a time; his car posed like a white confection in the usually bare driveway. She watched Mel's back. He was a big man dressed in some sort of one-piece thing, a cotton flight suit or something for attendants, a costume ideal for running presses, she supposed. (Stiff cotton, a person should add: he rustled as he walked.) Alice wondered shrewdly if, in Gloria's terms, Mel thought he was "meeting someone." He wore canvas shoes and did not lumber as a person thought he might. But for heaven's sake. Alice marched as no doe could march and cut him off at the door.

"What a help you are."

Her most loyal—bold, hungry—squirrel ran along the embankment wall and stopped before her. He raised up on his haunches. "Honey, I'll feed you later," Alice called.

"I'll be darned." Mel broke into a grin and the squirrel froze as a pelt.

"Goodbye! Thanks!" Alice barked to dispel whatever new Bambi images he might be hatching.

But Mel did not move. He beat lightly on his chest. "Whew. What a scorcher. I could use a drink of water."

Alice checked her bun and burned past the man, knowing positively that he wanted company. Water—neutral, lifesaving water. What cunning, to ask for water.

The porch opened into the kitchen, so Mel could stand right there the way paper boys had done every collection day for thirty years.

"You're a plant lover, Alice." Mel was all agog drinking the water, straining, swiveling, spying, inching, now bulldozing his way into her house. He drew back and gave her fruit-bowl needlepoint a long look. "Dark wood paneling. It's great."

Alice exhaled through the nose, but he took no notice.

"What? Mint grown into a bush." Mel set down his empty glass lest it impede his rambles: he took the dining room at a trot, pinched a leaf, and still Alice continued to stand by the sink holding her handbag to her as a time-to-leave signal. Any alert person would attend to it.

Mel broke the leaf and put it to his tongue; his eyebrows raised. "The taste of mint is heaven."

His voice ricocheted off the glossy wood walls and surely disturbed the very plants he claimed to admire. He was a large person, the largest person who had ever been in here, and Alice didn't know what might be wilted by that voice.

"I'll be getting along here." Mel dug for his keys and had to absolutely scrutinize them as he spoke. "I'm wondering . . . I know your husband passed on a while back." He looked at Alice directly. "Do you date?"

Shows, rhymes, cartoon panoramas blacked out. Of course it would come to this, all the hardy-har talk would lead to this very question. Meaning *the cheek!* Alice cried, "I'm bushed. My mother-in-law eloped today."

"Oh, well, now." Mel chuckled and rubbed his chin the

way men without beards do, and he slid her a non-Humpty look.

"I enjoyed the ride, but . . ."

"Plants, plants," Mel exclaimed. "I've got quite an acreage. You'd like it. I'll have you out to the place and fix dinner sometime. I'm in the same boat—a widower. Let's see here."

He looked to the telephone in the nook, a black desk model as old and novel as his flattop, while whipping a pen and pad from shirt pocket, and Alice was disarmed to see that his tiny pad of paper was the children's sort, rainbow newsprint sectioned by colors. He palmed it and on lime green wrote her number.

"I'm one of the few true soybean farmers around, Alice. That's not to say I'm a farmer who plants soybeans. Whole different worlds, you know."

"I'd imagine."

"You can read about it in *East-West*. Or do you see *The New Yorker?*"

"I take *National Geographic*."

The culprit phone began ringing, too gaily for Alice, as if showing off to Mel, who, thinking it in league with him, raised his semaphore eyebrows and took his leave.

CHAPTER 3

*T*he summer had turned upside down already, Carla thought, dialing her mother. The Jerusalem artichokes, which she did not tend, had grown into big-fisted guardian tubers long before a single Burpee squash blossomed. This was the most vivid wild-strawberry season in memory; out in the woods, hollows of berries could be mistaken for sunlight, a deer, or fire. And flies passed overhead in determined formations that never landed. Evenings she was rooted to Brian's telescope, tracking stars in a high black sky. Swooned by pine fragrance in that thick bug-free air, she sighted and imagined the dense weight of a planet, its perfect suspension; she saw Saturn's rings not as adornment to the planet, but as something mad and separate, spinning indistinctly, unforgiving and lonely. Carla reminded herself that heavenly contemplation served as an antidote: at thirty-four she fought emotions as wacky as a dream. Lately, she grew touchy in a flash, and these soaring, yearning seizures tended to displace ordinary emotion. No sooner would mournfulness be dispensed with than a carnival opposition took hold: little urges to be the sequined circus lady balancing tippytoed on a huge silver ball derailed her in the kitchen, and, exultant, she might forget, for once, fierce tiny trials such as how terrible she looked in hats. Washing up after berry-picking today she had admired her golden cheeks under the straw skimmer without remarking the balloon look that had dogged her since babyhood. And so antic was her energy, Carla had vowed to forgo honey in the tea; she had to do what she could to balance atop a shifting silvery motion. She had set down her berry pail and looked at her letters. Surely everything, especially the burst of wild growth, pointed to a psychic empathy with Grandma Morrow.

Her mother caught the phone on its third ring but sounded out of breath.

"Mother! Grandma Morrow has written to say she's married—as of today!"

" 'Eloped' is the proper term when it's utter shock. Imagine getting the news at work, yes, by letter," Alice said.

"But she must have hinted. Have we suspected something? Think."

Carla paused when her party line intruded with TV noise and throat-clearing on the line, but Alice threatened immediately, "We're paying. This is long distance." Alice was smoking, of course, and her words burst apart like pussywillows brought indoors. Puffs of something once solid flew everywhere.

"Party lines are ridiculous," Alice said.

"She's married!" said Carla. "I guess Morrows can't help being in the vanguard." She felt pleased but slightly perturbed, too, to know that no action whatsoever had been required of her to bring forth the extraordinary. She scratched the sweaty crease behind her knee and reminded herself that, of course, she had personally planned against any such requirement, but this news was just screwy enough to make her clench her toes, long bony perfect copies of her father's. No one cares, she thought, when the youngest generation goes bold, off the nut. Older people are covered by their natural tendency to rail and reminisce; it kicks into action and, really, they vent a runner's relief along with their spleen. But when the oldest goes wild? Everyone else might feel fooled and frumpy; and she did, just a titch.

"That earnest twang in your voice," Alice objected, but Carla plunged on:

"Daddy was the original househusband. And now his mother is the oldest of brides. We're always interesting. We act like we're normal, but we're extreme."

"Please!"

"My grandmother is a honeymooner."

"Please!"

Carla looked out the window past the clearing into pine forest and yearned to flash the romance news to her husband, Brian, this minute. A demand for their own best behavior was built into the news. Now a wee chest-flutter threw her off balance—the feeling of air travel—as she listened to Alice's quick cigarette sucks; she hated the "deplaning" sluggishness, rising to find herself rumpled and small no matter which clothes she had chosen to wear, and always the attendants looked above her head to engage the next passenger: Goodbye! Enjoy your stay! Reason enough not to travel so far that you needed a plane.

"An old woman is still a woman, Mother," Carla said gently.

"She's Mrs. Hazen Batten." Alice's voice came through the receiver dispersed to pebbles. Then an amending cough. With the receiver clamped to her shoulder, Carla was making a tiny braid of the wiry dark hair at her temple. She would not fasten the ends but let the thickness of hair hold itself in place, braids becoming little firecrackers all over her head. Then she'd comb it free with her fingers. Thirty-four, still no gray. If cigarettes killed her mother, she'd be an orphan.

"But eloping," Alice said. "She's broken rules we don't even have. I'm just surprised, that's all. We're very surprised."

"I'm sure she thought it improper to involve us, Mother. She couldn't afford to hear shock or doubt. First she had to decide that Daddy would have approved."

"He's not here to decide anything."

Subject closed. But her father had liked the odd event. Carla remembered the afternoon their neighbor Calvin came over sporting molded caramel-colored cowboy boots. "I've joined the sheriff's posse," Calvin said, interrupting James's plumping of a salmon loaf. Carla at thirteen was squirting on extra Worchestershire sauce. "Posse? What does it mean?" Her father's green eyes jeweled on the word and Calvin's toe-tapping. "We'll ride horses in formation at parades, Jim, and, if called to it, fan out on command through a field, conduct a manhunt. You know," Calvin said, addressing Carla then, "that's how lawmen caught some of the Barrow Gang outside of town here, years back. Bonnie and Clyde got away, but they bagged the brother." Calvin talked like the man who had come to school to promote auto safety by way of gore slides. He took a long time exiting in the new stiff boots, the salmon loaf went into the oven and Carla and her father whooped through the house, saying "Posse" and "Giddyup" and slapping their thighs. "In a town of two hundred thousand," James marveled, "they've got a sheriff's posse? What safety!"

But Grandma Morrow's eloping was a different story; no one among them liked a truly personal surprise.

Alice exhaled through her nose—her one dragonlike quality: a mother who, for better or worse, would not elope. "I suppose it's not our business—insofar as public pronouncements are no one's business. Public pronouncements deflect questions."

"I think," Carla decided, her head a rushing sandstorm, "it is our business to learn how the spirit breaks loose."

"New Age babble!" And her mother launched into a totally unrelated instance of what she called the "herd instinct," random physical intrusiveness wrought upon her: "Some poor soul at the bus stop this morning stood within an inch of me and wouldn't stop talking. I was tempted to say, 'This isn't Tokyo.' She began her life history with the news that she makes weekly payments on a stove."

Though talk was crisp and endless among them, Carla saw the Morrows as being in possession of one overriding cultivation, the ability to live in the fragile condition of permanent inhalation: they lifted teacups to lips with alarming steadiness, meanwhile someone died. Year after year, for half her lifetime, they had been given to understand that her father would die soon, and finally he had succumbed last year to a leukemia strain known for its insidiousness and caprice. After every postponement—doctors urging them to thank remission and their lucky stars ("Relax a bit now!")—the Morrow women filed from huddle soberly. Rather than don pink satins and break out the sherry, they would fortify their waiting postures: Grandma Morrow dusted her antiques; Alice the packrat heaped trinkets upon her house and peered out, smoking. And, once married, Carla likened herself to the leftover Japanese soldiers her father told stories of, men eternally in hiding: removed to the woods, she took a binocular view of home, disbelieving that the supreme war could end.

". . . and," Alice finished, "of course the poor soul sat right by the bus driver and began her wretched stove story all over again. Honestly! But, honey, here's one for you—what do you make of a man who calls himself a soybean farmer? 'I'm not just a farmer who plants the beans,' he says, cheeks working like bellows. A large man, you'd know."

"Great. Given a chance, soybeans will take over the world. Who is he, Mother?"

"No one, of course. Goodbye."

Carla beat on her oak table while laughing out the window to silent surrounding woodland, and chickadees flew up

startled from the feeder as yellow bursts of light. She wore
shorts and drew her one knee to her chin, pasting calf to
thigh.

The acrid commingling aromas of fresh zucchini bread and
simmering pinto beans filled her kitchen. She looked to the
shelves of institutional-sized glass jars: split peas, millet; oh,
the pinto beans she had carelessly returned out of order, next
to kidney. Black beans would contrast remarkably with millet. Let the pintos follow sushi rice, next to tomato pasta.
Every jar sparkled and was at least half filled. With a quick
application of scissors Carla denuded her windowsill chives
and threw them into the beanpot.

Before her on the table lay the day's mail: a contribution to
Group Against Smoke Pollution would be sent, as would a
card to her state senator urging action against the Army Corps
of Engineers; they had muddied the Mississippi in the first
place, and their continued fiddling threatened more harm. A
measure of wrath would go to the *Nonpareil* in Tillman for
suggesting a sexist Father's Day flower box ("lacquer with
ship pictures for a man's office"). The coupons offering
money-back guarantees were for maple syrup and herbal
salve. She had typed out a summer hint for Heloise: "Rubbing
jalapeño on chigger bites brings the swiftest relief." And resting on top of the pile lay Grandma Morrow's pure-white wedding announcement: "Excuse the plain notepaper, my stationery is being changed. . . . We've gone away for a few
days. . . . My dear, please call him Hazen. . . . Bushels of
love!"

From the stand of pines Carla strained to draw forth a
vision of how it was so, Grandma Morrow's wedding day. ("I
love a parade," her father had sung, laughing and tugging at
his nose long after Calvin's boots had retreated.)

This morning Jessamine Morrow would have descended by
elevator for breakfast, exuding an air of unswerving destination, a thick perfume. You would have seen her pause and
smile over the top of everyone's head, dreaming dreams of
girlhood and outrage, and she undoubtedly carried her break-

fast tray right past Hazen Batten without so much as a nod; it
was the least an imminent bride could do. Once back in her
rooms, she sat for a moment feeling fluttery with anticipation
of their being filled with a man and his astringent-smelling
things. She looked around the front room, to the china
cabinet, the ancestor ovals, chairs and tables all caned, claw-
footed, cushioned in velvet or needlepoint, polished black-
brown furniture that might have grown from the floor, so
absolute and wide-legged were its poses. She would be gone
for days, and so, with television on to the morning talk show,
she dusted, Carla was certain. In the 1980s, on her wedding
day, she wore high heels and dusted.

Had she bought a trousseau? An abbreviated version, Carla
decided, smelling the sweet mixture of sachet—a Craftique
perennial—laid atop soft clingy garments. Tucked into corners you'd be sure to find vinyl galoshes and bedroom slippers
curled like snails.

Jessamine Morrow and her Hazen Batten had gone off to
marry (where?!) and returned to Hillcrest briefly for well-
wishing. Right now you'd find leftover tea cakes and punch
which no one wanted to remove from the buffet table, hours
after Jessamine Morrow rode out of town under a plump rosy
sky. Away she went, garnering permission from the very aspect of this planet.

Oh, what—I'm crying, Carla realized. She pushed aside
the wedding announcement, so tears fell instead on Heloise's
note. "Chigger bites!" she scolded aloud. And whereas
Grandma Morrow's life had unfurled in color and fragrance
and a blessed rhythm of propulsion, her own was reflected in
the post-holiday look the woods had taken on. There was no
one yelling, "Giddyup." Against a lessening sun she saw
lumps, shrouds, things on hold, her dimmed and distanced
epistolary province. As I have wished, she admitted. Which
is old-ladyish in the doomed, noneccentric sense.

It was a character flaw evidently, aggravated by the Morrow wisdom: the less you do, the safer you are, and safety
counts terribly, therefore change into good cotton pajamas as

soon after dinner as possible, read something absurd, and be asleep by ten in a house of decorations.

Once as a child she had been made to wear her good cotton pajamas publicly. The family detoured to Kiddyland Park from a drive-in movie theater washed out by a hard rain. And even though she'd chosen the most conservative (she thought grown-up) ride, a VW microbus that taxied around a small asphalt circle, she had looked out to the fuzzed neon that flattened the sky, then down to her teddy-bear flannel, and thought they'd all better get home.

Sometimes she wished to hurry up and be truly old, experience a time when nothing would happen, but of course things happened. Look at Grandma Morrow.

Carla looked keenly at herself in the kitchen mirror. The pintos were cooked. She rinsed them. She brought butter from the refrigerator to soften for dinner. She rubbed her elbows. Reshelving the pinto beans brought no pleasure, and her kitchen was spotless otherwise. Before the mirror Carla unbuttoned her blouse. Her breasts were white scallops against a tan throat, no cooler for the exposure. She lifted them. The nipples hardened. They wanted to be kissed to a deep tickling soreness.

Brian's truck announced itself with the high screech, bass groans and tin hollow kicks of a one-man band. When he walked in whooshing Mississippi River air through the yellow kitchen, his monotone, "Hi, honey," charged an agitated Carla with dark raucous tenderness. Holy, how holy was the mundane, how invisibly anchored Brian was, walking with a spring that charged up through his body and even shook his curls. She loved watching him peel a sweaty tee shirt off, innocent of cataclysm. As he untied his boots one-handedly and kicked them to a corner, she ached from the trust expended and did not bother to check her inner voice against an inherited penchant for lumping life into rhymes and cartoon ghoulishness—Alice's legacy.

"Home again, home again, jig, jig, jig," she sang. "Brian, my grandmother has run off with a man. Eloped!"

He snapped a bandana from his face.

"With a man from Hillcrest."

"But that's great, honey. Let's hope they make it to Reno."

She hugged Brian at the waist and smelled the river that employed him. In Mark Twain fashion, he directed traffic at Lock Number Nine, his job being the raising and lowering of the water level, presto, as conditions demanded. In the beginning he had demonstrated the system for passing barges and pleasure-boaters on downriver, but, even as she watched, Carla had preferred to imagine a Godlike petulance dropping the *Delta Queen* in a free fall to shallows, all the passengers shouting, "Whee!" as on a carnival ride; a great tunnel of love naughtily raising summer skirts and all the women on deck extravagantly posed as upended umbrellas.

Something sharp in Brian's shirt jabbed her heart. He had been gathering river data and now withdrew from his pocket a little calculator.

Carla moved into the living room and flounced onto the couch she had measured and sawed and bolted together all by herself. Jessamine Morrow had lived to her eighties simply dusting figurines; she had not joined furniture and had never occasioned her hands to look spotty with walnut stain, as Carla's did. Everything in the room was textured and earth-toned, a bore, bore, bore, Carla was alarmed to hear in the tattoo of palm against fabric.

"This is a beautiful couch," she said, thumping it harder.

Brian peered in from the kitchen. He had learned to ask, "How do you really feel?" but, being unsure of his timing, he resumed drinking apple juice from the bottle, raising and lowering it snoutishly, with his shirt off. He had a buttery smooth chest, and up from the pants came a perfect pine tree of hair that stopped right at the belly-button star. His wavy gold-brown hair was thick beyond belief. It haloed his head. She had understood from the start he would never go bald.

"I've been thinking," he said, "why don't we go ahead and buy that south twenty acres now? I hear someone's been asking after it. We'd be sick if they built right up against us."

Brian's river-cadence voice flowed assuredly in calculation.

That pine-tree hair tattoo, so familiar, so a part of him, never-theless stood out in relief against his otherwise smooth front.

Carla looked at the woodstove, clean and ornamental in early July. An idea of adventure made a tick in her left cheek, but what could you do really startling with someone you'd been married to forever—buy great moats of land? It seemed impossible to go speeding into the night singing Frankie Valli falsettos, roving over Iowa blindly enchanted. When you've been married ten years the very sight of your husband's hands on the steering wheel could set off fifty frayed emotions. And, oh, could Brian drive a truck! Steady and sure and one-handed, tonight he would drive her into the pine-walled dark, away down the dirt road; they'd rattle past the Little Dipper, a shacky tavern whose neon shot away like a star, and they'd ride in silence with Brian's fiddle resting between them like a baby, speed on down the road to Community Hall, ablaze and beckoning them to the contra dance. On a breezy night the long curtains whisked and billowed through open win-dows suggesting a peek-a-boo good time; dancing might bring the whole world to you. A grave amateur, Brian would put mathematics and jiggling kneebones to his fiddle-playing on stage while Carla, band widow, swished her long skirt among friends and pleaded, "I need a partner!" Just as the caller yelled, "Line up for Dip and Dive," someone would come forward. She especially desired a man who could spin her, one arm firm under her breast and, oh, that was the part she loved, the tango of contra, when she had to yell, "Don't let go!" and the room whirled out of focus; they arched their bodies away from each other and somehow it worked like that. If you kept your right foot planted against the other's, toed off over and over with the left, held fast, pulled away from each other in earnest, the force of gravity powerfully balanced you for that one hot moment. And she could see to the souls of her friends. Having skinny-dipped with the lot of them, she knew the droop and scars and moles, sorrows of relationships; and she could even talk to Melanie Green with only the tiniest bit of squeamishness as she nursed her baby on the sidelines. Practice was everything. Women in flat shoes and cotton skirts practiced the contra, and their men in boots became gallants. Just as living by the seasons promised order. Over and over, with practice what you earned after so many seasons' passage was a tame knowable future.

But Jessamine, peeking in on the contra dancing, might shake her head at the past itself and say to her Hazen Batten, "I expect we should drive on down the road."

Jessamine Morrow had chrysalised overnight: she was a monarch butterfly. And a thought fleet and startling as the season's first monarch sighting came to Carla: in her boldness Grandma Morrow had set down the teacup and exhaled. She had released the tight, hard death-watching Morrowness still in effect, and set them all spinning. The presence of her brashness felt like steaming your face too close to the pot too suddenly. You gasped and swore and reared back, but an unguarded corner of the heart was warmed to ask how? Will this make me better? You took the steam, hoping.

"Honey," Brian said. "We could manage a bank loan. So, why not?"

She paced. Her legs, forever white deflectors of the sun, had never looked so solid. Outside, the forest, even after dark with the Archer's belt slanting down on them from a miraculous sky, was not the right kind of boldness required now. At this instant, you could bet that the Little Dipper was alive with low lights and golden drinks, big stretchpanted womanly hips jouncing to wild beats on men's laps. People there wanted surprise; they ripped and roared for something in the spirit of scandal. They would whoop to know of a grandmother bride. Carla slapped her foot on the kitchen floor.

"I don't want to think about loans. I want to dance at the Little Dipper."

For a moment, Brian's tufted head and still-straight body suggested the loneliness of a deciduous tree fleeced by winter, standing among pines, gracefully stiffened against a chinook wind, but no, he was Brian, flushed suddenly, compassionate even in the quiver of nostrils, priestly gentle as a husband, asking, "What?"

"It's just an idea!" And the limit of her idea of daring was what appalled her into silence.

Brian stared at her like a stranger, like a man you would read of in Ann Landers, who, having just trudged home from work, dulled and hungry as always, deep in figuring acres and loans, is greeted at the door by his wife fiercely out of her mind in a black negligee. He didn't know she owned one. I didn't until this afternoon! she cries. (There'd been a sort of Tupperware underwear party down the street.) Jesus, God, he thinks with shy horror, what is she trying?

"You're staring at me," Carla said.

She turned a hot face to the cranberry juice and zucchini bread she had already packed for contra dancing; and she touched her hot breast.

In the southern part of the state, heading into Missouri and its inklings of Ozark jungle, they'd be gathering salads every night and getting out the canning jars for green-tomato pickle. And despite the strawberry-wild summer, Carla's garden managed little so far: a whiskered row of new carrot tops; baby squash vine and lettuce still bite-sized for rabbits. Eggplant remained nonexistent, but she saw hope on the snap-bean trellis.

Saturday morning she knelt on a spongy little contrivance Alice had sent her, and troweled along rows; she tweaked a weed between canvas thumb and fingers of her work gloves, and pulled. She did not feel the sun raising itself high, directly overhead. By habit, she was oiled with Cutter's. Her head was shaded by the straw skimmer, and she'd brought out the jar of natural bug deterrent in which cayenne pepper figured as a key ingredient. When she was done weeding she would sprinkle the garden red. A certain weed, a prickler, worked loose, but as she drew it up and away from the ground a web of roots revealed itself as holding firmly. She broke loose what she could; with enough rain and steamy sun the ground would

push a new prickler to the surface by next week. Her job was
vigilance, not victory; and the miracle of the garden was that
things to eat grew out of the ground just as determinedly as
pricklers.

Sweat had begun to sting the corners of her eyes. She
daubed water from her jug onto a bandana and wiped. This
was the kind of weather that prompted her mother, who had
traveled nowhere since descending from Minnesota for college
decades earlier—got married and stayed—to declare, "Nothing is hotter than Iowa. We are record-breaking." As the TV
weatherwoman pointed out the humidity, 98 percent, and the
temperature, 95 degrees, Alice would triumph with her self-
styled sociological exposés, jetting smoke. "Dry heat doesn't
count," she'd say of a 110-degree Las Vegas reading. And,
"The South can't blame any of their problems on climate.
They're no hotter than us and someone should tell them to
cut out the nonsense." Meaning fried foods, drawls, their
particular rituals. "And these people I work with," Alice
would get around to saying, "the stupes dress in polyester and
never know what's hit them, why they suffocate if they step
outside. Then off they go, dying, to their catfish fries!"
("Scavengers," was her epithet for all fish native to Iowa.)
Alice's superior—insider—geographical knowledge somehow
offered justification for her life in Iowa and an imagined access
to transience which until now Carla had never known one
Morrow to possess.

Across the yard Brian was leaning under his truck hood
which resembled the jaws of a movie shark poised to devour
the innocent. You would expect the organ music to strike a
lingering dissonant chord.

"It's hot," she called, just to see him raise up. Rescued, he
waved his wrench, but went right back down.

Last night's dance had ended with an arrhythmic stomping
of her slippered feet, and Carla had needed to gulp juice as if
a flood of natural sugar would wash the agitation from her.
Brian, happy with having put wit and industry to a new tune,
"Pigeons on the Gate," rode home whistling it.

Carla jammed trowel into ground. Really, Brian looked un-steady, disappointingly so, though he didn't waver. She was seeing something behind her eyes. She wondered if she was falling from the grace of accepting vast moments of love as dullish routine.

"Making progress?" she called.

His head bobbed so slightly this could not be considered a rescue.

Briefly, before meeting him at college, before her epistolary self surfaced, Carla had ventured into action, what she thought her father would call (and approve of if he could understand the daring it took) the front lines. She had marched and chanted and leafleted. For two weeks she even chose to eat free-kitchen gruel over dormitory meals while camping out to protest the school's planned razing of an ornate Spanish-tiled philosophy building. Where a science lab was planned, Trotsky was reputed to have taken shade on a hot summer's day long ago. Carla had missed the Kent State upheavels by two years, but the protest mood lingered and the older students rushed to rekindle what they might: science labs were declared the enemy; flyers saying so papered every surface and were sucked like masks against the high box-elder limbs. This was a small liberal-arts college in northeast Iowa, affixed congenially to its small town for one hundred years. Rock musicians and baby orators began performing at all hours on the tent-city "liberated" campus green. An offshoot protest to legalize marijuana resulted in Carla's falling in with marchers, circling the town square for hours, urged on by a bullhorn-wielding hippie in the band shelter. That evening she was horrified to glimpse herself on the city news, scowling and waving a Tootsie Pop in the name of legal dope. It's true, she realized, the camera adds ten pounds.

She bought a slimming black raincoat, and in the familiar Morrow manner excused herself permanently from what seemed to be a giant messy gym class. She hurried inside. There sat Brian, feet up, stolidly at work on the historic-preservation project. His bold charts papered the walls, and

he spoke convincingly on the phone. "Mandate," he said
often. His hair crackled, bushy as any head of hair belonging
to the older, real radicals (jailed or fugitive by then); he wore
wingtips without socks, and other students copied him. His
sweeping reference to "our activism" flattered Carla, who had
retreated.

She believed they fell in love as the wrecking ball slammed
into and fissured the north stucco wall of the doomed Spanish
building. She confided to Brian, "It's awful. No matter where
you are, something is ready to destruct!" "You've got to live
in the right place," he answered easily. "That's why we never
make plans," she continued, coming the closest ever to dis-
cussing her family situation. The ball struck again and now
Carla stood with her back to it, snuggled against a man's
flannel shirt. Brian's chin dug into her crown; he looked
straight ahead and pressed their bodies together. Brian was
the first person she knew of to place a razor blade within a
pyramid structure and dare it to rust.

What relief and exhilaration she felt on being removed,
political conscience intact, to a perfect epistolary stance: the
woods. What a long way to have come from Alice's ominous
breakfast ritual: serving cereal from those little variety packs,
milk poured directly into the foil-lined boxes. (And why not?
Alice would have demanded, if you questioned her. Why
make a futureless family endure the humiliation of economy-
size Cheerios?)

At rest on the spongy little Craftique garden kneeler, Carla
thought of what a long way she had traveled, from Cheerios
to stockpiling pastas and legumes so beautifully and econom-
ically. Yet, it was as if she had broken some householding
pact by marrying and moving. Her parents, especially her
father, had managed to imbue her with the sense that, really,
their generation was the last of a certain fundamental adulthood; they had really taken care of the world, and you
shouldn't worry yourself or strive too much now. Carla,
they'd named her, emblematic of the times. Bright as candy.
At least they hadn't named her Candy.

She patted smooth dirt over a weed hole. For weeding, you had to be regular, methodical, set aside a portion of the day to approach the garden with humor, otherwise risk obsession or neglect. Weeding suited her. She jiggled the fringe of a carrot top and pulled free a tiny carrot. She ate it powdered with dirt. Sweet baby carrots. You needed that dusting of dirt on it to eat a baby carrot properly. She ate another carrot and continued to watch Brian, his slope of back, the truck's Jaws-mouth still hinged indecisively.

A flame of bile convulsed her and burped out raw and stinging. She jumped up, covered her mouth and tore across the yard to the outhouse, and just in time. She vomited into the black hole that seemed to drop to China; everything from Kiddyland to straw skimmer fluttered batlike across her eyes. She moved weakly over to the ledge and rested, waiting for the quivering to stop. Brian had built an irreproachable out-house of sweet stinging stalwart pine, high of beam and splashed with sunshine through its great picture window. She looked out the window and held on; this feeling of sandbags being lugged to one side of her head kept her off balance. She dared not close her eyes, but sat blankly. Sugar-craving, ex-tremely sore muscles, weak knees, sweat, the ripening of breast—her life fading behind some looming flying force to the beat of "jig, jig, jig" that singsonged her mind—every-thing snowballed to a bright white moment when she ac-knowledged her phantom period. "I'm pregnant," she said.

Straight up the nose went the sharp pine fragrance, an accelerated pungency like the carrot's. Her eyes teared on the view of Brian's sunkissed back—complacent, unknowing, a back that would dive into the shark's mouth, then come right out again whenever it pleased. A perfectly male back, tanned without strap lines from day one.

Pregnant! Already her body had gone half-mutineer: she was sitting like a pregnant woman, legs wide and anchored by feet pushed into the flattest dirty sneakers. She tucked a leg quickly to chin, but let it drop as fast. The wrong body part might get squished. Too late, complacency was gone, the same way it had fled with her father's decline. The care a person takes, and even so—plotting warding off, or ignoring a possibility altogether, for years on end—that was over. I am pregnant! It had never even warranted real discussion, but was known, just known between them, that she and Brian would not have a baby. Because of the past and the future; because of the tenuous hold of land and sky; the planet's sure plummeting. They were too dutiful to raise a child. But zero population growth backflipped now in one dumb moment. She was chilly from the drying sweat; it was a fuzzy chill, though, that allowed to burn through itself a pure nugget of female relief, the golden realization: I can conceive. Pure mystery and wonder were buoys; then the mess and fear of a wildly unknowable universe came up fresh black. In an outhouse. Bold or regressive—she couldn't imagine which it was in an outhouse.

She walked, offering a choice of trembly fists to a husband's back. Left, right: it's a good thing; it's a bad thing. Let him remain in half-swallow position, a distance, while she addressed every sweat-pearly vertebra.

"Honey, come up out of that truck and listen to me. Look at me, Brian. I'm pregnant. Oh!" She was giggling, despite herself. "Without a doubt, I'm pregnant."

She heard a deep cavernous gasp.

The news swung like a sickle, high and wide in a dizzy streak. Her voice dared the trees, especially the big jack pine that forever looked ready to snap in a storm and crush the house. (There is no protection!) Brian swung around. The wrench he held was in open-bite, skullish and laughing, and she tasted metal and carrots way down her throat. She coughed and looked straight into his eyes, which seemed pasted on, the look Brian got whenever he tried to dance. So that's how it would be. He'd picked the bad fist, and an icy spray shot all up her arm like a reverse heart attack.

"Carla?"

"Don't make that face, Brian. It's true. I can feel it." Her breath was all chinked up; she groaned trying for a calm swoop down. "Quit staring." Her voice rose again as she backed away, automatically shielding her front. Maternal instinct or mutiny, the arms and legs and her insides headed in all directions on the circus ball. "Will you please stay calm?" She was shrieking.

Over tea last night they had listened to the public radio station's report: a study declared that fetuses sense everything; unwanted babies grow into teen suicides. Be very, very positive if you are pregnant, was the message. Brian had shaken his head at the news; and Carla remembered now how she had continued to butter muffins, but hadn't she paused, hadn't she even squelched an urge—fey subterfuge!—to laugh herself sick? Where did "jig, jig, jig" come from, if not from the new condition? Now she breathed in and out rapidly, with concentration; she must calm herself and fool whatever monstrous intelligence spied from within her.

"Carla, calm down." Seeking to loosen the air with his twirling wrench, Brian looked perfectly culpable and powerless. Failing mechanically, he pointed at the jack pine and probably realized too that it could bash the house to smithereens no matter how smart, good, or pregnant you were. "Honey, listen to yourself. You don't just decide something like this. Wait a minute, oh you're upset, I know. I'm sorry. Come here." He meant to hug her but was mindful of his greasy hands, so he encircled her without touching at all: Saturn's rings, attached but not really; a lonely man edging around magnitude, with greasy hands. "This is straight out of the blue."

Brian looked kind, he looked gentle despite the wrench and his not holding her, and his rapidly forming analytical equations. Rabbit-keen at the nostrils, trying for sensation. So put his head in a cabbage patch! Someone needed to exclaim and be strong here. All rationality should fall away, and Carla's could not. To be a proper husband now Brian should babble crazily and affect huge wet eyes, leap to deliver her chocolate malts, or vow, "We'll ride the river," fling scratchy tourist leis around her neck. He must kiss her and declare her a wondrous

angel before lapsing into practicality; do anything at all that
signified wonder, dumb slapstick acceptance; show her the
ability to go beyond a self-centered world; react sponta-
neously to the sheer miracle and lunacy; then, finally, then
and only then, whisper fantastically a Herculean "What do
we do?"

But she had not chosen a man known for leaping out of his
head with pleasure. If truth be told, her man had taken up
the fiddle because he could not manage the contra dance steps
and abhorred being politically abject among his woodfolk.
Carla saw the two of them as they had been all along; they
should have worn little blue Mao jackets all these years,
Chinese cotton pajamas, yes, so in thrall to their work, so
earnest and believing in their order. For the good of all man-
kind, years ago they had filled a Ryder truck and exiled themselves far from even the mini-metropolis of Des Moines, and
they had sworn "back to the land" and "zero population
growth," and taken up dancing in the good clean contra way.
Now here was proof of solemn belief jelled at its advanced
stage: intractability. Which could no longer be. Work, back-
breaking work, had not beat out havoc.

"Well, I'm blown away. I'm flabbergasted. The honest
truth is that I'm shy, Carla."

And he was purely earnest, that she could see.

"Let me just—I don't know—can we get one of those drugstore tests? I mean, just because you say you are, does it really
mean you are?" he asked her ratty sneakers. "Pregnant," he
said, hardly even a question.

Of all times, a great blue heron flew overhead. The pines
waved. Carla gasped but could not say, Look at it, what's that
beauty doing here right now, so calmly coasting the sky?

"I'm going to Des Moines."

Brian dropped his wrench. "What are you, nuts? You can't
just make this declaration and then leave me . . . everything.
Carla?"

"I'm going to Des Moines to see a doctor. And my mother
and grandmother. I'm going for help."

She was going to Des Moines pregnant and she thought, I know this forest, I could swallow this forest, but I'm not bold, and boldness is required—Grandma Morrow has surely decreed it. She had never asked for this, not even as a girl with a doll. She had wanted the doll to go away. She had wanted a rocket to the moon. Carla exhaled with a force that shuddered her from the inside out and especially back of the knees, though her feet didn't budge.

C H A P T E R   4

As soon as Maintenance finished carting his things down from third floor, Hazen took up position in his brown leatherette rocker and looked at TV.

"But look out the window," Jessamine urged, swiveling him by the back of the chair. "That sugar maple's so close you can see the remains of a robin's nest." A little half-coconut thing perched in the fork of branch. Jessamine had monitored the whole business, from the glory of speckled eggs materializing to the parents' own winged desertion. "Next spring you'll see chicks," she told Hazen. A week of marriage had turned out the world immense with future again, and Jessamine's dust cloth was at rest.

"Powdered milk, gad!" Hazen said to the screen.

Since James Lawrence's death Jessamine had taken a permanent notion against visiting Allie Morrow, though really she had avoided the house in his last years as well, drawing James to her, believing in the curative properties of deeply felt familiarity: his delight in the way she polished the brass candelabra or the taste of a Grimes Golden apple which she always had on hand. A perfect sanctuary of trust might return him to good boyhood. She believed that whenever a parent outlasted a child the good earth suffered a convolution. And whenever Jessamine pictured the little Wakonda house absent of James Lawrence, her heart broke to pieces. At James Lawrence's house she didn't know what might seize her. But now with Hazen as escort she could do it. James Lawrence would want Hazen Batten to take her to Allie's. Jessamine decided not to wear gloves but to bring an extra hankie.

"Now, then," she said, turning off Hazen's program.

Hazen looked around in surprise.

"Remember, it's Allie Morrow we're going to visit. My son's dear wife."

Hazen mistrusted the freeway, so he chose long winding back roads that swept them into the rural territory along Cherry Creek. Fields of tall grass grew on either side of the road, and red-winged blackbirds perched all in a row on the high wires slung overhead. Jessamine knew how territorial they were this time of year; if she and Hazen got out of the car the birds would dive-bomb, even peck at them. A turn off gravel pointed them back to town eventually, to Allie's neighborhood by way of great stretches of shrublands sporting billboards about development—the telephone numbers were stout as trees. The city's central park ran along here, canopied by maple and oak; their regiments made a dark thickness that fenced the grassy flatness of a field and laid down shade carpet for as far as you could see. Bicycle paths and such had been added at some point, and young folks rode just inside the park wearing little more than visors.

"We'll spin through the park, Jessamine," Hazen said.

It was a parade, with youth on bicycles scooting past them, and Jessamine waved even if they were indecent.

"I'd expect they'd be worn out in this heat," she commented, inwardly thrilled to know that youth would not be.

The gravel roadway snaked through the park and suddenly opened out to where a high narrow wooden bridge would have to be crossed. Like a wise horse, Hazen balked.

"Looks more like a walking bridge to me," he said. "It's about as old as us, bound to be rickety."

A car nosed behind them, so there would be no backing up

on the one-laner. Hazen stuck his chin high over the steering
wheel and urged, "Come on, gal." Jessamine knew from the
buck of the car—its lurch forward—that Hazen had been
talking to it, not her. "Gal" was not a word for "woman" from
their day.

Each slat snapped under the weight of the car, and then,
despite the air-conditioning whirring at her, Jessamine heard
something else, a low groan and splintering as she looked
down to the small river, so slow and dark it appeared to mold
the rocks. A piece of guardrail clung to the antenna, bent
around to her side, then both snapped and did whirlybirds
down to the water. She felt yanked this way and that in the
pit of her stomach, but light as a leaf, too.

"Hazen, stop! Things are breaking."

Now a trembling seized Hazen's arms. They were on the
down slope, so he'd been steering just fine. The old boards
made an unnatural roar from beneath them, but he was heading off the bridge now, wasn't he? Jessamine might have forgotten the deal with traveling on a wooden bridge. You
expected eerie sounds. Hazen could see straight ahead: grassland; and he moved on, fast or slow, it didn't matter, with his
eyes fixed on grassland. There. He got them off the bridge,
that was the thing. He braked and held on to the wheel. The
small car from behind swung out onto the grass and passed
them at a beeping whiz.

"Darn, Jessamine, what do you mean by screaming?" He
looked all around and found himself without landmarks,
seated in his large car, heart in his eyes. "Don't ever yell at
the driver, Jessamine," he said in gulps. "It's like 'fire!' in a
theater. I held on, didn't I? I held on."

And Jessamine, feeling as though the entire world had con-
densed to a roiling sun in her head (this, she thought, might
be how you die, this must be an attack of some sort), found
her tiniest voice. She breathed, "Yes, we're fine, Hazen.
We're fine. Now you must be careful to drive just so. Hazen,
dear, you must be very, very good at it or they'll stop us.
They'll take away the car and leave us shut up. Shut in,
Hazen."

Hazen's car seemed to contract with her sharp inhalation. Using memory more than muscle—she was so weak all over —Jessamine got herself out of the car. She surveyed her side of it, and the front, touching the sunny metal. She saw nothing that corresponded to the unearthly sounds she'd heard on that bridge. She held her arms and felt the splinter-prone bones; the mystery of a tree's age. At times like this a person should be allowed to walk away from a car and say, No, thank you, and flag a trolley. This frightful heat. She got back into the car. Hazen was squeezing the wheel, then fanning his fingers, squeezing, then fanning.

Signals, that's it, she thought. "Hazen, I should be responsible for signaling. I will be a better guide." Hazen's eyes were closed. He nodded. Jessamine used her yellow hankie to wipe his brow.

Hazen drove up Wakonda slowly. Aimed at Allie's drive, his car hung on the hill while he maneuvered the screaming power steering. Jessamine advised calmly, "Watch the rhubarb over on my side." Hazen parked so close to the embankment wall he had to work his way across the front seat to get out on Jessamine's side. Jessamine gripped her pocketbook. Come visiting, she waited.

The neighborhood was quiet—the foliage did so much in the way of splendor here—though Jessamine could never understand what had gotten into James Lawrence, buying a house on the side of town known for Italians and floods. The street had none of the pleasing levelness she associated with marriage itself: she'd moved from farm to town and started life with Lawrence on a great boulevard lined with elm. Well, Wakonda would *not* flood; the houses were dug out of a hillside, their driveways made possible by firmly bricked embankment that held back the swell of yard. If Allie had a car she would drive it directly into her basement to park. And at least Wakonda had access to the main street below and, Jessamine observed with a slow 180-degree head swivel, a patrician view of downtown. Jessamine recalled her first trip here. Somehow Lawrence had lost his way in the tangle of streets higher up. They had come upon grape arbors and more grape arbors and tomatoes growing right to the curb and small children hosing each other, screaming. She had thought, These streets are burro paths, paved Italian burro paths.

Across the street a young couple sat on kitchen chairs, shaded by a cottonwood, tending a barbecue grill. If Carla could visit, the young life here might draw Allie out. But she is very busy working, Jessamine reminded herself.

Hazen's car blocked the steps cut from embankment, so they backtracked to the street and had to walk uphill to enter the yard levelly.

Jessamine called to the young people, "How are you folks?" She swung the pocketbook forward, glinting sun off it. She secured Hazen's elbow and hoped her voice was strong enough to banish James Lawrence's ghost.

"Good day to lay low," the young man said. "Let me give you a boost, friend."

As a young man can do, he sauntered from the yard and, in no time, had guided Hazen into Allie's yard. Jessamine noticed a design of red and blue swirls on his muscle. A fad, she guessed. A more mature man, someone distantly familiar, one house farther up, stood hosing down a yellow car. He waved. And Allie's yard! What a lovely landscape of flowers and ornaments. And here came Allie, running to meet them.

"Allie, you've become a landscape artist behind my back," Jessamine swore. "Iris, lily, nasturtium."

The young man said, "Later," and was gone.

Jessamine's sweep of arm took in the short forest of rhubarb, flowers, and long grass fattened by humidity. A pink bird statue was radiant above the fronds, just radiant. She pressed her arm against Hazen's side and stalled. James Lawrence's voice could come blazing through the pastoral . . .

"Hazen, I'm so glad to meet you," Allie said. She was a cheery slip of a thing, with hand extended. Jessamine sent her chin to the sky in admiration. What brilliant pants Allie wore!

"My pleasure," said Hazen. "I like meeting kin."

"Then you're in luck. My daughter Carla is coming to visit."

"Why, something told me." Jessamine smiled just above Allie's head.

Allie's kiss and Hazen's touch got Jessamine to the house and through the door. She let out her breath. She had done it and now sat gratefully with Hazen, on a thickly textured beige couch. She approvingly thumped the cushions. "So comfortable, Allie."

"It's the old one."

"Not the ancient thing I gave you folks years ago?"

"Yes, I've reupholstered."

"I should say." Jessamine threw her hands up in salute.

Hazen said, "Good. Working with the hands beats the devil." He stooped to touch his polished black shoe, then looked up. The squiggles on his forehead gave Hazen's face the look of fine new packaged clay, furrowed because that is its perfect state, Jessamine decided.

"Take shoe repair," he said. "Who does it now? Who can you trust with your dress shoes?"

"No one." Allie's voice grew loud as Hazen's, Italian-loud. "We're supposed to toss them!"

In moments of excitement Hazen had a way of chewing at the words before he released them, a habit that displeased Jessamine.

"Same problem with clocks," he said. "And what about milk delivery? Do young men care? No, they don't want the trouble of long routes, all-weather driving. We've got profiteers running things."

"A crying shame!" Allie leaned toward Hazen in rather frank delight. "And I've just read some news I can't believe. I haven't told Carla. It's atrocious . . . " With a quickly rolled newspaper in hand Allie swatted Hazen's checked pantleg, then leaned way back to say, "The dime store is going out."

"Forced out of downtown, you're right. I've heard." Hazen

chewed and chewed. Jessamine looked away. "Imagine any self-respecting downtown without a grill. Where will my friends go? It's a travesty."

Jessamine had become engrossed in the needlepoint sampler directly across the room. "Bananas, grapes, bing cherries," she said tunefully.

"Kresge's is the only place I can get all-cotton shortie pajamas," Alice said.

Oh, how unbecomingly Allie's voice rose, speaking to Hazen of nightwear, her hands on her thighs like that, her elbows bent out. Jessamine did not mean to think of frog legs. Allie's little arms were such fragile, furious supports. What a mighty little person. But *nightwear*.

"They're tearing down a perfectly good building, Kresge's, to put up a new one. Nuts," said Hazen.

"The stupes want skywalks between buildings. Cattle troughs to feed people from parking lot to office. Why? What's wrong with fresh air?" Allie asked.

Jessamine wondered: had Allie ever thought to have her hair done? Allie kept her glossy hair long, wrapped in a good working-woman's style, but still she wondered what a professional shampoo—that atmosphere of personal luxury—might do for Allie; then add a stylish comb.

"Germ breeders, those skywalks," Hazen assured. "Wait until winter. Well"—he turned to Jessamine and took her hand—"looks like we'll be stuck at Hillcrest, come winter. Least we're married," he said to Allie. Her face was thrust quite close now and arranged to question.

"Money, money," Hazen kept on. "I tell you, these old folks' places love to take it unless you're too old. They say we're too old for the apartments over on Grand built specially for old people."

"Hazen!"

Allie and Hazen turned toward her sharp cry.

"I meant to say, Hazen . . . " Jessamine paused, helpless against the feeling that her mouth would now behave like a drawstring purse letting out one coin onto gloved hand. "Carla's first job was at Kresge's."

"Good girl!"

"Well," Allie said. "Well, well, and well again. How about refreshments." She sprang away to the kitchen and commenced a clattering of dishes, humming something from the early days that Jessamine couldn't quite place. She returned with a plate of cookies, and Hazen took one in each hand.

"Watch out or you'll founder yourself," Jessamine warned.

"Oh, dive in," Allie urged and definitely winked at Hazen.

After filling up on ginger snaps, Hazen slumped groggily to one side of the transformed sofa, and Allie helped Jessamine prop a pillow behind his head for his snooze. Jessamine declared the house to be perfect for Allie, full of marvelous innovations, right for a younger generation. For instance, here was a decorator hobby stand—she supposed that's what you would call it—a brasswork behind an end table. Something very unusual. The high protuberances gleamed.

"Oh, it's a deer," she realized. "And, hmmm, what a fragrance."

"Eucalyptus. It covers everything."

"And the sword on the wall. Allie, don't tell me it's something Japanese that James Lawrence never showed us?"

"That's a machete. I got it in Mexico," Alice explained.

Mexico! Jessamine put her hand to her throat and indicated speechlessness, a miracle. She passed a fresh lilac hankie unfolded from her pocketbook over her eyes, then asked for coffee, no cream.

On second thought she followed Allie to the kitchen, a bright room snug as a bug for one person, but a working woman's kitchen that, really, she had to dismiss as being no kitchen at all. In case Hazen wasn't soundly asleep she lowered her voice. "Allie, I have a legal quandary."

"I'd hope it wasn't illegal!" Allie winked as she got the coffee and made places for them to sit at the dining table. "Here you go."

Allie dealt in the business world, Jessamine reminded herself, though it seemed not until James Lawrence passed on that her job acquired such career dimensions. She had trav-

eled to the West Coast on business—a widow! She would not
be shocked easily.

"Hillcrest is ecstatic," Jessamine declared. "Everyone loves
us married."

"Hazen is a gem," Allie said.

Jessamine relaxed her straight-back pose enough to sip coffee. She set the cup down quickly and folded her hands on
the table and worked at her beads. The necklace hung too far
down her front and she straightened, remembering suddenly
that this was a strand she usually wore doubled.

"Allie, I need to speak to you about burial arrangements."
She spoke in a whisper. "We have family plots there in Minneola, you know. Next to Lawrence there is . . . *space*. We
bought a double plot years ago, you understand. And James
Lawrence is right there, of course. Allie, I am now Hazen's
wife. I must make other arrangements."

Both women looked to the living room where Hazen Batten
slept, a snore away from death or gallantry. Alice was at a
loss to imagine either, considering his loose sprawl and the
fresh blue socks. An old man upsetting the applecart.

Jessamine searched Hazen inch by inch. Evidently satisfied
with what she found, she assumed a halting low urgency. "I
am sure God loves to take an old woman who is married. He
wishes to."

"James would have liked Hazen," Alice hurried to say.

"Bless his soul. Now, Allie, would you mind terribly as, I
don't want to pry, but evidently a space for you was never
exactly confirmed . . . ? Allie, would you agree to go to your
resting place next to your father-in-law, by your beloved husband? The plot is for a Morrow. Would you take my place,
Alice Morrow?"

Cremation for me! Alice had vowed at the end of James's
funeral. That dour minister eulogizing a man he'd never
known, and the organ music was full of false thumps. Cremation alone made sense, though even then, as she'd plucked
lint from her watch-plaid wool, she'd caught herself thinking
that thanks to burial—the gruesome, somber spectacle—the

world had zombie stories. A person would not want to do without zombie stories. She had read the latest "scientific" fuss over whether they really existed: another strong-arm approach, heaps of niggling rationalization, as if that's the way a person could secure the truth. As with the moon, science should leave zombies alone. Cremation for me, Alice repeated.

Jessamine's face was a crumbling rose. "I've discussed everything with Reverend Lyton. This is proper. Not without sadness, but proper, Allie. I didn't think of everything before the . . . decision. Oh! The necessity hadn't occurred to me."

"Yes, bury me!" Alice declared loudly, causing Jessamine's hand to flutter from her beads, and Hazen on the couch stirred; he twitched and muttered, "Now, CoCo."

"CoCo, indeed," Jessamine cried. "Who is she?"

Oh, what a person wouldn't give for a cigarette amidst Jessamine's earnest propriety. This octopus, marriage. What had Hazen forgotten to tell Jessamine, that he used to go out to the Val-Air Ballroom on Seniors Night with the other old guys to meet single grandmothers? Something might have started with his approaching a tableful of overrouged ladies, the loud chunky-beaded one being CoCo, being a mite too sure, in the end.

"Thank you for offering, Allie." Jessamine's head was tilted back from the force of applied ethics, and CoCo. "Allie, the problems and exhaustion of recent days . . . the expression 'second husband' slithers, just slithers off the wrong tongues. Someone asked me, was it true I had been divorced? Really! Not everyone at Hillcrest is ecstatic."

"I suppose they wonder what gave you the idea."

"Idea? Allie, love is not an idea." A sternness of spirit, what must have girded her through four years of James's soldiering and all that followed, marked Jessamine now. With burial arrangements in the bag, she was again completely armored, yet pure: sun rays were flashing off her beads and rings and glasses, and even her pearled lips wore a coat of mail.

Bury me not on the lone prairie, Alice wanted to shout, but she effected an inquiring nod as she swore silently, Thanks, James. The trouble with accusing the dead was that it didn't work; you couldn't get debate, defense, or submission. Something like an all-over bee sting grazed the skin, heightened her temperature. Her breathing came in gasps. She stretched finger and thumb into a chin strap that held up a smile. A person absorbed shock. Hazen, she'd seen instantly, was a gent, no hillbilly, fine, but next—bubble and splat—people were arranging her burial. Too much was asked of the mind. The emotion forbidden when appealing to the gods or the dead is anger. And anger was the creature surfacing, shaking free, doing back dives off her spine, cheeks, elbows.

"Divorced," Jessamine repeated. From a high hill of voice the word swooped low, accent wrong but perfect. And Jessamine proceeded to recall the summer James Lawrence learned to swim.

"He was six years old, Allie, and the lake was huge."

A legal quandary. Final resting place, please! As soon as Hazen and Jessamine left, Alice was outside with her hair loosed from the bun—a gleaming, bright bell of hair she let embolden her looks at home. She was tearing up a loaf of white bread, trailing crumbs from porch out to the back yard, where rabbits grazed at sundown. The fattest squirrel watched from the wall, having already claimed his share. Bones spooking the underside of the earth was idiocy, barbarism. *Build a great Hindu pyre, let ash and spark peashoot themselves into the night sky, send me to space.* Past the hem of her Capri-length pants, which she knew were not called Capri now or pedal-pushers or even deck pants, Alice admired her firm trustworthy legs. Health. In her own body, she had known only health. A blast from a motorcycle spun her back toward the street in time to catch sight of spangled helmets—twin moons—launching down Wakonda. Saturdays were busy motorcycling days; back and forth they went.

She had kissed Hazen goodbye, wanting to ask how he had

done it. Had he approached Jessamine on a Sunday afternoon, shoes shined, a box of chocolates at his back, ring biting his fist? Had she protested, or was this really Jessamine's orchestration? Marriage. Where had the impulse come from, Alice would genuinely like to know. In the yard, Jessamine had blown Alice a final kiss and wheeled Hazen to his car with a look that said she intended to learn all about CoCo.

And now Alice tore at the bread, thinking of all the Hazens who would become invisible with Kresge's closing, all the old-timers in fedoras who lived on valiantly in the remaining downtown hotels with no thoughts of malls or skywalks. Their daily convocations at the Kresge's grill raised and settled half a century's issues. Alice loved to attend at a respectful distance, watching as she sipped her coffee the old men's mirrored faces; she listened keenly over the hiss and scrape put to grill-tending by the hairnetted old faithful who would break debate, cackling, "Two number fours." The Hazens waved plain doughnuts, spilled their coffee and might pay in pennies, but they knew what they were talking about; and on the first day of real spring weather a breeze called forth a flock of blue-haired ladies to roost downtown, perhaps with CoCo among them. You would see them alight from the buses, flutter through streets and shops with plastic rain caps bonneted over their hairdos, just in case. Approaching Kresge's on her lunch hour and seeing this brigade—her future—Alice would feel her throat go cakey, the way it always did when a marching band broke out the horns.

Thrift with dignity, sales-ministering executed by ladies who could honestly match a package of Rit dye to the shade of cloth you desired, that's what went on in Kresge's. The dime store, Alice believed, had saved her family. Inexperienced in anything but housework and light typing, at her Craftique interview she had thought to say, "I'm good at math and know dime-store thrift." "Ahh," Dr. Rand said wistfully, "and such perfect teeth." James congratulated her. Finally it was settled, how they would be. (A family, Alice could see now, grew into itself.) James smiled the smile that belied ambition or doom. The man who had saved the world was next destined to bake a great pie.

He could bake it and sing about it and spoof himself and kiss magnificently. "Can she bake a cherry pie, Billy Boy, Billy Boy?" The slatting on top was always thin and uniform, a near-eruption bubbled at the middle, and James left no signs of having floured himself or the kitchen. With windows thrown wide he would pop it into the oven, turn on his heel and look perfectly masculine, his shirtsleeves rolled high. Next he might climb onto the roof wearing rough blue gloves and shake loose the old wasp's nest. When Alice came home from work she would see him up there, flame hair like a weather beacon or some bright tropicality; he'd be balanced strangely as if playing that Twister game he and Carla loved, waving, and truly he was king of the hill. James loved Wakonda. He loved the house he had chosen for them and kept it painted a cool dark brown. "Protective coloration, Alice." And Alice, even when weary or suffering flashes of ancient girlish notions of married life, redoubled her belief in the sense of things as she walked up the hill watching James. Yes, this is the way, she had had to say of the heretofore unimagined, and her heart would be stilled by the fragrance of good cooking. The cooking and housework—it was true—she had never taken to in the least, and James, in charge, would scold gently, "Honey, look at how you left the stove!"—thrilled to seize upon a mess with his cunning new cleansing formulas.

In the beginning many new ties had been knotted at James's tan throat. Careers were heralded. And each time, after a period of severe half-lidded humming, James told Alice what he had unearthed. At five o'clock, with tie ripped from his neck as if he had just escaped the noose itself, he ticked off the horrors of insurance and advertising and banking: inefficiency, an air of corruption and, by the way, air so stale as to be lethal. "Robots, Alice." In these offices mindless schemes were rigged and controlled by a few. It was a miracle this country was what it was. The details—walls of puce, rusty fountain water, a boss's inability to speak without spitting—

were horrid. This was what he'd saved the world for? James came to favor the simpler idea of a job. "An honest job, Alice," with a future where you might end up owning the company and thus have a career after all. From Sears, Alice ordered a stack of gray work pants. But it turned out those jobs were sticklers. You couldn't count on the dummies, all related to one another, wives bringing hot-plate dinners at noon! Enlightened, James clanged his lunch pail down with disgust. So, jobs out of the newspaper, without bosses or underlings, he realized, were the way to go. Driving: rural delivery, seeing the countryside you could breathe. (He may have passed Hazen Batten.) But before you knew it, the leased truck broke down and they gouged you on mileage anyway; schedules were unreasonable; winter driving sheer treachery. He detested smelling like fish and carting onions.

At some point the family slipped into the theatrical belief that James was between jobs. After school there he'd be with Carla, dipping candles or solving math, and Alice would find the roast in the oven crackling with extra trimmings that Jessamine had suggested by telephone. In fall, huge leaf-raking operations went into effect; at the first sign of spring James climbed high on a ladder to paint the trim. James had planted rhubarb and James had put up Carla's tetherball pole. Alice might hear James pause in hosing down whichever car and call chirpily to the neighbor Calvin cleaning his chickens brought up from a family farm, "Can't find a thing. It's a jungle." Certainly James did not join housewives for morning TV or Stanley parties. He was busy, endlessly busy in and around the house. Even Jessamine breathed a sigh of relief and approval once the routine was established. Keeping track of her son, that's what counted after all. Who could forget the four years of separation, spotty communications from the South Pacific, all the wondering, all the dead boys? How time had stopped then and frozen everyone. Having James Lawrence a captive phone call away became the perfectly sensible and superior advantage: careers were a nuisance once careers were deemed impossible. And much, much later Carla

reinvented the life all over again with her militant cheer,
"Househusband!"

When they learned of James's blood disease—mysterious,
unlikely to "really affect him outwardly for quite some time"
—nothing, indeed, changed outwardly. If anything, James
became more industrious, the family insularly polite. And the
neighbors such as Calvin's wife, who shepherded her kids
with a flyswatter and the threat "Wait until your father gets
home," did not see any dramatic folding of Morrow wings.
Alice, whose office experiences were mild compared with
James's, won the Craftique position and began lugging home
everything under the sun. A landfill of color. James poked
through all of it, hung and displayed what he could, even
going so far as to stitch up the cork coasters with gold braid,
and glue and paint and attach ruffles to several Christmas
knickknacks out of season. He stored the dowels, sequins, and
decoupage supplies as efficiently as possible. He remained
thin and handsome and full-haired and prone to mission. Both
of them clucked when his thirty-fifth-high-school-reunion
picture arrived: "The others look so old! Fat! Bald!" Their
breaking outraged voices wondered, How could James be
dying? How can I be?

But one day when James forgot all about a cherry pie he'd
been baking—had simply dozed off—and presented a briskly
dressed homecoming Alice with the blackened crater, she
could see he had been crying. His flame hair that was never
to thin looked brassy. Vigilance is required, Alice understood; I am in charge of a large unknowable world in James
and must be very, very vigilant. Even in that instant of recognition it was as if a larger version of herself surrounded and
froze and took over the real Alice. "Let's just get rid of it,"
she said, and took the terrible pie. She threw it into the garbage, pan and all, and James was so delighted, so grateful
and childishly astounded—"The pan, too!"—he laughed
himself silly, and in his hair Alice swore she saw luster, pure
luster.

Now she threw down the bird bread, white bread once perfectly sensible for sandwiches. She could not remember exactly when she had abandoned white bread to the birds.

Two teenage boys emerged from the little house next door, downhill, where owner Londo Vedaducci had gotten in a new faceless renter recently. Sometimes in the night, going for water, Alice would notice a light. She had never seen these boys who came walking toward her and was wondering why, for heaven's sake, a boy would wear his tee shirt cut off at the nipples.

He balanced a TV under his arm. The taller friend, who wore cigarette tusks at the corners of his mouth, lit them and fitted one to the other boy's lips. They scrambled up the embankment wearing sloppy teenage grins and cut into Alice's yard seeming not to see her. The wind was an ally, flipping high the undersides of leaves and animating the bread wrapper in her stop-sign hand.

"Wait a minute," she called. "You took a TV from that man's house. What are you doing?" She threw a bread slice that flopped against the TV toter's back. Then something pelted her; an early, maniacally early, acorn. Still twigged to leaf, it clung, then tumbled from her shoulder to foot and looked up at her. A fringe-faced primitive.

The delinquents had picked up speed. Alice began to lope, too; then everyone was running toward the alley, then onto gravel, uphill. Alice's chin was tucked. Black high-topped sneakers—huge, clown-sized—shot gravel back at her; her breath was coming up short and raggy; she felt numbed across the cheeks; a boulder crushed her chest; yet she ran. If she could only catch up to this gall, a brilliant demon-slaying strength would be hers.

The boys beat her to the top cross alleyway and jumped into a car. *A blue car*, Alice memorized shrewdly.

"Hey," the one yelled out the window. "You're a stupid old woman, know what I mean?" He shot his cigarette at her feet. The kick of gravel was even more insulting as they vroomed away.

Alice's breathing had eased back to steady by the time she reached her yard. She ran to Calvin's. As she pounded on his screen door his TV seemed to grow louder.

"Calvin, come quick. Help." She was breathing rust, cupping her hands in order to locate him, which regrettably resulted in her seeing his bare back. A forest. And a TV half the size of Calvin's head threw laughter onto the kitchen table.

She had already sprung back when Calvin yelled, "What did I miss?" He heaved himself into the old cowboy pose, but gone were the days of Calvin's posseing. And when his kids had grown, his wife took off with an auctioneer. Now, when she thought of it, Alice could swear she had heard a television going nonstop for a decade. She remembered when this rusted screen had been a fine new mesh.

"There was a break-in downhill." Looking anywhere but at Calvin, Alice recited: black, brown, purple, green, orange, yellow, blue, red, the enduring order of Crayolas in the standard small pack. A proper recitation served to exorcise gray shock. But she felt lightheaded, at a standstill suddenly, chastened by the rusty screen and the perverse little TV. And now Calvin stood in the door holding the most hideous sandwich in his palm: open-faced white bread, two rounds of thick pale meat (ring bologna?), terrible blind eyes. She prayed: sequins, ten thousand to the pound.

"I'll call the police and get my boots on, Alice. Be right out."

She went home for cigarettes and headed on down Wakonda. The dusky sky had released but one lightning bug into action and Big Rusty was umber, a color that resides only in the largest crayon pack, she recalled. She stood in front of the mystery man's house and called, "Hello, if you're in there."

The owner, Londo, roared up Wakonda in a big black jeep-sort-of vehicle with a lightning bolt painted on the hood. A short man, Londo did a free fall from his seat and hit the ground already speechifying and fisting the air. He was a bulldog, too old for retraining, Alice thought. He came at his house and kicked the aluminum door. Who could imagine such a person asleep? Did the scarlet in his ears subside to pink? He turned to Alice and Calvin, who was now buttoning a shirt over girth.

"I was at the Frankie Boy for steaks, first time in months, and I get word through a friend on the force there's a break-in over here."

Calvin re-posseed himself, sought clues. "The Frankie Boy," he repeated, with precision.

The squad car cruised up Wakonda with its red light flashing. As the officer took the embankment at one bound, Londo held a palm to him. "It's about time!"

"Give me the key and stand back, mister," the officer warned.

Londo complied, then banged a fist on the walls of aluminum siding he had recently erected. He still lived over on Parker with his kerchiefed old mother while buying up homes to rent.

People shifted and murmured and smoked while the officer unlocked the door and went in. Above his head he brandished a nightstick as absurd as a candy cane. At least, Alice thought, the brick house Londo owned across the alley from her own back yard was impossible to abominate with siding.

Returning to the yard, the policeman pushed his hat back and frowned, but was too young to produce a respectable wrinkle. Alice observed the tendency of navy-blue short sleeves to rob a man of authority when his arms are thin and white. He addressed Londo.

"The guy—your tenant—is in there. He's shaken up, that's about all, but won't come out. Those damn kids stole his TV and took some cash, pushed him around. Entry was voluntary. He was expecting them, is the thing."

Even as Alice watched, a lowland mist of perspiration was forming cover between the few hairs atop Londo's egg-shaped head. His eyes fluttered, suggesting mania or a faint.

The cop raised his voice. "Listen to me. The man had a misadventure, okay? He's sick over it. Some boys took advantage. What can I tell you?"

Londo was breathing heavily. "He means a fag. I rented to a fag." His eyes went sideways and gritty. "Jesus, I grew up here . . . "

"He's a man who pays his rent," Alice said.

Calvin coughed needlessly.

The officer lifted his cap so slightly, with such delicacy, a person might think he kept a trained canary under it. With his free hand he smoothed his light hair. Still no wrinkles. "Let's move on now," he said. "I'm saying you people can move along, forget it, okay?" The officer mustered a stern look for Londo. "He said he wants to clear out, Mr. Ved . . . here, spell your name." He thrust pad and pen at Londo.

Londo's fist slapped his palm. "I'll get my cousin back down here. He hates the Twin Cities."

"Then he's a fool," Alice hooted. "It's live and let live up there." Having come outside minus her usual ashtray, she took the opportunity to grind a cigarette out in Londo's idiotically butched lawn. Downtown Minneapolis was thriving and that was a fact.

"I have a description," she said. "Two hoods driving a blue car. I tried to catch them."

"Ma'am, that's not the smartest thing," said the young officer, younger than her own daughter.

"I've got a machete. I'll go out waving it," Alice declared, but already the policeman was walking away. Typically, normally, audaciously, a policeman or a doctor, anyone who did not wholly figure in the situation at hand, would, of course, declare himself and then walk away. A person must be vigilant, especially when the hair was all cattywampus. Alice had forgotten that hers was.

C H A P T E R   5

"Stupid old lady" still burned the ears and gave the Sunday paper an annoyingly fussy look, spread as it was on the dining table the next morning. Alice went outside to take stock of things: she found bumblebees clustered in hollyhocks, the hollyhocks themselves like great fluttery gossips, nosing this way and that, the tenderest pinks. A bird had splashed most of the water out of the large fake-delft bowl she kept for their bath. The sky was all cotton balls. In the sweet air just on the verge of thickening, the iris rose straight as gazelles. Looking at the ground more closely, Alice saw an ant army, a ruddy patch of clover and the yellow slenderness of new shoots of grass. And her young neighbor was wrestling with his motorcycle as if with a live thing, an upright animal sleek and feral in his arms to be tamed only by spinning the wheel over and over, to the point of exhaustion. Pieces of metal, eerily bright in the deep milky light, lay all over that drive. Now he let the motorcycle down and circled it, smoking, puzzling out some mystery of motion and power unfathomable to Alice. Didn't these people ever sleep? She had heard faint motor sounds—comings and goings—in the night. She peered at the base of her massive bur oak. Her bluebells were making a comeback.

She couldn't say exactly when these two with the motorcycle had moved in. At some point families had begun leaving Wakonda. Calvin's wife went to a farm town with her auctioneer; that had been the beginning of something. Restless determined buyers seemed to hold on for just so long. They came and went during James's last years and gave way to earnest renters who, in turn, deserted, leaving tenants of shorter and shorter duration. The last year or so had been particularly fuzzy with strangers. Going out to weed around her sunflowers one Sunday past, Alice was surprised to see a fleet of motorcycles crowded into the drive over there, picnic tables set end to end in the yard. Bikers, as contained and hungry as the next picnickers, were bending their biker backs (jean jackets with sleeves ripped out, lurid stitching everywhere) over drumsticks and potato salad. She could see a huge tray of deviled eggs and laughed to think of a biker kitchen full of yolk-mashing activity. Music at the lowest volume came from somewhere. In that house, her daughter's best friends had grown up.

Now the woman burst on the scene in halter top and jeans, carrying drinks. Her arms, more than the legs, seemed to be instruments of propulsion, reminding Alice of the new kind of jogger who grips what appears to be car handles as he runs over the viaduct. As the man stooped over the cowed motorcycle, his back broadened and the tattoos high up became shoulder epaulettes. His hair was rubberbanded into the tiniest ponytail at his nape. It was a crime, Alice thought, now turning from sunflowers, the way paint peeled off that house, once kept fresh as Monday laundry.

"Oh, you, hey! Hi, over there." Like some huge puppy broken loose, the young woman came galloping at Alice, not smiling so much as fixing her bite unwaveringly on target. Alice ducked sideways, sure the woman meant to plow her down, but she stopped inches short of collision. Still, Alice stepped back. *This isn't Tokyo.*

"I'm Mary." She was all head-bobbing and shoulder stuff, even at a standstill. She barked from the throat, "I hear something happened yesterday while we were gone. Kit over there's my husband."

Mary looked to be in her late twenties, a bit younger than Carla. She was tanned and pretty, though she should wipe her eyes clean of the black stuff and do something about the dark roots showing.

"We had a misunderstanding next door. Friends of the renter robbed him, essentially."

"Wouldn't you know." Mary's weight went all to one hip

when she snapped her fingers. She nodded at the house slowly and her face took on a series of contortions—sun-squinting, lemon-eating, a baring of Kennedy-size teeth in a floss position—before settling on what seemed to Alice a disgustedly wise pose of the lips.

"Did they rip the place up? Was it sick thieving like what made us move last year? We were out on a run. Someone who knew us broke in. Revenge, Kit thinks. Stole our wedding pictures, collector Elvis records, my b.c. pills, besides the major appliances. They even made off with our Eldorado."

A person could not imagine a wedding album for these two. A stark picture of stuntmen in the desert came to mind: tourist cars forced off the road by motorcyclists wearing eye patches. Alice lit a cigarette. She fervently hoped this Mary's "b.c. pills" had been replaced and were in effect.

"You know what they did with an Eldorado, kid?"

"What in the world?" Alice jetted smoke away from Mary.

"Stripped it and burnt it to a crisp. Cops haven't done dick."

With staccato punches, Alice put out, crumbled, obliterated her cigarette butt in the ashtray she carried. She might stamp out vulgarity, or the noise of it anyway.

"Hey," Mary said, lifting the ashtray right out of her hands. In the moment of drop-jawed examination, Alice acutely regretted the years and events, all the changes that left a person with neighbors she would not invite in.

"Cool. It looks valuable."

"Nonsense, not at all." Was this the eye of a thief? Alice spoke quickly, explaining that Mary was admiring the mosaic chips that a very young Carla had pressed into a rubber-cement-moistened dish. James and Carla had made batches of such dishes.

"I'd like that," Mary decided. Her look of disdain had to be unintentional, a habitual pose, or the result of tonguing a bad tooth, if Mary could have such a thing as a bad tooth. Her eyes were so bright she might have been on drugs, Alice realized, calling up newspaper accounts. No, Mary was smil-

ing and exclaiming, and suddenly, truly, Mary was a young
woman who simply lived in a rented house and responded to
color and design with an open, sensuous mouth.

"Wait right here and I'll fix you up," Alice told her, already
hurrying toward the house to marshal forth supplies. "I have
plenty of mosaics," she called from the door. "I'll get you
started."

When Mary marched back home, her shoulders squared,
she was swinging the bag of mosaic chips at her "old man"
and his "bike." Alice watched from her kitchen window. Kit
raised up and nodded, then stooped again. Mary stood in the
drive talking nonstop, shaking the bag. She set it down to
elaborate, to point back at Alice's house and run her fingers
through her hair, to suddenly wave as if shooing the cottonwood tree. She kept darting looks over her shoulder, one of
those women in constant trauma, thumbs in and out of jean
pockets and belt loops, relaying the break-in news, Alice supposed. With a cigarette stuck in her mouth untended, just like
that, Mary would hold a mosaic dish before her, Alice believed. She'd squint through the smoke and harshly cry,
"Red. It needs some red." Alice liked Mary for that. She
would be eager to see the first mosaic dish made in that house.

When Mary leaned down to the motorcycle her back looked
like a glossy brown package tied up by string. Kit spied it.
Slowly, scratching his belly, he rose. He reached for her back
and yanked: "Toot, toot!" Mary's top flapped like a bib and
loosed a big rosy-nippled breast.

In her fumbling the other breast wobbled free and the lump
of cotton knit got lost there between the breasts. She bunched
the material to her, clasping each breast, and sprang back,
letting fly a wide-open vulgarity that shuddered and seared
itself, hoarse with sexual challenge, across the street, smack
at Alice's face.

Alice spun around and charged from the window. She
grabbed cigarettes and newspaper from the dining table in a
house suddenly tiny and combustible. She conducted herself
out to the back yard, swatting the rolled newspaper on her

thigh. She settled into her lawn chair with a force intended to eject the picture of Mary's disgrace. No woman wants her top ripped off. It doesn't happen on Wakonda.

Sun was raising higher. Her ankle itched with the bother of little creatures made bold in the fat reveling grass. Overhead the sky was more leaf than sky. What a miraculous frill managed by the old elephant-skinned oaks! It would do to sit calmly in the shade and feel the peculiar mini-hurricane of breeze that seemed to manufacture and contain itself in her back yard. If those mosaic chips had souls, Alice had just consigned a thousand to hell, she believed. What did Mary care about mosaics? Alice hoped they would be left in the yard, forgotten. She would go over and whisk them back home.

Out in the alley Londo was struggling with a long roll of carpeting, bright as Easter-basket grass. His girlfriend—poor soul—came from the shed which was perched there on the edge of the brick house's property. Londo had bought the place last year and transformed the shed for his own purposes, nailing on a porch, painting the whole thing twice, installing furniture, an air-conditioner and a daytime girlfriend. A cat-house for a man who saved money by living forever with his old mother, that's what the upgraded shed was all about, Alice had realized on a fair spring evening, taking garbage out back, when along came Londo and a woman wearing heels that matched her dress, returning from somewhere like the Frankie Boy, returning to the shed as if to a home.

"Alice!" he yelled, spotting her. "That guy's bailed out already, can you believe it? He called me from over in Rock Island. It's the middle of the night when he calls up. So I get my cousin on the phone—by now it's two A.M.—and he says he'll come back, fine, just so long as I clean the place good. He'll like this sidewalk carpeting."

"Bully for you!" Alice called.

She settled behind her paper. Through slitted eyes edged over the top, she glimpsed the girlfriend trailing Londo, lugging a thermos. Londo's green baize unfurled as he came through her yard. It shaded the real grass nearly black. The girlfriend's calves were hard and white as bowling pins, spotted blue warnings that she wasn't born yesterday. When she sat, the ridiculously tight cotton-knit shorts rode immediately crotchward. She drank and used a free finger to work the shorts down, hooking like a rug. When had people become so fleshy?

Alice opened the entertainment section. An Alfred Hitchcock movie was playing on her side of town. Matinees! the ad touted. Film classics this month! Her heart leaped an inch. What greater bulwark against the tacky, bludgeoning pursuits whirring on and off Wakonda these days than Alfred Hitchcock? Alfred Hitchcock was personally inviting her to experience the proper laughs and shivers. And just because Sunday bus service had been suspended (a person was expected to drive to malls) didn't mean she couldn't walk right out of the house and see a movie. Two miles to the Lincoln Theater, if that. A very good jaunt. If she walked quickly, which she always did, she could make it to the noon showing. What an idea! She had never gone to a movie alone in her life. Alfred Hitchcock beckoned. How quickly an idea could overtake a person and become action, perfectly conceivable, the only right course. In this mood, Alice could nearly imagine how Jessamine had married.

It was a hike requiring loose cotton pants, flat tie shoes and Kleenex in the pockets; and Alice set off, wallet in hand, tickled as a schoolgirl, through the alley, past Londo's shed and downhill to the main street. She paused there at the juncture where hillside homes boxed off the left side of the street, parkland sprang up across the way, and bridges to downtown ran away to the right. The world had a visor-tinted, slightly unrecognizable cast to it.

Alice turned left. She had not walked this way in years, since the grocery went out. The houses looked darkened, as if after a rain, and they were not automatically known to her by facade or inhabitants; some had gone from frame to aluminum and back to frame; they had been razed or abandoned; turned into a Mister Tax or a beauty salon; sided in earth-tone slats or painted purple; all this without her knowledge. For once, ignorance relieved her and she walked even faster. When a car honked from behind, Alice turned smiling at a group of boys who became immediately stricken; they'd seen the age in her face that was impossible to gauge from behind. "Pooh!" Alice yelled in the prickly heat. She allowed it to be an honor, rather than a disgrace, to have the entire overgrown sidewalk to herself, block after block.

She stopped short at Carla's elementary school. Mercifully this one had not been shut down. The old Victorian looked the same as always; its benign narrow-windowed facade was set back from the street and, of course—being integral to what schools were then—looked down from a hill. Reeling back in memory, Alice heard the clatter of hard soles on floors varnished to indestructibility. She felt the little warm hands she had held the first day of the year. And she saw the tiny green chairs gathered in a story circle. But empty. The children were grown, her vision a memory. The liveliness of that circle was long since charged upon the world, leaving the clustered chairs to present druidic remains, silent spare divulgence of what had been sent forth. From Gloria's asides, Alice gathered that now the very idea of chairs was out of fashion at school. Couches, pillows, and who knew what all, had replaced chairs in the schools. And these days, Alice further understood, every child ate cafeteria food. She had noticed the horrid menu next to Kraft cheese coupons: chow mein, tacos, spaghetti, sauerkraut and wieners. But for the grace of Friday fishsticks, you would think the school was celebrating some kind of International Week. What had happened to peanut butter? To Campbell's soup? Her thoughts went back to those empty chairs. She had known those little green chairs kinetic with energy, and now she did not. Her family life was over, she told herself, gripped and disbelieving. The school stared down at her. James had died; Jessamine had fled. And Carla lived permanently in some kind of wheatberry dream.

But silly. Carla was, in fact, coming to visit on Saturday. Continuity mattered, and there would be continuity despite the jolts. Alice had always seen to it. She checked her bun.

And even though one of her pockets bulged with cigarettes and her thoughts swung around in a chest-thumping rhythm, Alice retained a notion of pre–World War II female propriety that prevented her from walking and smoking at the same time.

She took a moment to adjust to the Lincoln Theater's low lights; but the air-conditioning sign reminded her, pooh! She'd forgotten to bring a sweater. She crossed her arms, anticipating a chill, and called herself a ninny.

Deep in the lobby a small amount of popped corn climbed the corner pane of the machine, and a very young woman seemed intent on scooping it even higher. Alice's entrance had caught a man in brown leisure-style jacket leaning into the mirrored wall, pressing both palms to his hair; he was wiggling his fingers the way a person would for the eentsy-teentsy-spider song: "Out comes the sun and dries up all the rain." She smiled. Now the man jerked at his squared jacket hem and made eyebrow signs at the girl, who did not notice. "Melinda?"

The girl left her popcorn and came forward to the ticket counter. Alice was already flourishing her money: a mere two dollars, this bargain matinee price.

The girl was a new employee, Alice surmised from the way she kept glancing at the man: the putting away of exact change and advancing of one purple ticket from the roll took little dexterity and no cunning whatsoever.

"Thank you," Alice said, applying extra cheerfulness. The girl should know she was doing fine at her very first job; she must know the day as glory.

Now the man stood as if to block entrance while he accepted Alice's ticket, then tore it in half. "Alfred Hitchcock," he announced heartily. "*Rear Window*." Then he looked about. "Er, just the one?"

Alice caught herself turning, too, toward a flicking motion, but it was the wall mirror, her reflection cluttered by gold scrolly designs. She despised looking "antiqued" in mirrors and had squelched the idea of a Craftique kit of that nature. She stood alone in the lobby. A punctual person is often alone. Lips pressed, she gave the man a curt nod and breezed past him and the refreshments.

A pungent intimacy rose from the empty auditorium. The hushed, earmuffed feeling pillowed sensation and banished the world. Alice loved how the carpet made a regal-red slope of the aisle and sprang back from her feet. Only in a movie theater did the word "usher" resound straight from the heart, sending the person forward, half dreaming and surrendered. The dots of light on the aisle seats were ornamentation— baton hurrahs, not mere fire-law installations. And before her a rich tiger-striped curtain was drawn up slightly in scallops. Alice took the best seat: back row of the front third section, aisle seat for quick getaways, if need be, though she expected no onslaught. It was her conviction that a prehuman trigger in most people's brains motivated them to sit exactly in front of earlybird theatergoers or to one's side on the bus, despite numerous empty seats; they crowded you for perfume samples, and at public washstands, and always at bus stops. It was the herd instinct.

She was dabbing her forehead with a tissue when she heard the footsteps; but she did not turn until they stopped dangerously near. She composed a whammy-look to shuttle whomever from her radius.

The man in brown.

"Er, hello. I'm the manager," he said, bending as if to take an order. "I guess you're the only one today."

"Really." Alice did not like looking up to him.

"Er, Sundays can be like this." He looked around. So did Alice. No one had sneaked in.

Alice said nothing and turned toward the curtained screen. Did he feel sorry for her? Suspect her of being a kook? Was *he* a kook? She exhaled through the nose.

"Well, then." He retreated up the slanting aisle.

Alice watched as the curtain was raised a mite, then dropped with a shudder. Her floor space was not sticky, which made an excellent argument for always coming to a first showing of the day. She cradled her wallet in her lap and waited. In moments she felt, rather than heard, the hovering presence of the manager.

"Er, ma'am?" he said from slightly behind her. "I'm sorry. Well, I'm sorry, but you see, I just can't run the movie for one person. I have utilities to pay and all."

He had brought a flashlight along and now he bonked it against his palm. Two puckers had formed on his forehead as he gravely repeated the motion, flashlight to palm.

"I've never heard of such a thing. I walked here and I've paid for a movie." Her wallet fell from her lap and the man was quicker than she, used to floor retrievals. She detected a triumphant geriatric condescension in his balancing it on her armrest without touching her.

"I'm sorry."

"Honestly!" When Alice rose the man threw a path of light up the aisle. She walked away on bobbing yellow, thinking, Off with his head.

In the lobby, back on the level land of gold octagon carpeting, the manager brightened. "Say, ma'am, I hate having you go without a movie. We've got rentals now, you know. For your VCRs. Look here. Sherlock Holmes."

"Pooh," Alice scoffed as the man clacked his plastic movie-things onto the refreshment counter. She had gotten only as far as the counter and stopped to take a deep, tension-fissuring breath. She saw what she had overlooked in her eentsy-teentsy-spider zeal: the man had slinky eyes.

"Refund her, Melinda."

Already Melinda had emptied her corn popper and turned off the light.

Now the sun was hotter, harder, pressing her cheeks and brewing an anger and thirst. Alice stood on the pavement

suffering inhalation of fresh black tarring from the supermarket lot next door: stinging smooth, sparkling asphalt, still
cushiony, still crumbed at the edges of the lot. If a man had
escorted her, the manager would have shown the movie. She
had dampened everyone's day with the discomfort of aloneness. This was not the Orange County buyers' fair, where
individuality took top billing. One person and a giant movie
screen was wrong; the man wouldn't hear of it. She was back
in the glare, turned out of the theater onto a day in which
people made love in driveways, grown men fashioned a hut
for trysting, eighty-five-year-olds married.

The supermarket was a madhouse of women pushing
loaded carts, their faces set on monstrous time-saving
schemes, lacking househusbands, of course, and probably
lacking husbands altogether; an inordinate number of children
were crying and doing monkeyshines. Alice walked up one
aisle and down another to dry the sweat of angry embarrassment and calm herself. There was too much, just too much,
of all of this. You could cut the place down to five aisles and
still have what you needed. An entire aisle looked made up of
eggbeaters and pie pans. They belonged in the dime store.
Here, they were conspirators of the Kresge demise.

She ignored the refrigerator cases of drinks, rather she considered eating an orange for her thirst; but there in fruit she
spied a perfectly good group of kiwis, bagged and discounted
to nothing, as if no one in this town knew enough to eat kiwis
and they must be thrown at a person. California had drenched
her in kiwis. She swung the bag off the counter and jauntily
passed an untended child rattling the daylights out of a cereal
box.

Her back was seized with a terrible itch in the unreachable
zone between the shoulder blades so acutely that she twisted
and winced and hurried to attach herself to a surface. The
drink-cooler handle. She scooched this way and that against
the long door handle, and as relief melted into her bones she
considered the masked emotionlessness of the theater manager's face. The doughy man pitied her. He pitied her this, the

back massage you could not administer to yourself. Anything
else of necessity a person could manage. She would return to
a movie theater alone and watch a fool movie, any movie. She
would bet the manager a new brown suit jacket she would.
But she could not manage a good back massage without help.
This she admitted. The cooler door poked unless she took
care to move evenly. She incorporated that sharp edge into
some up-and-down massage, absolutely ignoring the flash in
her mind of Kit and Mary, hands and breast and back. The
need for back massage was the indelicacy inherent in aloneness that no one wished to see. This was what the theater
manager had known and hated. He preferred she leave the
movie theater lest she remind him of his own past, present, or
future.

"I need Pepsi from in there!"

Alice reflexively jerked sideways with one shoulder
hunched in a block. How long had the snappy young woman
been huffing and revving her tonnage of groceries back and
forth with a golf-tee heel planted in the floor? No more than
a moment, surely. The woman hauled out a carton of clattering bottled drinks.

"Glass bottles, good for you!" Alice cried. "Drinks taste
better from glass bottles. I've never gotten used to milk in the
cardboard, let alone plastic."

But what ferocity in the other woman's eye, in the final
look she threw at the obstacle Alice. The younger woman
took in the kiwis, Alice's no-cart status, and she looked at
Alice as if she simply had no right, was some old *thing*. To
her, the kiwis in plastic were a shrunken, hairy, wrong purchase and she pushed her cart onward.

"The nerve," Alice shot from under her breath.

But they were everywhere, these women, battering cucum-
bers and squeezing limes, defying perishables to wreck their
shopping schedules by giving out midweek.

She flung as many disdainful looks as she could and still
Alice arrived at the checkout counter spitting mad. In the
elongation of cash register reflection, she saw how her hair

had frizzed, and though it was only the trick of surface, her face was wrapped-around featureless. The one curl stuck on her forehead; this piece of hair had stopped growing at some point. She had walked and walked and wearied of this day. The supermarket had the big bland, mixed-up smell of a man-made lake.

She paid for her kiwis. The checker placed them in the depths of an oversized paper bag. Evidently a small bag, as well as a single person, was obsolete at Sunday shopping. Alice called a taxi. When had her shoe come untied?

Outside, without bothering to check for soot or anthills, inches from a leashed dog, she sat on the blond rock parapet, a woman close to sixty with no Sunday busyness. She removed her shoes and brought her legs up, Indian style. She slurped through the kiwis, one after another, letting the bright green juice run freely. And let that Pepsi drinker see her, let all the young housewives savaging the day see her. At a certain age or time, convention gives way. You have no reason to keep it up, and without duty you slip from its hold. She had no duty to another person. There was no duty to her day, whatever a day may be then. She was released into—she admitted—patternless motion. She waited for a taxi and pretended to bask in the free state of California.

CHAPTER 6

Wakonda Hill went on alert the minute a taxi pulled into Alice's drive. She was watching from the kitchen window, and neighbors spied from their yards, everyone home on a Saturday. Calvin's chest was burly, an unsightly thing rising out of lawn chair. It struck Alice just how much he had swelled and mossified over the

years. Smartie Kit held the inevitable piece of chrome in hand
as Carla's legs and full skirt swung from the car. Mary
strained forward but seemed to think better of it: she planted
a boot heel in Kit's direction and watched. The sun oiled and
slowed movement, and the bur oak flattened beneath the
hummocked clouds. Thank goodness her daughter, as short
as she, had inherited long lean legs and arms. Stunted legs on
a short woman were the end, a person had to admit.

Carla twirled once in the drive. That skirt, an African sort
of design put to limp cotton, was out of style now even for
the antistyle age group, unnecessarily of waltz length. Carla
frowned at the raggedy grass, then at the plastic delft water
dish, once the property of a dog long dead, now filled primly
for birds. She grabbed a fistful of hair, then let it drop as fast.
Next, Alice's new addition, the single pink flamingo nodding
among tiger lilies, which Jessamine had admired so, caused a
slump of shoulders, a pause before Carla butted forward with
memory sparking off her as visibly as if every single ribbon of
color from that skirt lashed out on its own and flew, helium-
filled, into the sun.

Carla looked every which way, bollixed by questions and
defense. Except for the brief visit at Christmas with Brian,
which Alice recalled as more hours spent away from the house
than in it (they'd shopped, of course, but Carla had insisted
on sampling restaurants and nearly bulldozed them into going
out for Thai food on Christmas Day), she had not visited since
the final long hospital vigil, and of course no one had known
how to behave then. They had ironed blouses and set off
briskly in the morning, but faltered with the first whiff of
hospital air; they dropped into the green automaton hours,
fluffing James's pillow, saying "Aha" to his chart; and they
wilted into dreams before nurse faces who graciously behaved
as if their sole reason to be was the care of James Morrow.

Doctors traced James's blood aberration to repeated malar-
ial breakdown, South Pacific duty. By means of a diagram
and bric-a-bracked foreigner's English, the one had assured
her, "This business is nonhereditary." In white coat, the mus-

tachioed doctor was like a car mechanic who stood beneath hydraulically suspended cars acting as though the process of wreckage was more important than Alice's knowledge of it.

Backfired patriotism killed James. That's how she saw it.

Alice hurried outside waving. Something was wrong with Carla. She is young and glum, Alice thought, going to her daughter. Raised on restrained alarm. Forgive us! "Welcome home," she cried.

They hugged identical slate-firm backs. And Alice kissed a cheek still smelling of bus travel. Carla drew back.

"Mother, what's with the pink flamingo?"

"Why not?" Alice cried, faking wonder. "They came as a pair, but that would defeat the purpose, you know. I'm sorry about the plastic, of course." She had loved ordering from the ad that dared, "Ruin your neighborhood!" "Don't look like that. We can always dig it up, for heaven's sake." She lit a cigarette and made a production of putting out the match. Naturally, Carla turned up her nose. This was the generation that had lost humor, Alice had to remember at times.

"Did you get a bus seat to yourself?"

"Yes. The bus was nearly empty."

"Aha, they're all on cut-rate flights, I suppose."

"There aren't any planes flying from the towns I passed through, Mother."

"I've got fresh lemonade. Come on."

At the kitchen window Carla peered over a swinging begonia. Alice saw that Mary had taken up a hitchhiking pose next to the motorcycle. She was croaking and thigh-slapping; the sound carried through curtains of humidity, as did the bike's noise. Mary was undoubtedly raising drama from dust to compete with that motorcycle. Thank goodness she wore an ordinary blouse with buttons and sleeves.

"Who are those people?"

Alice handed Carla a glass of lemonade. "The newest neighbors. Motorcycle enthusiasts, as you can see."

"Is the bike broken?"

Alice thought a minute. "They would dust it, if nothing else. I'll bet they're injecting it with more noise."

Such grimness caused Carla to shake her head. She swatted aside the begonia again.

"A biker may be like a doctor—on call," Alice hurried. "The word comes, 'Be in Utah by sundown,' and away he goes on a perfect motorcycle. You imagine motorcycles in the desert."

"Utah," Carla said through a thick slur of lemonade, "is full of Mormons."

Alice studied this tone of voice. Besides the hair and the legs, Carla had inherited her eyebrows—slivered curves that seemed to start far in over the eye, making the look, any look, parenthetical. With such brows neither mother nor daughter could ever manage ferocity up front, and this was what generally threw off husbands and others. They couldn't read the fury. They mistakenly saw the merely quizzical when in fact all hell was breaking loose.

"Another glass? My, you're thirsty."

Carla's hip bumped a large grassy plant on her way into the living room. "There's stuff everywhere. There's hardly room to walk."

"Watch out for the mother-in-law's tongue." Alice had elevated it onto the three-legged stool Mel Gifford had barged into her house with. She pointedly moved two boxes of jute nearer a wall.

The two of them sat on the couch facing the old window fan that bulged and rattled; it had been built in the days before the streamlined box models you could remove from windows. At bedtime the old fan nevertheless had the power to send a breeze back to the bedrooms while drawing out the stale trapped air. The blades at rest looked like the head and shoulders of Nikita Khrushchev; Alice had pointed this out to Carla long ago when it mattered. However unpleasant, a person must know what matters.

A squint at the machete, silver against the dark wood walls, triggered Carla's slow survey of the room. Again, the unsus-

pecting would be fooled into thinking that as a bus ride casu-
alty Carla was only relieving a stiff neck. Carla almost laughed
—a high thin sound shot from her—before she put a frown
to Alice's bookshelves. Most prominent were the thick vol-
umes Alice had received when she briefly subscribed to the
hardcover Tales-for-Late-at-Night Club.

"I've been brushing up on zombies," Alice said, following
her gaze. "Poor souls! If a sharpie gets to them, they're made
to cut cane forever after dying. In Haiti, you know. It gripes
my soul that the word has been so misused. It can mean
anything from uninterested to a very strong drink. Think how
often you hear, 'He's a zombie.' " No, the etymological slan-
dering of *zombie* did not faze Carla, though her face might give
rise to another misapplication of the word: *blank*. She looked
woefully blank.

"Wait till you meet Hazen Batten," Alice tried. "He can't
stand skywalks! His shoes are polished. He has a nobility of
spirit, there's no doubt about that. I like him. With Jessamine,
it's hard to tell what's going on. She's full of design and order,
terribly proud. Funny how tradition seems suddenly radical,
yet Jessamine is Jessamine."

"Are they in love?" Carla asked. Little blooms had replaced
the bus-ride sallowness of cheek. Her voice registered its
dense sound of social consciousness.

Alice picked up her lemonade glass. "A person doesn't ask."

Carla resumed her head-rolling.

"Tell me what on earth Brian is up to. What projects?"

"Brian is Brian. He talks about learning blacksmithing."

"For heaven's sake. And the garden—any asparagus in
sight?" Alice pressed on. She had one eye closed from the
sting of her smoke. She expected that her chin was thrust too
far, for the sake of sincerity, but better this than the weary
sag she felt. Yes, Brian would be Brian, a snowplow of a man,
thorough and steady, blacksmithing. One of those souls ded-
icated to pointless regression. She smelled the idiot biker's oil
and metal. She lit a fresh cigarette off the end of the first
without Carla so much as twitching. Carla's hands in her lap

were horrid little nesting birds. Scatter, fly, Alice willed them.

"Good heavens, I think you're sick, honey. Tell me outright." They both jumped at Alice's blurting, spluttering lemonade and smoke and fear everywhere.

"I've never been sick, you know that. I've never been sick or— Mother, guess?!—I'm pregnant. That's what's, well, wrong. That's why I'm here." She'd shaken the news right out of her hair and continued to shake her head silly.

"Ahh-ha!" Alice sprang to her feet and stood rooted. Once a person has sprung to her feet, no matter how impassioned, there is a moment of foolishness—you're too obvious, too ready, too spontaneous in the face of something that must be absorbed, not swatted. Pregnancy! It might have been a buffalo herd, the rolling thunder of stampede, a huge, ancient, forgotten onset. This was her house and her life in some newly limitless realm of surprise. Jessamine had eloped, and Carla was pregnant. And pregnant with wide wondering eyes that shot forward and back in generations. With quick blinks. She must have given up imagining Carla pregnant years ago if, to be honest, she had ever imagined Carla pregnant. Well, she must have, there must have been moments, say, during the wedding in City Park, during the flute-playing, the kite-flying, a moment of terror and recognition when she'd noticed that some guests were barefoot? She couldn't remember a vivid speculation she'd had on Carla's being pregnant. What with their constant preoccupation . . . poor dear. But I'm hardly a bad mother cat, lazy with the litter, Alice reminded herself. She had always kept steady. Someone must now and she would, she told herself, vowing to hold on from the center and rein in the wildness of fear.

By great chest-heaving effort, Carla said, "It's an accident, Mother," then fell silent. But for Alice the silence was the rich family kind that allowed for, encouraged, the eating of bushels of kiwis.

"Pooh."

"Brian can't even say it."

"But what would he know?"

"Mother!"

"Men. River-running, rumrunning. Look at your little hands; they're teentsy, not at all like mine. Give me that little hand." Alice clasped a hand and hugged her narrow-shouldered daughter. "Divine," she said. "That's what this is."

Now she began to pace. She hummed with her face set against the fan; her voice issued back in little waves. Then she turned and came at Carla with her hands winging her ears, beaming. "The song, remember the song? You know." She framed her face and sang, "And the eentsy teentsy spider went up the wall again."

"Mother, be serious. I have no idea what to do." Carla's eyes were wobbly with tears that would not spill. Alice dropped to her knees and took up both little bird hands.

"Accidents happen, but this is not one. You're gorgeous and we'll celebrate. You're great!" That unstylish skirt, how-ever, was a foreign culture enveloping her daughter. "Let's see, let's see." Alice paced again.

"Mother, I'm with Brian every day. You go along thinking you know someone, then this huge thing happens and what did I see in his face? A flat foreign look. I wanted to run. It wasn't the look of a future father."

"Pooh!" Alice told her. She felt Carla's eyes following her, accusing and burrowing; a mingling of hope and hostile un-certainty. Great flashing hope that was not apparent to Carla yet, flashing outward. It must be threshed, bundled, pre-sented to the sun. How? Carla was asking her. How? She had come to ask how. Thresh, bundle. Alice gathered to her heart, like a great bouquet, her wits. She was always good at making up outlandish rules to fit peculiarities of temperament and the rudeness of situations. Authority without more than a dash of condescension, authority that is a rush of sound and motion overriding immense, unknown horror; what else is mother-hood? It is the tossing of bad pies, the belief in a little green chair.

She shook a finger at Carla. "First we need a day in which to be absolutely royal. We'll celebrate now and answer all the questions later. Shopping makes the best sense." Alice clapped loudly. "Of course. And I mean we'll *shop*, honey, because midsummer sales are on. The timing is perfect."

Yes, she thought, first you must always put a rainbow around the body. Make a person look good and from there let emotion seep down deep, fuse, make its way to the bone in proud, crackling color. First and always attend the body which in all likelihood is scheming to deceive you. It's a grump, the body. It's a permanent baby and worse, but worship it, mollify it; God have mercy on us. She had outfitted James in a splendid camel robe, the brightest and best, at the end.

"Don't think a single other thing. You're not allowed. Today is the day for new clothes and nothing else. Oh, what a day."

Too-crazed laughter spasmed from Carla. She began rocking herself, arms hugging the chest, and those tears would neither shake loose nor dry.

The motorcycle screech jerked Alice so her cigarette ash toppled. A person would think the air was sheet metal being torn apart, and Carla's strangley laugh blended with it. Alice pulled her to standing, vowing to herself, I am Peter Pan, Oz, a grandmother! Now the imaginary jam-smeared children, so recently gnattish and suspect, arced above Alice like glittering sweet-pea angels. Duty. She had regained the possibility of duty and it went way beyond the pose of a full grocery cart. True, it eclipsed men entirely.

Shopping had always triggered hope and raced their hearts with purpose and possibility, through all the years' celebrations and alarms. Shields, armor, weaponry, outright trickery against a bruising, convoluted world—that was the purpose and effect of shopping. New clothes cured the curable. The plundering of a moonlight-madness sale hours after James's funeral ranked as their all-time coup; they'd spent hundreds,

and the three-beat click of MasterCard machine sang with
each purchase, "Good for you." Alice remembered how much
she'd loved hearing that applause: "Good for you." She was
humming in her bedroom, leaning into her mirror to sweep
powder over her cheeks. She raked her hair into a high fat
doughnut and changed into skirt and blouse. A cloud of perfume and the buckling on of a wide belt reminiscent of a
calmer time brought her back to the living room.

Carla washed her face in steaming water and emerged from
the bathroom blotchy and meek, to Alice poring over her
illustrated bus map of the city. A different color traced the
route of each bus, and all over the map animated drawings of
landmarks caused Alice's pointer finger to twitch with interest. "I didn't know the University bus line went so close to
Roosevelt Shopping Center. See how easily we could get
there, but why? They've only got a few good shops. Well, we
know downtown doesn't have anything. Let's hit a mall,
honey. We have loads of time and if we get hungry we'll stop
in our tracks and eat."

Carla could guarantee that her mother had never eaten a
bite of mall food. She ignored the battle cry, but went along
with the reasoning: they would go to the West Side mall, the
biggest one.

They were able to catch a bus at the bottom of Wakonda
that would take them through downtown, out to the mall
without transferring. They sat as always, as they seemed to
have done forever, mother and daughter off to scout the sales.
Alice was already feeling fidgety; the knowledge that smoking
was not allowed could cause this. They lurched through
downtown and were approaching Kresge's—papered over in
big ugly yellow signs, smudgy with black printing: CLOSE-OUT
SALE! She diverted Carla. "Quick, over that way—see the
woman with the nose? She looks exactly like Bullwinkle the
Moose. See?"

And they rocked away from Kresge's unremarked, with
Carla laughing, "Okay, Mother, okay." She opened a window
and leaned into the breeze.

"Every man in this state is named Dale or something worse," Alice announced. "You wonder where they get these names. The women, too. In the morning paper I came across a LaJune. Imagine. What if Bullwinkle is LaJune."

"Don't forget that you named me Carla."

"You *are* Carla," Alice replied, refusing to fan the fire of long-standing contention. She had recognized her daughter as Carla at birth. A person did not guess such things in advance.

They bumped along through the neighborhoods before the bus turned onto a woodsy stretch, and when it gassed itself uphill Carla felt her mother stiffen. The VA hospital would be the next thing around the corner, and if they were lucky the bus would zoom on by. But no, the air brakes shrieked. A woman in uniform got on and the bus hovered there, a big dog panting, making sure you took a look: Colonial pillars stuck onto an otherwise ordinary doorway created an antebellum monstrosity among the oaks. If an evil plantation had been called for in *Gone With the Wind*, something opposite Ashley Wilkes's Twelve Oaks, this would do.

Alice did not take her eyes off the front of the bus, where the uniformed woman settled on a lengthwise seat, her legs like furniture, her eyes flat as pennies.

Then they headed swiftly down a long strip of commercial development where a bowling-alley-turned-supermarket wedged next to a dental park; remodeled laundries, martial arts, dog grooming and every kind of chain restaurant formed a long, sleek anticipatory prelude to the big one, the Westland Mall.

And it seemed immediately they entered the mall that Carla's head swirled with a kind of discombobulated anemia. In a thrift store it was always easy to choose, but here she would have to be sharp, watch and trust to Alice so that an overload of choice would not bring on stupor and despair.

"See the new flat heels, Carla. What do you think of such pointed toes? I *like* the ornaments on dress flats. A buttercup —good. My arch is too high for this, but you'd look cute."

Then she was already appraising another window: "The big-shirt look. How much of it can short women manage?"

Muzak conducted them over to a shoe sale where racks and racks of shoes were price-coded on the inner sole with dots of orange and yellow and chartreuse. "Plenty of size six," Alice noted. "How about something sturdy but fun? Oh no." She drew her head back as if struck. It was the boot display that galled her. Boots not even racked by size, but heaped woefully among themselves. " 'Wide-calf boots,' " she read aloud off the sign. "Well, I guess there's a demand," but you could hear in her voice that Alice pitied anyone cursed with outsized calves.

Carla suddenly felt like a glum teenager blindly resistant to her mother's prom suggestions. "Let's go on. These shoes are ugly."

They passed a cafeteria where Alice would never set foot, and she commented as she always did when passing it, "Why do they come all the way out here for hot beef sandwiches and pea salad? And that horrid grasshopper pie the stupes at work say they crave!"

Old people sat in the window booths, sure enough, with knives and forks going at meat patties smothered in gravy. The time Carla came here with Grandma and Grandpa Morrow they all three ate meatloaf dinner.

"Would you like this? This?" Alice sailed through the stores, instinctively "up" on where each one's discount racks were positioned; she fell upon tumble tables knowing at one toss whether or not it was worth her time to plunge deeper. "Try this on. Here, let me get you something bright." Then, "What in the world?" She held up a little black loop of knit and checked the label. "A tube skirt? Well, if Europe is still the fashion standard, and I believe it is, here's the leanest peacetime look ever."

Neither said a word as they passed a maternity shop.

Mirrored facades tracked Carla-following-Alice. How dowdy I am! she thought. It seemed she had never grown up at all, was not really an adult in the way she'd always imagined adults grew to be. An aura hovering around Alice declared her agelessly female, adult female. Something haloed her presence and ensured against a blush. The fragrance of maturity, a smoothness of calculation tasseled the stupefied mall air as Alice passed through. Something crackled in response to her. Carla feared that this something, ritualistically and safely female, had been lost on her group, the thirtyish to fortyish woodchopping friends. Her build matched her mother's but Alice's carriage bespoke an era: she was at ease in spectator pumps or any high heels; jewelry flattered; her powdered face enhanced her looks and she had learned it all young. Victims of school dress codes and pre-pantyhose days, Carla's group had abruptly defected: 1970 had declared the ultimate fashion revolution, so you thought, and you didn't bother to rethink for years. No more A-line heathers! Garters and nylons banished! Her group had thought to dress a certain way forever: shop the sale tables in Juniors, India Imports, thrift-shop bazaars. Now even the much younger women walking by, mere girls really, emanated a cunning fashion sense; they looked grown up in fashion, free of petulance, as knowing as Europeans. I'm the youngest adult here, Carla wailed inwardly. Everything seemed impossible.

"Shorts!" Alice called from beyond, as if reading her thoughts and pulling her back into rank. Shorts! Forward! Alice was walking unbelievably fast, faster, surely, than at the sale they'd shopped when her father died. They'd stormed the mall and replaced their hospital clothes, Alice going up several notches in color and design. Carla had stuck with her old familiar styles; even so, the purge had been grand.

"Over here, over here." Alice guided Carla through the department store and, with that instinct missing from Carla's psyche, made her way straight for costume jewelry, to a sale table where she zeroed in perfectly on the quality amid junk.

"Let me get you something frivolous," Alice said. "You deserve decoration."

The urgency of decoration eluded Carla. She wore only her wedding ring. Jewelry itched and caught on washrags, turned her wrists blue; it broke, sprouted rashes; and mostly jewelry made her look blatant in a way that just wasn't her.

Alice scooped something from the table and inspected, holding it high. "A moon sliver. You should like that. I'll get one, too. Here's to a wide indigo sky."

They had trudged through every last store and now swung many bags at their sides; they had come to the food row at the far shopping tier, all ajump with uniformed kids frying, slicing, blending, cheering each other on in code.

Carla wilted onto a bench. "I'm just weak. I'm desperate for a hot dog."

"Sit," Alice commanded, dumping everything. She stepped forward and with a certain gravity and flair, and really too loudly (you'd hate to think of someone from the co-op walking by), addressed a little ferris wheel of wieners under glass. "Two hot dogs with everything."

"Then that's superdogs," a paper-hatted boy explained.

Bags and shoeboxes swung against their thighs as Alice and Carla walked back through the mall. Carla hugged a sack of blouses. Big shirts, they'd said without really saying, would be great for the pregnancy.

"You know," Alice said, "there's got to be a theater here. Want to see a movie? I don't care what's showing, ha! No? Well, maybe another day. Before you leave town. Look, here's Arnold's. How did we miss Arnold's?"

Carla sighed and shifted her weight to one side. What was the consequence of a pregnant vegetarian eating a hot dog? And should she have directly changed into the spongy exercise shoes she'd bought at The Athlete's Foot? Arnold's. She hadn't shopped Arnold's in years and remembered it as a land of high-school heather coordinates, and now they'd added a "queen-sized cottage," hardly an enticement, the florals and blueless blues.

"You never know." More the shopping veteran and true believer and scout, Alice forged into Arnold's, eyes on the horizon, and Carla followed automatically. A rack of blouses revolved in Alice's wake, and if she hadn't put the brakes on fast she would have slammed into a monolith blocking the aisle. Misguided, beached, a whale of a man.

"Good grief," Alice cried. It was Mel Gifford.

"Alice," he said happily, with so little surprise as to peeve her to the hilt.

"Of all things." So, Mel *was* the oblivious mall shopper Alice had construed. There he stood in his one-piece tan jumpsuit, arms extended—those freckly furred arms shaped and colored like (anyone would see) turkey drumsticks—and across his hands and arms lay *in Arnold's* a length of seersucker pink polka-dot nightgown. Like a Frankenstein, he held forth some unspeakable evidence.

And as if he weren't totally ludicrous and possibly perverse, Mel swiveled and said hi to Carla. His smile shot up one side toward the wink, and his graying eyebrows went to peaks. He just held that thing.

"Here's my daughter Carla. She's visiting from the woods near Tillman. That's north a ways, over by the river. Carla, Mel Gifford."

"Tillman, yes," Mel boomed. "You've got the best soil in the state over that way."

"I have a great garden usually," Carla said.

"Just what kind of a setup have you got over there? Any farming? Livestock?"

"It's mostly wild, except for the garden."

"Hey, I've got something for you." Mel let go the support of one arm and crooked the other so the nightgown draped like a towel. He began rummaging in a zipper pocket, Alice thinking that if he pulled out his pad for phone numbers it would be the last straw. Rock-and-roll music hammered down, loud in the pause. A person could never tell where this music came from, but in stores like Arnold's Alice often avoided corner racks, having had the experience of thumps and cries leaping more violently from there.

"Seeds. You go over to the drugstore, you'll get them

cheap," Mel said as he spread his seed packets like a poker hand on a display case filled with panties and bracelets. "Turnips—Purple Top White Globe; pumpkin—Big Max; beet—Early Wonder; tomato—Golden Boy." And Alice was thinking thank goodness he had never called her at home or this would be more embarrassing. "They're good cheap seeds," Mel said.

Did he really nudge Carla or was it his overall bustliness? Whichever, Alice disapproved.

"Now, Alice, you go in more for flowers, don't you. And rhubarb."

"I don't have a garden," she replied sharply.

Too late. Carla's face had grown little detective blossoms of color.

"Sir?" A young salesgirl, all bangles, slipped behind the counter. She lowered eyelids the shape and color of Craftique's little conch lamp, and opened them again. "Did you find something, sir?"

"Oh, Alice, here, can you help me?" Mel grasped the nightgown by its ruffled shoulders and thrust it at Alice. She stepped back, feeling distinctly like a denuded matador, with beast avenging.

"Something for my sister recuperating from an operation. I think she's about your height."

"I'm sorry," Alice mustered.

"Just about your height, yes."

"Height, Mel—" Alice began, but stopped herself. True, in a nightgown such as this, unless the sister was Two Ton Tessie herself, height would be measurement enough. Under the circumstances it would be best to assume that the sister was not Mel's identical twin, and Alice approved of the way Mel kept his eyes fixed on hers even as he measured her height. She thought of James's superb hospital robe, and softened.

"Yes, if she's my height, Mel, that's going to be great."

"It's pretty and cheery," Carla added.

"Cotton," said Alice. "It will lift her spirits."

"Along with her face. Sold," Mel told the clerk. "Oh, what about something else, well, fun? She's being cosmetically enhanced." Mel squinted and indicated quick slicings under the eyes and chin. "But the lady is in the hospital, after all. Hmmm," he thought, looking at the clerk folding the gown, "jangly bracelets?"

"Here's the jewelry expert," Carla said, indicating Alice.

Without the gown to hold, Mel's arms hung funny at his sides, a large person's problem. Well, he was rotund and solid, not really fat, Alice had to admit, and as he turned in his canvas slip-ons, squeaking on Arnold's fake-brick floor, it was a dance step.

"So?!" He was giving Alice the old look that meant he had more to say. "Did you take a bus clear out here?"

"Yes, and it's time we run to catch one back." Mel must not be given the time to show bad manners now: apologize for his not yet phoning her; make another plan.

In the moment before he spoke, Mel seemed disoriented; his face thinned and paled. Alice feared that the bricking-up of air might begin. But, "See you in the salt mines," he boomed, and "Goodbye, Carla. Remember to weigh your pumpkins. They're always heavier than you think."

Alice knotted a drawstring bag tighter over her knuckles. She took off at a clip.

Carla hurried after her mother. The Muzak was a drill in her head and if she didn't get to sleep soon she'd pass out on her feet. She followed Alice out of the mall to the bus chugging in place, doors open; the driver stood on the sidewalk, dressed in the chromatic greens bus drivers here had always worn.

"Perfect timing, perfect," Alice crowed, showing her pass.

They flopped into seats and piled everything across the aisle. They were the only passengers. Alice opened a window despite the air-conditioning. "This new vinyl, ach. You can taste it."

Above the windows posters reminded riders of associations that dealt with every part of the body: heart, lungs; the Easter

Seal child stood in her braces; and a Planned Parenthood provocation overrode the youthful crossed fingers on its poster: LOVE CAREFULLY.

"Who is Mel?" Carla asked.

"Someone I work with."

"Obviously. But what about him?"

"He's a friendly soul."

A kook, Carla translated. Her mother thought most people, especially "friendly souls," were kooks.

"Seeds! Mother, he's the soybean farmer and he's visited you."

"Oh, aren't you the shrewdie. Yes, he gave me a ride home, unasked for. Now look at that abomination." Alice tapped the bus window. A sea of sun-baked cars, all sanded white across the top from intense low rays, stretched on forever and undulated in the heat shimmer. "It's a crime with all these empty seats." She patted her seat and exhaled through the nose.

The driver settled his seat cushion and lunch pail. He leaned over the big flat steering wheel and began looking this way and that, pulling from the curb.

"We have the bus to ourselves," Alice declared, as if to an intruder, Carla thought.

"Well, Mother, here we are: Grandma Morrow is suddenly married; I'm pregnant; I wonder what's going to happen to you."

"I'm going to enjoy seeing a hundred movies alone." So saying, Alice put a swift hand to her bun and gave two quick snorts.

And Carla read this whipping relish in her mother's voice as a flirtatious rebuke of the soybean farmer who, as the bumptious ride commenced, occupied a space in the spirit of things.

C H A P T E R   7

"*H*ere he is, dear. Now, you remember Hazen." Jessamine held the door open for Carla. By the tilt of
her head she indicated the interior. A glassy earring
twinkled. "When you visited last Christmas he stood right
there in the lounge, by the shuffleboard. As we walked by he
said, 'Introduce me to your people.' "

"I was supposed to act casual! You were being spied on!"
called a rusty, chuckly voice from within.

Jessamine's earrings shook all the more.

"Sure, I know you. Hi, Hazen," Carla said, entering.
Hazen did not look familiar in the least, and though she'd
tried to think nothing she could not imagine her grandmother
with anyone but her grandfather, a wiry little man in starched
collar, and here was Hazen Batten, tall and soft, wearing
cowboy-cut shirt and checked pants.

After kissing her grandmother's poochy cheek and giving
Hazen a big handshake, Carla sat on a deep-cushioned brocade couch that raised her legs with hydraulic force: her toes
barely reached the Oriental rug, and her calves, showing beneath a straight lavender knit skirt, were flattened out like a
child's against this precarious gravity.

"So," Jessamine said. She smoothed at her own skirt. She
sat on one of the chairs that had famously traveled the prairie
a hundred years back, with a widow and five sons and bundles
of hidden money. Jessamine could tell the story as if she had
been there. Everything she owned was antique, but family.
Carla knew that the china slipper on the lamp table was inscribed with an eighteenth-century date.

Jessamine stood again and pressed at her lap. "Now, then."

Carla moved to sit toward the edge of the couch and crossed
her legs. Jessamine unfolded and placed a TV tray before her,

then served little cakes and juice. These trays had to be an addition that came with Hazen, as did the big leatherette rocker he was plopped in, smiling. Jessamine continued to hold Hazen in a smile at once as open as a field at dawn but utterly private. A third person was clumsy and intrusive against that look. Even me, Carla realized with a start. This is romance, exclusion, fervor!

But Hazen wasn't so rapt. "She's always feeding me." He chuckled and patted his shirtfront. He reached into a bowl of lemon drops, which might explain his clicking speech.

Jessamine lifted a clump of Carla's hair and put it behind her ear. "What news do we have from the river?" Her question rang out for the audience. Hazen should take note.

"Brian's on early shift and he's studying birds at home. He manages to tag chickadees at the feeder."

"Birds." Jessamine went around the world with her head to express the wonder of birds, Brian, family. You could as easily describe snake charming, puff-pastry baking, or a career in origami. The fact of accomplishment and testimonial to family structure set Jessamine aflutter, no matter what. She had been known to declare of a distantly related but favored California boy who suddenly left college, "He is a *journeyman* carpenter. With such skill, he need never worry. Educated men should be so smart."

Jessamine lifted the prize of hair and looped it toward Hazen. "Carla, Carla," she said. She had a story for Hazen in the flesh: a granddaughter.

A low hum of air-conditioning, a view down to garden, and the array of perfectly dusted family artifacts froze Carla into stiff-faced granddaughterly eagerness, but look at how Grandma Morrow had outgrown herself. She'd sprung a new identity on the family and now she was distinctly Mrs. Hazen Batten, stepping lightly in oxblood squash heels, at once forgetting that anyone else in the world was in the room besides her Hazen. "Dear," Jessamine called sweetly. She passed ornate snacks to Hazen, a woman loving a man. She clasped her sparkling necklace to her throat and twisted it. She alternated

looks of tenderness, shaded by degrees of vivacity, between
family member and the chosen love, and attended to Carla
as to a small child which, helplessly, Carla blushed and
became.

"You'll want to hear about our trip," Jessamine said, folding
her hands with utter self-command. No mention of the elopement; the marriage might always have existed. "We drove
down to Walnut Grove and spent two nights in a roadside inn
thereabouts. The little country church is still standing. On a
hunch I asked an old lady sitting on a bench in LeRoy if she
recalled what used to be there. Did she remember the livery
stable? 'The Stanleys' livery, if anyone's,' she responded, obviously pleased as punch. And I told her, 'I was a Stanley
here.' "

"She's hooked up with Battens now." Hazen's voice came
in as a high wheeze, a sweep out over plains. "She had me
driving her all over the place, combing the back roads. Lucky
I'm an old homing pigeon. Used to run my milk clear down
to Missouri. But I tell you, girl, I've never done so much
driving in twenty years as I've been doing now with Jess here.
She's a regular sightseer."

Jess?!

" . . . picnics with each family spread out on blankets,
there on the west side of that little church, Carla, my dear.
When I was a girl," Jessamine emphasized. "Rows and rows
of us. Families brought their fried chicken and their drinks
and what-have-you. Berry pies. Biscuits. Sunday biscuits. I'd
say that was our idea of fun. Pretty simple, weren't we?"
Jessamine laughed a secret laugh, and Hazen's reverie shut
down to gutturals. Carla said she could only imagine the fun
and began to mention contra dances, but what she saw on
Jessamine's face was a little smile that said, "They haven't
invented anything more fun," and, as always, in Jessamine's
presence everything beyond her radius seemed of a lesser
world.

Hazen sat with his hands gripped to the arms of the deep
cushioned rocker, pushing forward and back. His fidgety

puffed fingers might have been reliving the drive. Imagine Grandma Morrow or Hazen Batten ever knowing romantic hesitation or raising a voice in political dissent. They would faint dead away upon hearing the abortion mutterings that thrummed a gray space of heart. Carla pressed her feet down hard lest she faint dead away for the newlyweds.

"Gene Stanley," Jessamine pronounced in that way she had, a slow enunciation perfect for dealing with the world's foreigners, none of whom she'd known. "Now, he was a tall man who did poorly at farming because it simply wasn't his vocation. Gene Stanley prospered in the service area."

Taken back to Jessamine's childhood, vivid with threshing parties and lengthy beards, with a decided emphasis placed on millinery fashions, and the sensation of heating bricks snuggled to cold feet on a sleeping porch, Carla was rendered mute and lightheaded, turned out of her own future. The family story had no beginning or end, only Jessamine's nuance and emphasis.

As the tartness of red June apples was described, Carla had to suck in her cheeks. And when she was supposed to be picturing biscuit dough rising under oilcloth in Jessamine's old pantry, she felt an oven door open on her face, the baking and scorching attacking her eyes.

"I need a tissue," she said, rising quickly, patting down the beautiful skirt that tended to cling. (Alice had scolded her into buying it.)

Jessamine's bathroom was abloom in yellow: towels, toilet cover, fuzzy wastecan, tissues and holder, snail-shell soaps and shower curtain, creating a weird sense of solar storage, a shut-in's idea of capturing the sun. Carla rubbed her cheeks. They *felt* yellow and her jaw would not relax. She stood on the furry-covered scale: five-pound weight gain, though nothing showed. But anyone would see a doctor before letting such news sail onto display along with the china bootie. This was Jessamine's day; the meeting of Hazen and Carla, no more. It was not duplicity, just a bad omen, to behave otherwise and break the mood. Let this visit be like the others. The comb Carla tugged at her hair had to be Hazen's: long, dark and plastic.

"The garden is under way but slow," she said, now back on the couch. "This year I want to can lots of relishes."

"You little scoot." Jessamine nodded at Hazen. "From my old recipes, I'll wager." Then, "Oh, look at your pretty shoes, Carla."

Carla turned a sandal—a mall sale—this way and that while Jessamine recalled a story of buying shoes for a nine-year-old Carla. "A little girl wanted gray shoes, Hazen—just like her teacher's, she said—and that was impossible to find in the better stores. I won't say *where* we ended up finding gray shoes for a little girl."

"Nine years old? About that time some of us country boys went to school barefoot and the town boys envied us." From the ceiling, Hazen recalled his life. "Yes, and my feet spread to runners. I wear extra wide."

"Hazen." Jessamine turned deep perplexity on him. "Carla doesn't want to hear that kind of thing."

"What boy wouldn't want to sit barefoot, cramped up in school's bad enough." The swivel rocker launched Hazen this way and that as he fisted the air like a sports fan. He grabbed glory from where he pleased.

Jessamine turned to her walnut cabinet and scanned the top row's cut-glass ware.

"Three deer have been coming to our feeder," Carla interposed.

"Oh my."

"But were they healthy?" Hazen pressed a palm as if tightening his hair over the ear. "They're getting scarcer in these parts. Crowded out."

Close up, Hazen's face was a patchwork of colors: blues, and whitish dots, wide swaths of needly pinks, reminding Carla of a childhood project.

"Of course Carla's deer are healthy," Jessamine said. "But now, dear," she said to Carla, "shall we take a walk in the garden?"

Jessamine clamped Carla's arm and indicated to Hazen that he should rise. Hazen gripped the arms of the chair and hoisted his big square body, but he fell back into the cushions with a great squawking sound. He tried again; his arms quivered, and he sank. The cushions continued a minor squawking.

"Well, what's the matter, Hazen?" Jessamine spoke sharply, not altogether kindly. Hazen pushed and got to standing but needed immediately to grip something for support. His legs made a wishbone. He reached for the chair, which rocked and spun from him. One step forward and his leg wobbled loose. His bulk swayed, then he started a backward stumble. Carla rushed to catch him as Jessamine screamed, "Hazen!" with real terror in her voice.

"I've got you. Okay, Hazen, it's okay. Hold on to me." Carla battered and strained against Hazen's slumping weight. She was butting into his armpit and trying to grab a handful of stomach.

"Don't you hurt her!" Jessamine cried.

Hazen's arms had gone to wild propelling, latching on to Carla's thigh or hair or back for an instant, then swinging into the air again. She got his stomach in hand and gave Hazen a tremendous rude shove—a great punch into bread dough—that sent him upright and steady for a moment. She swung the chair around and tapped him on the chest, toppling him toward the seat, which she now rushed to steady for him; and Hazen fell safely, loudly, his scared crab limbs flashing.

Jessamine stood over Hazen twisting her ring and brooding on him head to toe. She put hand to his forehead and whispered incantations Carla could not catch from her place back on the couch. Carla's helplessly elevated calves trembled, and she was breathing hard. It's the stuff of miscarriage, anyone would say so, she guessed. It was the sensation of Brian turning the wrong look on her abdomen all over again, and again adrenaline seized and cleared the passages for a moment of instinctual response; but as quickly as she'd felt protective, so calmness began seeping into her bones, and the other truth

fled the heart. Already the familiar crafted attitude was back:
I don't know how to have a baby and that's that.

"Hazen, what is it?" Jessamine rasped urgently. "Is there
. . . Hazen, is there something I don't know? Tell me."

"Whewy." Hazen's face now shone waxy pale, all colors
drained to no color. "All I know is I feel like I've taken too
much sun. I ain't ever had a dizzy spell."

"Never?" Jessamine asked, rising to face Carla. Carla, who
had never heard "ain't" in her grandmother's room, trained
her eyes on the three-hundred-year-old majolica plate in the
china closet, half expecting it to shatter.

A snap upward of the chin, a gossamer veil put to the eyes,
and Jessamine was composed. "Hazen, Carla and I will walk
out of doors without you. Rest a spell, my dear."

In the hall Jessamine's posture and deliberate step gave her
dignity and more height. "He drives a nice car with perfect
air-conditioning. He's healthy. I can't imagine," she said, determined to imagine nothing.

Behind Hillcrest, meticulous landscaping rearranged the
sloping lawn into a formal miniature: stylized squirrels scamp-
ered in a frieze up a bird bath; if a breeze came up, a sunflower
weathervane would twirl, and a parade flag would whip up
patriotically from a grotto of sorts. Even the boulders lent a
preposterous calm as if basking in an idea of salvation. And
the residents of Hillcrest who had wandered briefly into the
heat of the day held their bodies motionless under awnings,
in broad swings fixed to move just barely, no matter how
much madness a reminiscing rocker might intend. Roses flung
mass fragility sharply into the air. Jessamine passed along,
bestowing faint smiles on the seated.

"He has his programs," she replied to an inquiry on "your
husband." "And I my granddaughter." When she linked arms
with Carla her bosomy fullness nudged Carla's little rock of
breast. Another genetic devolution, Carla thought: she had
not grown "up" to have her grandmother's breast. This generation had not. (Those young mall girls, she realized now,
had looked both stylish and buxom.)

"That was Mrs. Jennings," Jessamine whispered. "Half the day I'm made to hear about her son the Catholic priest."

After a measured walk to the far corner, Jessamine again smoothed at Carla's hair, then produced an envelope from her purse. A bill clearly showed through. It would be ten dollars, and didn't ten dollars still cover a nice silk scarf?

They kissed goodbye. On Jessamine Carla smelled a certain cologne fragrance apart from the roses. She thought of a livelier preserve, of cranberry chutney.

"Oh, but you're pale as a flower. My dear, don't tell me Hazen hurt you. I'll never forgive myself."

"No, Grandma, I'm fine. And Hazen is wonderful." She kissed Jessamine again and left her on the sidewalk to watch, as was her habit, every inch and twitch of her retreating granddaughter. Carla went back inside through the foyer to head for the front door. All the glass doors were reflecting Jessamine's stance: thin legs widely positioned in the elderly way, making a cradle of her skirt. She might gather apples or petals or a sobbing child in that skirt as she strained from the waist to catch the very last look of her granddaughter. Until the departing person was completely out of sight, a Morrow would peer and wave and wonder. Even Brian had taken up the habit.

·   ·   ·

Finding a knife sharp enough to cut vegetables in the kitchen was victory, discovering turmeric in the cupboard was a miracle, an ancient dusty orange tin box Carla sniffed for tang. She cut a block of tofu into cubes, working on a speck of clear counter space. The kitchen did not lack for countertops, but they were choked senseless with rubberband mazes, loose marbles and tacks, sales slips, free samples of tea and candy hearts. A tower of pennies rose from a corner; the cellophane on a boxed knife set had never been removed. Here and there, little notes proclaimed events: "Younkers noon— free food samples!" A coupon for process-cheese slices was weighted by a walnut. An electric can opener served to elevate the spider plant, and the poor hanging begonia had been knocked about so much it listed on a permanent basis.

Here, growing up, she had watched Alice peel her red-skinned potatoes directly into the pot and slice perfect coins of bananas over breakfast cereal, a sleight-of-hand flourish put to the act, a lusty chorus of "My mama done told me, when I was in knee pants" sending her into a rapturous dream of some new white-sweet world that might come on, open up and rain joy on them.

Maybe Alice had defied her own debris by ignoring it for song, but she'd better watch out—soon the very airspace would be snatched right out of the house. In the kitchen was bred the house-at-large's problem in mini-form: junk armament. Trick countertops and trapeze plants, all crazy.

The wheeze of air brakes announced Alice's homecoming, and once the bus passed by you saw her, dressed in smart skirt and dolman cotton sweater—her jacket draped on one arm—struggling up the hill with something inching from a large bag. (Had she ever in her life come home from work empty-handed?) Every now and then she'd hop and her knee would poke sharp edges back into the bag. "Darn," she exclaimed in clear high spirits. All of Wakonda might note another day's triumph.

A curl waved across her forehead. In a minute she would step into a house filled to bursting with knickknacks gleaned from the office. School projects and gifts had been forever fashioned out of this stock. Name an object and Alice would be rooting through boxes and bags muttering, "I know I've got one here . . . " and she would come up with whatever the personality or occasion required, potions or alms: a tea cozy shaped like a hen, a rock-tumbling kit for children. Last Christmas in a twinkling Alice had fished out a brocade clutch for Jessamine, do-it-yourself-monogram hankies for distant Morrow relations suddenly come to town.

Once, everything had been boxed and kept out of the way; but now the house was on a creep forward, daring you or

asking for help, looking nuts and brazen. What had looked
lumpish and dim against her own predicament when Carla
had arrived, scarcely a week later winked and sparkled and
protruded with all sorts of specific absurdities. Even the classy
dark wall paneling, formerly smooth and bare, was demented
with needlepoint samplers. Craftique must have had a run on
needlepoint samplers. Never, not even when Carla worked at
Kresge's, was a stitched-together fruit-bowl picture something Alice would badger her into using her employee discount on. But free was another story, so here it all was, the
tasteful and the tasteless, the free: oddments bunkering
against some unseeable chaos. It made her think of ownership
as a form of terminal exhaustion.

Alice rustled her bags through the door. "My arms are
killing me. I've got manhattan glasses, these snifter affairs.
For you, picture frames of all sizes. Wait, you're going to
need them."

She dumped everything on the living-room floor and kicked
off her heels—"Finally!"—and sashayed to her bedroom.

Carla left off stirring to brood over the glassware that she
knew her mother would never use; she glimpsed Alice flinging
her expensive suit and sweater onto her bed, irreverent as a
teenager; brushing her hair loose. Alice hummed the "Wash-
ington Post March" and did one elaborate stretch exercise.
Carla went back to the kitchen to guard her stovetop tofu dish.

And Alice emerged in a change of outfit that might have
been assembled at Craftique: drawstring pants bloused and
tied at the ankles with looped white cords; designs of grapes
and bananas climbed up and down the legs. "One ninety-nine
on an odd-lot rack. The price of an idiot giant Coke. Who
would believe it?" She modeled with pointed knee, hand on
hip, and Carla thought, How can she help me? She's a girl
sorcerer.

"That's amazing. Mother, I've been thinking, why don't
you let me help clear out the house some? Let's put it on a
diet." The stab at humor only made Alice's knee bend more
sharply and her eyes close to slits.

But Carla imagined a fleet of Goodwill trucks trafficking on Wakonda. "Things pile up and you don't notice. I'm that way, too. Honestly, the three of us couldn't get around in here even if, you know, we were all here. Mother, look at your ivory from Grandma Morrow—it's just tossed in with those chiffon things. And your vampire books take up all the shelf space. We could at least rearrange," she added lamely. The house would one day exceed capacity. In her mind Carla saw doodads exploding over the Wakonda sky.

"I want order," she cried. "It's the nesting urge."

"The back yard is perfectly ordered, perfectly," said Alice. "And I want my so-called vampire books within reach." Case closed and Alice clapped her hands as she often did to change the subject. "We'll relax now. I've got a salesman's sample for us. A perishable."

They sat on the couch sipping exquisite alcohol-free grape juice poured from what looked like a wine bottle. Carla felt the bubbly coolness in the back of her throat, and at the temples.

"Charles Addams's *Homebodies*," Alice said, reaching for the bookshelf. "How long has it been since you've seen it? I love it, just love it." As she flipped through, Carla moved closer to see. Ghoulish and wry, it was the cartoon book that had superseded stories of romping animals and fairytales, and even now it smelled of childhood. Every page was in black and white; curious, Carla thought, that it had held her child's attention, with its characters so owlish and slit-eyed, hunched over quirky and diabolical schemes. A man wished his smiling wife into the wishing well as he tossed a coin. On the opposite page a girl was setting her dollhouse on fire so that the brother, it appeared, could bring down an ax. Carla wondered aloud what she had thought, and whether a child should read this kind of thing.

Alice raised up with a missionary look and snorted, "Of course."

The yin-yang of childhood had slung Carla on a boomerang path between Alice's cartoon revelations and James's bedtime stories. ("We ate C rations, food from dark-green cans. Camouflage was everything. The nighttime jungle is as black as hell.") She realized abruptly that no life is a middle ground and wondered if this sense of revelation could count for maternal instinct.

What was this spindly brassy thing across the room?! It was sculpted into big loops that formed nose, eyes, antlers. It rose behind an end table staring, from a cartoon or a jungle. It was grotesque.

"Why a deerhead?"

"Horrible!" Alice cried, but turned a slavish delighted look on it. She had very likely forgotten the existence of this deerhead altogether, the way other people do the color of their mattress or a water stain high on the wall.

"Take it as a souvenir when you finally leave those woods." Alice's throaty cigarette gurgle thickened as she laughed at her own cleverness.

"Dinner's ready," Carla said, heaving an unnecessary sigh. She would mind her own business if only she could bear to.

"And eating is your job." Alice pushed off from her thighs, sprang to her feet and slapped shut the book.

At the table Alice scrutinized her salad of cabbage flakes and chickpeas from on high before sitting down. "Honey, health food may not be enough to sustain you. Your father used to feed me thick malts. Mountains of fried breakfast brought you to term."

"This isn't watercress." And dishing up the main course Carla said, "You can fix tofu as fast as slapping together a sandwich."

"Tofu," Alice considered as she speared a piece and pushed it into soy. "I had expected chicken texture. Funny." First she ate around the tofu, revealing an aster on the plate. Never mind the china passed on when Jessamine entered Hillcrest; they ate from the supermarket dinnerware Alice had amassed plate-a-week with elaborate fanfare ages ago.

"Bland, isn't it? Excuse my imagination, but what perfect zombie food. Don't go looking funny. Really, there's a rule:

no salt for zombies, and never, ever meat. In a word, they're health nuts by definition, poor things." She held an impaled tofu cube on her fork. "Spice up their food and it's a nightmare. If given meat or salt, zombies are sure to walk about wreaking havoc; trying to get back to the grave they'll even trample relatives. There, I'm full. I'm healthy. Now let me bring out the Mystic Mint cookies. Yes, sugar. You need a touch of decadence and I know you crave sugar. Honestly, honey, your cheeks look like ball bearings. Relax. I order you to laugh. Everything's in magnification, the good and bad now. Pregnancy—it's fits and starts you'll get used to."

"What *will* I get used to? Tell me what to expect and everything you remember."

"Give me a good back massage."

Alice sat on the ottoman eating cookies. Carla vowed not to eat a single one, tried not to smell them or see the silvery green box or watch Alice's half-moon brandishing of one after another black minty cookie. It was an old ritual tale-telling position. Carla stretched her legs to either side of the cushion for balance. Her mother groaned happily and her head bobbed lower and lower to make twin runners of her neck cords, while Carla massaged.

Besides Melanie Green, with whom she planned to discuss nothing, her mother was really the only other woman Carla knew to directly ask about pregnancy. Either she had drifted toward childless people or else the baby boomlet was coming late to the river. She lived in the vast sea of measured accomplishment, an order exclusive of such acrobats as babies.

Alice asked, "What was the problem with being pregnant? A person can't even remember. Short-term amnesia sets in and protects a person."

"I wish you wouldn't call yourself a person all the time!"

"I'm a person who certainly didn't take pregnancy classes."

"They didn't have classes then."

"And thank goodness for unenlightenment. Pregnancy is pregnancy. Nine months of sluggish, glorious time out. I felt —let me think—invincible, supreme. Hitler was dead, the bomb dropped, and we refused to notice Korea. When I walked outside the air parted around me. That's what it was like to be pregnant, suddenly everyone was, and so anxious to get on with life. The new houses were pink and green and yellow. Life was going to be a vacation."

"Everyone purposely ignored the bomb."

"I should hope so. And could people ever be so happy buying those little box houses now? Pink and green and yellow. I doubt it."

But they were off the subject. Carla meant to say, What was Daddy like? Did he love you enough? Did you ever feel so alone?

"The human race runs largely on faith, no matter what it does to itself," Alice declared. "Cookies won't kill a person." To prove it, she took another.

"We're at the mercy of the seasons in the woods. That's faith."

Alice rolled her head down and then way back, mouth open in a sort of neigh that could mean pleasure felt or contentiousness.

"At any given moment we're subject to extremes of conditions." Carla could not stop herself, though she wished Alice would quit munching while she spoke. "The big jack pine could smash us, just topple over in a storm and smash us."

"Tree attacks baby?! Oh, honey, you're mad. Here's the difference between my age and yours. We had facts on our minds. We said in July, It's snowing in Argentina, how fun! And the fact was enough of a delight. Now it's analyze and predict and tofu. Spare me the woods. Men ran away to those woods to avoid the draft. Woods are for running away and tramping about. You know yourself all the communes are dead. People do reenter."

"It's a lifestyle, Mother. It's choice."

Carla found herself drawing circles and lines on Alice's back, now that the first round of massage was over. The sound of Alice's cookie-chewing and murmuring continued. Gently she pummeled her mother's back in the manner from

years and years ago when she had told "back stories" that
were acted out in great sweeps of motion, tappings, gallopings
and travails along the spine and the shoulder blades, the fields
and ravines of the back. Bridges and cavalry and folk dancers
and the extreme terrain of two hemispheres figured in
the epics of Cecil B. De Mille vigor. And Alice would be
provoked to neighs and gasps, and shake the earth itself
as the story demanded. Carla had parted the Red Sea on this
back.

"Imagine Asian women who squat in a field, have the baby
and go back to hoeing. I don't inhabit the same kind of body!"
Carla cried. During the Vietnam War young women had
whispered this news among themselves, chastened.

"Think of the babies who survived the Mexican earthquake.
They didn't know any better," Alice said impatiently, "so
they stayed alive. Now, there, under the right shoulder blade,
please! Ahhhhh."

Carla was rubbing fists like mallets up and down Alice's
back. When she thought of Brian, how he would stand there
above her in a hospital bed, what that would be like, she got
berserkly angry and she poked too hard.

"Carla!"

"Sorry."

Standing around, a man with a cool dry brow and open
palms doing what he was told to do, unable to shed his self
into action, maybe thinking the theoretical or measuring the
experience somehow—that would be Brian. He would retain
choice, that's what frightened and irritated her.

"Brian might not be much help."

"As if you can change biology."

"But I can be angry. What was Daddy like?"

Alice stopped chewing and took a deep breath. "I came out
of the hospital carrying you, and here was a ceremony with
flowers galore. He had run through the neighborhood digging
up flowers. The roots wiggled, I swear. The dirt smelled as
sweet as you. The car, a black Ford, was spotless. He had
probably been waxing it for days. Nerves, you know. He was

waving and smiling wider than you'd think a person could. You were a little flower that could wilt. Imagine a heat wave in May. I covered you all up, and Jessamine and I walked to the car, saying, "Surprise."

"But in the hospital, did he just stand there the way I imagine, or what? What help was he?"

"None at all. He waited until afterwards, for all that." Alice's mouth was full of cookie, her words took chopped detours. "The man's role *is* minor at the crucial moment. Then it grows, maybe."

"Daddy wasn't even in the hospital?"

"Pooh, no. You'll see how a person gets all tossed in the head and needs to be led around. Jessamine took over, really, and she thought for James's sake—really, she just had a feeling of what would be best. Who cares now?" Alice chomped on her cookie. "We came outside and there he was, ready to be your father. No, it didn't seem odd, days had passed. You were born. That's what mattered."

Alice's back had become the land of severe tomtomming, and Carla's breathing was staccato as if a rhythm, the right rhythm, would kill tears and draw up the beauty of blank thought.

"Quick, back to the shoulder blades, please. There," Alice said. There, enough said. A person didn't dwell on all that, and why upset her daughter, as obviously anything, any tidbit at all, would upset her. Alice reached for the cookie box on the carpet and made a racket taking out another. A baby comes to a person, that's what's important. Carla will see. Forget the blather. She'll see, oh, if there were another way, a mother would pass it on, teach her daughter, for Pete's sake. But this is where you let go. She remembered all too clearly how she had lain there on a bed propped so high it seemed her head had flattened, as if just a breath of air, one thin streamer of it, lay between her and the ceiling, really a silver thread or straw's worth, and her work was to suck it, keep going, keep gulping in the exact right spot. From that, she had to inhale all the news she would ever know about how separate and strange is a man. The hospital—Carla will see this—is for and of women and babies. The doctors in the form of bushy eyebrows appeared at the very last moment to do drama with their hands, and then they were gone, all of them men. The nurses had done everything, the dirty work. The nurses had scolded and championed all in one breath, and were always a beat ahead of you, those nurses. Whitely dressed, with rubbery faces, they might block the light or swing it round to scald your eyes. They stood there flipping down the dominoes of everything that had ever made sense. Whatever girlhood, whatever pride and pose and cover-up a person had come in with, was flung away in sweat and rags and jeers, all wadded and disgorged. She had screamed into the faces of strangers who looked upon her with, and then without, emotion. It's me! She kept struggling to tell someone the story. I'm sinking, but it's me! She'd screamed and not even sounded the tiniest alarm. Nurse faces lit up from within, and the scream was something giant visited upon you rather than a howl up from the gut. The scream was the world. No, you didn't forget, for Pete's sake, but for sanity you did not go around drawing this up to you and fashioning conclusions. When you saw the baby it all floated away. And Jessamine, who had been through it with kettles and eider-downs and a midwife neighbor, said you were fine. She knew *it* and she knew her son James. She kept him away; and James, for all a person knew, was soothed into thinking, as he stepped into the car that morning, that some magnificence of "female trouble" had taken place quite neatly—ice packs and red rubber water bottles were applied, frilly things draped and worn. For all James knew at home, still combing his hair, birds hopped on the sill as the baby was born. Heraldry, that's what he could provide, and he did. He stood by that waxed car. His face was a sun. He stood dressed beautifully and had flung all four doors open so that the car was just a frame as you approached it. She saw an endless horizon of rooftops out the other side, and an early-morning turquoise was doming the land. James tenderly helped her and the bun-

dle she called Carla in, and the way he cooed as if he'd always
known how trembled her with deep, relaxing pride. Jessamine
heard him, too, and tilted her head on which she wore a felt
maroon hat with a razor feather pointing up.

Carla brought Alice out of her memory. "We were always
waiting, because of Daddy—watching for changes we'd pretend not to see. Looking forward has always been fearful,
impossible! Bodies scare us, you know that. Cover them!
We're stricken to see them change."

Carla feared she had gone too far. Alice's back was shrinking. It folded in on itself like a duck, wings high, head
invisible, sheltered. But she sprang up, saying, "Ha!" and
went for her bookshelf, leaving Carla's hands to massage thin
air.

Alice flipped through something with a bat on the cover.
She peered closely for a page or two, snorted and closed it.
"Thank goodness we don't live in Haiti. We'd have to worry
about jumbies. I'd forgotten them. They're raised by the voodoo like zombies, but they escape the work life. Jumbies are
abroad causing mischief."

Her mother's bun was a knot. She stood terribly straight
with the bat-fronted missal tucked under her arm, her lips
pressed to invisibility. She snorted. She was thinking hard,
and when she turned a bright hawkeyed look on her, Carla
understood that with memory pried loose her mother might
calypso or cry, you didn't know which. The book must be
held.

Carla pressed her eyes shut and saw fifty wavering suns,
hot balls of sorrow. She had stirred memory up greedily and
in her mother's own sorrow seen future responsibility. Alice
needed her.

They both started when the phone rang.

"Unplug it," Alice said. "I'm not talking."

But Carla picked up the receiver to Brian's unhesitating
"Hello!"

"Oh, I didn't expect you. Hi, Brian. No, I wasn't expecting
anyone. We're both here, yes. Yes, we're fine. Wait a minute.

Mother?" she called, but Alice had scooped up her cigarette pack and slipped out the door.

"I *think* we're fine," she told Brian. "We're very busy. Talking."

"I've been visiting Melanie Green and her baby, honey. The way she explains everything, she's a big help. Yes, it's sinking in that we're having a baby! I sent you one of her books. Read it on the bus coming home. Soon, Carla?"

Brian's voice was a river rushing at her, all current and starlight, a bit too much lapping at the edges, a presumption of territory. "I haven't seen a doctor yet," she said.

"I've changed little Sam's diaper." Brian's laugh held the unmistakable pride of a nursemaid's. His earnestness as good as knocked the wind out of Carla.

"Great." Her fake voice flattened and rose up in the sinuses, causing a pressure the same as any lie would do.

"What else? We've got snap beans growing wild all of a sudden."

"Imagine," Carla said. "Snap beans," she repeated as she hung up the phone.

Outside she found Alice sitting sideways on the lawn chair, awkwardly, so where the legs of a relaxed person would stretch, the plastic weaving sagged with all her weight.

Carla touched a shoulder, and Alice dropped her head into massage position.

There was a broad hum of activity in this yard, Carla couldn't figure it out. Not even a rabbit was in sight, but a breeze kept everything—the long grass, the bushes and fronds, the oak leaves—jittery, busy with a talkiness that had turned Alice rapt.

"Everything's so lush," Carla said. "The spirea bushes have coattails. They're very formal bushes."

"You'd have me trim them?"

"No, never. Let them go wild. They have coattails because they're wild."

"I hate trimmed hedges. Bushes weren't made to be sheared like sheep. It's a spectacular yard, don't you think? And it's certainly not Haiti," Alice said, with the sunlight dappling her proprietary smile.

• • •

"Know now that a soul of sturdy suspicious nature inhabits you; one of the spirits who has held back in the cosmos shrewdly waiting has zoomed at you. Here is your baby!"

Carla was reading from the book (Melanie Green's), which arrived the very next day, and plowing through the remaining Mystic Mint cookies. The unsuspecting mother is the blessed one, she read.

Melanie Green had bewitched Brian with one of her theories. So be it. Carla brushed her hair, all of it flung forward, then she threw it back and caught a glimpse of herself in that surprised, flushed, wild-stalk moment in which even she looked a little bit like a model. Melanie Green had found a philosophy to suit her. After years of claiming that young wanton living had rendered her sterile, two years back Melanie had stopped telling the story altogether: she found a meditation path that suggested celibacy. Melanie Green pumped her own water and lived rent-free in spiritual soundness with a view of the river. She wore her hair wrapped in a turban, and only a few blond dreadlockish ends fell free. On moving to the river she had left behind a life that was "all materialism and high heels." When a surveying team came through she suffered a lapse of faith, and six weeks later—she could not *believe* it—at thirty-seven she found herself pregnant. "And pregnant and exultant beyond meditation's grasp," she told Carla, adjusting the turban. "Come on, let's face it. We're not men! We're different and this is what it's all about." So went Melanie Green's ability to clasp whatever situation to her heart and rationalize with a brazen steady eye. She brought her baby to the contra dances and she went about thrusting him at men, saying, "Here, hold Sam. He needs the feel of a male person now and then."

Carla brushed at her hair a bit more, and read on: "Expectation cancels out mystery and only mystery matters. Very

special people are set apart from those who scheme and plan
and get what they want; that which is wanted becomes dimin-
ished and circumscribed by the author of desire." And, the
book counseled, this applies to matters other than pregnancy,
too. If you're a Carla—not looking, hoping or desiring—and
still a baby comes, rejoice absolutely. You've been chosen.

Carla ate the last cookie and went back to the mirror. The
whole spiel sounded not so very different from one of Alice's
phantom stories: zombies and jumbies on the loose. She
laughed suddenly and fully at herself. A swashbuckling ca-
pability to see others' lives with perfect clarity was hers: she'd
come in the nick of time to diagnose Alice's problem. Clutter.
A strangulation of clutter. The house needed a giant emptying
out. Carla would attend to it on a new purposeful calm wave of
energy. The visible world drew her out of the cosmic mumbo-
jumbo with its capacity for arrangement and rearrangement,
purchase and discard. She fixed a comb in her hair.

When Deborah from Hillcrest called to ask would she attend the midsummer birthday party—"Your grandmother's
soon to be eighty-six"—the conversation became a conference
between two prime-of-life, confidential, knowing adult
women. Bring a cake? Of course she would. She would bake
Jessamine's favorite. Big airy boxed cakes, slathered in frosting, sprinkled with silver; delectable clouds of cakes suspended themselves in her mind. She wished to eat layer cake
right that instant and over a second piece confide, "I'm pregnant." Jessamine's favorite angel food would be delivered to
her as affirmation that, indeed, lives were changing; Carla was
drastically grown up, and Jessamine would be reminded that
she herself had passed from the realm of having the facility to
bake. Dressed crisply, exuding the evidence and wiles of
duty, of a new order, Carla with severe housecleaning energy
would deliver her grandmother's cake to her wearing three-
inch heels, pregnant or not pregnant, if only she owned a pair
of three-inch heels.

Carla walked into the front room carrying a pinkly iced
cake. No one had answered her knock. Hazen, wearing his

checked pants, was swiveled toward a television game show, intent on the m.c.'s rewarding a man for recognizing place names that Hazen had probably never heard of. "Oaxaca. Dun Laoghaire. They don't sound the way they're spelled, do they, audience? Eddie Bale, you are smart. A winner."

"Hello, hello," Carla called over audience fervor.

Hazen spurred the floor with his heels to get a good swivel going and swung at her. "Hi, there. She's in the other room." He kicked back to TV position.

The bedroom door was open. "Grandma?" Carla called into the sleep-stillness. Grandma? She peeked in. Jessamine sat at her dressing table, hand-held mirror and brush dueling silver crosslights above her short curls that were always soft and never blue-rinsed. She paused and held fast to her image, whether in defiance or surrender, Carla could not guess.

"Oh hello, dear," Jessamine said, flashing Carla into view and setting mirror and brush on the table. She reached for the box that contained a trove of earrings. She had overrouged her cheeks and was as intimately exclusive with her mirror as she had been when serving Hazen his treats.

"I can't imagine what went wrong," Carla said, presenting the cake.

Jessamine rose on her heels to get the full picture. "Perfect." She sat right back down.

Most of the icing had soaked into the cake or run down the sides. The surface was shiny and set, a spackle of cake crumbs. Riding the bus hadn't helped; the pan cover must have created a little sauna in there for the cake. Dream Mountain Angel Food Cake. It looked more like the relief map of the moon's surface she'd made as a child, concocted from baking powder and water, pasted to construction paper, a 3-D effect. It was a failed boxed cake.

"My dear, sit a moment and tell me what you think. Here I am, made to celebrate a birthday. Isn't that the dickens?" Jessamine tapped a pearl on the mirrored tabletop. "We're the first generation of this freakishness. What will it be for you dears, I wonder."

Jessamine raised her eyebrow inordinately on her question

and Carla scrambled for something to say. She noted the absence of the fiftieth-anniversary photo which used to wing the dressing table. Its display, she supposed, was rightly sacrificed to the Hazen Batten marriage, but a starkness did not lift even as Jessamine tipped open her gem box.

"To live far into your eighties is a fact, but no accomplishment. I forgive youngsters for the misinterpretation, but Hillcrest should know better than to insist on these parties."

"If you'd rather not go down, Grandma?"

"My dear, we're too civilized to resist." Jessamine sighed and fished through the cornucopia of earrings spilled before her. She held a miniature gold gong to one ear, dropped it into the pile and plucked out red raspberry clusters. It took two tries to fasten the left one just so.

Her voice dropped to a hush. "When your grandfather died, in the heat of loss I forgot myself and said, 'Take me, Lord.' I landed at Hillcrest. Then it was *James* Lawrence he took. Ah, we're such crones here. No, don't protest, my dear. As a group we really are, but who sees it?" She checked her profile in the mirror. "You adjust. Lawrence and then James Lawrence, gone. But I'm here and the desire to live a certain way wins out. I spent five constrained years here and now it's different. I'm a married lady." Jessamine drew her seated carriage to its greatest height. Stiff-cheeked granddaughterly platitudes fit nowhere. Carla said nothing.

"I'll celebrate. As a married lady," Jessamine said. She flashed her earrings and next considered her tray of lipsticks. She applied color to her lips and kissed them at the mirror.

"I bet you think of my father's birthday at times like this." Carla's face went hot the minute she spoke. This was a very low way in which to instigate pregnancy talk, akin to a bill collector calling up and posing as a hearty old friend.

Jessamine turned around, paused and said with thrilling confidentiality, "I had a wonderful confinement. Did you know—his first dressing gown was entirely hand-embroidered." But an X-ray question rose in Jessamine's eyebrow and accompanied her very lacy glance at Carla. Carla flushed again. Her doctor's appointment was in three days.

"At the party it's barbaric the way those younger than me will gloat; the older ones will exhibit a vicious glee toward anyone catching up. But if I didn't show, my! They all revile the person who doesn't show. The grudge would last a year with some of them. Dear, we're a small group with large emotions, and we have no one to anger but each other. Mostly we can't speak of the unspeakable. When Hazen came here it was because a fellow had passed on. Hazen was next on a list. You understand that this is the way it happens nowadays, but back in my day we would not have imagined ever quite so frankly dismissing those who had passed on. A room was retained. In Walnut Grove and Minneola too, everyone had a place here and hereafter. The family took care to see."

Jessamine made her hands into a perfect steeple and for a silent moment considered herself in the mirror, lips relaxed. She closed her eyes. Presently she stood and took Carla's hand and pronounced in her lowest tone, "I'm not sure, Carla, that my Hazen can distinguish a nectarine from a peach. Really! But what magnificent defense against the birthday party, a husband. And you."

The three of them walked, Carla wearing an oversized shirt and cropped pants (elasticized waist), holding the cake, and Jessamine, in nubbly short-jacketed summer suit of a misty blue, guided Hazen by the elbow. His one leg remained stubborn. He called out to a man in suspenders, "Hi, fella." The vacuous hallway emitted a low-grade sunniness and an electrical hum. Down the way a woman beating cane to floor would have to travel night and day to make it to Jessamine's door.

Carla stood in the elevator holding her cake. The door stayed open forever, accommodating the hesitant and a man on wheels. She looked out the window to the cornfield across the busy street, noonday-bright and fresh in the last corner of undeveloped land in this not-so-long-ago rural area. The stalks posed like a chorus line, arms flung wide, lavishly garnering praise.

"Oh, a cake made from scratch," someone next to her said.

"Only kind," Hazen said. Carla loved his wide smile that saw only her intention.

Slowly the elevator descended. Carla clutched her cake platter and tried not to breathe the comets of wildly disparate perfumes clashing almost visibly before her. Jessamine smiled slightly with hands clasped in front of her, implying good will and a conspiratorial distance all at once.

The birthday women (and one man in bow tie) were to occupy a long central table in the dining room now festooned with honeycombed papier-mâché lanterns and long twists of crepe paper. Everyone else would forgo assigned seats, Jessamine explained. Bright-green plastic chairs were being scooted and scraped, and groups were forming. Jessamine showed Carla and Hazen to an empty table, then, carrying the awful cake, walked to her place of "honor." Three old women, gladitorially frisky, descended on Carla's table as one massive chin.

"Who are you with? Oh, she's Jessamine's." They pulled chairs to the table, and the one whose voile shoulders reached to her ears gave a clubby laugh. "Hi, Hazen."

"Ladies." But Hazen, "the defense," seemed not to hear, really, so busy was he flagging Jessamine. You would think she was pulling out of a train station, gone off on a long trip. All that waving and yearning. "There. Caught her eye." He waved harder now.

A large pantsuited woman with freckles and color still in her hair took her place at the piano after Deborah, ablaze in kelly green, greeted the roomful and indicated the birthday table. The woman hit the keys, one foot at a trot, with "Happy Birthday to You . . . happy birthday, dear friends, happy birthday to you."

The group sang in drifting, cracking voices. Cooks came forward and stood to the side of the guest table. As each person's birthday—but not birth year—was announced, they would hoist the appropriate cake. Why had she frosted her cake in glaring pink? Carla winced at the sight of it and gripped the table. It had imploded, was a fizzed volcano, the work of sad fortune. Otherwise, cakes of all glorious descriptions graced the table. Bakery cakes were sculptures suggesting hats and ice floes and steep-walled gardens.

"Jessamine Batten, August tenth."

Jessamine leaned forward as everyone clapped. Her eyes flickered at the pink thing, then she swept her arm over the table, motioning the cooks back, indicating that not one but *all* the cakes saluted her. A wand, her arm swept back and forth, back and forth, gracing the cakes until at last "Dr. Bob Wittemeyer, August nineteenth" signaled her release. A cake was hoisted for the doctor, and Jessamine relaxed back into her chair. She did not cross her legs at the ankles the way the other women did. Rather, her knees poked sharply at her skirt; her legs were bent in rocket-launch position, turning her body from the table. Carla felt the quiver in her own knees, felt how Jessamine meant to spring away from that cake.

"We have lovely, lovely cakes," Deborah intoned. She spoke into a stand-up microphone. "Sit tight and you'll be served."

One by one the cakes were cut, pieces wedged onto paper plates by cooks who worked with acute joviality and were sure to scoop extra frosting alongside. The sick pink cake remained before Jessamine, who, Carla was certain, now leaned with desperation away from it. Poor Jessamine was marooned out there front and center with that cake. She was probably forcing herself to remember: "I am a married lady. My family is in attendance." What she must have endured these five years in the way of parties. And was her "real" birthday any better? On those nights after dinner she had probably hurried to her rooms telling Mrs. Jennings and everyone not to knock, company was coming! She set out paper plates and napkins. She shook Spanish peanuts and pillow mints into fluted cups, and she waited alertly for Alice —and Carla, if in town—to visit. She would keep looking at and be needlessly twisting her silver watchband and smiling way in advance. Offering her cheek at the door, she did not allude to a dull day or a miserable group party. Instead, in

her granddaughter she would be seeing new shoes and pleas-
ingly thick hair and the breath-catching proof that her son had
lived. "Happy birthday to me," she often said in greeting.
Couldn't they have rented a car, borrowed a car, just once
taken her out for the day? But no, the Morrow women did
not drive. They visited briefly in the evening and rode the
late bus home, past empty shop windows, down dark streets,
with a sense of having outwitted all that's bad in America.
They left behind a bouquet and bath salts and something
from Craftique. The open bags of Spanish peanuts and pillow
mints Jessamine, alone again, with TV news on, secured with
red rubber bands. Not until months had passed would she
throw them out.

All sins of omission could be rectified with one impossible
clarion call: "I'm pregnant!" And the cake would shine like an
Oscar.

Jessamine turned to smile and wave at her family. Hazen
signaled back, a little windshield-wiping motion. Sheer white
slices, marbled squares, the iced flowers, were showing up
everywhere in the room, and Carla's inadequacy remained
squat on the table, baldly pronounced, shiny and singular in
its pain. How could she have a baby? Jessamine seemed to
look everywhere, but everywhere was the cake looming in
front of her. Mercifully, knife was finally put to the angel-
food disaster, and some slices disappeared to a far section of
the room.

But now came the problem of the Dixie Cups which had
been removed from a heavy refrigerator box and set at each
place, wisps of cold steam swirling up. With small wooden
spoons Hazen and the others jabbed the bricked ice cream.
Imagining resistance to have everything to do with a failure of
elderly muscle tone, they jabbed on long after Carla had given
up. The ice cream would not budge.

"People, your ice cream is frozen," Deborah announced.
"Use your hot coffee to melt the ice cream. Just a drop or
two, and put the cup against the ice-cream carton. Keep the
coffee cups filled there, Annie and Jolene, will you, girls?

Let's applaud the cooks Annie and Jolene while we're waiting. And Claire at the piano. Claire, strike up a tune, will you?"

Outside, clouds reached over the still green corn and low-ered shadows onto the street. Cars running in a smooth silvery stream past the building reflected the gentled disharmony within. Beneath the jostling, a hard current of limited time ran through. Did they feel it, Carla wondered, as she did, pushing low across the brow?

"Roll out the barrel, we'll have a barrel of fun" gave way to "Daisy, Daisy, give me your answer, do," during which Carla caught the little drooped-chin woman winking at Hazen.

Then, "Darktown Strutters' Ball," Claire called and took off with a lusty start. "I'll be down to get you in a taxi, honey, better be ready 'bout half past eight, now dearie don't be late. . . ." This was a table-thumping song.

"Coffee's so hot," Carla exclaimed. She coughed, but the tablemates were heedless of her dabbing napkin to eyes. Ha-zen's eyeglasses made twirling kaleidoscopes, sweeping in arcs to catch at Jessamine—you couldn't tell what all he saw—and the song continued: "I'm going to dance off both my shoes, when they play those jellyroll blues, tomorrow night at the Darktown Strutters' Ball."

Carla lost her voice in a lumpy throat. Hillcrest kept on and on, the piano threading the tune through a web of high and low, weakly determined voices. A huge warbling symphony, this singing for the long-gone-away crescendoed within her. She thought how crippled the Morrows, how lunatic and val-iant and small their universe had always been, and this chorus seemed to mock it. Now watch: follow Jessamine, she de-cided. After all, Jessamine leads the family. And Jessamine was singing, with a hand on her neck to ensure moderation, and her Dixie Cup was removed altogether. She sang along with her eyebrow raised as if against dissonance. The group was singing louder and louder, gaining on harmony, too, warmed to the birthday party. But Jessamine was straining. She touched her throat and hung on to the necklace. Her mouth opened a smidgen wider. The difficulty of joining in was apparent, as it should be, Carla felt, straightening herself. Relaxing, joining something like this, was impossible, really. To hesitate made sense: she was pulling for Jessamine, for the old reserve that was numbing but known, their way. She wouldn't have minded seeing a touch of sorrow in the group exhibition. The bubbled mouths sunk in "ohs" made her nervous. They seemed to cup her ears and breathe the music deep, and if she caught someone's eye—as she just had Hazen's—the person would sing right at you, straight on like a child, for way too long. You felt that something had fallen off your front. Her face burned. Jessamine paused to drink coffee.

The singing grew louder, in fact the group's singing capacity seemed extraordinary, limitless; they had hardly caught a breath at the end of a song and the old people were calling out for new songs. More! Round faces that never grew flushed. More! Carla hunched among the good fellowship, feeling that sharp singing faith pinch her ribs and her ankles. They all knew the verses of "She'll Be Coming Round the Mountain" ("She'll be wearing red pajamas when she comes, when she comes!"). And they sang, tilting their heads like wildflowers in a storm, reaching for inflection. The singing kept growing like a gale whipping a path between tables, overhead, freely, with nothing held back. The singers were set loose in the song, given faith, a reason to tap knuckles and hope. They were proclaiming love. Love, love, love, it seemed they kept singing. Outside, the cars going by cut away the world; beyond that definitive silvery edge lay the dull nothing. Here inside was captured the breeze and color and thrill of many years ago, steamrolled into the moment. Harmonious orthopedic-shoe stomping racketed the linoleum. Let the voices rise as one and crash the heaven they believed in, tease it with wobbly vowels and consonants hissed free of the dentures. We are alive! We are here and so we sing! they proclaimed, a great forestallment of meeting the Maker. People do not die singing, they were explaining to God.

During "Sweet Molly Malone," Carla saw that Jessamine

had quit altogether. She had no intention of resuming, of trying. She'd given up the effort as surely as she had quit baking cakes. She couldn't. Jessamine controlled the set of her chin, nothing else, no one. The Morrow center was gone; no one knew what to do; yet life galloped on. Carla stifled a sob with her napkin. Her father had sung, really sung. They'd better remember the way his baritone could sweep over you like a wave, stir up the butterflies that she felt in her stomach right now. It seemed, after all, a dark family sorrow not to sing, an ugly secret kept, a killing kind of secret if you couldn't sing for him and beyond him. A beat behind, a shade too loud, as if she carried a perfect cake high above her shoulder, Carla joined the chrous: ". . . crying, 'Cockles and mussels, alive, alive oh!' "

CHAPTER 8

*T*he cupboards over the tub hadn't been opened in years. Cobwebs veiled old decorator soaps, cough remedies, and a hair spray long ago removed from commerce, due to its toxicity. Carla recognized bath salts she'd spent a child's allowance on for a Mother's Day eons ago. "Heave ho," she said. With hair tied up in a kerchief, she dropped everything into a giant trash bag, grabbed it shut with one hand, spun the bag—"Where she stops nobody knows!"—and secured the twist. With Alice at work she would purge the house, topple encumbrances from ceiling to floor, liberate the bathroom for starters. She sponged down the paneling again and again, singing to the radio she'd unearthed from a bedroom stack of disuse. "I miss you most of all when day is done . . . " It was a station of slurry old songs that didn't come in too well.

Opening the medicine chest launched torpedoes: Vaseline, toothpaste, floss. A crusted calamine-lotion bottle broke in the sink; gauze came billowing off the spool; tweezers and razor blades pinged against porcelain; a cadre of motel soaps dove as one. But the sickening, unbelievably worst sentries lined the top shelf: stoic, forbidding bottles and bottles of her father's medicine. Shiny buglike capsules and speckled football-shaped pills, a container of stomach-coating liquid, monuments to his grief, filmed over with dust. The typing on dusty, faded labels: James L. Morrow. Take two. Or ten. Take before, or after, or q.i.d. to get the day in order, stave off death on an hourly basis. If he were just here to take these mummified pills and get the day ordered.

Crazy! Alice was waiting it out, believing that the pills, with some zombie-jumbie trick put to them, would just file out one of these nights, give her the clean, quiet slip. Carla ran from the bathroom feeling a kick in her head. At the kitchen sink she bent low and splashed cold water on her face. She bumped her crown on the faucet, sending her hand flailing at the counter, loosing rubber bands and marbles into the sink. Crazy, she said, shaking water from her hair, and she looked out the window toward further incursion:

That biker woman neighbor. She was marching bronzed and booted through Alice's long grass, straight on for the door; and even at a distance you could see that her eyes were widened by thick liner and bravado. Was it a law of the universe that an exercise in civility must follow shock? This woman slogged through the heat of a Friday afternoon as if to say, *Yes, Carla, ha!*

Carla opened the door after the first thump against porch screen. The woman greeted her with mannish fist in the air; she was the sort who would pound and pound right up until the moment a door opened.

"Hi! I'm Mary from across the street. Alice isn't home, is she? I got a surprise for her, I guess it can wait. So, you're Carla. She told me. Oop, flies. Close the door. Here, I can come in for just a minute, kid."

She hustled past Carla and made for the dining room with a distinct sense of chewing her way into the house. White tee shirt and heavy jeans constricted all they covered. Denim rubbed denim: thighs and knees wanted free. She sat, leaning all her weight on her strong summery arms, and underneath the table clopping noises were made by the boots. Her gum-chewing and wide-eyed staring were so intense as to draw Carla's shoulders up to self-conscious alertness, even as she sat down opposite Mary. Her heart beat in a still-higher rhythm to that gum-chewing. I'm ready, she thought fool-ishly, as if switchblades were to be drawn.

"Your mom just cracks me up. Like with the break-in next door? She should of been on the news."

"What break-in?" Carla's shoulders might as well have been strung to her ears. They stayed up there, high-hunched.

Mary shook a head of heat-curled hair and flipped a creamy palm at Carla. "That's what I mean. It figures! Your mom didn't even tell you how she chased some punks. They'd bro-ken in downhill and she chased them up the alley, bare-handed. Yeah, I told Kit and he said that's unbelievable."

"Yeah?" Carla said. Yes, she meant, of course. Yes, Mother!

"It's epidemic. We had something like that happen at our other place, but it wasn't kids. My old man is still after them." The gum-chewing sped up. "So now you're visiting your mom, what are you doing? She said you split from your old man."

"My husband's at home working." Carla could feel in her chest how chopped and off guard her retort sounded. What was Alice doing, volunteering her life history over the clothes-line?

"Say no more." The woman held her hands high to crash invisible cymbals. She did not shave under the arms and Carla approved.

Mary got a sullen sneerish look. "I know a few things. Cooling on the counter is the best time to get away."

"Now, listen—"

"Kit's and mine's five-year anniversary is coming up next month. I look at him, you know, brushing his teeth and I say, God, I can't believe it. Know how we met?"

"How could I?" were words Carla had to swallow as Mary plunged on, louder, savoring her romance history, gum-chewing juiciness adding immediacy, or urgency, to the story. Maybe this had all been chewily explained to Alice, and Mary assumed her mother would have rushed to inform Carla.

"At the State Fair. I'm not kidding!" Mary sat back as she slapped a hand on the table. A good game-show answer. Carla jerked her head slightly to mean that she had taken in the fact.

"Down at the Plaza Stage, you know where they have the free acts? I wanted to get a look at this chick Elvis imitator they'd advertised. I mean, a chick. Of course she was bad. The sound went off. She was standing there lip-synching with the sound off. I could of died, but I had to laugh too, you know. Hell, farmers who'd just sat down in a free place wanting to prop up their feet, even these farmers were blowing her off. Kit heard me laugh." Mary took a deep breath and chewed several loud revolutions. "You notice this voice? It comes from having polio in the neck as a baby. I was in the paper, about the last one to get hit. I grew up hearing how lucky I was to be alive. In my mind I still hear it. Kit loves this about me. Anyway, at the fair Kit goes nuts for my laugh and comes on directly, like a wild mother. He blew a hundred bucks on me right off, on the midway and drinks, I don't remember what all. We're coming up on five years together. It's unbelievable, I tell him. Our anniversary's an automatic party, thanks to the fair." Mary narrowed her eyes. "What about you and your old man?" It was unnerving the way Mary did not seem to blink, ever. "How'd you guys meet? That's the good part."

"Oh, just at college. There was sort of a protest." Carla was fumbling, caught off guard again, actually blushing at the word "college," or at her life, but Mary was nodding and nodding as if catching at some drama Carla hadn't gotten to yet, maybe did not even know of.

"The school planned to tear down a historic building. Everyone marched. Brian and I worked in the same office. Well, it's complicated." She trailed off. This milestone didn't sound the least bit complicated.

But the wide eyes had hardly blinked, just like the Hillcrest people singing. More! "I bet cops came. I bet you got to shout at the top of your lungs. Who won?"

"I'm afraid they tore down the building."

"Ha! But you guys had gotten it on and didn't care anymore!" The boots whacked. The gum did a pink squiggly trick between the teeth and perfumed the air with fruit aroma. Mary was still seeing color and strife, and Carla could almost believe that, yes, she and Brian had been wonderfully endangered. She would think of an example for Mary.

"Don't ask me to tell you about the guy I was with before Kit. Jesus." Mary's jaw dropped. "Come on over sometime. Visiting parents can turn into a drag." She considered with her bottom lip sucked over her teeth. "Alice is different, though. She's cool."

She stood suddenly and reached as if to sling Carla over her shoulder. "Here." She took her by the arm. "Let me show you what I've got waiting for Alice. I'm starting a home business from supplies she laid on me."

Carla followed Mary across the street. Of course a mother lives beyond the child, she told herself in the wake of Mary's boots. Especially an adult mother with an adult child, the two people having lived together and separately for very long spells. Alice lives here every day, she reasoned, and she does whatever she pleases. But it takes a mother being drastic, she conceded now, to make a child of any age really comprehend the facts; it takes elopement or a chumminess with bikers to impress upon the child the true otherness, the mystery and real truth that everyone is separate and whole. Of course your mother is, she said. You don't notice the subtle changes afoot because you're happy in a fixed notion. Then the mother chases vandals. She brings new people into the picture—this Mary whose boots bludgeon the grass they walk on—as if to whip the idea of understanding from you in favor of acceptance.

But she was gratefully being led away from the cleaning project, that was the main thing. The house would never be right with those pill bottles in it; deep wrongness beamed a path straight off the medicine-chest shelves. If Alice couldn't touch those pills she'd better let someone else do it. Let this two-fisted confidante Mary.

In the house where her best friends the Wallace girls had grown up, a Confederate flag blocked light from one window, a nude centerfold sprawled across a brown wall, boots lined the edges of gold pile wall-to-wall carpeting. The matched furniture was brassy green plush. In the kitchen a gleaming set of Revereware pots hung from the pegboard. Carla recalled the pitch of the pots-and-pans salesman who, years ago, in this kitchen, had hit up the senior-high girls. He was an artist with gadgetry, slicing a ripe tomato into transparent perfection, speaking to them as women, even as future wives. Aluminum looked like love to Kay Wallace. She might still be making payments on the octopus kitchenware set he'd conned her into.

Above Mary's sink a motto read: "Don't Look at Me; You're the Problem." And on the wipe-clean kitchen table Mary was pushing around a heap of colored tile chips. She poked a finger at something. "Yes, this is dry. Look, kid." She showed off a saucer with mosaics packed into the surface. "Look familiar? It's like your mom's ashtray. You use it for a candy dish or just as decoration, too. Multipurpose, that's why they're going to sell. I'm making three sizes. Your mom says craft fairs are the way to go. I've got one lined up."

Alice's booty. Carla's childhood project. She'd pushed these tile chips into rubber cement for days on end. She'd made dozens, and her father had gotten into the act. Gift dishes were sent to everyone. Alice designated one as her favorite ashtray, and Jessamine kept a plate, used for nothing at all ever, still propped in copper holder in a cabinet next to her priceless cup-and-saucer sets.

Mary lit a joint, smoked and handed it to Carla.

"Oh, no, really."

"It's past noon," Mary said.

Carla took the cigarette and puffed quickly. There. She thrust it back at Mary. What was she doing? But a few hits couldn't hurt *things*. Heat filled her lungs and little flakes of the weed got stranded on her tongue. The sweetish smell to the air brought back the old carefree times when there had been hours, days, in which to sit, listen to music, smoke, speculate, before she and Brian had gotten serious about lifestyle. She swallowed, dry-mouthed. She took the cigarette again. "Yeah," said Mary.

As they passed the marijuana back and forth, Carla's head filled with long, vivid memories. "The lady who lived here was famous for her homemade noodles." What else had they eaten? "The air was always wet from steaming water. I can smell it."

"Noodle water!" Mary flourished the pot and started a long slow nod at the stove. The rhythm and length of silent speculation on noodle water panicked Carla.

"Once I marched to legalize pot," she exclaimed, feeling great and surprised, feeling so very young. (Let's talk, share!)

But Mary stopped in midpuff and shook her head with funereal sadness. The room was quiet. It was Mary's turn to speak, Carla was sure, but when would she break this silence and speak?

"Forget it, man," Mary said. "If the government gets into pot it's going to ruin people's lives."

Mary's voice chased after the chilly marijuana fog, a light. She sounded sensible enough, vital. What had been wrong with the old friends? How was it they had all wanted the government that invaded Cambodia to regulate their pot?! They had been wrong stupid meddlers, not liberal, and she should apologize to Mary. If Carla could muster up the words she would explain all of it to this woman who kept her copper-bottom pots on display, gleaming. Whatever Mary cooked, surely she put it on boil and dotted it with Tabasco.

A snapshot of Kit at rest on his bike was posted on the refrigerator with a guitar magnet. He leaned back against the sissy bar and grinned into the camera. The hem of his jeans was frayed.

"Did you ever want to take off on his bike and go ninety? Just fly?" Carla asked.

"You bet!" Mary leaped up and began an animated tale about abduction that caused her midriff to peek from beneath her short top. She'd run off with another guy, nothing serious; she knew Kit would be coming along. "Then I broke a beer bottle and threatened three black dudes on a stoop. Ha! They said, 'Go home, white thing.' Was I ever glad to see Kit ride up on his Harley. That's exactly what I said to him: 'Kit, go ninety, I don't care.' "

Mary narrowed her eyes on private tough times Carla could not clearly imagine but felt her heart beat toward in a dream. It was like Hazen's weight dropping on her in Jessamine's room: loud noises, definite ballast, immediate and clear-cut danger were forces you rose to grapple with, find relief from. But the pot was so strong she couldn't think whether it had to do with outsmarting death or life.

A picture of Mary cooking noodles swirled up from the fog. Carla giggled.

"There you go," Mary said. "This pot's two-toke." She took the joint. "Are you going to be in town for the fair? The tenth through twenty-first this year. But you know—hey, I'm offering seriously—come on over and party one of these nights. Who knows, you might get yourself all charged up for going back home. What are vacations for? After five years with Kit, believe me, I know how it works."

CHAPTER 9

Pregnancy should be a crusade. It requires the brave rich loneliness of a tiny desert nation: the Arizona Hopi is buffered, yet put upon, by vast surrounding Navajo-land. Pregnancy, Carla translated from her own esoterica, means you had better know the world. Carla's father had been to war, but her mother hadn't known the parts of the body. When pressed, Alice admitted she scarcely knew from where Carla had come. ("From over the rainbow, then. It was a doctor-and-nurse job. I simply followed directions. Yes, in the wake of the bomb came the babies. That's right. A flood of babies came after the bomb. And thank heavens the order was correct!")

Carla sat in the waiting room at Planned Parenthood. It was a clinic named for hope, but the savvy woman pictured on the home pregnancy kit she'd bought without looking the Tillman clerk in the eye was nowhere to be found among the black teenagers sinking into soft-design chairs, and her nerve was failing. Babies covered the powdery blue carpet, claiming the day as surely as sunshine. She would peek sidelong at their huffing faces and wiggly fingers, agog at all the working parts, the little doll clothing; girl babies tented in pastels, tossed about like wayward cocktail umbrellas. One sexless crawler had, so far, learned to use only the right arm and leg; the baby tipped, rolled and launched itself all over again. And here was a mad bottom-scooter losing his diaper to no one's concern. All of them crawled at the feet of girls who slouched over fashion magazines venting nonchalance and proud powerless-ness in the steady rip, rip of pages. They were beautiful scary girls. Men and boys had fallen away, were distant generics mentioned in the magazines. Eye makeup would be applied for the sake of the eye, and nothing else, by the girls in this room.

Carla had hardly touched Melanie Green's baby but re-membered that his little hand looked sweet as pie. She would love a dessert right now. Three desserts. The wait went on, endless, wrapping her with shopping-mall anemia. Of course Planned Parenthood would be the most inconspicuous and egalitarian way to approach pregnancy, and of course you would have to wait and wait.

She tried to concentrate on the magazine she'd opened. All the models were wearing pajama-type clothes and looking wholesomely surprised to be caught doing so. Across from her a girl was shaking her beaded hair. Carla felt wildly alert and old. Risk would be routinely noted in any health matter; but she did not constitute an epidemic as did the sullen teens with their bumper crop of babies, all of whom she admired enormously. (Look at how the one sticks a bottle into the teensy baby mouth without losing her place in *Glamour!*) You hoped this was not racist, or ageist, or sexist, or just plain wrong, but you knew—Carla thought positively—that an instinctual attitude guided these girls. They were too young to be wary. All of them, however, were waiting to be told what to do. Just like Carla.

A thirty-four-year-old white woman would attract no sociological surveys unless someone wished to explore the darker side of the new baby boomlet, poll the fallout, the seekers, the still-bewildered to whom life simply happened this way or that because an age had been reached. It seemed, really, that time or *the* times had gotten her pregnant. Once, everyone had taken to backpacking. Now they strapped on babies.

She knew about nutrition and would surely grind her own baby food if, indeed, a baby materialized, which, despite hor-monal roller-coastering, she didn't for a minute believe would. No welfare benefits, please. And amniocentesis would be down the road a few months as insurance of a sort. Her kind might terminate a pregnancy but would never abandon a baby or trade it for a convertible, as a girl tried to do, according to a recent wire-service story. ("I got confused for a minute is all," the girl protested. But she had not protested motherhood itself and that was the telling fact, Carla thought now. The newspaper pictured the girl performing a huge gitchy-goo thing, her nose against her baby's. A quick mistake! All forgiven! Now motherhood! To Carla, an impossible elasticity of spirit.)

Despite feeling older and wiser than the girl, Carla thought she had lost her place in line and gone back to some sub-basement of sexual growth: being pregnant, accidentally, protestingly, at thirty-four, a hick among the healthy urban baby-eager mob that had become her age group. She embarrassed herself. She should be happy. She must remember Melanie Green's idea of the shrewd waiting spirits in the highest stratosphere, the cosmic adoptees. One out there was intent upon choosing her. The theory insisted that we all choose our parents. The cosmos had gotten her pregnant, really, and it was too great to protest, according to Melanie Green, to whom it had happened first. Carla remembered how whenever Melanie was called to task on the extreme claims she often flung at people between dance sets, she would reply fiercely, "Believe in what keeps you sane." At Planned Parenthood, a low-level hum of Muzaked rock tunes descended from overhead speakers and it was understood that no one here had mustered the wits to "love carefully," as the bus poster asked. Belief as hindsight was insanity.

Dr. Ellen Hollingsworth determined the status of the pregnancy: positive, eight weeks. She checked Carla's blood pressure, breasts, teeth, all the while doing a cha-cha with her own abnormally white teeth. The new tooth-polishing craze Carla had just read about in the magazines piqued her with the realization that her teeth were yellowing and today you were supposed to do something about that. If she moved into a city, fifty traps of fashion would age and mock her. And was it true, for that matter, that in pregnancy your teeth might fall out of your head?

No older than Carla, Dr. Hollingsworth was tapping her knee now, encircling an ankle, cheered and attuned to subsur-

face mystery. Where have the years, so cyclically and assidu-
ously attended to in the woods, gotten me? Carla demanded
of herself. What do a handful of repeating seasons add up
to?

"I am feeling your ovaries," the doctor announced as she
scrunched and pressed.

A person is not a garden, Carla continued silently to the
ceiling of a thousand dots. Dr. Hollingsworth would agree.
She might argue that in turning to the land today's intellect
got buzzed down to mere reflex. Today's intellect needed a
town for top performance, a career. You might think of it like
a car leaving gravel for the highway. Yes, you could work a
field, but when it came to the Asian women squatting, dropping a baby, going right back to the hoe, the Western brain
would shut down. It knows nothing like that; it's uselessly
Occidentally wishful. Not living in Asia meant you would
not function like that. Over ten years' time, Carla would volunteer, I have hauled, canned, repaired, kept the jump on
the seasons, yet a baby! She could plant acres of tomatoes,
run a California fruit farm, oversee, feed and shelter
migrants—speak to them in Spanish—before she might
fathom a baby.

Dr. Hollingsworth continued to name the inspection. "I am
feeling your thigh. I am spreading with my hand. This is the
speculum being introduced, warm but not too hot."

In fall, once everything was canned and laid out in a pleasing design on the cellar shelves, Carla would briefly will it to
remain so forever—perfect, undisturbed. And no matter
what, here came Brian's wholesale devouring, his forking out
of pickles and peaches and whatever else, the minute she had
put it up. "It's only October!" she'd cried more than once as
he dug in happily. Food. If she could just keep the food
supplies shelved properly, on hand—grains and pasta, relishes and compotes, supplies as decorative as useful—she'd
feel a greater safety, and it had nothing to do with hunger.
She just did not want to be low on food. And here was another annoyance with Brian; whenever they received a fancy
box of chocolates Brian ate by the blind handful, one gulp per

candy, no pause, never checking the centers. They were obviously incapable of parenting.

Now the details were done and Carla was to sit upright and behave truly expectantly. With sheets of tissue swathing her middle, she dangled unevenly hairy legs: they looked glaringly irresponsible under fluorescence, and her eyes fell next on a pigeonhole compartment on the doctor's desk. A chorus of diaphragms petaled outward. All they needed was tuxedos and cheers.

"You should shut that drawer," Carla said.

Dr. Hollingsworth seemed to listen to a faraway voice, a chickadee at the feeder. "Yes?" she said slowly, but with her eyes fast on Carla.

"I'm married," Carla blurted. "I have a college degree, there's income, I don't take drugs. I'm thirty-four. This wasn't planned, and I'm trying to imagine myself as a parent. And my husband." The performance of her double-jointed toes helplessly undermined her blunt logic. She tried to crank them rigid. "We live in the woods without sidewalks for roller skating. Everything's impossible."

The doctor shook her head wildly without mussing her sleek hair. The cut allowed for serviceability and drama. And medical education of course made her swiftly no-nonsense. "This baby isn't going to roller skate for years."

"But when I told my husband he stared at me with a wrench in his hand." Carla's voice was rising against the doctor's. "He wasn't threatening me. Please, don't think we're like that. It's just that he was working on his truck when I ran from the outhouse knowing I was pregnant."

Dr. Hollingsworth's hand puppeted around in her white pockets, but her expression did not change. The outhouse was neither horrific nor amusing. "Men don't experience the news as instant thunder. Who knows what emotion went into that wrench."

"Now he calls long distance. He wants me to hurry home. He wants me to know he knows all about babies. He's changed a diaper."

"Good for him. The caution and concern of mature parents

is truly special. Your visit makes my day. So much of the time . . ." said the doctor with a frown directed to the greater babydom beyond.

But lest she think her patient entirely above the hordes of teenagers out there, Carla confessed, "I don't even know the parts of the body."

"You're afraid to hope, I think. Is it impossible for you to imagine a future?"

Carla frowned at the doctor's gullish sweep of white-jack-eted arms, the melodrama of truth.

"Hope didn't run in my family. We had projects. We were great at varnishing and baking. My father had cancer for twenty years." Carla gasped. The news sprang free with such force that she gripped the exam table's edge lest she too fly off.

"The future was a flat idea," said Dr. Hollingsworth with a nod.

Bright as a bubble, a sob popped out. "Excuse me. I'm sure it's terrible to cry pregnant. There." Carla tried to make snorty laughs of her sobs.

The doctor's hair required a mad swish as she touched Carla's shoulder. "What kind of cancer did he have?"

"A leukemia." Oh, her legs were a fright and she hoped the doctor wasn't noticing. Hairy, indicting, what do men think, that accepting equal hairy legs side by side in the bed forgives them the major failings? "I'm too old. Let the Third World carry on."

"Leukemia." While the doctor searched her mind for the medical implications, Carla concentrated on demystifying those teeth: were they polished, capped or natural? Probably natural. An extreme of evenness and definition must mark a doctor's psyche and appearance.

"I'm giving you vitamins and sending you on your way. It's early, just wait until the pregnancy takes over up here." The doctor tapped her head. "I have a fourteen-month-old. I do know the parts of the body, but I've felt like you. Parents aren't stable, they die. That's your experience. They fail their

children and you'd rather do anything than fail responsibility.
Take the vitamins, that's all you need to do."

Carla thought aloud, "Yes, I'm a responsible person. My
letter writing is important, political enough . . ." Ugh! The
teenage girls would hoot down a woman who sounded so
drear.

"Take the vitamins."

"I have to want this baby desperately."

"You'll admit to hope. You'll see."

Dr. Hollingsworth bloomed with the opportunity to insert
such tidbits of philosophy, to go beyond stressing the Basic
Four and flat shoes, as she must confine herself to doing with
the most rebellious pregnant teen.

"The future simply *is*," she said. "Every day it gathers its
hem high and jumps the puddle. It's really fabulous, no matter what. The *what* isn't the point, do you see?"

Believe in what keeps you sane. Melanie Green's motto was
racing in Carla's mind as she came walking down Seventh.
She believed most staunchly that she would not live another
day of her life with hairy legs. Hairy legs on a pregnant
woman were as fundamentally damaging to a fetus as a woman's precipitate frowns and moods—public radio's explanation for the eventual teen suicides.

Kresge's windows were plastered over with long sheets of
yellow newsprint as if some exciting display were being assembled in secret. When she'd been a girl working in
Kresge's, she had always loved seeing the floorwalkers window-
dressing mannequins. The men's sheepishness—and later,
she realized, vulnerability—had to do with being grown-up;
if you came close to them smoothing at a mannequin's dress
front, danger took on a whole new meaning. And she had
more than once felt herself smiling in a new thrilling way.
But she was closer now, and the signs were shouting CLOSE-
OUT! CLOSE-OUT! Shadows moved behind the papering. Her
Kresge's, a fossilized low diffidence, was perishing at Seventh
and Walnut. "No!" she cried and swung around, half hop-

ing for assurance, but she talked into the vacuum of downtown that Alice had been griping about for years now. A cry here could only swirl pigeons nearer the curb or enrich the soliloquy of some mental adventurer who was reliving Calvary.

Inside the door, high above the counters, a four-sided lightbulb affair rose from a slender pole—a giant wand, it flashed blue light over everything. The contraption was rigged onto a cart being wheeled away, deep into the store. A man in a cheap summer suit nervously jerked at his microphone cord. "Shoppers! It's a Blue Light Special. You've got five minutes in Ladies' Accessories for a special Blue Light Discount."

Carla followed.

A smocked woman stood with discount marker in hand under the light. Ladies' wallets were sixty percent off. A binful of wallets made of fake leather suffered the blue-light inspection; the wallets were shiny and huddled as the unwelcome beetle life under wet logs in the forest, sought by a flashlight. "Unbelievable!" Carla cried, hoarse as that neighbor Mary, but she dug into the pile. A maroon billfold creaked as she handled it; the cellophane wrappings for photos were all stuck together. These were sad wallets meant for people without photos.

Another shopper had trailed the blue light. "How dumb do they think we are?" she asked Carla in a nasal voice. "If they're closing shop they'll go to seventy-five, eighty percent off." She threw a wallet back into the bin, hard, disrespectfully, downright hatefully.

Carla spread her arms over the poking, crackling wallets. "Then leave them alone. Go on."

"Will you look at it," exclaimed the woman, who was obviously wearing a wig. "You're more proof that short-order maniacs are taking over this town." She gave the wallets a punch and left.

Carla scooped up a handful and let them drop. "How can you close?" she accused the clerk.

"They're tearing down the building, that's what. Going to

raise something taller that hooks into the skywalk system. Kresge's says it isn't worth staying in town. They're all over, they've even got a store up in Montreal, Canada, but it's not worth staying in Des Moines, they say. We all lose our jobs."

The clerk consulted a kitchen timer ticking away on the cart while the blue light continued to signal the bargains at hand. The microphoned voice blared, "Shoppers, you've got one minute left of the Blue Light Special. Only one minute in Ladies' Accessories for great bargains!"

Acting as if Kresge's weren't disappearing did not keep Kresge's from disappearing. Alice had withheld the sickening news. See, Carla could have told the doctor, we dare not even look at a dying store.

Muzak came into focus as a doughty rendition of "Girl from Ipanema." She must have heard it a thousand times back when she worked here, in high school. The blue light spiced up and flicked over the xylophone sound and then turned off.

Carla smelled all the Kresge's smells, the heightened ambiance brought on by a beehive of materials and activities, of foods subject to casual ventilation: popcorn, grill grease, the dusty chocolate of malted-milk balls and coated raisins; she smelled the sewery smell of the goldfish and the hot metal dust of keys being made; something waxy—shelf paper or sliced ham. Someone was using hair spray right off the counter. A sweeping glance took in the great glossy colors of throwaway paperbacks there on the wire stands, bright Third World–wrought shoes (perfect for contra dancing), and— still!—pink sponge hair curlers in sizes to guarantee you ringlets or bouffant and everything in between. Next to those, brush rollers. Here was a world of transformation and possibility for the young and old and disenfranchised; Carla's history as a shopper and a girl, pungent, powerful, dying.

The clerk took off her glasses and laid them down, chained, for a rest on her bosom. "They've got extra discounts over in Makeup. I don't know why he didn't announce that."

Carla went directly to makeup.

And it was the lipstick model's face on the faint-aqua card

that did her in. She knew that face. It was the face of an older
girl—you wished she were a confidante—who smiled hope
on you when you were fifteen and ugly. It was the face of a
top teen model twenty years ago. Now it was a liar's face.
Flip hairdo, bangs that were foreigners to greasiness, a velve-
teen bow. This girl on the BriteGlo lipstick had appeared on
page after page of the magazines. Carla could suddenly recall
her name: Colleen. Colleen-somebody had offered a million
fun promises. Once she'd posed in a sailor cap, eating a hot
dog, captioned by "I love to cheat!"

An uncomfortable lack of dignity claimed the lipstick picture. Had the company pirated Colleen's face, or was she
grotesque and nostalgically hawking herself? Surely not!
Carla could write to BriteGlo or Consumer Fraud. Years and
years have gone by, she raged blankly at the youthful Colleen.
We don't look like that!

As early as age ten she and her friends had begun shopping
alone. The lady with bootblack hair who'd supervised nail
polish here might have been waiting just for them. "Hello,
girls!" She explained sales tax and told how she had met her
husband: "At a club." She was meticulous and smelled of
flowers cut and placed in a very small room, wildly, joyously
rebloomed. She set out and rearranged her rows and rows of
nail polish in color-coordinated order on a counter slanted just
enough so that if you bought a bottle the others of its kind
came scooting down an inch for a noisy farewell. It made you
want to buy another bottle. (At that time cosmetics were not
carded.) You felt grown-up when this woman said, "The new
lime green will catch their eye." She winked. That was
Kresge's through and through: young girls silently being encouraged to puzzle through the buying of hideous straw
purses and swoop-up sunglasses, choosing between fad socks
with names such as Twist and Popcorn.

Now, facing this Colleen, Carla had become a little hot
spring of sweat, but the heat steaming from her pores was
thrown immediately back on itself by the air-conditioning
which feathered along the surface of things.

The question for twelve-year-old girls is: How big can breasts get? She and the Wallace girls had studied the biggest bras and thought, Is this it? Is this the future? They were in Kresge's figuring out bras, silently blessed by a phantom wearywise saleswoman who was probably hoping along with them: Not *too* big. Brian could have been found in the hobby shop.

She had come to boys' socks. Brian was Brian, as she'd told her mother. Some sort of translation switch in Brian took the language of the heart straight to an information booth where it was leveed to problem/solution status and then came forth slate gray. Admit it, she told the shower caps racked high over the next counter, once you were glad that hard questions weren't asked. She and Brian had presumed to tackle the world properly, to trick themselves out of the imposition of change. They'd disallowed it, like refined sugar and smoking in the truck. They had not, she admitted, broken into the mad regions of each other's heart. We have not really broken down; we never really have, she said.

These boys' socks in front of her were sold in unwieldy bundles as if the very nature of *boy* could not be constrained. It flew off somewhere. It flew off and left girls. She came back to the uneasy idea that mothers are mothers fundamentally and fathers, these days more than ever, are fathers by invitation. How would Dr. Hollingsworth brighten that news? (The teenage girls would hoot their understanding: "Girl!") With terrible swiftness Carla missed who she wanted Brian to be, closer than close, Siamese close. She stumbled against boys' socks. She unhooked a strapping set of boys' socks and bounced them onto jockey shorts folded like envelopes.

Blue Light Specials had not yet been introduced when Carla got her first job here. She'd walked into Kresge's on a summer afternoon wearing a heather A-line skirt and jacket, shell top, nylons held up by girdle—a teenage convention that the garter-belted Alice deplored. Carla was sixteen; pantyhose would come out the following year. "Do you have any job openings?" she asked the first person who looked at her, a

woman standing behind bottles of globular creams. The girdle
was unbreathable rubber against the backs of her legs, and
her Social Security card was brand-new. The woman became
all neck. "Mr. Anspach!" she yelled. "Toiletries, Mr. Anspach!" She told Carla, "He's the floorwalker."

A man with money wrapped over his knuckles hurried their
way. He had hair like Ricky Ricardo's.

"I'd like to be a cashier," Carla told him.

The toiletries woman helped out: "She means a salesgirl,
Mr. Anspach. The cashier is who pays us, right?!"

Carla was hired on the spot for the usual schoolgirl hours,
Monday evenings and all day Saturday, and her job brought
Alice downtown shopping to revel in employee discount.

In its final days the Kresge's grill was going by the name
Snack Shoppe. The high dark booths Carla remembered her
legs rubbing against, sticking to, had been replaced by teetery
plastic-mold tabletops and chairs. At least there was still a
fountain, and the counter. Kresge's had updated itself but
failed anyway. The name "dime store" signified a trinkety
bygone innocence. "Grill" and "Carla" bespoke the same era,
Carla thought. She used to scold her mother with the idea
that a baby should be named as if eras and calendared time
don't exist. (At the moment, however, she could not think of
a single such name to attach to her theory, let alone to a real
baby.) From within their pink and green houses her parents'
generation had miscalculated what the future would bring:
their children would grow up, age. What would it be like
when her group reached Jessamine's age, when retirement
homes would be crowded with Cindys and Sandys, a wobbly
old DeeDee and deaf Melody, incontinent Bobbi and Wendy,
instead of the dour Delores, Agnes, Mildred milieu that seems
fitting to old age? What would they sing at their Hillcrest
parties?

A girl with thick red braids delivered her a Coke in Styrofoam cup. Above the grill were the pictures of the old ways:
a faded hot-fudge extravaganza in tulip dish, Coke in a Coke

glass. The girl drifted off and leaned elbows on the counter. If Carla had had a kid at the age those Planned Parenthood mothers had, it would already be as old as the fountain clerk facing unemployment. It seemed a perversity of nature that the girl's arms, incandescent with freckles, could not spare her unemployment.

"What will you do when the store closes?" Carla felt insistent as a bus passenger and didn't care.

"Supermarkets pay."

"I worked here when I was sixteen."

"Yeah?" The girl lifted a braid off the front of her dress and began picking the split ends from it. Carla was an "older woman," boring. The girl slipped deep into fantasy.

"We get ten percent extra off everything," she said presently. "It wouldn't be fun in a grocery store."

"Right. Discount grapefruit, who cares?" said Carla.

"We get a big going-away party and some money." The girl screwed up her face and still looked adorable. " 'Nobody knows how much, Victoria.' That's what my boss says."

"My boss worked here for thirty years," Carla said. "The only female floorwalker." She had once put Carla to work racking an outsized lot of pants, and when Carla asked Alice if sizes thirty to fifty meant waist or hips, her mother had quipped, "When you're elephantine it's one and the same."

The redhead, too young for historical amazement, scrunched her face again.

"I have no idea what I'm doing here," Carla said abruptly. She nearly crushed the Styrofoam cup.

"Drinking a Coke." The girl was used to difficult old customers who lost track. She sort of smiled. She was undoubtedly sexually active.

"You're right, Victoria. You are absolutely right. I'm thirty-four, pregnant, and I'm drinking a Coke. Victoria's nice. I *mean* Victoria is a beautiful name."

She was much older than the girl, jubilantly so. For once, she knew exactly how old she was. Unlike Jessamine or even Alice, this girl would believe that when Carla brushed her teeth the slightest pink could be counted upon to tinge the rinse water. And her calf, a sturdy calf, would be assessed next to the girl's as bony, recessed at the shin. The truth of their age differences was secure, absolute knowledge in the girl's heart. Of course Carla was a mature woman; if anything, her proffered evidence of having once been this girl's age was not quite to be believed.

"I nearly forgot why I'm here," Carla cried. "I need a razor. Where can I find those throw-away razors, Victoria? Do you know which aisle?"

C H A P T E R   1 0

Gloria had the suspiciously contrite, dressed-up look about her that Alice associated with her leaving the office early due to "PMS." She would not stop pluck-ing at an outsized cloverleaf neck bow that matched her flow-ered skirt.

"Come with me after work, Alice, and let's take a look at the Seniomsed celebration. I'll drive us over."

"Not if it's another discount warehouse." Alice was sitting at her desk.

Hilarity for Gloria meant producing choking ninny sounds. When she recovered herself she wiped carefully beneath one eye and said, "Alice, that's the sidewalk gathering I told you about, the new Friday-afternoon outdoor cocktail hour around the fountain. Tonight's the first night."

"They should call it something better." Not exactly the Frankie Boy, but something, for Pete's sake.

"It's Des Moines spelled backwards."

"What smartie thought this up? Now we're as bad as Ne-braska with their Ak-Sar-Ben racetrack. Honestly!"

Gloria stopped wobbling one ankle. "For once everyone will be at the same happy hour. You'll meet people you never get a chance to. Alice, come on, really." She frowned at her neck bow. "I wish this were a normal office."

Meaning she would not have to resort to asking a sixtyish lady with hair bun for companionship, which is how curtly Alice felt she would be perceived and dismissed by the Seniomseders—businessmen and -women, their unbuttoned suit jackets a sign of availability. Des Moines spelled backward! Wasn't it enough that "Iowa" meant, in the original Dakota language, the sleepy ones?

If only Gloria would get a man, this sort of wheedling would be put to rest. Beaming a look into her desk drawer, Alice asked her sachet voodoo doll to find Gloria a man because deep down she was a good heart who did up every holiday for her kids and followed the sensible parts of Ann Landers ("Do not belittle your ex in front of the kids").

"It's a mixer," Gloria declared brightly. "For all ages, everyone."

"Who wants to promenade around a fountain in work clothes? I'd rather jump in. I'd really rather go home and throw off the clothes."

Gloria's face fell. It would take colossal nerve for her to go alone, though it would be simple enough on arriving to abandon her female company for "a prospect," as certain men were called. Alice added with more warmth, "Really, Gloria, you don't want me along. Someone around here will go."

But fellow she-hunters were scarce at Craftique. It was difficult to imagine the Smith relatives venturing beyond a family steakhouse for public entertainment.

Alice lit a cigarette. None of the Seniomseders would jump into the fountain, she was sure. Instead, they would be sizing up the mate potential of the nearest entry-level manager. Insurance company employees would go to Seniomsed; pairs of men affecting surprise, women in groups of four to ten wrecking their apartment-pool tans with frosted makeup. And why so many outfits in peach and baby blue? Drudgy with neck bows and light twill blazers (the cut hopeless), the women would exude patience as if they were forever cutting from bolts of fabric, applying pinking shears and Simplicity patterns to a dream of good girlhood they had relished on the farm. Carrying the foil-wrapped remains of potluck might provide for witty openers. ("These are called Hello Dollies," a Craftique woman had once told Alice while thrusting bar cookies at her.)

Oh, I'm mean! Alice said. Or rather, I belong in a more slapdash society, possibly a resort town where each person parades off season as a well-appointed and finally quite deliberate shipwreck. The craft buyers' fair in California had given her a taste of what could be, and someone there had even listed for her a string of renegade towns, all of which she had later discovered in Rand McNally to be posed on inlets, capes and faults. If a person could look forward to California as an annual event, stupes and Seniomseders wouldn't bother her a hoot.

Under Alice's tutelage a quiet sloe-eyed girl from Office Helpers sat in the storeroom recapitating a shipment of Hong Kong plastic acorns that had not kept their glue. Alice checked on her. Heather wore earphones and hummed and had a little pile accumulating. Alice returned to her office and lit a cigarette.

The world at large could do without plastic acorns, of course, but so what if some of Craftique's stock was trash? It had nothing to do with how a Craftique subscriber felt sitting at the window waiting for the postman to deliver the package. You stop what you are doing and gladly lay out the plastic, the glue, the ribbons. You get that swimmy post-shopping feeling in the chest. By dinnertime, place mats vined with green yarn and made novel by tacking red wooden cherries to a corner will be set on the table proudly. The thingness of life is a comfort, Carla should know; and having created the object is a projection of the soul. Put it on the shelf and it will not change, that's the beauty. The customer correspondence file, which Alice turned to, confirmed the seriousness of the act, the dedication to the process, time and again.

Today her file yielded up a confused lady customer writing on lined notebook paper. The Christmas-tree skirting kit had confounded her: "My daughter's skirt fit her just fine, but I look about like a circus bear. Do they come in half sizes?"

If the woman had dared follow even the most basic directions, in Freeport, Illinois, she could be found butting about her house in a skimpy red felt skirt trimmed with braid and tassels.

People! Honestly, people! It was worth all the craziness of unstuck acorns to be privy to such hope and earnestness.

Three small potatoes followed: a bad hook-and-eye had been received by a ten-year customer; a varnish packet was missing from someone's wood set; a woman thought there should be more blue and fewer green threads in the seascape embroidery. Next, a poor innocent's confusion over his wooden Dutch shoe planter: "Naturally, I ordered a pair. Why did you send two left feet? What good is two left feet?" Gently, Alice would explain. She would expect a sheepish response, or even a life history.

"Alice!"

She jerked her head up. A person did not expect privacy here, but she did not expect to see Mel Gifford unannounced either, his arm raised on a covered platter that might sport the head of John the Baptist. That grin! Must he always carry things oddly? she thought in the space before responding. Alice had the cool advantage of sitting in her stocking feet. With utter civility she said, "Hello, Mel."

"Surprise, Alice. I've come over here with something for Smith to take a gander at. You never know, Craftique might want to expand operations one of these days, tap those subscribers' other interests. I've got a food experiment here. Actually, they're cupcakes," he said gamely. "I took a vacation day to drop by."

Which explained exactly the buckskin shoes, pink oxford shirt (courtesy of his face-lifted sister?) and white pants pressed to free-standing. They would contain a good deal of polyester to be able to make such sharp rudders of themselves.

Mel thrust a domed Tupperware sort of thing at her. His

piney cologne scent assured her he was simply a man with cupcakes. She smiled and rapped the desk.

"Sit down, Mel. Please."

"I'm looking for taste testers," he said, and looked all around the room, but not at Alice.

"Eating is religion here. You'll be mobbed."

Mel lifted the plastic dome straight up to reveal a pyramid of beige-frosted cakes in multicolored papers. Alice remembered that he had written her phone number on lime-green paper. He had mercifully, though rudely, not dialed that number lo these several weeks. But however unwelcome, really a man's promise to call should be carried through. With miles of phone wire between them, she should have been allowed a proper "No, thank you."

"This is a business experiment," Mel stressed. But it was a struggle to sound businesslike with cupcakes on the lap. Alice wanted to laugh, marvel and scoff. She wanted to smoke a cigarette.

Gloria thrust her head in the door. "Oh, so it's Mel you've got in there. I wondered what was going on. Break time, good."

"Yes, come on in, Gloria. You ladies help yourselves to a cupcake and tell me what you think of the frosting especially." Delicately, Mel handed each of them a cupcake.

Gloria obliged gracelessly, holding the cupcake as if it were inching away from her. She leaned toward it, oogling, but this was her way with sweets. Goodies snagged and drugged her. Now her taut pinky maintained the tiniest protest as she wolfed down the cupcake. "Delish. It's canned frosting? Betty Crocker?"

"Tofu. I grow soybeans."

Gloria licked her fingers abstractedly. "Tofu" did not ring a bell; for all she knew, it was a house brand.

"I can't eat this before lunch," Alice told Mel, but she dabbed at the frosting, tasted it and said, "Mmm," the least she could do for the poor thing's self-esteem. What could you do about a man who had mashed beans into icing?

"That's right, you live in the country," Gloria said to Mel. "I saw a special on Ireland last night. They have more bachelor farmers than they can count. The show started off with this flashy news to make sure you'd watch. There were fields and more fields; they talked about magic. I was figuring how to *some*how take my two weeks there, when they admit: these are old farmers."

Because Mel was not a "prospect" Gloria could confide freely and Alice feared next would come jokes and innuendos. She tucked her feet back into shoes, steadied now for whatever vulgarity.

"I'll test that pink one," Gloria said, helping herself to another cupcake. "My thirteen-year-old would kill me. She's set on eating herself fat." Gloria leaned toward Mel, licking her fingers, purple nails and all.

"Reward her with these protein cupcakes," Mel suggested. "Trick her."

Over the top of Mel's head Gloria tried to engage Alice in a quizzical "He's cute" look.

"Mel, will you tell Alice she's not too old to meet people?"

"Too old?" Mel swooped a look up at Alice, then down to the cupcakes. A cupcake paper needed tidying.

"Pooh!" Alice's feet were firmly in her shoes.

Gloria explained her horrid Seniomsed to Mel. "And I think it's just the word Alice hates."

"Des Moines backward? Since when?" Mel's voice boomed around too loudly, but thank goodness he laughed at abomination.

"You're invited to sit on cement and look at the fountain," Alice added.

"I give up on you guys." Gloria clipclopped from the office.

Mel slapped his thigh and seemed ready to leave, then he sprang blunderingly at the desk. Alice thought he had tripped, but it was a gesture of camaraderie apparently: he was straining his neck in a way that let her know he held back an enormous laugh. He propped himself on the corner of her desk, and the silver flat-topped hair slanted this way and that.

A moment of secret, intense complicity thrilled her, staunch in the arm that balanced Mel. Alice's desire to snort left her. The two of them were sailing down Wakonda again, Mel's feet off the pedal. But not knowing what to do with such a moment, Alice wrecked it:

"Gloria!" she hollered through the wall. "Get the temp. girl to go to the beer party. Heather's her name. She's home from college, bored stiff."

She scooped her little hoodoo from the top drawer for a hard look and a satisfied pinning. Too late she remembered herself. Mel's eyebrows were at top alert and his mouth had gotten that lasso-look it took on when he'd watched her speak to the squirrel. His head bent so close she smelled his breath, which was no smell at all but a tickle; no, the tickle was his thick peasant's finger touching her bare arm.

"You're funny, Alice. You just don't know how funny. This is great."

This isn't Tokyo, she said to herself. Mel was sitting too close or too obviously staying here for too long. Some rhythm was off, even as a loud pleasant music filled her. She rapped her knuckles. "Life *is* funny. I'm busy here trying to rescue a woman who is traipsing about in a red felt runner meant for her Christmas tree."

"Is that right, Alice?" Mel finally seemed to be moving along. He was off the desk and kicking free a pantleg whose stiffness had tucked itself into an Argyle sock. He gathered and redomed his cupcakes and now held them at a lesser elevation than when he had come in. The mad energy that had brought him through his quirky project and necessitated the stiff pants and jokes was, of course, ebbing, and any moment solid embarrassment would take hold. He stood with the cupcakes and *would* stand forever with the cupcakes, suspended in a kind of mournful accusation, if she didn't snap him out of it.

Alice swiped her cupcake off the desk and peeled down the blue paper, watching Mel. She took a mouthful. "Very, very good." She held her pinky the way Gloria would.

Mel had shifted around now so that his back was to Gloria's

wall, and he seemed to know about lowered voices, after all: "You're making a face I've never seen, Alice." He hoisted his Tupperware a bit and asked, "You really like that cupcake?"

Her feet were firmly in the shoes. "The frosting especially."

"Good, Alice, that's great. If I didn't see you with the doll and eating the cupcake, I just wouldn't know what to think. And I do want to know you, Alice."

As if a person should tell life histories at work. There is proper behavior. Mel should know what was proper behavior, Alice thought as she waved goodbye. She was waving the cupcake, a downright maudlin signaling once Mel was out of sight.

C H A P T E R   1 1

"*T*his is the one time I wish I drove!" Alice paced to the edge of the yard and put a hexing look to the foot of Wakonda. "Your friend is late."

"Ha, Mother. I'm just the buffer here, I'm just the chaperone on this excursion."

"Callow youth." Alice lit a cigarette and read the smoke signals: in the long run adult children are the ultimate curse of motherhood. Just when a person has them somewhat squared away and disinterested in rebellion per se, their problems redouble and they bring them home. And they do not hesitate to arrange your life. Carla had guttily arranged for an afternoon at Mel Gifford's acreage. A daughter with manners, or a guileless daughter, would have explained that her mother was sitting outside: please wait a minute, or call back. Instead, she accepted the invitation, then broke the news: "We've been invited out," which, once Alice got the details, she interpreted as an afternoon shot.

"One Sunday afternoon. You never go anywhere, Mother.

It's okay. Go on, have a friend." Carla had flung advice at her like a shrew.

Then Alice had brought her lawn chair to upright position with slow definite clicks. "I'm bushed after work and my weekends are my own business." Carla was too firebrand to note the ploy, the old trick of involving a person's daughter.

"Why do you get so angry?" she'd demanded. "He's friendly, Mother. It's one simple afternoon." Carla had begun the horrid grabbing of hair, fisting it at crown and temples. Then and there Alice had decided that the habits of non-smokers might be observed more closely by the medical field.

"Call him up and decline, then, I don't care. I'm going. I'll go alone. I can't sit still, I can't go home yet. I can't help it, I need diversion. A picnic sounds great." Carla stamped her foot as Alice had not seen her do since childhood. "I'd love a motorcycle ride. A fast one. Maybe I'll ask the neighbors."

A final upright clicking of the lawn chair Alice meant to be taken as a signal of assent. What Carla was hanging around for, over three weeks now, a person could not guess and dared not ask, or risk a tornado-fit. August was in sight. Carla was newly pregnant and away from her husband. Duty dictated that Alice take her to Mel's.

The sky was the colorlessness of blanket heat. Poised, heavy, it could rain torrents or shrivel the earth equally fast. The long grass was tinged yellow and of course the temperature would be upped by ten degrees in the country. Already her underarms and nape and backs of the knees itched. And if the sky opened in showers Alice would hate to be away, miss seeing the downpour crack and cartwheel on Wakonda, then swirl and pool at the bottom. There were so few reasons to be away. For once "Big Rusty" looked honestly dimensionless, and a battalion of bikes shone in the neighbors' drive.

She put James's old watch back into her bag and hurried to finish her cigarette. "Not now," she told a squirrel coming at her in the mechanical high hops that trust had produced. On spreading out her city bus map, Alice had discovered that Mel's acreage was nowhere near the end of a bus line. It was situated several placid car-dependent miles from town, and this was exactly what she liked to avoid, getting trapped by friendly souls.

"God, it's a limo!" Carla cried.

Noiseless, the supreme car came up Wakonda, Mel's arm a raised truncheon. His flattop slanted sharply toward the other side of the street and caught light off the motorcycles, those glinting sharks' teeth wondrously aligned. The women moved toward him.

"You ladies live in the thick of things."

"I certainly do," Alice said in her voice for strangers. Carla hurried to take the back seat. Alice, suppressing any notable emotion save polite alertness, got in front. As Mel pulled away, Mary galloped onto the street chasing a volleyball.

"Summertime," was Mel's heralding of the day. For a moment, Carla expected him to sing.

Alice directed him up the street, then through the top alley and along down a parallel sharp hill where apartments, their roofs rising one on top of the other, ran an accordion skyline down the hillside. Each apartment building was an outsized conventionally shaped house built before the complex boom. The last, newest building—ranch-style one story, now twenty-five years old—sat on a corner lot, apart; it was constructed of mottled pinkish brick. Way back when it was completed, Carla had wished to live in such a home graced with ornamental ironwork. And now a critical glance revealed that the bricks were the exact color of Spam, the building a mushroom-capped cheapie.

Hormonal highs fluctuating with dream-stillness was her experience of pregnancy so far. Now on high, she itched for constant change, entertainment; she wanted to be chauffeured forever in this powerful car. Forget pickup trucks. She would speed away from the pregnancy in such a car, then some-where—way out in Nevada would be a likely spot—she'd stop and see about the situation, watch the future coming up on her and say, Fine. But first, a stretch of mind-blowing speed.

"Lose your brakes around here and it's goodbye, American pie," Mel said.

"Mmmm," said Alice. She'd have no idea that Mel referred to a song, and for that matter, Mel might not have the foggiest notion of what he referred to. Carla wiped her eyes and cleared her throat. Hysterical, all of it: her mother going on a date, sitting an ocean's length from Mel, her bun a fist.

Carla got a fit of giggles. She could not look at Alice's head or Mel's arm resting across the steering wheel or the burro statues carting geraniums in the yard they were passing.

Mel slowed. "Berries. Look at the bushes. They're black raspberry, aren't they?" He leaned toward Alice to glimpse the shrubs. "No one picks them?"

"*Red* raspberries are my favorite," said Alice, now sitting militarily. "They're wild everywhere in Minnesota."

Oh, Minnesota. Carla covered her mouth. To sober herself she thought of Brian, but today he was as funny as the icon state, Minnesota.

As they wound past the railroad tracks Carla could read in Alice's neck-straining the search for hoboes. Her mother loved hoboes. Or the idea of them.

They drove along the back side of the city's central artificial lake, in which toy-sized sailboats made caps on the water. Carla waited for Alice to comment on how this was nothing compared with Minneapolis's natural city-interred lakes. Alice snorted. Then they headed into the park that stretched all the way to the edge of town, past the Izaak Walton League ("Friday Nite Catfish Fry!" the sign proclaimed).

"Imagine it!" Alice said, a thrill of disgust in her voice. She began shifting on her seat.

The calm, the girth, the clean car: Mel was a nonsmoker. Carla was just settling back, wondering how put out Alice was, when her mother held up a roll of mints. "Anyone?" "No, thanks," they told her. Alice used a fingernail to slice open the roll. In no time she'd chewed them all up.

The combination of Alice's low-grade agitation and the calm ride made Carla think of ancient family outings, an era of alert fleet observations that ended with her father's wrecking the beautiful blue-black Dodge. For ages after, the house ran extra-heavily on innuendo and silence. His leg cast shone against the smooth dark walls. It was a bridge heaved from rocker to footstool, an exertion recalled to her years later by Brian's waterfall demonstrations at Lock Number Nine. "Carla, bring me my right slipper," James had urged softly. "A bowl of Cheerios." (This, when economy boxes of Cheerios were still in favor.) And Grandma Morrow would visit and pace in her open-toed pumps and lament that James Lawrence, such a brave soldier, Allie, did not need sorrow in this decade too.

They were riding in the countryside under a sky turned china blue, on a road walled by cornstalk. The soft air-conditioner song dissolved before a crackerjack burst of gravel. Mel had turned into a long drive lined with tall grass; it swayed and racketed with the high pitch of beetly voices familiar to Alice. A good omen, she conceded. And the air was so green with growth that dust could cause only the slightest tempering of color. Mel stopped the car in the midst of a lovely powder cloud, a country driver's creation.

"Watch out for Riley," he said.

A monstrous black dog gallumphed and swerved, head-ducking, his tongue a whirlybird, and the moment Mel stepped from the car the dog reared up wagging and crying, to wrap his paws over Mel's shoulders.

"Thatta boy." Mel patted the dog's side only to raise another cloud of dust.

The front yard was shaded by oaks on one side, but a great weeping willow conducted the wind.

"Mel, this whole area over here is wildflowers," Alice said.

"You like it, ladies?"

Carla said, "Yes, it's a perfect garden."

"I found the darndest thing called Meadow-in-a-Can. All the fixings for wildflowers came in a can, no kidding. Look at

the wizardry." Mel motioned them near. They all crouched
over the meadowworks, Alice bending deeply from her waist,
now Mel on haunches tweaking his pantlegs up, and Carla
sank into a cross-legged position. They leaned closer as if to
spot some failure or evidence that Meadow-in-a-Can was de-
fective, an outdoor version of a fake fireplace log. But the
flowers blossomed wholeheartedly, and the fragrance was
real. Riley snuffled and rooted and snapped free a petunia.
He tossed it toward Mel.

"True love," Carla said.

"I should have known about this product." Alice's voice
was sharp in professional self-reproach.

"Bachelor buttons, yarrow, blue flax, shasta daisy, prim-
rose, lots more," Mel said in a voice that guaranteed you a
carnival from this can. When he curved his palm lightly and
stroked a bed of pink buds, they quivered. "Ahhh," he said.
As if he could fondle them into growth, Alice thought. She
crossed her arms over her chest and stood quickly.

"I'm parched," she said.

"Follow me."

The house was the squat, two-story white square common
to rural Iowa, long-faced and stoic; the raised roof and the
very squareness of the windows gave the house a surprised
look as when a person exclaims and shoves a hat far back on
the head.

"Remember the Sears-Bilt houses, Alice?" Mel said, leading them onto the porch, its shade and butternut swing inviting. "That's spelled b-i-l-t. They had a catalog of homes, all
prefigured," Mel said to Carla. "The Depression wiped them
out; they hated to foreclose, considering they were Sears. The
houses were named after flowers. Mine's the Acacia. I was in
Chicago once. I got eighteen pages of blueprint from that
Sears Tower. It even tells where to put the piano bench."

"A house from a kit!" exclaimed Alice.

"Cool as a cucumber in summer, warm in winter. I've never
had to replaster. No complaints."

"A kit," Alice repeated for the benefit of her daughter, but
Carla had wandered. Do you see? She wanted Carla to think

about this. Even a house can come from a kit. "I love it," Alice declared, stepping inside.

The kitchen was nearly as large as the front room. Mel brought a pitcher of iced tea from the refrigerator, with Alice's approval. This would not be some bleary boozy thing, thank goodness, and she was aware of a watchful aspect gracing the kitchen. The abrupt calm of a woman suddenly called across town on an errand lingered here, but she felt sadness, too, in the museum-calm. Curtains were starched, reminding Alice of Mel standing in her office with his cupcakes, and on pegboard every appliance that could be hung was. Mel poured three glasses and squeaked them into Styrofoam holders.

"Come on out back."

They followed through the house on creaking floorboards bright with throw rugs. In his own home Mel's walk had a rolling and gathering aspect to it, Alice observed, so casual and open; it was a startling intimacy, watching his back, and she kept watching. The throw rugs were obviously hand-made.

At the back door Riley was whining and bucking, and as Mel stepped outside the dog took off, ears flying. The flimsy screen door whacked to behind them and here was the gateway to farmland, behind a frenzy of black dog. A thickly shaded yard held lawn chairs. A pyre of whitened briquettes smoked on the grill. The perfect green lawn grass was paled by the more brilliant sea-rolling emerald beyond, a dense leafy roll of hills riding to the horizon. Way out there hidden birds were letting loose long proprietary trills. The greens were golden, devoid of blue shades.

"So here are the soybeans," Alice declared. "Aha." But how peevish a discovery. A verdant green, yes, but how was it so special—a soybean farm? Really, the Sears-Bilt house held more interest. (Who hooked those rugs?) A house kit was surely the ultimate kit. That might be a new direction for Craftique. Much more significant than peddling tofu cupcakes, a person would think. Dr. Alan Rand himself, sailing the Caribbean, might grin and bless the idea.

"Beauties," Mel said. "That's right." Taking his hands out

of his pockets, he left sails of the lining. "But let's eat. First
things first. Seat yourselves, ladies."

Alice sat on a woven lawn chair. As Mel left, she sought to
give Carla significant looks, which were, annoyingly, ignored.
Her daughter shook her head at her in the way that meant
"Relax."

"Here we go." Mel came outside flourishing a foil-wrapped
platter. He uncovered what looked like hunks of light meat in
dark sauce. They hit the grill with a sizzle. "Best barbecue
going."

Of course Alice was quick to understand that a person's
perspective took a turn when living alone. Of course a person
would have the habit of eating foreshortened meals. She tried
to let sympathy, even empathy, kill off irritation toward Mel
and his chicken-fried steak. That's what dinner looked like:
breaded precut unnaturally squared tricked-up cheap meat.
She had relinquished a good day of solitude for this. It had
taken Mel a month to invite her here to eat these . . . *slabs*.
She struggled with her hair, going so far as to replace a bobby
pin publicly, to hide her greater peevishness. However cheerful the kitchen, this was an indication of what it really means
to be "older." A person has no idea how foolish he has become
by habit and solitude. Dare you have a "date," it is all revealed, how far you have listed from, for lack of a better
phrase she thought, *the romantic seas*, the center.

"Chicken-fried steak," she said tartly.

"Oh ho, Alice, you've got a long way to go guessing."

Carla peered at the grill from her chair and got up nodding.

"Then tenderloins," said Alice.

"Noop."

Noop, stupe. It would be like Mel to boom, "That's sweet-
breads (cow brains, tongue) you've got there," just as Carla
bit in.

"My daughter and I do not eat organ meats!"

"Smart ladies."

Carla was grinning now, grinning and braiding at her hair
with that smug look generally reserved for mention of woodchopping.

"It's safe, Mother. Watch." Carla pocketed the woeful meat in a bun, topped it with tomato and bit in. "Yummmm."

"It's tempeh," Mel announced.

"Pooh. What on earth? Speak English." The sandwich Mel handed her smelled of spicy sauce.

"That's soybean curd, a variation on tofu. It's the highest, most efficient protein source, the lowest in fat, and look at it all dressed up." Mel took a huge demonstration bite. "Tempeh. Some other cultures know how to eat. Go on, Alice, munch away. You're not going to hit any bone or gristle. And know what a sandwich like this costs you, buying tempeh at health food stores? Fifty cents tops. If people only knew, really cared. Families could save a heck of a lot." Mel faced his fields and ate like prayer, a big slope of man silent until the finish.

"I'm Iowa rep. of the National Edible Soya Promotion Team. I run off a newsletter after hours out at the plant, they don't mind. I'm experimenting," Mel told Carla. "Alice has tried my tofu-frosted cupcakes."

"I fixed her tofu the other night. Stir-fry," Carla said, waving her sandwich. "*I* eat it, of course. I'm vegetarian."

"She ate a hot dog, too, Mel."

Carla shook her head. "I'm no fanatic."

"Alice, you know the five sacred grains?" Mel asked.

"My memory is poor." Enough of the fawning vegetarian self-congratulatory spiel. Food was fuel, period. She ate. Thank goodness for the sauce. Otherwise, she didn't think she'd taste anything in the cakey texture entirely capable of exonerating itself from the cow-brains idea.

"Anyway, soybeans are the most exalted in some cultures. Bake them, whatever you do, they're nature's highest gift out of the earth, a true miracle food." Mel finished and sat down clasping his hands between spread knees, like an athlete or a promoter. "Heck of a miracle. And the varieties? Two hundred, no lie."

"Really." Alice drowned herself in iced tea.

"Manchuria is soybean heaven, and those fields out there, I want you to know, are on the same meridian, same climate,

as Manchuria. Alice, we're more exotic than you'd think. We
are China. I didn't grow up farming. I'm from Council Bluffs
and what did I know or care? Now I hire these local men to
plant and harvest. I take a real razzing. To them, soybeans
are pig food. Biggest shock to me was to realize the fields of
corn and beans you see everywhere are pig food. My farming's organic, by the way. Well, I use potash but no herbi-
cides."

Carla was having a heyday of head-shaking and beaming,
entirely in cahoots with Mel: two food zealots thrilled over a
boring victory. But Mel was sincere. Alice gave him that.
Still, thank goodness she didn't feel like Carla, because this is
exactly the way a person throws over a life and becomes a
fool: one idea or ideal or habit in a person floods another one
with such relief (tempeh? me too!) that they are won over
lock, stock, and barrel, assuming that all else will fall into
place. Tempeh will bind, carry, sail them. Tempeh, or sur-
viving a war. Love, she feared, was a manufactured state that
had much to do with finding relief in a niggling coincidence
deliriously exalted. A song, a color, a taste shared, a war
story, and the impulse was supposed to carry the years. Impossible.

"Corn and beans, all pig food," Mel was saying to his fields.

Alice eyeballed the man. Evangelical tones, no matter what
the cause, set off her alarms. But in fact as quickly as Mel had
cranked up into preaching beans he now lapsed into silent
reverie. He relaxed heavily in his chair. His flattop was a neat
silver lawn, and only the twitching of his fingers revealed
furious thought.

"This heat," Carla said. "We need rain. I'm so tired."

"Is anything wrong?" Mel asked.

"No," she said, darting a look, mischievous and warning,
at Alice. "I just need a moment to lie down, if you don't
mind."

"Siesta hour, of course." Mel took Carla inside and returned
—with a new swagger in his walk. He carried bowls of ice
cream melting perfectly and a little blue saucer of strawber-

ries. "This is tofu ice cream, Alice. I made it myself. See what you think. I'd like to get a little processing business going out here. A couple of good products." The slatting on Mel's chair bulged fearfully as he settled himself.

"It suits me to sit here and watch the beans grow," he said.

Alice sat forward. The ice cream tasted exactly like ice cream. She followed Mel's gaze to the beanfields. High on Wakonda Hill her back yard manufactured an ellipsis of vitality. Peculiar breezes swirled through the top limbs, but did not escape into the neighborhood at large, and she always got the feeling that maybe next time, if she could sit a moment longer, so much would come clear, that everything, a pattern, could be deciphered right there in the back yard. She'd stretch her head back, forget she was Alice, forget to think; she'd be spirited up to where a canopy of oak leaves twittered and played fingers against the sky's face. An old Indian woman was quoted in the *Geographic*, explaining why moving away from ancestral lands was impossible: "Our mother earth knows us here." Alice could say this about Wakonda. High in the sky a fast-moving creaturish cloud perfectly advertised this day. Did Mel know any of this?

"I've always enjoyed sitting in my back yard, too," Alice said. "Since my husband's death I sit outside more than ever. We always did. But I feel like I'm waiting for something. I realize I still act like I'm waiting for news of him. We never knew what was ahead, for years. Excuse me, I'm just going on, aren't I?" She coughed. How appallingly confessional. These crazy beanfields she spoke to! She was used to addressing squirrels, the newspaper, the stupes at work. But a palpable presence, a deep orchestrating revelatory hum, was ghosting in from over the crops, calling, making her volunteer her heart.

"I heard he was sick a long time," Mel said. "I never got the specifics."

"I didn't discuss them."

"I had the opposite with Betty, nothing *to* discuss. Eight years back she went in for a shot of penicillin. Allergy had been building all along. They figured this out afterwards, after she died right there in the office. Instant reaction."

"For Pete's sake, Mel. What a shock. I'm sorry." She looked to the sea of beans, all patchwork shades of green in the lap and swell, ruffling and settling of a million leaves. She had never sought out empathetic health cases. It seemed terrible, but now she could not recall ever having been aware, truly, despite all her newspaper reading, of feeling anyone else's personal tragedy. Not vividly. (Had Craftique passed around a card when Betty died?) Death coming with no warning at all was totally inconceivable. Mel and Betty had simply lived and one day Betty died. She died with plans and a full refrigerator and tomato seedlings on the windowsill. It was too gruesome. Alice could see Mel moving back in memory now, but not into mourning.

"But you're happy here, with Riley. The fields, everything."

"I'm single."

"Of course." She checked her bun and to further her approval she said, "I still don't know what got into my mother-in-law."

Mel shook his head and grinned. "When it hits it hits."

If he meant love Alice was grateful for his sensible use of the word "it." She looked toward the fields as if he had said nothing. (His rubbing of palms on thighs was a dubious gesture.) Betty, she thought, would have been a plump simple woman known for wise acts at the merest hint of catastrophe. Alice looked at Mel and saw a man who had been chosen, lived with and loved; and she felt a twinge of envy for the simple Betty who had had the faith to love this man. Sure, she had loved James—the beginning was quite romantic— but she had soon enough come to think of people, adult people, as singular, as separate small tornadoes cutting tortured paths. Thanks to the glitter and paste, she had managed as best she could, thinking it was how people must live, after all. Betty and Mel were different. They had been a team. That's what a person felt in the kitchen and saw in the bright throw rugs. The rugs were there to be walked upon, and when Betty did not return from that doctor's office, Mel continued to nurture those seedlings as opposed to tossing them in grief. Betty might even have subscribed to Craftique.

They continued to sit as if at a drive-in movie or at the precipice of a breathtaking view—a stormy sea, something Californian; yet it was the beanfields, low-lying, ruffly dense impassive green, they faced. Alice sucked on ice cubes and strained, shading her eyes, to see the beans. Mel was over in China:

"This old American doc went to Manchuria and started it all. Once he saw what was there, he took his soybean crusade all over. He converted the Japanese. Now, *that* I admire. I've got a gambling streak, Alice, a bit of snake oil salesman in me, if you like, but this isn't snake oil. It's an honest deal. It would profit me to help change this state's eating habits in more ways than one. It really would profit me."

Alice wondered what Betty would have thought of Mel's scheme.

Mel clapped hands over a mosquito, and he gave no indication of being a man after a woman.

"I exist on cheese sandwiches, Mel, but I promise to try some more tempeh. Oh, listen." Alice jumped up. A hum rattling her ears, a leaping in her limbs, she took as signs of having gone too long without a cigarette, but she felt a deeper agitation out here with the soybean crusader. The humming, crackling, a long roll of birdcalls unfurling from the fields, intensifed and roared through her. They were crazy beanfields. A sucking sound she imagined composed of moisture, energy and color being funneled right down to the nub, in order to feed the beans. The sky was drained of itself, and beanfields, incredibly luminous, greedily drew breath.

"Let me see these beans. I don't know what a soybean looks like."

Mel marched her forward. Her temples throbbed and the man in pale-blue jumpsuit swished along with his arms swinging. Did he whisper or did the fields? There was no breeze

now, just a liquid bathing sun. They walked quite a ways and
then stood smack deep in a beanfield. Mel's light blueness
looked protectively cool. The fabric, its give and weightless-
ness, was right for working the fields high in Manchuria, a
person could believe that. A pungent sour-mash sort of smell
prevailed and the leaves gave off sweetish chlorophyll luster.
Alice recalled Mel's testing the mint leaf at home. She wondered if there were snakes, but would not ask. She kept following.

Facing west, he was large enough to block the sun. With
his arms raised to encircle the beanfields, Mel looked like a
bursting blessed scarecrow, and now Alice, her insides dissolving from nicotine need, the backs of her knees sweaty,
weak, felt the earth as a great swell. She braced herself. On a
far hill she could just see the square rise of white farmhouse
cresting.

She remembered going kite-flying with James in an open
field when they were sweethearts. It had been her idea, probably dreamed off a greeting card. "No obstructions," she'd
said, pleased with what they'd found at the end of the Green
trolley line. They stood in the field, James with rolled shirtsleeves handling the kite, and looking like a cross between a
workman and a wisp. He guided the kite against the wind. Of
course it would fall, but this seemed to sadden James too
much, and oh how touching she'd found that, how she'd just
loved him triple for his crazed jerking of the string and his
crying out. She'd plunged right in with silly gambler shouts
she hadn't known she remembered from her father. "Lucky
dog come to me!" And "My baby needs a new pair of shoes!"
But James did not laugh. He kept the ball of string looped
around thumb; he scanned the field. "There's no cover," he'd
said, and all the fun was out of him. These were hints, Alice
told Mel's beans. But I could not read them. Later came the
cherry pies. And James's leaping from the bed at the first
crack of thunder, yelling, "Get in the foxhole!" She had forgiven the fright, called it a nobility of spirit. A young dummy
I was, too, she told a million beans.

"Adventuring," Mel was saying. His arms were still uplifted, catching a mood. His mouth opened and closed in agreement with the sky. So brimming with flesh and appetite.

Alice crouched low to examine the beans. They were a miniature bean forest at that height. How fragile, the little gold-green ornamental growths; the bean pods dangled from leafy dress. By enlisting these long-necked beauties, Mel aspired to pearl and save the earth. He would pay homage to the diffident grace of beans by enlivening their image. This field had no business calling Jessamine to mind. Jessamine! As Alice rose, blood rushed to her head, her chest spasmed and a bubbly sob broke loose.

"Alice?" Mel was at her side, a dance partner, she thought woozily. The smell of beans and earth and sun was so strong, closing up her throat. Mel put his one hand in hers; the other rested across her shoulder and took her weight. Someday they would twirl, glide, win something; but for now she could only shield her eyes and continue to sob; muffled noises filled the air, noises that hurt her so badly they should boom and ka-boom. But they were pillowed by the beanfields.

"Treacherous, beautiful beans," she cried. Mel was blobby through the tears, courteously looking away to beans and more beans, and the hand he extended back to her as she followed along toward the house had the decorous integrity of a Sears-Bilt house, and the roominess.

"You can come out here anytime. Come back. Watch them grow."

She breathed deeply: convex, concave, over and over slowing her beating chest the way she did during long hospital visits when deprived of cigarettes. Tension broke to bits in her chest. In her calves and fingers and elbows she still died for release. As they reached civilization she broke from Mel.

His house was cool as a cucumber, he was right. Alice found Carla lying directly under a ceiling fan, looking weirdly alert in her sleep due to the stippling effect of light and shadow on her. Her limbs were fillylike, tossed everywhere.

Alice found a bathroom. She disapproved of the fuzzy gold-

and-blue wallpaper, post-Betty obviously. She would not look in the mirror until she'd patted water on her eyes and rubbed off the lipstick. She had cried. She had cried in front of that man, in a beanfield, and if nothing else was required of her she would like to sink onto the floor and sleep. She wondered what Gloria would do, what those women did who wore eye makeup and suddenly cried. Her hair frizzed bossily as if it were set free in her emotions and were outraged that this was so.

"Quite a nap she took there," Mel was saying when Alice emerged. She was determined to look keenly polite. Carla was sitting up, a red spot on the sleep-turned cheek.

"Yes,' Alice said.

"Ladies." Mel actually bowed, indicating their departure.

On the ride home Alice developed a splitting headache and an urge so strong to skim a hand over Mel's flattop that she sat with hands clenched in her lap. She expected any bright word would make her sick. Any reference to her emotional outburst would be cause for bolting, hailing a taxi, denying the moment.

"What sort of a driving record do you have?" She'd made Carla take the front seat this time and spoke directly to Mel's neck.

"Why, none at all, Alice." The neck reddened.

James had had a driving record and Mel Gifford had made her cry.

Mel turned the radio on. They all rode silently, terribly intent upon an interview with a famous painter's twin.

CHAPTER 12

Alice sat in the cool back-yard twilight and smoked all the cigarettes in a row that she had sacrificed for a scalding walk in a beanfield. Safe in fiefdom, she had already ironed a week's supply of office outfits. Her entire sweep of vision took in only trees and sky and stillness; no activities on Londo's turf, and Calvin never used his back yard. Once frazzled with kids and toys, power-mowing and fence-painting, it had gone to forest. He had more trees than she. More pelting trees: black walnut and buckeye, one apple, and oaks that rained their acorns downhill. Two white oaks were positioned just right to swing a hammock, but no one had ever done this. One of Calvin's trees, something from the willow family, was so severely camel-humped it had once been photographed for the *Register*. Alice consulted with all these trees, and their dark cloaking of the sky assured her it was good to be home, to sit right here.

She put a mother's double-vision to Carla's movements in and out of the house. Carla moodily watered the lilies, and she even filled the disdained delft bowl for the birds. She carried out garbage and pointed to the sky. "Venus." Alice nodded and watched Carla do all these things and make her busy gestures in which history showed itself as acutely as the present moment. It was no effort at all to call up Carla as a little red squall in a crib or see her as a straight-shouldered girl in a school program, or walking down Wakonda swinging unsure teenage hips and one of her horrid big basket purses. The whole thing flew at a person without regard for dimension, time or space.

Carla bent and smelled the spirea. Here was a daughter's back curving to the earth, invisible from Venus. James's back had firmly remained James's back until the end, but eventually in the hospital Alice had not been able to draw an ounce of meaning from his face, his gentle saucer eyes. Manhood was totally eclipsed by the gosling look.

And loving as hard as you can has never guaranteed perfect illumination, that she knew. Carla's fidgety furtive start to pregnancy might be something only her own mother could abide, being a titch reluctant (she'd confess only under the hottest tar torture) to let her girlhood go. Carla's hesitancy was unpopular, and Alice suspected she would not confide in other young women. What could a person tell her? Perfect love, especially mother love, does not, does not guarantee illumination, rather it binds you to the absolutes: trust, and the deep fighting belief that your offspring is forever and ever the fine angel you delivered. Every convict's mother swears from her heart, "He didn't do it!"

And when in love you thought—she had thought in the beginning with James—that every glance, motion, word and deed, however cockeyed, related to a deep order, a communion that would deliciously wrap itself around them in clearer and clearer, brighter, neater ribbons. She was a young coed after the war, a bobby-soxer correct in rolled jeans and men's shirts and white, white socks; and she believed that the men walking across campus in Army uniforms who wore such remote intensity on their brows were miracles. She had seen in the newsreels what they had survived. In the movies, with feet propped on the seat backs, she and her bobby-soxer friends had watched Europe go mad, and grew to fear the Japanese. The men who were practically thirty years old walking around the campus had witnessed and performed miracles. These men—James Morrow sitting next to her in Advertising and using only full-length slate-blue pencils for note-taking—had a facility and grace and uncanniness. They talked about markets and designs in a way that let you know they meant the world. They had risked everything to pry open the earth's shell and go for oysters. "Marry me?" he'd asked, sweet enough to break her.

But it was as you went on together that the clues came; the

strangeness had revealed itself fathomless. Logic, she saw now, was hindsight put to bewilderment. James's wacky spirit prefigured the body's doom.

"Let's take Carla out for miniature golf," James had cried one Friday night. He'd turned a slightly surprised and delighted smile on Alice, there at the table folding laundry. "Carla's eight. Sure. Why didn't I think of this before?"

Alice had pushed back the curtain sheers and looked out to a very still evening. Funny, what you remembered of childhood evenings, yours or your child's: it was always summer when you remembered the evening. In summer a child's evening comes in blues and greens and sparkles. The sky winks with the diamonds called bugs and stars.

Carla was a woman now walking in circles in the back yard, yet still, like a child, she would pull the descending darkness to her in wonder. "It's a whole different sky here," she said, brushing at it. "Too many lights. And this haze, Mother. I don't know how you live with this haze. How did I?"

Alice jetted her smoke straight up. It was a great sign, Carla's impatience here. She would return to her own home, however monstrous the woods, and surely, quite normally, have her baby. Alice's duty was simply to believe this.

That Friday night she had looked out the window and said, "I don't know about the weather, James." The sky had gathered a woolliness about it, shone yellow at the horizon and was fuming yellowness higher up. "We could have a downpour."

". . . just give her a taste of golf and see, yes!" James was saying more to himself than to anyone else. "She may really golf later." His throat and left arm were bronzed from driving all day. He was in that phase, the last phase of jobs, a time when Alice was used to sewing curtains and doll clothes and piling recipe books up from the public library, copying everything out in her eager, scrawling hand onto cards placed in a flowered index box. She owned fifty spices in miniature tins and kept the tops dusted. And she might have known she was getting the house into an order she could neither maintain nor enjoy: it was a kind of orthodontic work that might just as easily pan out as backslide later.

Family outings had always been James's affairs, and there was something so tender and noble about the three of them on parade as a family, driving into the world, luxuriously on display in the dark beetle-humped Dodge. A family!

They had all piled into the gorgeous car and rolled down windows immediately. A quaint stinging fragrance rose up from the leather seats and fabric armrests, from metal itself, thick enough to cushion a person's head, to blur questions, and steal energy. The car was old enough to have been a bargain; but it was going antique. Even Thunderbird owners expressed envy. James had told Alice this, bringing it home the first night. "Come out and see the surprise," he'd said, making Carla guess what it could be. ("A Shetland pony? A big, big Hershey bar!") In the dark, beyond the streetlight, the car just gleamed. Alice couldn't say what color it was. It was grill-gleaming and body-gleaming. All chrome and dark gleamingness. And James told her right then, "If you're going to smoke, you'll have to blow it out the window. And toss the butts."

The sweet smell was surely peculiar to cars, but it reminded Alice of Jessamine. Did a family fragrance get passed on, along with speech and eating habits? Now years later it came to her in the back yard as a whiff of hospital smell.

The way James drove them to Airport Miniature Golf that night a person had to think life was perfect. He sang! Back then, driving was the only time in the world James Morrow was known to sing. It was, she thought now, the soul covering for itself, for its imminent failure to thrive. Get him behind the wheel and he'd sing with such hope and cleverness. Alice joined in softly so as not to drown out his baritone and rhythmic slap on steering wheel. She willed Carla, who sat in back (always on James's side to protect against flying ash), to absorb this, to have the singing father tattooed onto her mind. I must have suspected, she thought now, watching Carla. Carla's walk was changing. Carla didn't know it yet, but her supple body was leading from its center. She was parting air as she walked pregnant.

Once in a windstorm the hood of that car flew up, and for ages they swam in navy-blue blindness. But with James leaning farther out his window he one-handedly got them safely to the curb. Using spare things, he fastened the hood and continued on, singing, "Pony boy, pony boy, won't you be my pony boy? Don't say no, here we go, far across the plains. Nothing to it, Alice!" Such pride and absolute knowledge of the universe, such pearling of fear into faith! Alice had flung herself into his lap, weeping, laughing, in love to the heavens and back.

The sun hadn't set, but like the sky Airport Miniature Golf had affixed unnatural yellow lighting to come up from the earth. And the overheads were on, making everyone look lighter than day. At first the green course was nothing but a maze to her, but she noted strangely cut banks of earth and ever increasingly complex sets of plastic trellises, windmills and bridges. She stood to the side and lit a cigarette while James came out with golf clubs. "Here's your iron, Carla." He insisted on showing off some real golf swings before admitting, "But here you want to putt. Keep a steady arm, eye on the ball, and you've got it." He stood behind Carla and swished her club and her equally skinny arms: left, right, left, right. ("A pro golfer came to Minneola," Jessamine had told Alice a dozen times. A pro golfer wanted James—just a teenager—to tour. He was a golfer before he was a man, Allie.")

"I'll watch," Alice volunteered. "If I knew how to keep score I'd do it." James shook his head, shifting his flame hair forward. This was between father and daughter, what he might transmit to Carla from his Minneola country club days. Sports clothes for the amateur were not de rigueur, but James rolled his soft cotton shirtsleeves to doughnuts and wore loose pants of the palest blue. And Alice loved to stand apart, in her long circle skirt and red cummerbund that matched her lips. She noted other families—men in bermudas (thank goodness James would not wear them, his legs were a fright), women in patio pants; and she looked gloatingly at Carla's long-legged eagerness, her ruffled midriff top.

"Look at her go, Alice!" James bent back at the knees and thrust his "iron" high. Carla was jumping up and down.

"Mommy, did you see? I did it, I did it." A hole-in-one or whatever you called it in miniature golf, right from the start. Carla kangaroo-leaped all around her father. Alice smoked and smiled and knew that, though the victory meant nothing in terms of future golf-life, still it meant a dreadful lot.

It was all drama with James. "Into the stream. Hey, over the hill, there, there, you got it!"

At the end, James looked to the sky streaming purple and seemed to listen there, not to Carla who was pleading, "Can we play again?" Then she switched to "I want some root beer, Daddy."

"We'll go watch the planes," James decided.

Just once, later, she had gone out there to look again, as if she might get a clue. Upon leaving the doctor who admitted, "He's dying," Alice took a taxi straight to the airport and accused the planes.

There is no longer an open-air observation deck from which to spot planes coming and going. It's probably no longer a sport or pastime now that everyone has ridden one or seen a thousand jets on TV and in the papers: crashing, burning, doomed skeletal birds. That is the only kind of airplane picture a person sees now, it seemed to Alice. Boredom and terrorists have spoiled the mystery. But with your first family car, taking the family somewhere, you ended up at the airport. You went to watch the planes. It wasn't as if James was the only one with this plan, Alice had consoled herself as they climbed the boring metal stairs.

"Hold my hand," she told Carla. With the other she lifted her hem. James had sprinted ahead and when they emerged out onto the deck, there he stood.

"Look at it!" he cried. As the jet took off he leaned away from the railing; his thick flame hair lifted sure as a wind sock, and he seemed full of a boy's glad wonder. More wonder than he'd displayed at Carla's birth. A resentment not named until that moment kicked in, but Alice lit a cigarette and exhaled all puzzlement into the sky.

"Holy God!" James called to the sky as the jet swung back on itself and plumed white into the darkness. These were not very fat planes and the front of the one still on the ground had a fine dolphin's face.

"Tatatata, Daddy. Got them," Carla yelled. She was shooting down planes from all directions with her finger.

"You bet," said James. "This is great."

Even in the wind and at 9 P.M. Alice was dripping. The sky, she felt certain, was bound to burst its seams any second.

Sure enough, lightning fissured the blue-blackness and thunder rolled overhead. James gurgled, held fast, and Alice thought that maybe, just maybe, he imagined himself lifting and flying, too. His heels had begun jerking up and down. Yes, the lightning touched him peculiarly. It convulsed him. He held the railing tighter. "Here we go!" he cried.

"James?" A giant drop splattered Alice's cheek. "Oh, oh, we'd better get going." She wrapped Carla in her cardigan. "It's starting, it's going to pour."

"Hey," James yelled. "I know that sky. I know it from its rooftop. I'm looking down."

"I'm sure I don't know what you mean, *honey*," Alice called. She made nervous brushing gestures at Carla's hair poking from the shawl-cardigan. This is how the abandoned look, see how little it takes to turn a child into an urchin.

"Whew, well, let it rain. Let it, brother. It won't even touch me. Hold on, baby. I say, hold on to your horses. I could wrap things up. Fly over that ocean . . . you know, things were never wrapped up." James went up and down on his heels, smiling, slapping the railing. "Something got left behind. It needs fixing over there. I'll go."

He called to the sky. He shouted from another universe, from the soldier's advantage.

Alice shot her cigarette over the railing. What could you say to the hero, the blessed who returned home when so

many, many did not? But, oh, how it turned on you, and
sometimes Alice looked forward to their coming through the
years, being absolutely ancient, having forgotten all that. And
then he would no longer be ten dramatic years older. He
couldn't be a soldier forever, could he? Not after they'd
shared decades, he couldn't.

And she had no idea what he was talking about anyway.
Her days were full with the recipe books and arrangements
and imagining the day into some goodness that was family
life. Part of the day was spent in preparing for the night. A
half hour with Pond's cold cream. Her own mother, for heav-
en's sake, would storm around the house reviling the father,
but minutes before he came home from work she'd apply
bright lipstick.

"James, it's raining." She spoke gently, touching his elbow.
"It's time to go home."

"No, no." In the dark, catching the blue lights of the airport
—a knowledge of metal and weather detected therein—
James's eyes grew large. "Part of me feels nothing, Alice. Part
of me—you know—is still over there and tells me, Come on,
buddy. Come on over, buddy."

"For pity's sake, it's raining. We're soaked. That's your
daughter in the rain. Soaked!"

Carla held the sweater tightly and her little face worked to
sing the four-leaf-clover song. James was stuck on the sky.
Everyone was oceans apart. Songs, whispers, pleas all clashing. Carla's little finger darted out to shoot the airplanes. Alice
hated the night sky. She dug her fingers hard into James's
bronzed arm.

"Damn, honey," he said.

"We're drowning. Move. Watch your step."

She led them down from the observation deck. She had
never meant to lead anyone anywhere, and if she knew how
to drive the car she would drive the car home.

The car humped like a giant beetle there, alone, in the
parking lot, a blue-blackness. James started it up with a jerk
that sent the glove-compartment door swinging free. Its inside

was molded to hold two cups and a square tray, for drinks and burgers. You were supposed to have fun in this car. But James was a test driver now, going from zero to forty miles per hour from red light to red light.

He knew better than this. He knows more than to do this, Alice thought, hanging on as James took a corner. "James, watch it." He shook his head like she was hopelessly ignorant of the situation.

"Oh, slow down!" she screamed finally.

In the back seat Carla whooped as a child will do in the face of illicit fun, glad to find her own mother stumped for once. "Ha, ha, ha!" How quick to turn. Alice sighed, supposing her voice dreary, the voice that kisses away cuts and fears is dreary when protesting thrill. Carla sat way back with her feet up on the front seat tickling her father's neck. Then she switched and sat on her haunches. Even without root beer, the night was absolute adventure now and a mother's care was lost on it.

They got off the main roads, thank goodness for that, Alice prayed. But now James really gunned it. Lightning flashed up ahead. And James seemed to race for it.

"For chrissakes, let's open her up," he cried, zooming harder into the rain. He was not on this continent, but he got them home.

"Let us off at the curb. Right now." They hadn't paved the driveway yet. Usually packed dirt, it had turned to puddles while they were away. Let James park at the top of the hill. But he sped away with such screeching, Alice's heart leaped after him. The car's taillights were red slits, disappearing meanly behind a veil of water, up the hill and gone in the sound of the rain.

"Where's he going?" she cried.

"Daddy!" Carla shouted.

Grabbing Carla, she realized how wet they were. "Quick, run." Lightly, she spanked Carla along toward the door. She put her into a hot bath and combed her moppy hair and braided it. Later, tucking her in, James still not home, she

said, "I don't know where he went. Daddy needed something." And Carla's round-eyed look prompted her to say,
"Tomorrow let's shop for school clothes!"

For ages, she smoked and paged through *Look* magazine.
There was no shred of evidence in the magazine, no clue to
James's behavior and nothing on how to be a wife who offsets
phantoms. The centerfold showed celebrities standing over
"the biggest pizza pie in the world." It ran the length of a
ballroom. Men in white ties dazzled her.

Hours passed and she began to wonder what a person
should do. Call Jessamine? The police? The airport? Then
the phone rang. It was the Veterans' Hospital. The beetle-
blue car and James's left leg were smashed. "Something short-
circuited," the hospital spokesman allowed. "But he should
be fine."

"Mother."

Alice sprang forward. "You scared the daylights out of me,
sneaking up." And in fact the daylight, she saw, was totally
dissolved into dusk.

"You were fantasizing. You *look* different now that you
know Mel has a crush on you."

"Baloney!"

Carla sank onto the grass with a laugh. "I'm not sure exactly
what to ask my own mother about her suitor. But you should
thank me for needing a nap this afternoon. Things happened,
I know."

"No you don't. Nothing happened."

"Plenty is happening, Mother. It's okay to like him. *I* like
Mel. You've forgotten how it works. Sure, he's not another
Daddy, but that's no requirement, is it? He's a friend. No-
body says you have to *do* anything."

Do was the pushiest word. From the dusk sprang Londos
and bikers, a rage of slinging halter tops, doing, doing, and—
ridiculous but true—she could not think of anything specifi-
cally terrible to say about Mel.

"I wouldn't want to encourage him, though he's brighter

than a person would think with all that hardy-har talk. I don't know who he is, but he's definitely without malice of forethought," Alice said.

Carla sat so close that Alice lost her double vision. She could only see Carla as an adult, right now grabbing up tufts of grass, picking the yard clean, choosing carefully which tufts, as if it mattered. She was a soft blot against the darkened sky, with the new pregnant-smooth face.

"Then tell me one thing, Carla. What would I honestly *do* with . . . him?" Alice performed the fake coughing they'd always managed in order to gain a moment's thought.

"Mother, juggle grapefruit way up over the moon. Quick, *flirt*. They say that everyone who dies earnest gets reincarnated as a slug."

"Honestly." Alice hooted. "You are your mother's daughter." And the night was cozy and familiar and contiguous with, built upon, a thousand family nights. It stirred these visions.

"Do you remember your father singing that song 'Pony Boy'?"

"Of course." Carla stood in the shadows and sang clearly, like a straight-shouldered girl in a school program.

C H A P T E R   1 3

As usual, Hazen awoke with the sun and Jessamine did not. She felt his kiss, a tickle on the cheek that ran a skittering sensation up the bone to her temple. As Hazen squeezed her hand under the sheet and rolled himself to sitting, she continued to let her head rest very still on the heirloom embroidered pillowcase. Hazen's feet swam themselves into his slippers and off he went. Through the wall that separated bedroom from bath, Jessamine followed Hazen's morning preparations. First he gargled, then a little cough accompanied the fitting of his bridge to mouth. When he stirred up his shaving cream in the Old Spice cup she had given him, the attendant low drone meant he was humming.

Hazen progressed to morning chores. He could be expected to empty the trashcan into the hall dumpster if as much as one tissue had been discarded into it. Next, he checked the little refrigerator. From the sound of it the ice cubes she had frozen last night didn't suit Hazen's idea of proper ice cubes. Perhaps they had set lopsidedly or were too shallow. He moved back toward the bathroom, where he cracked the tray against the sink, then ran water to refill it. While Hazen ambled down the hall to the landing window for a clear view of sky and field, the condition of which he would report to her later, Jessamine put on her robe and went to the bathroom. Hazen's leather shaving bag and his tortoiseshell comb, the Old Spice cup and toothbrush (medium bristled to her soft) became a meditative presence by which to work on herself. Lilac soap bar was lathered, the face massaged, the toweling-dry undertaken with care. Back to the dressing table. Now powder. Now lipstick. Cologne was dabbed on the throat.

"Light clouds," Hazen called.

All set, Jessamine moved into the front room and was sorry to find that Hazen had put on the shirt from last night's dinner. She prayed quickly to the black-clad ancestor ovals on the east wall, *In due time* and *This too shall pass*. Early in their acquaintanceship Jessamine had confided in Hazen after breakfast, "Some of these people look like they've tumbled from bed and landed in the dining room." Her heart warmed with Hazen's mordancy: "Yes, Deborah ought to put mirrors at the tables instead of her darn centerpieces. Wouldn't that fix them, losing their appetites over their own looks!" Now she waited for Hazen to look away from the morning variety show to notice her.

Finally. "Jess, you're ready for the dance."

Jessamine smoothed at her no-wrinkle shirtwaist. Hazen

flustered her pleasurably with the nickname she had abhorred in girlhood. (Jessie: A woman without a bustle who could use some restraint back there. Jess: a boy's name.)

She went to Hazen with her arms extended, two bracelets jangling from the left wrist. He clasped them silent and tugged once, firmly but lightly, as if signaling a trolley stop. By now the sausage fingers were familiar as church. He leaned her against his side so that she half sat on his lap. His legs, Jessamine was proud to note, were perfectly capable when at rest, and hers were slim as a girl's.

"Good morning, ladies and gentlemen." Deborah's voice pushed its way through the loudspeaker and bounced all over the carpet, sprang up and spanked the walls and tremored Jessamine's earrings. The air *became* metallic, Jessamine swore. "Breakfast today is poached eggs and wheat toast or bran flakes. Sticky bun, a fruit selection and juice. It's seven forty-five, breakfast time."

"We're not deaf!" Jessamine cried, though turned away from the speaker. "My dear." She sighed and motioned Hazen to stand. She wished to be granted just one day in which to cook for him. At sunup she would tie an apron to her waist and stuff a turkey to bursting with her oyster dressing, baste it in sweet butter and roast it all day. Then right before the company came—a load of company—and after adding the relishes and the flatware to the table, she would change into her smooth black skirt and the white silk blouse with pleated yoke bodice and glass buttons down the front. Yes, she would. She had schooled Hazen on the use of a five-o'clock teaspoon.

"Let's get along now, Hazen."

Jessamine and Hazen were earlybirds in the serving line. Side by side they carried their trays to the table-for-two they occupied near the front of the dining hall, a distinction afforded them as a married couple. This was the walk Jessamine adored. She shuddered, recalling her routine of five years as a woman alone at Hillcrest. The blabby Margaret Jennings had been assigned her former table, and a shrill Easterner who had been let into Hillcrest sat there, too. Generally a good class of people resided at Hillcrest, but to eat three meals a day with the same six meant that having even one bad apple at the table devastated the peace. The situation had anguished her to no end; yet she had perfected the inward path of anger that allowed her to sit in a full room, furious to death at the woman to her left, with none the wiser.

Though the eggs required little effort, Hazen winged his elbows in order to eat. "Ahh," he said when finished. He pushed his plate forward and took his coffee black.

Jessamine paused and looked across the table at Hazen. She easily imagined her old light-filled kitchen into being, despite the stark fluorescence etching him. Daylight had spilled onto her spic-and-span floor tiles in a room rimmed with checked curtains and seasonal fragrance. The table was set with English Blue Willow and cloth napkins. A memory of unbounded privacy warded off the Hillcrest stares and speculations always whispering along her spine.

Hazen said, "Ahh," again, and with his eyeglasses flashing in the fake morning light he announced, "I've been thinking. There's only about one thing in the world I guess I can say I've got over on you, Jess. Want to guess at it? I'll give you a hint: it doesn't have a darn thing to do with your hand-painted dishes or whatnot."

Jessamine sipped coffee and prepared for the game. "Let's see." As a lifelong farmer Hazen was rightly energetic and fanciful at the breakfast hour. "Hmmm. You've had your travels. I expect you know the roads north and south and everywhere. I've always meant to visit my people in California and I believe you could drive me there, or even to Alaska, if you put your mind to it. And I'll say that because you're a man you've had certain experiences pertaining to earning a living that qualify you to speak on a range of subjects." Her glistening coffee reflected the cagey cheer Jessamine felt at such times. She worked to educate Hazen through photo-album sessions and examination of family artifacts. In turn, Hazen, a man of few possessions, used the guessing game to

shore up his past. From his broad declarations Jessamine proceeded to glean the stuff of his days, and then educate him
further. Smiling, she jangled her bracelets and waited.

"Can't guess?"

"I give up, Hazen."

"I have great-grandkids. We're four to zero on that score,
Jess. Being on top of four generations, that should make me
feel old as Moses, wouldn't you think? But darn if it doesn't
make me think of all the good times. I want to touch their fat
happy elbows and such. Wouldn't you like them to visit?
We'd have a real party." Hazen looked around the room and
let his voice deepen. "Bunch of old croakers." And some people were staring back at Hazen as if accusing him of the very
same thing.

"Hazen." Jessamine sought a whisper with backbone. "It's
only breakfast and most folks haven't reached stride yet. Will
you listen to me? Don't glower at them. Great-grandchildren?
Why, you act like you've just realized the extent of your
family." Jessamine pushed forward at the bust. "We've been
over this ground before. Yes, those children live in Kansas. I
can name them. Crystal and Robin. Matthew and Justin. You
see? I really don't count this as having something *over on* a
person. We're hardly in control of such events."

"Battens are like oxen, that's what they used to say about
Battens. You know, same as a dairy herd, something gets
passed down the line. On and on. You can't stop the Battens,
it was always said."

The purple plastic African violets between their plates were
safer and not as sad to look at as Hazen. How often through
the years had she waited, at first confidently, Jessamine recalled, then in prayer, for news from the river: a baby, Carla
and Brian expecting. She had stopped alluding to her hopes
quite some time ago. How fragile the universe of Morrows.
Once a cavalcade of pioneers matched with stout Stanley
blood, the generations had winnowed the family. Morrows
had become few. Allie was left with the name, and only Carla
carried the blood.

"Hazen, breakfast is over."

"Oh, oh, Jess. Are you huffing up on me? I didn't mean to get your goat. It's a curiosity, that's all. And a fact, like horses eat hay."

Jessamine made sure to keep smiling as she stood.

They took the elevator up to Two. With both hands Jessamine clasped her beaded coin pouch which contained the room key, and sometimes her fingers would snap up stiffly, snap down as fast, giving the impression that the pouch's contents wished to speak. She watched the number on the wall light up from One to Two. She walked down the hallway with her arm crooked automatically for Hazen while her heart tumbled back over itself in memory, seeking Lawrence Mitchell Morrow. How he had rejoiced at the birth of his granddaughter. "Carla." He had pronounced the name as if speaking through rich chocolate.

So, when everyone gets to heaven, then what? she'd like to know. But, silly! Couples and what-all were earthly matters. Some high order of society would be heaven, and up there she thought you would behave like a bird more than anything, glorious and tropical, traveling in arcs and spirals and dives, breathing lavender, then soaring on to the zenith of fragrance, more soothing than sleep. Lawrence Mitchell Morrow would not spite her the Hazen marriage, not in heaven. Besides, she planned to beat Hazen to it, and all would be smoothed over by the time he arrived. Our Father, I wish to die a married lady, Jessamine reiterated.

Her heels echoed smartly and Hazen's shoes made a scooting sound. Stubborn as a dray horse, that was Hazen, and she'd be the last person ever to suggest he use a walker. Jessamine's nose stung from the chemical solution fuming out of the beauty salon at the far end of the hall, and she wished as she had never wished before marrying Hazen that Hillcrest would all go away. She wished they could walk into their rooms, shut the door behind them and be assured of ultimate privacy and loads of space. Let her entertain Hazen in a proper home and she would know exactly who Hazen was.

Banish loudspeakers! Never again admit a Margaret Jennings past the threshold. Install a rear door that leads to her very own fenced back yard and a discovery of fruit-bearing trees; good sour cherries begging to fill a pie. Lawrence, her heart called. Oh, James Lawrence.

Hazen resumed watching the morning show. A girl dressed in leopard spots swiveled to point at the guest who wore a turban; he drew his legs up under him and raised his dark hands. He was barefoot on TV; the girl's shoulder was naked. Both looked directly into the Hillcrest living room where Jessamine now dusted. As she moved from the majolica plate to the hand-painted cup and saucer given her as a child, she feared to think that her cheerful little Carla had inherited a wartime malady from James Lawrence. World War II devastated James Lawrence's very blood. Could the Japanese have finished off the Morrows, robbed Carla of motherhood? She must speak to Allie. To Reverend Lyton. To her physician. She had never understood that disease.

Jessamine set down the duster and dropped quietly into a plush wingback chair. She was out of energy, thanks to the Japanese. Seeing that Hazen's morning nap was in progress, she let herself weep.

• • •

Her mother-in-law stood outside Hillcrest clasping her throat, wearing a dress splashed with tangerine and bronze. She wore low-heeled woven pumps and reached out as Alice followed Carla from the taxi. You could lop ten years off the svelte Jessamine. Alice swore she had never seen Jessamine's hair look so racy-white. When had the gray shadings vanished?!

"We're all together tonight," Jessamine said, taking each woman by an arm. Being the tallest of the three even if she was born before vitamins, she led her visitors inside.

In the front room Hazen stood so that Alice and Carla could kiss him; then he whooshed himself into the abomination lounger Carla had warned of. He looked terribly incapacitated in that chair. Alice checked an impulse to yank him to his feet and sit him down in something with grace. She and Carla sat on chairs that could scoot on little wheels. Carla, thank goodness, reached for the TV and lowered the sound to no one's notice.

Hazen, deep in the lounger, kept his mouth open in a smile. Any glad movement caused a terrible squeak of synthetic fabric. This chair, surely the purchase of his first wife, was not meant for exuberance.

Jessamine had gotten to work setting out paper plates and juice glasses.

"Of course we've all just eaten dinner," Alice said, helping to unfold the TV trays. Jessamine was known for ritual overfeeding.

"Folks, I have a surprise," Jessamine announced. She rummaged in a paper bag and hefted a jar of popcorn; then she pointed at a draped tea towel hiding something lumpish on a cherrywood stand. Jessamine paused theatrically before unveiling a spanking new corn popper. It was shaped like a coffeepot, shiny yellow with gold diamonds running up the side to a bird-beaked top. "Air pops it. We don't need oil, and you see here, Allie, when you're ready you just melt your butter in the lid. I have sweet butter, of course."

Hazen fell into a wheeze of a laugh. "She gets me over here to the supermarket and shops my legs off me. What a contraption."

"Next time wait in the car," Jessamine said. She had to clear her throat from having spoken too loudly. She held the bag of corn to the popper and said, "Let's see. How does this work? My neighbor Mrs. Jennings got hers first. We went down the hall and ate popcorn with her a few nights back. The popcorn was excellent, though Mrs. Jennings can be a chore."

"We liked it when she shut up and ate her popcorn," Hazen added.

Alice read the directions marked on the popper. "Here, yes, fill to that line. See that, Jessamine? There."

Hazen had begun rocking. "You people know what they've

got in this grocery store? Whole aisles of socks and undershirts and things you wouldn't want mixed in with your food. Next aisle? Pots and pans. It's a mile on to the food. I keep an eye on Jessamine here. Who knows what she'll fancy? She was after gadgets, then wondering about recipe books—they had a collection of them. And fresh vegetables for which we have no use."

Jessamine rained popcorn into the machine. "We have use," she corrected, her back to Hazen. "But not the cooking facilities."

Hazen gallumphed the rocker. "I am busy, I tell you people. She's got me changing clothes five times a day to go look at vegetables or eat my dinner. I've got the gasoline bill of a Saudi."

"A person can get lost in those supermarkets," Alice assured Hazen, then quickly turned to Jessamine. "But there's so much that's fascinating."

Jessamine had turned on a heel and was holding a stick of butter high. "Why, Hazen Batten."

"I'm in new shirts! We're the high mucky-mucks!"

"Hazen!"

"Oh, the popcorn's starting," Alice cried, clapping her hands. The air clinked with a sound like tiny knives sharpening. "See . . . " A few little clouds floated out the popper chute.

"Hazen, I believe—" Jessamine began, but sudden alarms shrilled in over the loudspeaker vent, stopping her. Hazen rocked back in his chair, the TV was zapped to static, and the popcorn began spurting highspeed.

"My word. Help!" Jessamine cried.

As Alice went for the door and Carla pried at Hazen, popcorn sailed from the snout of the machine and shot far beyond the small bowl Jessamine had positioned under it, some pieces going so far as to strike and fall away from a madonna statue. Steady and soundless, the blizzard of popcorn increased.

"Wait, folks. Don't open the door." Jessamine yanked at the popper's cord.

Alice had already gone to the hall and discovered above the

frame a flashing red light. Sirens were looping the summer air.

"I said close that door," Jessamine cried.

"Look, the popper set off the alarm," Carla said. She pointed to the smoke detector, a little beige moon in distress, placed inches above the popper. "It's okay, Grandma."

"And the alarm rings in the hall for safety. Good," Alice said.

But Jessamine was lurching about with the arms of a puppet. "Allie, put that appliance away—oh, here." She slapped herself, then took the popper into her own hands and tossed it behind the couch. She fled to the bathroom with the bowl of popcorn, flushed it down the toilet, and was back in the front room, a dervish fallen to hands and knees, scrabbling for loose kernels that had shot from the popper.

"Jessamine?" Alice asked the figure before her so un-Jessamine-like.

The sound of heavy boots on the hall stairs made Jessamine gasp. Twinkletoeing back to the bathroom, she emerged once more, now shooting a fusillade of lilac spray into the living room. She held the can with both hands, her eyebrows raised on tragedy and resolve. The ultimate mother, Alice appraised, crazily protecting the lair, ready to eliminate it altogether, if need be. But it needn't be, she was ready to tell Jessamine. Carla has news!

The door swung open. Slickered young firemen piled in.

"Okay, everyone, let's move. How many, four? One, two, three, four. Good. Come on, ma'am, get out in the hall."

"But we were just . . ." Jessamine grabbed her throat. It shook like a gobbler's as she allowed herself to be escorted into the hallway. Then she stood stonily, with the legs positioned widely, and slightly bent at the waist in the alert elderly way that says goodbye.

They came to line the yellow hallway, all up and down, the flustered, agitated, reveling Hillcrest residents. They pointed to Jessamine's blinking red light, milled and swayed, hitched pants high, smoothed dress fronts, and tapped canes and walkers. A lungful of voice rose above the others. "Oh, Jessamine *Batten*, I told you. Didn't I tell you to be careful?"

"Margaret Jennings!" A proper name trilled piercingly was the closest thing to a curse Alice would ever expect to hear from Jessamine.

"We didn't burn you down," Hazen called out.

"Hazen, hush, really." Jessamine tilted her chin high at the firemen who might just as easily have been a firing squad.

The head fireman's blue eyes were direct and friendly. "You had a scare," he said, emerging from within. "The place is fine. The building's alarm rings right into our station, so we can get here in a jiffy, no matter what."

"It was a fake alarm," Jessamine explained.

"No, ma'am. Something set off the alarm. Maybe an appliance?"

Jessamine clutched her throat-gone-gobbler again. Her face got the crumpled-rose look, the look of pain Alice recognized as concerning burial property.

Still holding her pocketbook, which she thought later was such an odd thing to have retrieved considering the antiques, Alice whipped out her matches. "These culprits," she cried. "I was lighting candles. Jessamine here didn't stop me fast enough. We're celebrating a new marriage, you see."

"Oh well, ladies." The fireman nodded sagely and looked beyond Hazen, politely searching for a groom.

"Yes." Jessamine grew to giantess proportions in her doorway. "Allie, those matches are illegal in here and that could be trouble."

"Now you know," said the blue-eyed fireman.

"Indeed!" Jessamine was nearly shouting.

"My land, she's a card. Isn't she?" Hazen was all chuckles, turned to Carla. Somewhere along the way he had salvaged lemon drops. He said in a low tone, "Here's a joke: *I've been jessed*. Ha, ha. Jessed. That's a falconry word. It means hooked, attached. You know, I don't even like popcorn, but I go along."

The firemen left, grinning and trotting at each other's heels.

Jessamine gathered them all back inside, waved away
Hazen and took Alice by the arm into her bedroom. She shut
the door soundly and sank onto her bed. She crumpled into
great silent bobbing measures of grief, gripping her quilt, and
when she motioned to the room beyond, trying to speak, she
ended up shaking her wispy white curls. Alice sat beside
Jessamine and held on to the quaking shoulders. Through
them she felt a furious heart's tremoring, and she touched a
powerful mutual confessional yearning: Alice wanted to speak
about men, not popcorn. Abruptly, urgently, she wished to
speak of all the men in their lives.

Presently Jessamine stretched her head way back. Her neck
carried composure up from midsection and cleared all passages to reason; it was an amazingly visual transformation,
topped with the application of a great powder puff, restoring
an even pinkish composure.

"Thank you, Allie. You've rescued me. Yes, the popcorn
popper is illegal, but we have needs. Think of living by such
rules that exclude popping corn. Who was meant for it?
Sometimes I can't . . . just can't abide. I think of the early
days . . . Oh, I've been reprimanded by a fireman." She
bowed her shoulders, a schoolgirl.

"But how does Mrs. Jennings manage?" Alice asked, mas-
saging the bowed shoulders.

"Allie, I forgot." Now Jessamine waved white scorning fists
as random and angry as her popcorn. "Mrs. Jennings had all
her windows open despite the air-conditioning. *That's* not illegal, but immoral, I'd say. Mrs. Jennings plugged hers in
miles from the smoke detector, by the window. I forgot, I
simply forgot. I wanted you folks to see it pop and enjoy an
evening. I wanted to be a rightful hostess." Jessamine stopped
speaking, and when her frown smoothed itself to a swift retreat, leaving dewy eyes, Alice had an idea of what to expect.

"Allie, you know that we used to spend summers at a lake.
That's where James Lawrence learned to swim, and at night
we popped corn over an open fire. We sang. I taught him ever
so many songs." Jessamine clasped her hands and sang faintly,

"My truly, truly fair; truly, truly fair; how I love my truly fair." She turned to Alice, flushed. "You can never be closer to someone than you are when sharing the open land."

Sitting like this, Alice could almost imagine they were girls. The pressing confessional need bound her like a tight new bra. And though the time was wrong and the idea of men as a subject as startling as ever to Alice, she knew that Mel Gifford's existence on the same planet ("on a farm, Jessamine") was, would someday be, news meant for her mother-in-law.

She said, "Hazen's sense of humor is special."

"Yes, but—oh, monstrosity—how can he make light of this? What do you do when you're so furious at your husband, oh, who am I speaking to? Forgive me, Allie. You, of all people. But you have no idea of the difficulty. All of Hillcrest is watching over a coffee cup. I believe some are waiting for disaster between strangers. Because, of course, we are. I married Hazen on faith. The promise in his laugh . . . that car. At my age, these are enough. I describe serving my turkey dinner to him because I can no longer serve turkey dinner. We won't have time to know each other properly." Jessamine inhaled quickly. "We're summing up, really. With Hazen I can assure myself that everything that ever happened did, indeed, happen. We want to speak of it, Allie. Love allows us." She broke off and for a long time looked at her side profile in the mirror.

She patted her hair and frowned. "Allie, Mrs. Jennings and her bunch are still out in the hall, aren't they? Expecting confession, I suppose. That's what Margaret Jennings would expect. That Catholic!"

"Let me take care of things."

Sure enough, Alice found the Hillcrest residents still grumbling and pointing at Jessamine's door, waiting for the true explanation.

"All clear," Alice called. "I lit candles to be fancy. I set off the alarm." She hunched her shoulders to show guilt, then raised up smiling for absolution.

Slow-dawning acceptance, then laughter pecked its way along the hallway. Someone went into a sneezing fit and Alice heard the definite whack of a girdle waistband.

Back in the bedroom, Jessamine was standing, holding both hands out to clasp Alice's as she entered. "James Lawrence chose such a wife," she beamed. "Allie, I know that showing Hazen the photo album won't bring back the past. It won't make Hazen one of us. We're too old, after all. But for five years I tried simply sitting and I prefer the effort it takes to live. Every day there comes some small disappointment or exhaustion. Who *is* that man who will not be convinced out of his checked pants? Knit pants!"

From a drawer Jessamine produced the china slipper that had always posed on the cherrywood stand, its heel missing now.

"Jessamine!"

"Hazen had a dizzy spell."

Jessamine examined the slipper all around and indicated that Alice should touch the wound for herself. Doing so caused the finest powder to mist from the jagged edge. The eighteenth-century date remained plain as day on the instep.

"He's a Batten, whatever a Batten may be, Allie. Hazen's not a Morrow or a Stanley, but he is not a mistake. I've come to believe there's no such thing."

Alice continued to touch the jagged china bootie, the smooth deeply colored side, purple and gilt, and the bad edge. With one wild swipe, Hazen had put a hundred years behind him. Traitorous admiration hummed in Alice's head. "I'm sorry," she said.

"Effort counts," Jessamine continued, feeling along the shirred edge of her dressing table's flounce. "There's strength and protection in alliance. Living with someone opens up this world. I know more than you might guess." Jessamine's eyebrow was raising and she looked beyond Alice. "I watch all the shows. *Donahue*, and the others. Hazen sits right next to me and, why, I've come to learn about all the elements, all of them, even transvestite fathers and such. I have indeed. Effort counts on earth, Allie."

Jessamine's gauzy look had cleared as she murmured "trans-vestite." Then a little wry glory plumped the cheeks. This was how she must have looked riding out of town on her honeymoon: extravagantly modern. But the staring eyes now insisted Alice do something. She pressed a thumb hard to the jagged china edge and feared what it would be. An elevator might have descended too quickly the way her stomach swelled with a pang of anxious observation. She thought of the horrid State Fair ride that James and Carla had loved. The Round-Up effected a terrible circle of elevated, spinning illusion by tilting up, speeding, pressing bodies to its slim sides by the force of gravity alone. No belts, nothing but misaligned air held them. Alice used to stand beneath and watch as the bottom dropped out to heighten the drama. She went stiff as she waited to see her family tumble down from the sky. The ride inevitably, miraculously, would slow, right itself, stop. Carla and James would spring onto littered asphalt, wedded to gravity as surely now as the maniac operator of the machine. Vividly flushed, they looked on Alice with vague spirited pity.

"Bring Hazen to my house as often as you like," Alice declared. "We'll bake him a turkey."

"Thank you, Allie. I intend to. Now let's see to Hazen."

Jessamine stood and took one last look at herself head to toe in the dressing-table mirror. "I *do* need a permanent," she said, and mustering a lifetime of resiliency she stepped from that room. Alice grabbed a handful of pillow mints from the bureau and followed.

Carla was again fiddling with the TV.

Holding his juice glass high, Hazen turned a happy smile from the televised ice skaters wearing Indian headdresses.

"Jess, let me describe what happened here." He pointed to Alice and winked. "She lit a candle and it raised Cain."

Jessamine's shoulders relaxed. "My dear, my dear."

And Carla had the wits about her to hurry toward Jessamine, calling, "We came to tell you I'm pregnant, Grandma." The errant popcorn had derailed the night's duty. "Yes! I really am expecting."

There passed a moment in which Jessamine could only clasp her necklace and swivel her head slightly left and right, but never so far as to send Carla out of her field of vision. Shock broke in favor of delight. Majesty dictated a degree of confidentiality that screened Alice and Hazen neatly. Jessamine sank to the couch and removed her earrings. Carla perched on the edge. "My dear," Jessamine began, "let me tell you how the ladies, *we* ladies, used to proceed. You are a lady now . . ."

Hazen was rocking. "Yessir," he told the TV.

Alice tried to eavesdrop as she told him, "A person would expect that popper to malfunction anyway. That brand name had trouble with their hair dryers. My toaster won't adapt for lighter and darker. It's only three years old. That gripes my soul."

"It figures," Hazen said. "All these inventions in the age of profiteers. We've got trash heaps all over this country filled with plastic radios and whatnot. They build skyscrapers on top of these heaps. Dishonesty abounds."

"My dear, my dear," Jessamine was saying with a catch of severe restraint in her voice, familiar to Alice, coming to her as if from a dream: it was the singular tone reserved for the discussion of pregnancy, unfurled suddenly like a monogrammed hankie.

Alice reached for Hazen's lemon drops, her heart feeling stitched when she looked at him. The old man had shared a night of confusion and redemption. Nothing but family life would dare splice together the extremes of fire alarms and pregnancy news, and then settle a person back into his lounger without fanfare.

Jessamine called across the room, "We're even, Hazen. Four to one equals the same thing, my dear: great-grandchildren."

C H A P T E R   1 4

*C*arla sat in the back yard recalling sexuality like a dim vacation. The last time she and Brian had made love, the contra beat was still tapping on her bones, and the news of Grandma Morrow became a high dream she circled in above the Mississippi; a sweet swirly ride that made the earth look flat, but, really, she had Brian beneath her. She'd kissed him, thinking, "tug" and "barge" are the most ludicrous words for transport! Everything had tickled then, making her laugh out loud. She couldn't have known she was pregnant and hormonally doped.

Carla had drawn herself to the fringey shade made by two oaks crosshatching high up, leaving only the very end of the lawn chair and her feet basking in sun. With Alice at work, Carla sensed that she was behaving exactly like her: sitting in the lawn chair waiting, yet dreading to wait, seeking peace and distraction in the trees.

The windy music peculiar to the back yard started up its roar. Here, ancient oaks pillared the land; they were massive, all of them. The far cottonwood whose flaky silver-white bark Carla had dreamed of making into a canoe once—it looked enough like birch—had grown a sympathetic rough dark trunk; high branches remained the slender white arms of some other life. It was the only tree that showed signs of aging. How long did trees live? There were no new sprouts, nothing middle-sized or upcoming within sight. She closed her eyes. Someone should take charge of reforestation. If pin oak disease were to sweep the neighborhood . . .

A pleasant bird relaxed her with its soft song of "Ee-nee, ee-nee, ee-nee." Jess, jessed, jessing, she harmonized silently. She had looked up the words. So Hazen liked to joke that he had been captured by a falconer-Jessamine; he'd been "jessed." His ho-ho response to the pregnancy news, as she and Alice left Hillcrest the previous night, flowed cool and humorous to her mind now. His rusty laugh tempered the worship in Jessamine's eyes that had, nevertheless, reflected a specific green-eyed shock.

"So *here* you are. I've been knocking on the door."

Carla jerked forward, saw Mary all speckled with light, and dropped her head back against the plastic weaving. "Hi, Mary." Even standing still, even with Carla's eyes closed against her, a weird energy glinted off Mary. Carla's limbs tightened. Did Mary have to sneak up on her like this?

"Some vacation. It's bad enough you pick Des Moines, then you sit here in the shade. I'd at least go down to Gray's Lake or out to the gravel pits. Call up your old school friends, why don't you?"

The gravel pits were for teenage daredevils and the lake was a man-made thing, delusional blue and mucky. Carla felt pontifically like Alice, moved to say, "I'm thirty-four."

Bronzed Mary shook her head before inconsequentials. If this were high school, she might go at Carla with eye colors and blush. The Marys at her school, Carla remembered, carried notebooks to shield their sweatered fronts. In packs they slinked down the halls with their heads lowered, shooting looks out through the bangs, secret knowledge and scorn preserved by spiked mascara. There had been no reason to speak to anyone from high school for a good twelve years. Carla rearranged her legs on the lawn chair, smooth-shaven legs, Mary might please note.

"Kit's being a bastard."

In the adolescent way, Mary slumped all her weight onto one hip. "Tomorrow's the craft fair, my very first shot with the mosaics. I've never been to one of these deals. It's okay I sit at the kitchen table making fifty fucker candy dishes, it turns out. 'Great,' he says. 'Cool.' But will he help now? He'll loan me the truck, that's all. The rest is up to me. It's 'wus,' he says." Mary stared hard. Carla nodded as she was expected to do and scrambled for high-school slang. Wus: weak, womanly, a shorthand for pussy-whipped.

"Something like this, you don't do it alone." And in case of a surprise denial, Mary whipped her head back and forth. "So, I thought of you. Want to help out? It's just a few hours and I'll give you a cut, no problem. The flyer says usually it's two people to a display. Can you believe with our anniversary coming up in a couple of weeks he pulls this?"

So, why not? Carla asked herself again as Mary screeched them to the bottom of Wakonda early the next morning. Carla was holding on to the dashboard of the truck, fixed in the grimly cheerful vacationer's attitude. Visiting, weren't you always expected to be helpful in some off-the-wall way? Alice, who would spend this Saturday like all Saturdays among trees and squirrels, had asked, "Do me a favor. Write down what you see."

Mary's truck demanded constant gear-shifting, and she played the radio with a vengeance. It was like a video game you had to stay nimble with or take the consequences of exploding the world: the knob went back and forth between talky, thumpy stations. The minute a song faded or Mary caught the downbeat of something she hated, she'd race the dial onward. In the truckbed, boxed mosaic dishes clattered against each other. Carla could not decide whether it was grotesque, hilarious or a coup—a grown woman being mad to sell these things.

Mary rounded a corner and shook back her hair, the better to envision fame and fortune. "Move over, jerk," she called to the traffic, in her hoarse broken voice.

Carla's own voice seemed to mush out from the sinuses with the most inane observations. "Yes, that one really was a jerk."

Mary had to fling looks out the rearview mirror on Carla's side every five seconds. Carla tried to guess when to duck forward or suddenly flatten herself to the seat. You wondered what kind of energy Mary would put to real emergencies.

"Anyone coming? I'm changing lanes." The truck swerved

and clattered left. She would have constructed the mosaic dishes with such fury. Fidgety, swearing, head-tossing earnestness was put to the bright chips; the kitchen became a tornado and the rest of the world paled.

The two-block area out in West Des Moines was a renovated strip known for antique and junk shops; general nostalgia had dictated a reconstruction of facades in gingerbread or rough-hewn board. Mary cruised the strip slowly, passing a vintage clothing store, its windows all plumes and velvet; a doll hospital; a comic-book exchange. Everywhere, people were uncrating their goods. "Right here in front of the ice-cream store, kid. Perfect. They're going to all come here for ice cream. Get out and guard while I park."

Carla guarded the spot and Mary brought her boxes of dishes two at a time balanced on her hip. Back and forth she went, swaggering with cigarette stuck in the corner of her mouth, her chin pushed up and her eyes closed down. Wearing jeans on a sweltering day did not make Mary sweat. She managed a distinctly determined air among the khaki shorts and the sundresses.

Other earlybirds were bunching around them, in the good spot, on the street's shady side. To their left, an elaborate stained-glass display went up, constructed on frames. Large snappy pastoral scenes—oversized mushrooms, brooks, and a setting sun—towered over their heads. On their other side fleets of tiny dolls made of walnut shells and gingham were being set out on a table by a woman wearing a matching gingham skirt.

Mary muttered, "I hate those dolls. Low price, that's our competition. But, hell, we're functional." A tremendous yawn required Mary to fling both arms out, pushing away the boredom of dolls.

She set up a card table and tore things from boxes. She produced a shiny navy plastic cloth to smooth over the table, a pre-dampened rag for touch-up. She stacked the mosaics: wall-decorator size, candy dish, ashtray, then propped one of each face out against the stack. "There."

Now out came a bundle of newspapers for wrapping purchases, and an industrial-looking tape dispenser. Pad and pen
would be used for figuring, and a baffling porcelain frog
looked somehow as if it belonged. From some good home-
maker instinct still agitating within her biker heart, Mary had
collected everything useful. She positioned two canvas folding
chairs with such earnest attention to their angle that Carla felt
her own heart stir. All these tools and plans Mary had spread
before Kit, then suffered his scorn. The strength of Mary's
fruit gum aroma, her flash of hair and arm, worked to empha-
size Carla's sluggish assistance. She straightened at whatever
Mary set down, but could not outguess her.

"Hand me that frog. I'll need its weight on the wrapping
papers in case of wind."

Finally Mary tented a placard onto the table and stood back
squinting. Felt-marker block letters read: HANDCRAFTED MO-
SAICS! GIFTS! DECORATOR PLATES! CANDY-FRUIT DISH! ASH-
TRAY! UNIQUE PATTERNS! Great gum-chewing accompanied
Mary's admiring of her work. She stuck a pen behind her ear.
"You suggest what they're looking at." Then, "Forgot something!" and Mary dashed away, leaving Carla to snoop in the
cooler she'd parked under the table: beer, cheese in a tube, a
pepperoni stick. But already Mary was back and twirling a
lavender-billed cap on one finger. She crushed it onto Carla's
head and rapped her knuckles. "You get fried easily. This will
help. Now I want you to walk around to the other side of the
table, pick up a dish and start talking. You'll be the fake
customer. Man, you look geeky, kid. Just right."

The thing about Mary's eyes was their refusal ever to soften
or skim from point to point. They leaped, froze, bore in. Just
as when she'd demanded spectacle from Carla's story of meeting Brian, here she would draw drama from the ordinary craft
fair. Carla slung her purse over her shoulder and, feeling
goofy and envious and in cahoots, stood opposite Mary. She
picked up a big decorator plate and felt the blessing of a toothy
smile upon her. She raised the dish higher.

"That's just great," Mary whispered. "Psst, got some."

Three women were approaching. Mary bent to the table and did some showy scribbling which held their attention, then straightened and put the pen behind her ear, but stayed deep in simulated concentration.

Carla held the dish in a rakish way that only anonymity and wearing a lavender cap could foster.

"That's the decorator plate," Mary told Carla while the women hovered behind. They strained to hear and see but would not cross some invisible line of commitment just yet, and step forward.

Louder, Mary explained, "Each plate is handcrafted. You could serve fruit on that one, for instance, or put it on display. Get a wire stand. Or you could hang it on the wall. You see, it's art, and you're not going to find a painting for five dollars *are you, ladies?*"

Smart Mary had hooked them forward. Specially invited, the ladies were inching and smiling and suddenly three hands shot out to touch the plates. One woman, in the good sale-shopper mode, jostled Carla needlessly.

"I've got the darkest living room," Mary said. "I hang one of these and my husband says it's like the sun."

"I can see how that would be," the jostler said, nodding. "Yes."

"Mosaics are an ancient art," said Mary.

Not sure what was expected of her now that Mary was on a barker roll, Carla continued to turn plates over, trace the patterns and murmur, "Hmmm, the colors are so cheery." On a sudden wave of giggles she called, "I'll get my husband. He's carrying the money." She turned from Mary's astonished gum-chewing and hurried behind the stained-glass display. She doubled over laughing, though a spurt of nausea played a part in making her briefly sink to the curb.

Carla went on down the block past pottery and a man sketching portraits, past a clothes rack of woven shawls, next to it a display of bongo-type drums and wooden cars, past a stand of real feather dusters and lacquered novelty brooms. A man behind a leather display called, "Belts, purses. Well, have a good day." At the last stall she examined sachets, smaller, less pungent and varied than Craftique's. Alice would be pleased. Looking back down the street, Carla could believe it was all ancient art, pure and simple, that in their minds the shoppers felt they were traipsing a museum. They were let out of malls for once. Sophisticates, they smiled at themselves. Carla rejoined the crowd, smiling too.

From a distance the mosaic dishes shone like little saucers of light, and Mary had drawn a crowd. "Seventy-two pieces were slowly selected and fit into the dish," Carla heard as she approached. "It takes more time than you'd think. You make the design and then it's got to dry." As people walked by Mary felt moved to evangelicize: "Something everyone can use. For once you can afford what you need." And, "Christmas now. Avoid the racket."

The stained-glass people, playing low-volume symphony music, turned fuming faces on her. For Mary, who didn't even notice the glumness next door, Carla returned some scathing looks. She thought it a deception that people who made such sun-bright glass could scowl so. And with all that sun in her heart, Carla allowed that Alice's years of squirreling and scavenging might well have been propagated for the sole purpose of the eventual vocational salvation of biker-Mary. Fait accompli. Alice had used an ashtray for twenty-five years to some noble purpose.

As the early lone lookers gave way to a surge of strollers, Mary heated up. She might have been panning for gold there behind her folding table, staking a claim with her legs planted wide. The thrill of earnest huskiness in her voice fumbled people into behaving righteously: it would be rude to ignore Mary. What a masterful stroke—their believing they were accountable to Mary long before the fact. (Hers was the voice, of course, that had stricken a man with love.)

"Gee whiz, yes," Mary was telling a woman. "I make these right at my kitchen table; dinner's on the stove and I'm gluing. At first my husband complained. He hollered when he stepped barefoot on a chip. Aren't men babies? But, hey, he sees what I've got. I might have a future with mail order too."

What fathomless dinners bubbled in those copper-bottomed pots that Mary kept shiny enough to hang on the walls? Carla took off the lavender cap and scratched her damp hairline. *Gee whiz?*

Yes, the woman was agreeing. Her husband would be like that, just like that. "What about serving candies on those dishes? I make drop candy."

"First off," Mary warned, "if something will melt, keep it from the sun." The woman took this news as if it were brand-new. Her neck craned toward confidence. Establishing trust, that's what Mary was up to, automatic, shrewd carny-smooth trust. "You'd want to wrap the candy in foil or something that looks good. These are mosaics, remember. That's rubber cement holding them. You don't want food mixing in. But for serving, just serving? They'll look great. Slip some foil under them, but don't cover up the whole design."

Well, she'd take five saucers, the woman decided. Mary had them wrapped and money in hand, pronto.

"Man!" she exclaimed behind the woman's broad back. "It really works." She handed Carla a beer. This was a celebratory time. So Carla sat on a folding chair and hoisted the beer can. Surely she held it as a Little Dipper patron would. She loved turning to the stained-glass people, sipping. But it was really too vile-tasting, this beer, and she gladly gave it up.

She was sweating buckets, woozy even without drinking the beer. What would it be like to punch yourself through the world at every turn, to know, for not knowing what else, that you were gloriously right, loved and rebuked by a biker, living the only way to live? These Marys, Carla figured, grew up not needing braces, tanning safely, and ready. Guerrilla-ready, tensed for opportunity. Mary still wasn't sweating. She was a natural with the crowd. Carla imagined a terrific clash if ever Mary were to meet Melanie Green.

"Go ahead and check out the fair," she told Mary. "I'll take a turn selling."

Now Dixieland music rattled along the street from a band playing in the square. Oom pah pah! The crowd moved as one pleased undulation, and balloons dotted the sky. Carla stood squarely behind the table as Mary had done, though she still felt woozy. The sky was clear, forgiving of ice-cream eaters and walnut dolls. She faced everything out there with a pushy imitative courage she hoped would become her habit. Oom pah pah!

When a potential buyer removed her sunglasses and said, "Well, what are they *for?*" without reading the signs, Carla barked throatily, "Original handcrafted mosaic dishes here. Unique and multipurpose."

Sometimes people walled her in and she couldn't instantly match the voices with the reaching hands, mostly dimpled and spotted. But deftly she served them. Good will and the music inhabited her heart.

In Mary's absence she sold a raft of dishes. The cigar box springing open, lively now with money as she went for change, required the porcelain frog's weight. The day was needling hot and windless, the wrapping paper docile.

Finally Mary came thrashing through the crowd.

"It's going great. I've sold a bunch," Carla said, wishing Mary could have seen her selling a bunch.

"Good work." But Mary could as easily be referring to the mosaics as to the man she was hauling behind her. She had him by the belt, a wide leather belt.

"Speaking of old school friends, kid, look. I find this guy down the street tooling leather. Tommy." Now Mary's voice had more taffy in it than sawdust. She examined the man like a dish.

He was the man who had called to Carla. "Hello again," he said. His hair and clothes were that of a healthy faded hippie, which was to say he probably hadn't been one at all, not at the right time. He did not look so different from Mary's Kit, with his longish hair and flared jeans and boots.

So, let her take over. Carla gave in to drowsiness and sat

down. Let Mary hawk the day into passion or auction off her
mother. Carla cradled her head on one arm at the table's edge.
Mary's mother, she guessed, would wear a beehive hairdo but
otherwise behave with stunning practicality. Carla's heart settled low. And the voices were fading. Once in a while they
came back to her, as whistles. When her head jerked up she
knew she had been dozing. Her throat felt shrunken. Now
Mary's arm was around the man, her beer bottle up against
his back. A great spine-bending kiss commenced, this
Tommy with his hand in Mary's rear pocket, Mary bent low.
Carla fluttered her eyes and pretended to sleep.

"Who's your friend?" he asked at the end of the kiss.

"Her? This older lady got me started on mosaics and that's
her daughter. She talks a lot about having been in college
once. Hey, drink up."

Carla's heart pounded through a long goodbye kiss before
she let it be known that she—sidekick insipid nobody—was
fully awake. By then Tommy had left.

"How much did you make?" Carla asked peevishly.

Mary licked her thumb, the better for counting bills. She
whispered as she counted. "A bundle. As long as Alice can
deal me the mosaics, I'm in business. Bastard Kit," she told
a plate. She grabbed and threatened to throw it Frisbee
style. Her big teeth chewed a remnant of kiss; then she went
for the cooler and began drinking her beer like a virtual King
Kong.

"Are you thinking of leaving him?" Carla asked.

"What?" Mary lowered the bottle. "I'm in business, that's
what I'm thinking about. Tommy says he does okay working
these fairs. I've got to thank Alice. Suddenly there's a whole
new gig, like the world's bigger, you know? Thanks for helping out."

The lowering sun shattered color through the stained-glass
display, all over everything. Carla's sandaled feet were striped
red. Mary finished her beer. "Let's catch these last stragglers,
what do you say?" Mary shifted her weight back and forth a
moment, then cupped her mouth. "Half-hour special here.

Get a *set* of mosaic dishes, that's three of them, for the price of one. What are you waiting for? You'll never find these again, not in a store. Don't come looking for me in December. One-of-a-kind handcrafts here, available today only. Hurry."

C H A P T E R   1 5

*L*ed Zeppelin was *meant* to shatter the peace, Carla reminded herself, standing barefoot in the cool night grass across the street from her mother's. The music broke free of Mary's house to shimmy on up against a flat cookie moon that was blotting out the stars. On the last day of July a twenty-year cyclical phenomenon had popped a full moon into the sky a second time in a month. Mary had urged her to come to this "blue-moon" party.

Carla walked into the front room and was struck shy. She had no idea what to do at her first loud party in years.

"I'm over here!" Mary waved and pretended to struggle mightily to get off Kit's lap. Kit raised a beer can and grinned at Carla. The idea of a three-way conversation among them would not have occurred to Mary.

"Don't sit on the floor, kid. Wait." Mary dragged a kitchen chair into the room, catching its rubber-tipped legs on the carpeting. She was smoking pot. Pink combs plucked up her hair, enhancing her look of alert disbelief.

The only light besides the kitchen glare that blacked out anyone standing against the archway came from a lava lamp shooting patterns up a plastic casing. The lamp was so old it seemed novel. And you would suppose that Kit and his friends had been playing Led Zeppelin all these years, too. But contra songs were ancient, Carla admitted, often a hundred years old—older!—as unchanging and predictable

as the view of pine trees at home. She closed her eyes, wanting to forget pine trees, contra, everything, for once.

She took the pot passed her way and examined the lava
lamp. But these were not the old days and she could find
nothing marvelous in its colorful repetitious designs. She inhaled. Just this one more time. . . . Pot tasted delicious and
had a way of hollowing out tension, feathering her limbs
grandly in a good party way, and inwardly she thanked Mary.
She had felt flattered and piqued when Mary invited her,
finding that Mary knew about blue moons, wondering
whether reverence for the phenomenon or groundless ridicule
gave her party its name. Whatever, she had given Carla, who
felt herself bursting with hesitancy and restless wonder, a
reason to walk across the street and do something, join a
party. It didn't matter whose or what.

"Kid, remember Tommy? He's here and he doesn't have
an old lady." Mary yelled at the kitchen, "Tommy, hurry
up."

The man framed against kitchen light signaled and
launched himself forward with a push from the spine. How
he had heard Mary—now she'd managed to disappear—was
a mystery, but he came on jauntily, smiling, and planted his
feet so close Carla had to look straight up from her place on
the chair; she would have had to push way back on two chair
legs in order to get standing room. Even in the dark she could
appreciate the tooling on his belt, eye level. Tommy, way up
above her, had a grade-schooler's look: he wore a short-sleeved
plaid shirt, and his smile spilled unknowing eagerness. His
hair had been brushed and he wore better jeans than before.
Maybe he, like the woman who had matched herself to the
dolls she was selling, had been decked out in a sort of craft-
fair uniform. (Leather toolers did very well looking patched
and rustic?) Probably the small fairs took their cues from the
big Renaissance fairs, which, after all, depended on period
costumes; patrons happily bought turkey drumsticks and
Scotch eggs as long as "friars" and "lords" were selling them.
Carla puffed on the marijuana, remembering how Alice had

gotten her to attend one such production across the river in Wisconsin for Craftique-spy purposes.

Tommy dropped to his haunches and took the joint. "You're friends with these guys?"

"I just know Mary," she said.

"She called me up," he said, shrugging. His dimples made Carla remember the way he had kissed Mary, with such conspicuous verve. She couldn't have been jealous except in a general moviegoer sort of way, but she glanced away from the man, her prim version of rebuff.

"Some tough characters here, or what?" he said.

She liked the way Tommy rolled his eyes, spoofing the bikers. Maybe he—at last, someone!—could solve the mystery of why some men's jeans sling low in back (Kit's friends) even though the body looks too stocky to be buttless, perfectly capable of supporting jeans.

"Who knows?" Carla said, laughing. Her head went down to her knees, hair taking flight, and she raised one bare foot in a sort of pony stomp. Flirting at parties was not a lost art. The sale shorts Alice had picked up, khaki green and so loose-legged as to be skirtlike, felt so light, like nothing she had ever worn. ("An update," Alice had said crisply. "Three ninety-nine for no reason at all.") She wore her favorite white blouse. It was as old as the music, embroidered at the yoke.

The men exclaimed over album covers and joked in a low mooing chorus. They were as calm as if plopped before TV eating potato chips and fudge. Some talk of a bike trip went around the room. But the pot and their suggestions of outlaw behavior seemed more aroma than substance. Being frozen in the past with their music and lava lamps denied them full mystery. They nodded and smiled at Carla, but none of them really talked to her. A supreme little party jumped its way through her veins. One time, this one time, she would "party." She smoked and winked at Tommy quite conspiratorially, she thought. Men were tapping their boots and flashing studded wristbands, making a great pantomime of being tough characters.

"Play 'Ten Years After,' " she called toward the stereo, delighted with her nerve. Voices rose in approval. A pony-tailed man turned to the records.

She and Tommy stood against a wall of rough cream-colored stucco which, along with the rounded archways in this house, had caused Carla as a girl to expect that something fun should happen, but the room of cheap whimsical plaster-ing had been subjected to Mr. Wallace's careful reconstruc-tions of the day's insurance sales; and now it was hot and becoming heavily veiled with pot smoke.

Mary slouched across the room waggling her finger until she connected it with Tommy's plaid shirt. He grinned with-out showing signs of guilt or longing. Good. Their fair-kissing was history.

"Give me Carla a minute," Mary said, pulling at her arm. Carla trailed after her, noticing that Mary's back pockets sliced her rear into triangular frowns—the hipbones were made to look sharp and unflattering. Why did everyone here have a problem with jeans?!

They both cried out against the kitchen lights, then they passed on through to Mary's bedroom, lit by a small lamp whose base was a hula-skirted woman. The room had changed so drastically since the Wallace girls' bunk-bed days (their parents being kind enough to give them this larger room), there was no way to gauge it. In the dark Carla's senses heightened to the ambiance that made this an adult room: the thickness of fragrance, a bed centered in the room. The trans-formation and strangeness seized upon her rocky emotions; she went muzzy, and tears sprang up behind her eyes. But it had been a silly room, hadn't it? The Wallace girls collected Dolls of All Nations, and everywhere you'd looked these boxed dolls, in boleros and capes and gilt, stared at you through cellophane. Now time was all jumbled and tricky; Carla felt a hundred black eyes on her.

Mary kept fooling with plugs. After a moment of total dark-ness, great slashes of colors fell into the room: green, yellow, then red and blue.

"It's a color wheel like my mother had once," Carla cried. It had to be the same ugly bizarre thing: a flat round plastic surface sectioned off into different colors, powered and lit up from behind. It had been a sample companion to an aluminum Christmas tree; a sweep of color was meant to replace ornaments, but did not cause a sensation.

"Mine's from a garage sale. Wouldn't you know Alice and me would have this in common."

Carla fell back on a marshmallow bedspread and choked on hilarity, grateful as when she was first led over here, away from her father's pill bottles, for Mary's uncanny control of the mood. How much they all had in common! She laughed at the ceiling too, where a distorted peel-on mirror caught wobbly rays off the color wheel. Alice had set up her color wheel as if to sight criminals in pine boughs, and watched it bathe their short-needled tree, crying out, "Idiocy from Hong Kong!"

"Blue moon, I saw you standing alone," Carla miked with her fist and threw a leg high. It fell back and bounced. So this was the party. An old, old party with girlfriends talking in a bedroom, singing silly, the boys shut out.

Mary plopped on the bed and took the pot for herself. "If things are slow with Tommy, don't worry. I remember in high school two chicks fought over him in the back of social studies. Instead of bragging he got embarrassed."

When Mary pulled her to sitting, Carla had to grab her head to stop the mad surf in it. "God" Mary said, smoking, "he's still just as cute."

"Cute!" What freedom, to call a man cute. Yes, they were back in high school. With Mary, she was always back in high school, being taunted to do more, be louder, faster, gutty. "Kit and all of them are cute," Carla said.

Mary frowned. "Well, but there's a lot more to them. I'm Kit's chick and, believe me, I see some heavy things. I stick by Kit and don't have trouble." The pink combs, however, knew only cuteness, and Carla believed they were telling the true story. Cute! You could turn somersaults on Mary's wide lush bed. Giggling, she pushed off trying and rolled onto her side.

"Hey." Mary poked her. "Are you one of these people who thinks the Angels are the big deal?"

"Well, sure, I guess I do," Carla admitted, thinking of the Hell's Angels for maybe the first time in her life, and smoking again. On Mary's bed, Carla wondered intensely about Kit. She wondered where in the world you bought a peel-on mirror for your ceiling.

"Kit's club is called El Forestero. Have you heard of them?"

"No."

"Figures," Mary snapped. "Of course, you don't live here—" Music banged like a fist against the wall, making them both leap. "Listen," Mary said, yanking at her again, "let's you and me dance. Come on. I never get to. I hate it that Kit won't dance."

Being an exhibitionist strangely exhilarated her. Carla didn't care who all watched as she did things she knew they couldn't. She was aware of Tommy leaning against the wall watching while he lifted the wine jug, and she knew she looked better than Mary, who mostly did hip swivels and shouldn't let her jaw drop so, and one comb had fallen sideways to look like the extension of her ear. The dance had never left Carla, and incredibly smart turns and jumps occurred to her. She was anonymous and free.

"Follow me!" Mary grabbed her and like an older sister, teaching, took the man's part in jitterbugging. Her mouth was wide open as she spun Carla in against her, really mashing their breasts, then she pushed away. Carla's arm jerked, but she caught the rhythm, held on and kicked high. They did over-the-head twirls, three in a row that left them staggering and laughing. Carla broke then and did a full-circle turn on one heel.

The men kept shuffling around, doing whatever they were doing: mostly punching at each other's arms, it seemed. The music was so loud Carla felt plugged in; it seized and spun her. They were dancing to Led Zeppelin ("Gonna give you every inch of my love, oh! oh!"). And her hair was zinging across her face the way she'd danced a long time ago. Skinny-dipping after a contra dance was not this kind of carefree.

Carla danced by Tommy and waved him to her, a slight whorish gesture to her way of thinking, yet so slight, she knew, that she laughed high and loud, and gestured again. "No, I can't," he yelled. Everyone else had shuffled to one side of the room.

Mary stopped and gripped her arm. "Dammit, Queenie's here." Her harsh voice flattened in Carla's hair. "I'm going back to Kit."

Cheap wine in a tremendously heavy jug was passed from Tommy. Carla only wetted her lips, then handed it back. A few more steps of lone dancing quivered from her; then she looked across the room. The woman must have come in while she and Mary talked in the bedroom: a thin young woman swishing a white pleated skirt, beyond the men, shadowed in a corner; she moved her hips so slightly Carla thought of the hula lamp. And the men moved toward her, their jeans slung low, in a rhythm that was deliberately anti-dance. The woman's hair was finger-curled like an old actress's. The rhythm of a new faster song did not disturb her cadence.

Her clothes came off in one pull; then she kept up the motion, wearing a red bra and garter belt, nylons and straw high heels. Men began unbuckling and stumbling, bumping and cheering as they hurried out of their boots. Then they were naked around her.

Carla held her cheeks, which had begun to sting. Kit was bouncing Mary on his lap, watching, and Mary's eyes were closed.

"Tommy." Carla had forgotten Tommy. Now he'd come back from the kitchen.

"Jesus," he said, maneuvering around Carla so that they stood at an angle to the group. He could watch everything, but Carla would have to twist and gawk. Some chivalric urge had caused Tommy to steer her so, shield her. What a marvelous and silly idea, protection at a party. She swayed to the rhythm and laughed her flirtatious laugh, so long rested as to come out stuttery. Sweat ran hot and cold byways all over her body.

Tommy leaned close. "I can't get into that." He spoke without panic or apology, and took another swig of wine.

Carla's limbs stiffened. Tommy had killed the moment of make-believe by naming the distinction: them and us. Dance was no longer possible. Carla was all bones. She tugged at her hair.

"She's got to be zonked," Tommy continued.

Even with their clothes on, the guys had looked like apes, of course, the way they tended to lurch left and right before stepping forward. Their barreled upright bodies were useless, being more at home hunching over bikes, of course, and their hands wanted to curl over something, too. Carla laughed and something broke in her. She covered her mouth and laughed nearly to sobs. She might have been shrieking with laughter—the music was thumping her chest along with the laughter like some violent medicine pounding free the phlegm. It was all mixed up—breathing and heartbeats—when Tommy leaned down and kissed her. She felt the good spirit of the kiss and even so it felt like challenge. Any first kiss should, she guessed. In fact, she thought, bristling at an intrusion of Brian's face, maybe all kisses should be, forever. She determinedly kissed back, settling something between them. They broke away quickly. Kit and Mary were entwined; it was the simplest way to mark yourself off from the crowd. But after a first kiss you have to speak. You have to go on as if, really, you haven't even kissed, in order to decide whether it was a fluke or if you should stay with it. She began loudly asking Tommy, hadn't he ever learned to dance? Didn't he ever? She'd show him how to dance right now in the kitchen. He responded by kissing her for a good while. She guessed she smelled patchouli.

When the lights went on Tommy swore and pressed her close. "You don't want to see this," he said.

She turned and blinked against a back view of the woman

no longer dancing. Her pale butterfly rear moved above a man sprawled in an armchair, his head thrown back. *Limbo rock* stuck ludicrously in Carla's mind: the group mischief of a slumber party, that was the extent of what her own consciousness knew of such things and could bear knowing in this house. The biker's legs had never seen the sun. His knees jutted, immense luminous bone. He drank from a beer bottle. Led Zeppelin ended. Between records the room became hushed except for the wet kittenish noise of sex. A roomful of bikers went speechless up against that tiny signal and all eyes fastened on the couple. You couldn't stop looking. Tommy was taut and unbreathing at her side. She wondered suddenly where all the other women were. What kind of a party was this meant to be? Oceanic nausea, heat and pot and the sweat of hesitation, took hold of her. Sweat by the bucketload, like humidity, thickened the air.

"Camera's ready!" someone yelled. The ponytailed man, nude, held a movie camera on his shoulders and blazed light on the two. Carla darted a look at Mary; she was lost in the taming of her breasts against Kit.

The red-gartered Queenie turned everyone else to statues as she performed. From the back, her knees pointed out unattractively; crease and folds formed where torso met thigh. *Every boy around the world going to get a limbo girl.*

"Action!" the cameraman called.

The woman slipped easy as a fish off the man's lap and down to the floor. Someone moved to straddle her chest. She closed her eyes and opened her mouth. The camera made a moonlit spectacle of it and Carla couldn't not watch, going gaggy, pressing her lips together. The woman's face shone white and lazy and pebbly pink from the blusher beading on her cheeks. The camera went the length of her body and then the flat light jumped. Another man had dropped to the floor and was turning her little doll leg out.

Tommy spun Carla by her shoulder; she was moving, achy at the knees, holding her mouth tight, dizzy and stung with sweat; now they were going through the archway into the bright kitchen, past the copper pots hanging like captured moons. She was going on through the kitchen with Tommy's arm around her, hearing his muttering, "No way, man." And then she was being cradled in a dark room. She took big gulping breaths and was rocked side to side, her face hidden against the man. They had just stood there and watched. She hid herself in shame against a fine plaid shirt. The man's hand clutching her back felt like forgiveness and more. She curved against him. It made no sense to feel so hungered and repulsed, aroused; yet she was falling into a rhythm and plan as if it were the inevitable thing to do. It was some kind of mutually decided-upon absolution, a man's hands in her blouse.

She was the first to lie down. Not until Tommy sat on the bed taking off his plaid shirt did Carla comprehend the color wheel's madness, furiously slicking Tommy, as with warpaint, as he turned to her, naked. She raised up, tried the blouse, got an arm caught in the wilted sleeve, and gave up with a cry. She fell back on the bed and laughed and let Tommy take over. With an air of admitting to derangement, she relaxed to the point of bonelessness. Tommy was planting a thousand kisses on her, desperate to be a man like all men, in chivalry and lust. That's just fine, she told herself. The flying sensation from the last time with Brian seized her and she felt like something very small in nature, a chickadee that roosted by the house; and Brian stood there solemnly intent on counting her among the returned. She soared and alighted in a tree; from a bone-white birch bough she felt the whole earth as a shimmering throbbing mass that touches you crazily and crushingly in this life. She signaled to Brian and all the Mississippi River from this high place.

The man raised up a moment to look at her, his face catching a green streak. He held her head in his hands and kissed wetly. He muttered and dove back to his work. His smile had been genuine, though, that grade-school variety of happiness, close to moronic. She thought he was talking to her, and came up against his chest wonderingly, but the rock music was deafening; she lost hearing, and they tumbled back down. In the peel-on mirror above she saw an abstract blur of wavy color, something like the lava lamp in the other room. Her body was reshaped into long lines of color, simply dissolved. It made perfect sense to be invisible up there. Bodies don't levitate and they don't belong on ceiling mirrors, she insisted just as she felt herself flying apart. She knew a blazing heat back of her eyes. She was light as air, with a beautiful scorching sun shining through. But she couldn't see anything.

The man kept lugging at her, gripping, trying to keep their slickered weight steady and connected. The big hot white blankness was razzing her and the man who had triggered it could not even sense it. She remembered the time she had fainted from sunbathing. When she'd come to, everything was white and flat, marked by wobbly gray outlines. It was from this white, white dissolving center that now her baby hurtled forth; this crashing, jarring, thrumming surprise harmony that stopped the music at the wall. Her baby. And it was a jabbering indignation, soldierly in the way it meant to fight off the foolishness she couldn't. It took command of her, a fury proclaiming itself and disavowing all future denial, goof-ups and waffling. It was a wildness totally foreign and instantly true, blasting at her. "Baby," she said as if to the man. Yes, we're fine.

Just as madly, the fury left. She came to as if from a dream, lying drenched in sweat with a man propped on his elbow at her side. The color wheel swept over him—a long lithe tadpole frame, broad chest tapering to thin legs, and she didn't know what she was seeing. Tommy, she remembered, reaching for her hair. It squeaked with sweat.

"I could get us some beers," the man said, once her eyes quit fluttering. Remanded to the world after sex you'd want beers, of course.

She sat up wrapped in a blank chill. "No, I don't think so. No, thanks." The music hadn't stopped, after all; it crashed and crashed against the wall, and the beams of color scattered as they swept along that wall. She remembered the events in the front room and shuddered. She drew her knees tight, with her chin clamped down. If the man touched her she'd scream.

"I better get going," she said, loathing to touch him, but

thinking it was the kind thing to do, the obligatory thing. She tried to pet his mossy chest, but feared its dark life.

"I'll take you out," he said, raising up slightly. "Want breakfast? How about steak and eggs?"

"Oh no. No, thanks. I'm visiting my mother."

"Your mother." He considered. "But we could eat steak and eggs."

Wounded hope is what she saw in the man's blurred eyes. Some woman had left him recently. Careless Mary had hustled him to this party. She'd hustled the two of them, and now had a story to tell someone: "How they met at my party."

"Wait." The man closed his hand around her ankle as she was getting off the bed. "The second time will be better. Come on. Wait with me."

"Oh no. No, really." She was getting into her clothes as fast as she could and trying not to look at the luggish, fishy shadow twisting itself around on the bed. "Excuse me, I'm just done in. But amazed, really—oh, words!"

"Like I'm some learning experiment."

Reproach and disgust thickened his voice. She'd better get out or he might do something. (Call out to the others?) She tried to make the parting kiss a decent one even as she held her breath.

The man sank back on the bed and propped his hands under his head. Sliced all colors, he said, "I liked you from the start, seeing you out at the fair. That's what gets me. Tonight I thought, See, it's special. Here we were again and things were falling into place, you know? It's my bad luck you're only visiting. What town do you live in, anyway?"

"None," Carla said.

She ran on great springy legs to the kitchen. Mary was standing against the refrigerator frankly owlish, starting some deep significant nods that included jutting the lower teeth. Carla fled barefoot outside across Wakonda, believing that the streetlight was talking to her of imminent electrical explosions. Everything electrical was a potential explosion. The

moon had risen out of sight. As she let herself in, voices
spilled from Calvin's TV.

In her dream Alice took responsibility for rescuing a
beached whale. She alone among a frantic crowd somehow
lifted the monster and lapped water onto it over and over and
over. She spread soaked checkered cloths on its moonbeamed
back.

She woke to the splashing sounds of Carla's bath. It went
on and on, an all-night bath. She raised up to read the clock,
then looked out the window, down to the river where not one
hobo fire blazed.

Alice smoked, looking out the kitchen window; five minutes
to go before leaving for work. The biker house looked the
same as always, innocuous white frame; oaks, the muscled
cottonwood, the black central motorcycle. She had heard
engine-shrieking at some point in her dream, and all that bathing of Carla's, for Pete's sake. The streetlamp was fading and
sputtering in front of that house, hissing a faint suspicion.
She could imagine flames leaping from the lamp; blue, white
and orange, obliterating Wakonda. Perhaps a grand sweep of
fire would circumscribe Londo's real-estate empire, relieve
Carla of her disapproval of this houseful of things and put
everyone off Wakonda equally terrified. Where *would* I want
to go if I were to make a change, leave here? Alice asked
herself and with peevish clarity knew she couldn't think of a
single other place to be, only a better way: wrap wild fabric
around the body, put on gold slippers, and let a parrot claim
the left shoulder; and even so, let no one comment, let no one
care.

"Mother?"

Alice turned to see a fright of a daughter, hair all clumped
and at the height of summer she'd wrapped herself in James's
camel robe. She was jerking the belt tighter and tighter like
the unfavored boxer about to be mashed.

"Is there extra coffee?"

"Of course not. You don't drink coffee. You don't drink coffee pregnant. Or beer at a party." Where had she found the robe?

Carla shook her hair down into a mop. When she came up she mockingly cried, "Pooh!"

Alice shot her a deadly look. With icy precision she understood that her pregnant daughter had been promiscuous. There was a point past which any mother could blot the extravagance of a daughter's experience. This was it. She'd wash her hands of it. No details, she prayed. She crimped her thoughts into the minor alarm register of a fed-up mother. She held her cigarette high. "For God's sake."

"Don't stare at me," Carla cried, her foot stamping, the bare toes exactly like James's. "Don't ask questions. Don't stare!"

"I have a bus to catch." Alice stubbed out the cigarette, giving the biker house a withering look, and avoided Carla's eyes while she pressed her in a papery hug. Was it safe to leave her here? A person could not take an adult child to the office. A person could not do a single thing with an adult child.

"Mother?"

A gleamy, bizarre smile took over Carla. If sex did that to a person, Alice would *never* . . . Not that she had *ever*, but she would *never* . . . She wished as she had never wished before to smack her daughter across the face, smack and smack her. "I'm going to work. I honestly don't care how you live," Alice lied, swinging her pocketbook to her shoulder, "but will you have the decency to save your shenanigans until the baby is born? Give me that baby. I mean it, give me that baby to raise."

"You're serious. You would!" Carla's laugh was brazen and her eyes took on an idiotic New Ageish luster. "Something happened last night."

"In the dead of night . . . over there? Well"—Carla took a breath—"the baby began sending me messages. It did! And," she added quickly, frowning over her blush, "I hurried home." She was wrapping hair onto a finger, drawing words into the batty worn-out air between them, and she had never looked so much like James. But Alice would smack her. All these years, she had needed to smack and smack.

"Honestly."

"Yes, Mother. Messages. Something moved up onto my heart, I think that's how to describe it, and then on up, like a cloud, not like a thought. A thought from inside out maybe, but much more than a thought. It wasn't words or pictures. More like sound and weight than anything else. And emotion. It was a waking dream." Carla shook her head. "Now I know my baby." She draped her weight on Alice. It was staggering, relaxed weight.

"Good grief, sit down. You're weak." Alice pushed Carla into a chair. She wasn't sure of anything at all except the intrusion of filth, but she had had enough experience to know choice, and she chose to believe. "If you think so, bravo. Yes, I believe you. I know that feeling."

"I'm going to the library." Carla spoke like a sleepwalker having lost the initial terror of propulsion. "I'll get every book on babies. Where's your library card?"

"This baby needs a million things. Go shopping."

Carla laughed shrilly. "Of course, Mother. I'll go shopping."

If her daughter had been given the sign, so be it, despite the twitching body that seemed, still, extraordinarily childlike to Alice. So be it. Let Carla sail over sharky waters and everything else with her new knowledge. Alice ducked into the bag and fished for the card. She was drained, happy, terrified. She threw her head back in case of tears. Carla remained glazed, sweaty, and she smelled faintly of jasmine. Thank goodness for all that bathing.

"Go lie down. Get some rest. Here's bus fare."

There was the slightest bit of coolness, a breeze enough to flutter tendrils of hair across Alice's forehead, as she strode downhill to the bus stop. The biker house seemed to touch her spine all the way down Wakonda. With a mother's instinct for defense she wished for the sputtering mercury lamp to fall across Kit and Mary's roof in the very next storm.

Carla heated water for cocoa mix. She curled on the couch in the fan's direct aim, sipping, and after the cocoa was gone she sat staring, imagining her body at work, doing great shiftings and reroutings for this baby. She was growing octopuslike; there was a reaching beyond control now, a grasping and beating up against the sky, though her head was surely in the sand. If only she could block out the party, the man, and glimpse the marvel within her, untarnished. Her moment of beauty was predicated on revulsion and this did nothing to break her of her Morrow training: there is impending doom; hesitate and be lost. She assumed that most women experienced communion with the unborn while sitting in a rocker at sundown. It was admittedly hard to picture Alice placid, being filled with revelation just so, but her look had said that she understood the feeling precisely. The moment was true, despite all. She was to believe this. But in the future, in years to come, whenever pregnancy talk bubbled up, whatever gladness might spring its wealth, there she'd be, gripped with intolerable memory as well. Her sharp inhalations or faint coloring would be mistaken for pleasure recalled. A dirty rim around bright talk, that's what she'd have.

She felt equally sick and wondrous. If you go across the street influenced by a rare moon, take drugs and dance among bikers, expect sympathy for the consequences from only the most strenuous quarters. A little clamp on her heart squeezed it as far from the brain's insistence as possible: tell someone, was the nagging thought. Confess. To whom? Dr. Hollingsworth, and be remembered as far more malevolent and ignorant than the teenagers? How about a stranger on a help line —ten years younger than she? Or Brian! She thought the whole mess might have been foretold the minute she'd walked from the outhouse bringing the news into the open. Brian's raising of wrench, her yearning to run. There was violence in sloppiness and retreat. She wished she could blame Brian.

The house exuded a quiet dignity. Even that brassy deer head seemed to sympathetically cock to one side. A dignity of spirit was shining off all that she had allowed herself to see only as cartoon stuff. There was a hum of serenity and cheer in the house. Even the vampire books were brightly covered, happy to be vampire books. Peacefulness and a loopy order deeply suggestive of Alice reigned here. Her mother's glad heart, peopled by flamingo-zombie humor, graced this house. Anyone but her own daughter could see this.

Carla burrowed deep into the fabric of her father's robe and half-slept and cried in whimpers, exhausting herself. She closed her eyes tighter, wanting darkness. She nuzzled at a clean musty smell, some long-forgotten familiarity, and she missed her father sickeningly in this house.

When she unwrapped herself much later, she dared to feel that something of her father's heart was grafted to hers. She felt his deepest secret, and knew the exact capacity of his heart: he had opened a spare chamber of it to take in his tragedy; he had found a quiet soft royal-velvet place that stored just such knowledge as that of imminent and terrible mishap. Then he smoothed at his fine cotton shirtfront, turned on TV or stood to announce, "I've made a pie." If you didn't do that, she saw now, the mess would bang and clatter out there in the world, swing around and hit you in the slightest breeze, on the sunniest day, and in midlaugh you'd get knifed through and through. If you laid the misery down on velvet, contained it in this locket-chamber, you would never spoil a day. Doomed adventurers, the two of them, father and daughter, they needed the deep welcome of this home.

It was well into the afternoon by the time Carla trusted her bones and roused herself. She tied her hair up with red ribbon and made her way downhill. Her bus fare lay heavily in her palm. She said she would no longer stand by and hurt herself. She would be present in her life. She would love Mary's passion and forget that Mary existed.

"Purple Santas!"

As Smith came sputtering into her office Alice promptly

yanked her drawer wide and jammed a pin into the voodoo doll. "What in the world?" She spoke pleasantly.

"I don't know how it happened, Alice. Those blind bats at printing." Smith had crumpled the disaster and now tried to smooth it over Alice's desk: four pages of Santa stock had been printed in rich, unmistakable purple. Purple Santa door knocker, purple Santa everything. A penitential Christmas atrocity must be halted.

Gloria walked in with her Coke, and it was awful to see how closely her eyelids matched the bad Santas. As mayor of the world, Alice would kiss every Santa, purple or red, and banish every idiot gesture of less than life-giving importance that had ever wasted her time.

"We're going to the printers'," she told Gloria, already yearning for the day to end. She expected to return home to find Carla examining booties and sleepers and little barbell rattles.

"I'll drive," Gloria said. It was a fact so obvious, both women laughed despite Smith's bent shoulders that spoke of better days handling insurance adjudication.

Gloria's car, like Gloria's desk, suffered all sorts of personalization: a snapshot of her children—the one thin, the other fat—was decoupaged onto the dash; all knobs were fuzzily covered. A person could be sure that Gloria's bathroom would look just so, her medicine-chest mirror stickered with sayings like "Starring Gloria!" and inside a person would find all the latest beautifiers. The car lurched. Alice squinted her eyes against a picture of her own medicine cabinet, James's pills lining the top shelf. She willed them away and watched them tumble from the shelf.

"Carla is pregnant!" she crowed.

"Carla? My God, Alice. Is she all right? She's, er, happy?"

"What do you think."

"Tell her congratulations for me, but between us, Alice, oh, God. Imagine doing it all over again. I'm glad I was young and dumb. Oh, you'll be a grandmother. Fantastic."

The print "shop" was an immense concrete structure forested among acres of trees and brush in a barely developed industrial park back of which, Alice noticed for the first time, grew a beanfield. Two small supply stores were barely visible amid the growth. The minute these buildings were not maintained, wild greenery would rupture foundations and resume domain.

"I'll never live in a desert climate," Alice said. "Who needs Arizona?"

Inside the plant Alice made her way through to the large room where overhead giant rolls of paper whizzed at crazy angles on nightmarish machines. The smell of ink itched the tip of her nose, and a deafening syncopation of machinery portended operations wilder than purple Santas.

"Why not turquoise Santas?" she sang, knowing no one could hear.

Down an aisle, beneath flat checkered fluorescent squares, she spotted Mel and another man just stepping from the camera room. Mel was carrying a sheet of stripped-up negatives. In the moment before he saw Alice, he smoothed this onto a light table, balanced himself like a rocking horse with one leg forward. His bib apron pooched.

Alice buttoned and then unbuttoned her jacket. If the clacky-heeled Gloria got wind of her discomfort, it would be horrid. Flirt, Carla had said, for God's sake. But the key to emotional well-being was an impassive, stylish exterior, to Alice's way of thinking. Especially on business time. Or in hospitals. She buttoned her jacket again. She cupped her hands and yelled, "Gloria, why don't you go speak to Ted Biddle about the paper and ink? You're the expert there. I'll deal with Mel on paging and inserts, whatever we have to figure out."

Gloria brightened. As it happened, Ted Biddle was handsome enough and spoke in the same office-flirtation code as she.

Now Alice approached Mel, forcing each footstep solid as the wedgie meant it to be. The whoosh and shuffle of the presses belied her hesitation, made for ostentatious accompaniment. On one machine a huge roll of paper crossed itself halfway through the course into old-fashioned nurse hats, for giants, then *voilà!* At the very end, nicely ordered sheets flew into stacks.

Her jacket could not be buttoned any tighter and a person should not tug so. But could anyone else on earth feel so exposed? Alice had cried the last time she'd seen this man, and when he'd called her later she'd coolly disengaged him. Three times. She had trained herself not to cry around James. She didn't know a thing about crying. She carried with her the habit of a million days of not ever saying what it was all about: at James's insistence they were not to have spoken of the disease. ("Don't let's tell Carla," he had hoped at first, which led them to speak of beautiful pies.) Alice's carefully fashioned disregard of the miraculous now lay in her bones helter-skelter.

Mel turned. "Alice!" And a big arm immediately brushed aside the other man. "The purple-Santa hit squad." Mel did not have to yell to be heard; she wondered if his booming voice was a by-product of his employment, a printer's protective coloration.

"Yes, you're in trouble," she said with a great drawing-out of the words that made her cheeks feel the way they did blowing up balloons. Certainly, this would be flirting.

Mel closed his office door behind them and Alice found herself in a cool room where machine sounds were reduced sharply to cricket chatter. She touched her ears; they had suffered the equivalent of elevator stomach. Mel's walls were decorated with little signs exclaiming about Mondays and Fridays, stupidities and brilliances.

"Okay, give me the verdict," he said. He took a pencil from behind his ear (extremely pink, Alice noted) and laid it on the table. Alice unfolded the sheets of purple Santas. Mel supported himself by gripping the desk, and leaned close. His watch, thank goodness, had numerals instead of the digital nonsense. His hand hovered above the pages; it stayed in midair, quivering, not at all like the geiger-counter hand she remembered seeing test his Meadow-in-a-Can buds. They both watched with horror as the uncertain hand tremored above his desk. He couldn't manage to speak either. Alice clasped and stilled that hand.

"Guess what? I'm going to be a grandmother."

Perhaps Mel was too big not to react physically. Large people had their peculiarities. He caught Alice in a hug. No one so big had ever hugged her. Her automatic chicken-wing reflex went into effect, a pulling back, but as Mel tightened his grip a truce allied her jumping-bean bones. In grabbing Mel's hand she had let go something ancient and hard. She did not resist the illicit hug on office time, in a building mad with flying paper. Resistance would be dishonest. And she could not even touch her bun if she wanted to, the way her arms were anchored.

His breath tickled along her temple, to the ear. He kissed her cheek, looked at her, kissed the other, met her eyes, kissed the ink-allergy itchiness on the end of her nose as if he knew its problem and solution. Then, her mouth.

And as if she were trying on the luxury of fox, Alice wrapped herself tight and took the full effect.

Mel pulled a chair forward and she sat. She trumpeted to clear away the tulip that had grown in her throat. And thoughts turned to Jessamine, whose presence was felt: she as much as perched on Mel's desk ready to sing a torch song and dangled a slingback pump. Romance is courageous and humbling, if you dare to think about it, Jessamine advised; and you don't, Allie. Had marrying Hazen Batten made her so laconic?

"So," Mel said, "we're supposed to paint the town red, is that it? We'll start by doctoring a catalog."

Red. It was a luscious word. Scarlet, crimson. Challenging.

Gloria drove fast heading home. They sped along the park's edge, where flower gardens were groomed into square mounds, making pink and white cakes of the earth. They pointed and shuddered at teenagers and fanatics on bikes and joggers in the thick day's heat whose skin was spangled with sweat.

"They're asking for strokes," Gloria said. But to Alice it was miraculous to note that each and every one of these people had a grandmother. Might, should, have a grandmother.

"Why not spin through the park?" Gloria suggested. She turned at the entrance, where wide grassy fields swept away from the gravel road. "I'll still get home in time to catch a soap."

Up over the old wooden bridge they flew, Alice rubbing her arms absently, both of them laughing like girls when the boards snapped up. Big shaggy-dog willows nodded their approval. Delinquency was divine, Gloria a good sport. In a warm moment, someday, she might be convinced to change her lip color, tone it down at the eyes, and swear off the loser men. But not today, Alice knew. Today was a purple magnificence and Gloria fit right in.

At the bottom of Wakonda Gloria gunned the car— changed gears or something; the car rolled back, then shot up the hill. Cars, Alice understood, were built with personalities. Mel's was meant to approximate riding on a cloud, fine; she supposed Gloria's was meant to attract attention much as a younger sibling does, by having fits.

Gloria held her foot on the brake while Alice climbed out awkwardly. "Tell Carla I'm thrilled, Alice. I'll see what I've still got around the house."

Letters were stuffed in the mailbox. Carla was still out shopping. Right now she might be charging a bassinet at Younkers'. She deserved a special dinner. Quiche, if there were any frozen piecrusts around, would be fine. She would surprise Carla with quiche. It wasn't so bad if you fed the birds during the baking time.

She got the mail and came around to the porch looking at it, empty-handed otherwise, for once. She stepped inside, and something slammed her down. Like a ninny she was bowing to her shoes. Navy blue. Then blackness.

Carla got off the bus at Wakonda. The house, for all its oak canopy, still tricked her heart. Hadn't it always rung with disappointment, loss, fear, when she stood like this, coming home? Year after year she had looked up the hill wondering, not knowing what she might find.

She ran, forgetting the books frozen against her chest and the trip to Babyland downtown, forgetting the feel of the man that three hours of soaking hadn't quite removed. She sprinted up the hill and rushed her own house, charging around the corner to find the back door swinging on its hinges and a trail of small objects littering the entry. A stained-glass lamp lay on its side on the baked summer earth. Broken, jagged, it bit the ground meanly. She screamed at the sight of the shovel, Alice's ancient heavy garden shovel, bloody and wet, launched off the porch like some terrible, intractable tongue.

"I'm here!" Alice was yelling from somewhere inside. "Shh, they're on the phone now. Hello, police."

Her mother's head was gashed and cakey with blood, and she was waving the phone cord. She looked at Carla and spoke levelly. "We'll get the police, honey. Police, police," she cried, not exactly into the receiver.

Carla grabbed it. A dial tone. Her mother smelled like rust and she was blinking like a child, slow and amazed, staring at Carla. Her eyes tracked inward, though, questioning, then relinquishing, as if she had previewed the future. If she dies I'm an orphan, Carla read there, stricken. And I'm already her keeper. She swallowed, held her breath and dared not gag as she used her hair ribbon to wipe at Alice's face.

"Mother, sit still now. Please sit down." She pushed Alice to sitting and wedged her with a leg straddle until Alice assented, still staring.

"We need a hospital escort," Carla snapped at the operator. "We need police, detectives, the ambulance."

"Don't you get it?" Alice asked from dreamland. "I'm fine. It's the house. What have they done to my house?"

"Sit, Mother. Here. You've been hurt. Please sit still."

Gaggy, Carla ran to the bathroom. Under loud running water she dry-heaved. She moistened a cloth for Alice and wrung it out, looking at herself in the mirror, eyes red and sparkly. She yanked open the medicine cabinet. With its spewing of dishevelment came comprehension, and a huge hyena sob launched itself out of her nose, stinging, causing tears. She grabbed a bath towel and sobbed into it.

"What, what?" Alice was shouting from the other room. "I can see okay. I can feel all fingers. Today is Wednesday."

Carla leaned forward and swept the dust off the blank top shelf. The thieves had scooped up every single pill box and bottle that told James L. Morrow how to take his medicine.

She ran from there waving a dripping cloth. Alice lay back, eyes closed. This blood and swelling were externals, signs of healing, of course. Surely in the midst of the worst mess Carla had ever seen, the universe struck harmony.

"Call Mel," Alice said from a shallow gurgly throat.

C H A P T E R   1 6

*A*lice had lapsed into total unconsciousness and Carla's nerves went alternately to fists and jelly on entering the hospital. Mel was mutely Neanderthal, traveling abreast of the ambulance attendants who wheeled Alice down the hall wearing their sneak-soled shoes, a surplus of guile, Carla determined, where life and death were the issue. They would blunt all signs of expectation, of reason and dailiness here however they could. Silence, please! Reducing panic was the surface job of hospitals, and just as if you were in a casino, here you found no windows or clocks, as little reality as possible by which to gauge the gruesomeness at hand. The idea was to wear you down past sleep, to force a vacant acceptance so that whether your patient lived or died you eventually stumbled out in a delirium of gratitude for being allowed to stumble out. When she had left the VA for the last time, her father dead, Carla's clattering shoes had madly filled the world.

Alice lay flat on the cart, that one loose curl bouncing and catching on her forehead. "The halls aren't *too* ugly of a brown," Carla said. Her mother would want to know. "Just think, I'm pregnant," she said, but her voice quavered.

"Alice will be a grandmother!" Mel's voice was like a thunderclap. Carla ignored him. Who was he anyway? An abrupt faithful, whether saint or apostate, Carla could not gather the wits to decide.

"She'll be a good one," Mel vowed, his voice somewhat lowered.

Like so many stacks of dirty dishes, Alice's cart was pushed through swinging metal doors, off to the kitchen. The last attendant bowed, indicating no passage. Carla and Mel were left in the hall. The sweetish smell of manufactured air suggested rather than subdued the enormity of trauma. Carla and Mel sat on a bench rather than follow the arrow to a visitors' lounge.

Carla's cheeks were dancing. She pressed her hands to her face. Mel's arm supported her back. Let loose, she feared she might slowly tilt to the ground like those weighted toy clowns, go all the way to the floor, but not necessarily come upright again.

"There. She's going to be okay," Mel said.

Carla shook her sward of hair and began braiding it to firecrackers. But she gave up quickly; her arms dropped to her sides.

"One way or another, Carla, your mother's going to be okay." Mel sandwiched her limp hand between his two. She pulled away and undid a braid.

"She's special. She's beautiful," he said.

And Mel sounded nobly deranged pretending to know what she did not: Alice's ultimate strength. A proffered hairy-backed hand was not evidence of superior insight.

"I love her," he said. "I'm saying it out loud. I love her."

Carla bolted upright, flinging an arm toward the greedy doors. "She's lying on that cart and doesn't know you love her? You haven't said so?"

"Maybe she just knows."

"Ha!" But Carla did not choose to stare down this man's mournfulness, so she sat again. And no matter how much time passed and how their loves and fears swelled, there was not a single sensical word to pass. Do you love her enough? was not a question she had ever demanded of her father. How much do you love her? a child wanted to know. But like adoptive-ready parents laying open their hearts and pocketbooks and weekly menus, a strange man, her mother's suitor, had better confess and do something, do something.

"You'd better save her," she said.

In moments or ages, an intern with his face mask swinging at his throat pushed through the doors. "It's looking good," he said. "A concussion. A nasty abrasion. Go on and relax. Check back in an hour."

"I'm going to look at babies," Carla decided.

She went to the elevator with the sensation of walking on stilts; her feet were down there, not exactly dominant in the willfull act of walking. Mel followed. If he wanted to trundle himself along, fine, she didn't care.

The elevator raised them through space on a hum and opened onto a rose-red carpet. Carla's legs boinged back to meet her body, and freeze her. The air was an extravagance of peppermint. Mel waved as if he knew these people, and his strong voice vacuumed a nurse to them instantly. "We have an expectant mother here. She'd like a quick look around."

The nurse pressed on Carla's back, releasing her stiffened legs. "Of course, dear."

This was a funhouse maze ordained and orchestrated in someone else's dream. After years of simply living the right way, in response to the seasons and life's events—writing letters, planting food—it seemed that every possible shock she had banked high out of sight, every new discomfort outfoxed, was plowing right into her face; some once-a-century current was breaking the dam. Carla followed the nurse's bowling-pin legs sheathed in dream-white; a swish-swish undertone of duty, they led her deep into a corridor hooked by shadow and memory, and then departed. This was how you came to visit the dying. Carla's bones shrank away from what they had known. The hall was a soundless empty tunnel to which wraithlike men might flock, men in flowing seersucker, speaking to heaven, some in wheelchairs they could not budge. But not here, she insisted. I am looking for babies.

She stopped at the first open door. Here lay a great whale of belly, the woman's face gone thoughtless with waiting to begin. The lights were out, the shade was drawn. Something akin to sympathy pains gently stroked Carla's limbs, while a dream stirred her insides. With her eye on Carla, the woman flung an arm out—beckoning?—no, she raised it slowly and raked her hair. But in Carla's mind the arm remained extended; the woman's mind opened itself to her as oblong, rainbow-colored, a perfectly munchable cornucopia, and she felt the tumbling transference, an acceptance and embracing as her first original act in life. She strode forward. Pregnancy rose up in her mind as oceanic surf: a moppish, cleansing sea-green surface cresting, reversing the silvery tides so long steeled toward dying. She walked unsteadily on this new surface; it was as if, really, dying didn't count.

The nursery was a glassed-in oasis emitting faint squirming and mewing sounds; a heat-lightning gauzy pinkness glowed from in there. Nurses fluttered about, attendant drones. Babies were the great incubating queens.

In a room festooned with streamers, bunting and rag-doll faces, this giant coincidental celebration commenced. See, look, she willed her little-self, as she felt suddenly happy to call the pregnancy. All these instant friends await you!

A young couple approached the window, the woman shuffling, leaning on the man, her hair pinned wildly.

"Jerry's the one moving his fist. See over there? See his sweet fist? That's him, hon."

"Oh, Molly," gasped the new father. "My God. Am I old enough for this?"

"How could anyone be?" Carla added loudly. "I'm expecting in February." The younger woman now looked at Carla's abdomen, at fortune. "Seeing a hundred babies makes it seem more normal."

Molly drawled, "Once you take them out of here the kids get raised up just about no matter what you do. My mother always said so and I believe it. Hon, get me a pizza, will you? Olive and anchovy."

"Molly, that's not your favorite at all!" The husband's voice went teenaged high. He hunched against the very idea.

"I want anchovies." Molly spoke with the snapfire conviction of motherhood. Having come through the battle, she would be obeyed.

Carla watched the babies. Mothers and babies from time immemorial had flowered the earth, always more new mothers and babies. They made an exclusionary hive of the highest order around the perimeter of which buzzed, of course, men. Men argued pizza toppings and men waved wrenches. A great application of force accompanied these acts. So precise, the limitation of men; so terribly hapless. She felt a hot forgiving emotion. From within the infinite space of motherhood she could love the man's limitation as a humorous perfection. It was not her doing, her plan, this orbit they were all consigned to: someone with a wrench, someone else newborn. Thank goodness it was not her plan; she didn't control a bit of it. Protest and rationale were too nutty to fit here; she felt she was glimpsing deep stuff: monolithic laws, unassailable pilgrimages, sacrifices and spells, all this in microflashes, as in the floundered patch of no-land that runs between waking and sleep. In this dancing buzzing universe, Brian was Brian, forever prone to eat fancy chocolates the wrong way, unquestionably limited and complete as himself, as Brian. In this mood, Carla might call him up and say, "I want to blame you. And I know you're perfect." She looked in on the babies and wiggled her fingers at the sides of her face, showing them the eentsy-teentsy spider sun.

She found Mel pacing in the waiting room, eager to talk. "We can visit Alice soon. I went down and checked. Go on ahead of me. I left something in the car."

Alice lay with her head propped up. A fat white bandage was taped across her forehead. Her eyes opened.

"Tell me the truth," she rasped at Carla, sitting gingerly on the bed. But she caught sight of Mel peeking into the room. "No, no," she said and closed her eyes.

"You asked for him, Mother. He wants to be here," Carla whispered.

"Put on my lipstick."

Carla found it in her mother's purse by the bed and obliged, telling Alice, "Mel knows I'm pregnant."

"Of course. I told him first."

Coming through the door noisily enough to cover whatever he didn't want to hear, Mel weighed a heavy pot in each hand. "Here you go, Alice. I've dug up some cheer from my flower garden. Petunias. And here's a soybean plant." Mel set the pots on Alice's bedside table, then lifted her hand to his lips. Her arm fell, white on white, back to the bed. The smell of hospital vanished as a powerful earthiness emanated from the pots. No one mentioned the tear trickling from Alice's eye.

"They won't tell me anything," she said. "What happened?"

"The concussion is a slight one and you have a gash on your head. You're fine, Mother. You caught the thieves on their way out. The police suspect it was kids—they dropped stuff all over the back yard. They probably didn't even have a car. The house is messed up, but don't worry. They didn't even take much. Nobody touched your vampire books!"

Alice fidgeted the covers up to her chin. Carla noted that her mother's fingers, always thicker than her own, were gnarling over and gripping the sheet. She sat on the edge of the bed and placed her mother's hand on her abdomen. "Rub me for luck."

When you're a person lying helpless in a hospital bed, bandaged, wearing a gown not meant for anyone's eyes, ever, from that perspective even your own daughter—for heaven's sake—sitting there, looks hugely perfect, remote, impossible. No amount of fussing will admit her, or Mel, into the hospital world, as they can walk away. So now Alice knew, she clearly saw why it was that sometimes James, in the midst of a visit and much to her chagrin, would turn away and attach himself to another veteran. Any old man wobbling down the hall would do, and the smallest of small talk was not too small for James in this mood. "Say, Charlie, what'd you get there at the canteen? Oh, a Bun candy bar. Your favorite." There had sprung up a breezy, floaty wall of empathy among the seersucker-robed men, and the code was unknowable to visitors. Forgive me, James. Now I know this, Alice beamed at James Morrow, who, she felt in the twitter of hairs along her forearms, was not so far away.

"You're coming home tomorrow, Mother. You're done at the hospital, so don't worry. I'll call Grandma Morrow. And, get this—I've seen the nursery. It's a mirage, rows and rows of identical babies. I think they do it with mirrors."

Alice smiled weakly and muttered to the ceiling, "I didn't have one of those experiences, you know, seeing light at the end of the tunnel, so I guess I was just out cold, not dead and revived." It was consciousness that gave her the feeling of something cutting sideways at her. James moving swiftly toward her.

He spent days and nights, months, lying like this, looking up to see the various plaids, belted coats, flowers in hand—the only stars in a man-wrecked sky—wondering, maybe, what the feel of serge pants and a light cotton shirt might do for him. If only just once he could have risen and dressed properly, stood in front of the mirror and enjoyed the luxury of combing his flame hair with unwavering vanity and sport, surely he would have been saved. Forgive us for not trying, Alice prayed.

"Then go on, the two of you." Her fingers worked rapidly

at the sheet. "I need to sleep. After all these years, look how
I end up."

"Mother, no one is ending up."

"I'm on drugs."

"We all need some rest," said Mel. He led Carla from the
room.

They were gone. Fine. Alice's tiredness and a pinging ache
in her head presently orbited her past dizziness; she perceived
an infinite bright space encircling her bed. The windows had
been opened and the air was stingingly rural, as if a constel-
lation of soybeans speared the sky; and James came to her on
the fragrance. He wore his favorite striped pajamas and
claimed a corner of the bed she could not raise her head and
look at. Sneaky, hello! she thought. What does he want? She
continued to look at the ceiling, and soon enough his old
familiar smile worked as a compress on her brow. She listened
to her breath, steadied, and she felt cooled down. It was time
to piece this whole thing together. She flapped her sheet. She
said, I'm going to tell you your own story, James. No one
ever has.

So there you were, a slim man looking young and neat to
the end. Good grief, Jessamine was proud that your hair never
thinned. And you retained your soldier's wariness, a stringi-
ness, a rangy foxhole-diving urge long after the war, well,
honestly, forever. We tried so hard to tell you that everything
was fine, that you were just right. And whenever we doubted,
Lord, Jessamine was there turning that silver spoon in the
sunlight, telling the story of how you had outsmarted death
from the beginning. Newly arrived in the South Pacific, all
communications were disallowed you recruits. This was a
very big dark war, so how would your mother ever know
where they'd sent you? Good boy, you wouldn't let her
worry. Ha! You found your way to a trinket stall and bribed
the man to send home a spoon inscribed with Beautiful Mel-
bourne. That operation began in Australia; your family was
the first in America to know. Hearing this story killed my

heart every time, the way Jessamine would be turning and stroking the spoon. You would outdistance death, our miracle man. We weren't strong enough to think otherwise. And you needed to tell the story—abomination and monstrosity—in all its variations and episodes. You had to own up to your survival, over and over remembering how arbitrary and narrow your escape was. I just kept listening.

Alice pulled the sheet higher and turned her aching head slowly on the stiff pillow, the way she had always done to let James's punched-up bedtime voice come to her. She willed him to go on, speak, and she listened with her eyes shut tight as he said:

"Everyone expected to die over there, Alice. You didn't know that? Hell, all the soldiers did. That was the gist of the hype. Guys knew that dying might be their most important moment and the thing they'd be remembered for. They dreamed of style, not freedom. (He died in the war? Oh, *how?*) This wasn't any contradiction with the will to live, Alice. Knowledge and will are what put a guy out there ready, and, I confess, there's that gambler instinct racing the veins; it's a sensation that alters even your sight; it greens everything up. You know the guys who live right at any edge they can find? Take every chance? You know what happens, Alice? The thrill gets larger and then, good Christ, it needs to get larger. A certain kind of guy would've been better off dying over there. He comes home and wrecks a path every day, destroys everything. You get what I'm saying, Alice? They are the angry ones.

"But speaking of chances and close calls, Alice, let me tell you about the one time that stopped my heart. We were in camp. Tokyo Rose had been worming into, just eating our minds, but she'd shut the hell up now. I was shaving inside a tent—suddenly, an explosion. A man across the way fell into mosquito netting. His body did, but not his head. And, believe me, the worst was this: the severed head didn't look that odd. I recognized the guy's expression, ready to say, 'Fuck, I'm hungry.' He was known for saying that: 'Fuck, I'm hungry.' But it was just a head. Then everyone was running. Oh,

Christ, they hit the ground crying and calling for Mama, some
of them blubbering their heads off. The Japs were in our
faces, Alice. Hand to hand. But I felt this chilly calm. I felt
that everything was absolutely over, and so hell, what I
wanted to do—I didn't have a buddy next to me, and I'd
never see my family again—I wanted a moment of reckoning,
like they say. I had a mirror right in front of me, see, and to
hell with all the firing. What I wanted was to look at me,
square on, till the goddamned end, until my eyes were burning out. I wanted to face myself dying. Me! Not some Jap. I
saw . . . I have never since had that look, that grace . . . I
was exactly at the edge, and it's like God came right up under
the surface of my skin, swimming, and took a breath there.
Whoosh, came this glow spreading and it wasn't from enemy
fire. My insides lit up. I stood there with my insides flushed
pure, and maybe nothing showed on the outside; they
couldn't see me. The firing stopped. We were massacred, but
I hadn't been hit. I hadn't even been scratched. I think, to
this day I swear, I went invisible. I stared my way out of
there, is the thing. I sort of stared myself into a rapid transport, to safety way off somewhere I can't describe. What I
saw—and it doesn't have an effing thing to do with any kind
of church, Alice—was my soul in flight."

How could I forget this story! Alice said. Her head was
splitting, stuck on the pillow. Open or shut, her eyes were
pierced by galloping purple lights. She would not ring the
nurse, but lie in the breaking fever dream. She struggled to
continue.

James, if a man came home it meant he had survived the
South Pacific, angry or not, no one bothered. It was Jessamine's creed, the country's nervous cheer. But I took it up,
too, a dutiful wife guilty in milk-cream baths and dreams of
yellow kitchens. Without a doubt, I took it up. Blessings flew
like pollen. We blessed you, James, over and over, when you
needed recognition of the pain. Now I see it. Now!

You remember Carla bouncing in her bed, a one-year-old?
That apartment was a steam box. You never knew that I stood
in the hallway and listened, sick. "In the jungle, in the jun-

gle," you sang, insisting history already—then!—into her life. A free man in a tee shirt telling foxhole stories. I believed you had a choice. You could have found me in the next room weeping, had you looked even once for a future.

I say that you smashed the blue Dodge recognizing something of the dirge at work in you. Die, it said in a beetly foreign tongue.

You cried out, but we couldn't hear, and that's our shame. Oh, this country cashed in! We hummed and raised new curtains. We did anything but listen. Houses were pink and green and yellow. And yet you chose brown.

Our daughter was orphaned before birth; I, widowed at the altar; you never got past boyhood. A family, weren't we, though: masked and fashioned and avowed nevertheless. And when you lay down at the VA, finally in peace, you probably strained to say, This is nothing new; it's been me all along. This is me.

What did we know to say, having trained ourselves not to speak of deep disturbances? We couldn't read the news. Minutes before the end we turned on the television. Olympics. James, forgive us, truly. For heaven's sake, I didn't know a thing. But time gifts me with knowing you now. I'm telling you what I know, James. I know *you* and that's the whole story. Soldier! Mercy! Love!

C H A P T E R   1 7

"*T*his isn't rummage," Alice told Carla when the idea for a sale struck her. (As abruptly, as soundly as the shovel had hit her, Carla thought, roused from her book.) "I'm done with the excess." She strode through the house putting a radiant eye to her rooms. "We'll arrange a clearance, a yard sale. We'll call it Salesman's Samples."

"Saleswoman's," Carla corrected, helplessly trained in the battle of gender offense. From the library she had borrowed the latest book on baby names and was reading from the "crossover" list: Lee, Brooke, Kim, Brie. Or Bree. She read, "It is equally acceptable to name a child after a country—note the popularity of Erin—as it is a cheese. Brie. Aesthetics overrides origin today." Carla disagreed.

"Sales*man's*," Alice insisted, "or we'll scare off the women we mean to snag."

"You're probably right," Carla conceded. She breathed deeply, hoping to release the rank column of air that pushed hard against her spine whenever dread or family uncertainty crept into the hour. "Mother, you're not going to sell the house, are you?"

"Pooh, no."

Carla took the bus to the *Bargain Advertiser* office and placed the ad: "SALESMAN'S SAMPLES. WIDE ARRAY OF HOUSEHOLD GOODS. GIFT ITEMS. NAME BRANDS. NO SECONDS." She paid ten cents a word, firmly disbelieving that her old housecleaning dreams had in any way precipitated loss and upheaval and "Salesman's Samples."

Alice had never stayed up past eleven o'clock in her life. Disassembling the house, she puttered around in tinny lamplight, her thick white bandage glowing like a miner's beam against the midnight dark. Never, Carla noted, had her mother thought to buy the proper wattage bulbs.

She moved in slippered feet, having come upon some Craftique felt Santas. She fanned a set of potholders over her face, then tossed them in with a drink caddy, saying nothing. She hunched like the fiend in an old film—she would like to see herself so, Carla knew—her giant shadow wavering on the wall, cunning in its own right. In that bad light Alice scrabbled at the boxes and piles, the sets and pairs and mates to everything under the sun she'd entombed through the years. She worked speedily, mechanically, as if she had only so many minutes in which to find the elixir and save Egypt.

"So here's that cheesery kit!" she cried. "I knew I had one."

The woman pictured on the cheesery box wore bangs that rolled down stiff as a window awning, more outdated even than the BriteGlo lipstick model, Carla noted.

Alice scooped up a handful of bead necklaces. "Kresge's and us. Let the vultures descend." She used the necklaces as castanets and hummed, "Give my regards to Broadway . . ."

Silver ribboning zigzag glee energized Alice's voice. This was a far cry from how Carla had visualized an eventual housecleaning. Alice's eyes were too bright, her hands greedy and stung. She worked devoid of sentimental hesitation and consolation. This wasn't natural, was it? Carla had imagined, instead, a time like this worked up to with the utmost tact and caution. "The upending is for your own good, Mother," Carla was prepared to say at some future date. The unraveling of nonsense was to be sluggish and teary, but uplifting. As she and Alice wrenched loose the skeins of decade-old raffia yarn, the matched cookie and cracker jars, nursery books, picture frames, place mats—and nearly broke themselves by doing so —gratitude would wash them, a new simplicity sound a high note. So Carla had imagined. But, really, mourning was missing, and spooky irreverence predominated in Alice's creature look.

"Another rock-tumbling kit, great!" Alice cried. "Do you know how good this sale is going to look, Carla? How professional? We may have to extend the hours or even set up again on Sunday. I *think* just the two of us can handle it."

"You said Mel's coming. He'll be our bouncer."

"Of course we can handle the throngs," Alice said, touching her bun. She picked up a huge petaled bowl with a swan sculpture set in the middle. "It's glass. See the dipper? Some poor soul who never makes punch will buy this bowl."

Bringing Alice home from the hospital, Mel had wagered that the bikers were to blame for everything. He stood with Alice and Carla in the front yard briefly, as it was tacitly understood that no outsiders were welcome in the house. "These motorcycle gangs ruin the nicest people they can find. They seek them out. I've read about it."

"We have no contact with them," Carla retorted. She had looked to her mother for support, but Alice was a new dreamy Alice, gazing raptly at the brown still river below.

Mel said he would be glad to take Alice to a real-estate office and list the house. Alice smiled slightly, but didn't respond. "Even condos have their advantages," he said, turning to Carla, "though I hate to admit it."

"Mother would die in a condo."

"I mean something very temporary along those lines." Mel's eyebrows sought to imply a coded meaning, but Carla was weary of interpretations.

Alice said, "I smell like a hospital," and went inside.

In the end, the thieves had not taken much from the house. The mess was malice, but the hit on the head cold viciousness. Food, cash, and pills meant for a man with cancer; the cache was the work of rambunctious young junkies, a policeman speculated. (This time an older cop was sent to investigate Wakonda.) But Alice did not appreciate his use of "rambunctious" and "young" with junkie, as if, she told Carla, he were describing a Little League melee, an inevitability that she must—as a resident, a citizen—accede to. "You frightened them" was his explanation for the head-bashing. Never mind that dresser drawers were dumped, footprints gouged into sheets, a Tiffany lamp chipped, the machete still at large. Because silly things were taken—a plastic radio and a decorator Kleenex box—the policeman was led to conclude, "A girl was with them." Case deflated. Next came an insurance man's eager, lawful intrusion. He had sniffed dramatically, whether for clues or due to allergy or in disdain, no one guessed, but he had gone nose first through the house, squeaking in wingtips which Carla was astounded to find anyone still wore.

When she had called Brian and reported her mother's progress he'd listened so quietly her voice rose nearly to a scream. She piled on more details and strained to imagine them being charted in Brian's mind: on graphs, in colored blocks, with a whiff of ink in the river air aiding him coolly. There would be nothing else, no doubts lurking in his mind. Brian's mind *did* no lurking, she reminded herself. He offered to take a few days and come to Des Moines. "No!" she cried. It wasn't necessary, she assured him. "But give me some news from home. Something good." He announced that Melanie Green's baby was rolling over. "That's great! I'm so glad!" She was squawking; she could just as easily cry. She tried to swallow her tone of voice, redo the air in her mouth so that the deceit, apparent to her in every thin big word, would not slip from its locket chamber of the heart. "Our baby is doing wonderfully," she said. "I can tell. Do you believe me?" she found herself asking her husband for the first time. "Yes. Even the dandelions miss you." As he laughed she had felt how trust unhinged the guilty soul as quickly as fright did the innocent. Her jaw seemed to work independently of her brain. "When did you quit wearing wingtips?" she cried.

Jessamine had wept on the phone to hear of the calamity. "Why, your mother is too young for this. Your mother is full of life," she had added fiercely. She wept harder to hear of the Salesman's Samples event. "The public sale of a household? There has never been such a thing except in the case of poverty or death. Oh, don't tell me." Carla had rushed to assure her that essentials would remain. The reupholstered couch, for instance. Well, then. Jessamine was able to take a deep breath and manage a soft goodbye.

Mary hadn't shown herself in broad daylight since the party a week ago, but the minute Alice went outside to spruce up the front yard for the sale—she was stabbing the pink flamingo more firmly into her lily patch at the curb, Carla was watching from the kitchen window—Mary popped her door open. "Hey, Alice, bummer! I'm sorry!" Her feet were bare, her toenails painted deep magenta. Saturday, sale day, would also begin the State Fair. With knuckles to mouth, Carla stood back in the kitchen shadows and watched Alice anchor the bird just right: it rose several feet higher than her, on a black pole angled so that the beak slightly bit the sky. And her mother, in those grape-and-banana $1.99

pants she loved, paused, looked high and created her own
Iwo Jima.

Now as they worked through the house they drank gallons
of juice and water. Dust had woven itself together into thin
flannel that rose, floated, then disintegrated on contact. They
dug out and hauled and stashed everything on the back porch
and beyond, onto patio bricks, in the grass. Piled high,
cleaned and priced, the largesse of the house was considerable.

"A clean sweep," Alice said. "Now if a thief walks in, what
will he get? Me! Ha!"

Carla was reminded of a time in childhood when she and
her mother had worked like this. She couldn't have been older
than seven. "We were painting somewhere," she told Alice.
"For Daddy. Was it an office? Your yellow paint turned green
on the wall. It took forever to cover those dark-blue walls."

Alice cocked her head. "Cream, yes." She picked up a chif-
fon Christmas wreath.

"You let me eat a candy bar for lunch that day."

"Never in my life."

"A Clark bar."

"For a snack. It only seemed like lunch because we worked
so hard." She put the wreath around her neck. "An office for
your father. How lunatic."

"It seemed like lunch," Carla repeated. She could tear joyously into ten Clark bars. Rebuke with that wreath around
her neck signaled Alice's firm emergence from a dream.

On Friday evening Carla blitzed the neighborhood, cardboard signs and staple gun in hand. She walked up the alley,
passing the old Murphys' grotto, garishly floodlit since the
break-in. The Murphys were retired postal employees who
had brought Alice two heads of lettuce in sympathy.

Gorgeous oaks corseted every street, every humble home's
yard, with dignity, a *haute couture* incomprehensible to the
suburban manicurist. Pin oak, red, white, bur oak. She had

learned the names and features as a child. Some leaves were webbed, others spiked, some reached down like gloves. All the tree trunks were dark, ridged and widely skirted to the ground. And all around here houses had been built into the uneven landscape with respect for it, she realized now. Amazingly, even the Spam-colored apartments were fitted to the terrain as best they could be. Having been overlooked by the city due to its convolutions, the hilly neighborhood enjoyed autonomy; the streets rang with a clear proud outsider voice. The area adhered to its Indian identity: stealthy, lush and implacable, in spite of dilapidation. Ottumwa Street overlooked Wakonda, had a yet higher, more magnificent view of the river and downtown, but it did not signify the summit. Ottumwa must have been named at a time when builders did not imagine cutting higher still.

Carla clicked the staple gun several times as she tacked a sign to a telephone pole at the base of Ottumwa. In her youth she had never seen homemade signs posted around here, not even for lost animals, because back then pets did not get lost. Salesman's Samples. Carla's generation—she, the Wallace girls and the others—had grown up and moved away, dropped a generation out of the neighborhood, leaving the Murphys, Londos and Alices behind. All of their homes had to be full as warehouses. Would anyone bother with the sale?

Carla approached Parker, a stump of street that buckled high in the middle, then sloped at each end. She chose to walk the gravel alleyway as she had always done when young. The back yards here were built up by brick walls that raised vines and flowers and vegetables to majestic heights. Sunflowers in one yard leaned forward and down, watchdogging her movements. She looked up to see high wooden stakes everywhere marking the tomato patches, still thick on Parker. The street had always been Italian, and wouldn't you know, old Mrs. Vedaducci, Londo's mother and supreme tomato cultivator, stood half as tall as her stakes; and when she reached for a high tomato she sang hosannas to the sun. Her bare brown arm wrestled the leaves, and a bra strap swung free. She kept up a husky harmony, plucking tomatoes. A gardener's faith and a mother's faith looked like the same thing after all.

By 8 A.M. Saturday the yard glinted with color. "Samples" were stacked and arranged on card tables, on chairs, and on shelves fashioned from cement blocks and planks. Londo's building scraps, piled high in the alley, had come in very handy.

"The driveway would make a great display area—it's the only truly flat surface," Alice observed, "but I suppose people expect to park there. If anyone comes by bus, honey, give them a free gift. Ha! We'll see." Alice let healthy contempt crackle in her voice.

Carla stood behind the tallest display, ornamental yard statues, and looked across the street. At this early hour the bikers would be sleeping, or maybe they were out of town, or, ridiculously, camping at the fairgrounds. It doesn't matter, she reminded herself. Alice's own strength, a battery of froufrou, girded her.

Alice produced a box of daisy stickers. ("Dress up your notebooks, lamps, mirror, lunch box!" the label urged.) She pasted one onto her thick bandage.

"The third eye, Carla."

She set the brassy deerhead in a place of honor, apart and in front of the main table. She looped potholders and light-catchers off its spindly antlers. The frame caught sun and blazed henna. On his nose, Alice fastened a Santa that was meant to glow in the dark. She laughed with high agitation at her choices and made sure to place ashtrays everywhere: seashell, kidney-shaped, glass, ceramic. One was made entirely of cat's-eye marbles. She stood smoking, darting her head this way and that. If a customer fell out of an oak, Alice would pounce and barter.

The first arrival was a short pig-faced man wearing his hair winged into a Rorschach test. Alice marked him as being Carla's age. He came on foot, from uphill. He would live

alone in an apartment, Alice guessed, and he wore the guilty
look of a chronically rejected suitor. Women found him unat-
tractive and said so. He stared at Carla for too long, pretending to examine the deerhead, confirming Alice's worst
suspicions.

"Can I help you?" she said loudly, and broke his stare. But
it was thick in the air, thick as humidity, the surety of male
absence. This rude young man sniffed it; he knew that James
was long gone, that no man sat within the house watching
sports on TV.

"Just a minute," she called to Carla, refusing to name her
daughter in this man's presence. She went inside and rang
Mel. Yes, he still planned to get there by noon.

"I'll bring some lunch for you ladies."

Alice hung up and broke a mint leaf between her teeth.
Mint *was* heaven.

"I live over here at the apartments," the man told Alice
once she was outside again. Actually, he spoke to the deerhead contraption. His hair seemed not pomaded but alerted
inches above the scalp, catching signals down to earth. Testing, testing. Alice snorted so as not to laugh.

"Bargains galore!" she yelled. The man removed himself to
a row of mirrors. His lips rolled back in an attitude for bray-
ing as he examined his teeth. Alice took the deerhead from his
path and set it down nearer her.

"This isn't a sale item," she decided.

"What about the ornaments? And the potholders?" The
man's voice rose to a whine, exactly his problem with women.

"Those, too." Alice dragged the figure away from him,
which got the poor thing to leave the sale. Still, he insisted on
pinching the hollyhocks bordering Calvin's yard.

"We're a nation of feelers now," Alice declared loudly. "I
blame it on the discount-house mentality. Kmart is *not*
Kresge's."

This, thank goodness, removed him entirely from the yard.
He crabwalked uphill with much shoulder propulsion.

Next came Calvin, swinging his wide pantlegs down over

his embankment wall, yelling, "Hi, Alice. What've you got here? Lord, the burglars couldn't have gotten too much. You're running a store."

"Or an auction,"Alice said, not thinking. Calvin's face fell as he remembered his wife's desertion.

"Oh dear, Calvin. Look, take this wine carafe." Alice pressed Calvin's hand to it and squeezed.

"I'm a beer drinker, Alice."

Lonely grief was his problem and Alice struggled not to let the vision of Calvin's fatty-meat sandwich spoil her sympathy.

"It's a unique jar for hard candy." She supposed he ate hard candy.

Calvin grinned and hoisted the carafe. "Why not?" He turned to Carla. "Still having a nice vacation?"

"I'm having a baby," she called.

"Bravo!" Alice cried. "Listen to her. Honey, I love you." She threw a kiss across the yard.

Calvin didn't know where to look. "I'll get my money," he said. He rolled himself onto the embankment wall, was upright and lumbering toward his door. He held the carafe high in one large hand. "Peanut M&Ms, maybe. Yes, I could see that."

The cars with good brakes parked on Wakonda; others lined the top alley, the driveway, even down the back alley by Londo's cathouse. "Salesman's samples," Alice heard several customers remark with satisfaction. "Look. Rock-tumbling kits, Julie. I'm finishing Christmas shopping right here."

Gloria came midmorning in gaucho pants, or maybe, Alice tried to think, they were "updates," called something more contemporary. Gloria pushed her sunglasses to the top of her head and kept jangling her car keys. "To think that I let you off at the curb and just drove away." Gloria shuddered. "I've had two nightmares." But what a festivity; she'd been involved! She brought along Alice's get-well card from Craftique. It opened out like an accordion, the message escalating with sexual innuendo. A celebrity, Gloria looked all up and

down Wakonda but found no audience. Her lids were green
and she had three more sales to get to by noon.

Mostly a sort of hybrid Kresge's type came, one or two
women per car. The yard-sale circuit had its own, it seemed,
and the old Murphys from up the alley blended sweetly.
They belonged to some order of the day Alice had served only
long distance. These were the people whose birthright would
be proud thrift and a yen for invisibility. On principle, they
would not enter any mall store that went in for faceless silver
mannequins, low lights and fast music. No matter what the
sale advertised, they would spend as much for discount-house
no-label clothes because discount-house no-label clothes were
their clothes. Alice handed an outdoor-thermometer kit to Mr.
Murphy and a whole box of spice bottles to his wife.

A woman who suffered peculiar yellow crescents beneath
her eyes bustled forward. She picked up a glitter-glued salt
shaker and recalled what Burt ("my husband") had said last
night. She moved smoothly over key chains with little music
boxes attached, and a diabetic son's problems, on to quilted
place mats, and a fishing vacation on the river. ("Have you
ever seen a twenty-pound turtle?" she asked. "Good grief,
no," Alice answered.) The woman settled on the topic of
"rhubarb supreme," a concoction from her sister's recipe club,
after spying Alice's rhubarb, grown into imposing trees along
the driveway. Alice looked and was surprised at the broadness
of the leaves, the stumpy reddish forest claiming her land.

"Take what you want," Alice told her.

Londo and Sheila came through from the back yard. Alice
gave Sheila a decoupage jewelry box. Londo's eyes went
buggy with the plastic squirrel family she indicated, claiming,
"It's discounted for you." Sheila hugged Londo, evidently
thrilled. Alice felt moved to thrust two 3-D face mugs into
Sheila's arms.

To strangers she offered advice. "With this kilo of red sequins there's no telling what kind of Valentine's Day you'll
have next year," she was vowing to a shopper in hair curlers
when the winged man returned wearing crisper clothes, his

hair still dismally in place. He smiled, but Alice saw permanent distress under the surface. He was the kind of man who
would misinterpret a woman's smile as license to saddle her
with a lifetime's injustices from all who had come before her.
At this point he would never forgive a woman for loving him.
Sometimes Alice couldn't bear the insights, tender as a bruise,
that swelled her heart since kissing Mel in his office.

"Take this Chinese-checkers set. It's wooden," she told the
poor soul. "You're lucky these days even to find a metal set.
They're all made of cardboard. A wooden set is very classy
and rare. And popular with dates," she added, feeling it was
positively so. "Take it free." Finally he walked home in earnest.

Mary tried to slip into the crowd unnoticed, but Carla had
been waiting for her. Hunching ridiculously, Mary kept her
head down as she moved in among the generally more squat
shoppers. Her arms shone their magnificent gold-brown. She
kept one hand deep in her jeans pocket as she examined a
small woven basket. She looked and looked at the basket,
raising it to eye level, then just a bit higher to make wary
contact with Carla, who felt sick.

"Hi, kid. This is a nice setup you've got. Good luck." She
set down the basket. "You could get more than a dollar for
that basket, you know. Well! I'm glad Alice is okay. Hey,
sometimes tough luck keeps circling around. But it has to
break, right?"

Carla looked directly away from Mary. Across the yard
Alice was radiant, seemed the fortuneteller in her grape-
banana bloomer pants, a sage with the third-eye daisy, and as
Carla watched she prayed that her mother wasn't somehow
selling off her very Aliceness. Shedding skins, encumbrances
. . . And she, Carla, was going into parenthood as Alice
seemed to gain youth. Carla looked down to the river, such a
sluggish rippling brown, and she wondered what had ever
become of the hoboes Alice used to point out and shiver her
with tales of. Maybe all along her mother had yearned to toss

out this stuff, yearned for release from the householding life. Who else, really, would admire hoboes?

But Mary had not gone away.

Carla spoke firmly. "How's the mosaic business?"

"Oh, great!" Undulations of hip and shoulders commenced with Mary's sigh of relief. "More fairs are coming up. One's out of town, practically to Missouri. Keokuk." A humid silence walled off the news. Mary went to town on her gum, a fruit fragrance that soured in such thick air. She flung her head left and right a few times and managed to work up more breathlessness. "Tommy said that things ended all right between you guys, but I had to wonder." Carla's arms got a leaden feeling. She moved a banana ashtray a few inches to the left.

"He's split to Mexico," Mary hurried, chewing. "Something to do with a good deal in leather. I just thought I'd tell you he's gone and everything. Dammit, kid, things happen, don't they? What can I tell you?"

"I'm pregnant. I came to town pregnant. I don't have anything else to say to you. Please leave."

"Kid! God!" Mary yanked the gum from her mouth as if it were obstructing thought. "I can't believe it. Wait a minute— I should of known," she said once her eyes were normalized to nonblinkingness. "When I think back? Right! I should of known. There were indications."

Carla bristled to think what "indications" Mary meant.

"Congratulations, kid. That's just unbelievable. It's damn cool, Carla." Mary backed up, staring, and suddenly she flung her arms around as if scattering the denials she lived with. "Yeah, great." Her head seemed dangerously loose-necked. Guilelessly bobbing around, Mary was suddenly shy and young, stupidly young, and now she had to take Carla's hand and give it some kind of elaborate handshake.

"Then that's settled. Adios, Tommy. Who cares, right?"

"I said please don't talk about it, any of it. Go back to Kit. Kit! Kit!"

"Hey, don't spit his name at me. What's your gripe?"

"Nothing. But now that I know what goes on over there I pity you."

Mary thrust her bottom teeth into view. "Wait a minute. I'm not part of that stuff. Kit and me are together. I told you."

Carla realized she was standing with her legs spread, imitating Mary or bracing against Mary. And the women faced each other alone like that because Alice had attracted virtually everyone over to her side of the yard with a demonstration of encapsulated herbs. Carla would not look at Mary, but Mary found a way of hunching and squinting up at Carla like a weird terrible child, catching her eye.

"It's boiling out here," Carla cried, slapping her thigh. "Don't you own any shorts?"

Mary came to full height. "What do you care?"

"Cut off some jeans. You're not Kit. You don't have to be macho when it's ninety degrees." Carla's face was burning. She boiled, really, from the inside out, from a free-floating self-loathing she'd been too busy to feel. "You said yourself that he's a bastard."

Mary shrugged and rocked on a boot heel. She raised an arm slowly in what looked to Carla like the most absurd, the most amateurish nightclub gesture. "You know I've come over here to check on you and try to smooth out your bad feelings . . . say hello to Alice . . . see how you've been getting along. You never came by and I knew—I told Kit—this is how you'd be. I said, 'She's got an old man and she's guilty.' But you're worse than I said you'd be. Shorts, Jesus Christ. Don't have a stroke. Beat up on yourself, but leave me out of it, man. I could tell what you were after and I fixed you up with it. Things got too heavy? Tough. I was your friend. I'm glad you're pregnant, all right? And I'm glad you got that itch cured."

"Stop it!" Carla tightened her hand on a hideous milk-glass lamppost tagged one dollar. White bubbly glass, a deformity. Imagine cracking it over Mary's head, her own head; a clean hurtful confession, a shower of white glass relieving memory and guilt.

Mary threw down a dollar. "I'll take that lamp."

She had already wrenched it from Carla when Carla thought to say, "Good, you need it. And take these bags of mosaics. We don't want them. Go on."

Mary effected a casual hunching retreat. *Things happen, Carla* seemed emblazoned across her back, a biker motto mocking the screaming indignation of truth.

The Carla-Mary conversation had not escaped Alice's notice. She'd barked the browsers over to her, wishing to let the two fight out whatever, let them sand it to the grain and be done. She imagined a bag of mosaics swinging down from the bur oak, swatting Mary sideways on her bleached head, and Alice felt better. Even as she added prices and handed over sachets and a mermaid soap dish, she eagle-eyed her daughter. She admired the loose shorts—her own sale find—and the long thin legs and the mane of hair. Great inheritance! Thunder and bones and the supple muscle of determination, that's what Carla was made of, and, whatever else, she carried a baby.

Alice's intensity of emotion tingled Carla's scalp. She turned to her mother as Mary left, and found Alice staring with the ferocity of a cornered woodland creature.

"I'm okay, Mother," Carla called.

"You've got great genes, honey!" Alice yelled at the top of her lungs.

A bargain hunter raised her head. "What? I didn't see any outfits."

Alice hooted.

"Are you sisters?" someone asked, and it seemed to Carla that in this singularity of purpose, and living in this strange shifting of time, as she was pummeled forward into parenthood and Alice was spiraling back to resemble a girl popping from a cake, they were frozen exactly even for a minute, and surely showed twinlike.

C H A P T E R   1 8

While Hazen steadied himself on the boxed-cake counter Jessamine stood in Produce, across the way. Strawberries had come down twenty cents a pint and they were the luscious middle-sized berries that mark the height of the season and sail from fingers to mouth. Jessamine preferred to choose one at a time from the tipped bushel basket that imitated a farmer's spilled bounty, in which, she knew, the bottom berries would be squashed.

Despite his snorts from over yonder, Hazen obliged Jessamine as many supermarket trips a week as she required, and they were increasing in number. Those five years of good widowhood put behind her with a shudder, now Jessamine came to be among the commerce of daily duty wearing an accomplished heart. All of it, even the frantic young woman groaning over the meat counter, resisting steak prices, played music along Jessamine's cheek. Here was community, the promenade of old, and Jessamine at eighty-five blessed the Lord she was here, with a lavender cardigan flung over her shoulders and clasped in front by a jeweled bar, combat-ready for air-conditioning chills. She might scan the spice rack as an opportunity to recall exactly what goes into a date pudding. She was always pleased to find pastry flour stocked, and if Jessamine discovered a splat on the floor, a beet jar opened, a runny egg or a torn bag of navy beans, she reported it with haste, aplomb and the wisdom of years.

Jessamine kept her midget refrigerator at Hillcrest stocked with juices, fruits, and triangles of foil-wrapped cheese, for the sake of company. Today she thought how delectable would be a dish of strawberries and vanilla ice cream, right after supper. The vision of a ripe berry sliced and glistening atop white, white ice cream made her catch her breath.

"What about one of these?" Hazen held a plain cellophane-wrapped angel food from the boxed-cake counter. "With berries and whipped cream?"

"In summertime you want *ice* cream with your berries, Hazen. It has always been so."

He set down the cake with a definite "Gad," and Jessamine, pocketbook swinging like a reflector off her bent arm, continued to examine strawberries one by one. She held each briefly at a proper farsighted distance. She boxed the loveliest berries into a pint container and knew that in the time it took to drive back to Hillcrest—they had no other errands today—the bottom berries would preserve themselves.

She could think of nothing else to buy, and they should move along while the mood held. Hazen's tendency to speak his mind (foreign notions, more often than not here) was irksome. Sometimes handling Hazen as she would a child, Jessamine schemed to offset his rumblings by devising an advance treat or a mission for him. ("I wonder if folks can still buy the little syrup bottle for making home root beer? You've told me how you loved homemade root beer. Hazen, why don't you investigate?")

Here came a young man with children—who would have ever thought!—carrying a little calculator down the aisle and looking properly informed. And right now married people debated earnestly over the bin of mixed peppers and called out dishes Jessamine marveled to hear the names of, swashbuckling words that left a tick, tick, ooo! sound behind. And over here, gracious strife: "But your mother doesn't eat pickles, Mandy." And "Remember the last time you bought leeks?" It sounded like show tunes, and Jessamine hummed. Did her own granddaughter shop so with her husband? She imagined that, yes, she did. It was a new day, she thought, looking over at Hazen. And here we are, in it! And she was mystified to think how all through the years she had picked out every last canned fruit, stalk of celery, and rib roast for her family, every condiment and carrot; she had regulated and censored, yet she could not recall ever hearing a word of protest or suggestion. Not one opinion. She had exercised veto power, denied husband and son green olives (she favored jumbo ripe, pitted); new-brand cereals; choice itself. Well, it almost seemed evil if she dwelled on this, though the Lord knew she had shopped with love and concern as guides. But that little rise to power . . . Yes, indeed, Lawrence and even James Lawrence were absolute fiends for green olives at the Methodist Church smorgasbord the family had attended twice yearly. But they never made mention of it otherwise, as if home and green olives were mutually exclusive worlds.

Where were their palates, then, and their heads? If she had lapsed altogether, had become a slattern who set out, say, pickled pig's feet in jars, would they still have sat down to table? If she had taken the oft-imagined trip to California to see the distantly related young carpenter, on returning would she have found the Morrow men weak and mewling, with evidence that a large finger had cut a swath through the peanut butter? How was it they had delivered up to her the very essence of their lives? Mother or murderer, they made it practically one and the same. "Oh," she gasped and covered her mouth. She yanked the cardigan onto her bowed, educated shoulders.

Hazen's continued harrumphing carried across the aisle. He was tapping at the cellophane suspiciously. He cared about that boxed cake. Jessamine looked at the other shoppers. Why, Hazen's interest was as fierce as the young men's with their calculators and their leeks.

"Hazen, Hazen," Jessamine called. "You could drive me straight to California. You *could*." She blew him a kiss and did not care who was watching.

"Jessamine," Hazen said, grinning and wagging a finger, "you are the berries."

Of course a store-bought cake was past the limit, and Hazen was lucky someone knew this. The summer season, contrary to what she had led Hazen to believe, had nothing to do with her admonishment. From a reputable bakery you could purchase a cake properly—in a pinch, order in advance to specification—but you would never serve a cake from the supermarket shelf. Jessamine felt gushing gratitude for having her faculties about her to resist the cake-buying impulse. Imagine being too infirm to know that you were eating store-bought cake! She prayed: Heavenly Father, thank you, not that.

They moved toward the front of the store. Hazen circum-vented the checkout counters and leaned against dog-food bags stacked to his height while Jessamine, holding her straw-berries and the highest-quality vanilla ice cream ("old fash-ioned," the label said in vaudeville lettering), reluctantly espied the express lane. She shopped among a Friday after-noon crowd and felt unhurried, but then came a well-meaning pressure at her elbow. "Over here. There you go, ma'am," said a young woman, her cart loaded out of capacity. She as much as danced Jessamine to the express lane. Silly to hang back, but Jessamine would not have minded if Hazen had snoozed on the bags while she took up position in a real check-out lane.

As Jessamine's turn to pay came near, Hazen gave her the high sign—a shake of car keys—and headed out. He would bring the car curbside. When he triggered the automatic doors the electric burr quivered Jessamine's earrings. She pressed her lobes.

Sunlight hit harsh and low when Jessamine stepped out. She guessed it was later afternoon than she had imagined, and they were deep into summer, of course. The sun hung white-hot at that point when it bullies the other elements, blazing an indistinct fury in the moments before the hour forces it docile. Jessamine loosed her cardigan. Even in summer Hazen wore his long-sleeved shirts buttoned to the neck. Jessamine had discovered that often the buttons were not buttons in the real sense but disguised snaps. His shirts snapped up the front, at the cuffs, over all pockets, and sometimes down the collar.

Outside, she stood with her back to the sun, waiting for Hazen. An aproned grocery boy darted around her and with the magnificence of youth he slung bags into a car's back seat. He straightened and pushed the now empty cart to the line of others, commencing a gentle chorus from fellow carts. Jessamine smiled at his vigor and he stopped a moment, caught by her look, unsure now whether to speak or not. He was a well-bred boy, obviously, who understood that Jessamine's considerable experience in the world might lend him some insight, and did she need his attention? No, she smiled at him.

The boy saw Hazen first. As the old-gold car, blurred nearly to silver, nudged up and sent a shudder through the line of shopping carts, the boy sprang to Hazen's door calling, "Whoa, sir." He used hand signals to attract—and halt— Hazen. Charcoal briquette bags, stacked high as dog chow indoors, at the far end blockaded the cart that had been jarred loose.

"No problem," said the boy.

Hazen's head turtled out the window. His eyeglasses had gone mother-of-pearl blank, but Jessamine knew that the twinkle was there.

Time was not of the essence with Hazen. Time, Jessamine thought, looped your days like a funny lasso that shone only in the brightest light. And one thing she could say for not having a slew of great-grandchildren around: time—the years —did not notch up on you quite so obviously. At this end of life she knew no burning future; the present expanded and brocaded itself rich in detail and of a golden absolute hue.

The spangled seat felt warm against Jessamine's legs, and already Hazen was fiddling with the air-conditioning. She placed the double-strength bag of ice cream and the strawberries between them, where a bit of shade covered the seat.

Hazen let a multitude of shoppers nose from the exit before him. He regarded Jessamine's penchant for car-riding as a mandate to creep, creep along. Anytime now she might start in on a memory, recall a baptism or a stubborn first tooth, note the relationship of her son's hair color at age five to a covered-wagon expedition one hundred years earlier. Driving imparted a harmony to her renditions and revelations; Hazen knew this. Why, Jessamine took to car-riding as its being something from God, and would often see and think things on a drive that were impossible at home. So Hazen drove "at your service," ready to switch tempo, cruise or guide or get on home lickety-split.

If it weren't for the strawberries and ice cream, they might drive clear out to the west side park to watch the swans named Jack and Jill. That was a good summer drive, Jessamine mused, approving Hazen's letting so many cars by. Then it was Hazen's turn to nose into place on a street which half of Des Moines seemed to be traveling late Friday afternoon.

"I expect we've got caught up in vacationers' traffic," Jessamine said. A parade, you could believe. Here, not even a mile from Hillcrest, the street broadened unrecognizably; it shuttled cars directly to the highway heading west out of town, where farther on you came to the lakes. Jessamine looked for cars approaching them filled to bursting with children and beach balls, and in the hampers you would find cold fried chicken. Off to the lake for a day or a weekend, a parade of them. Discreetly, she waved. On one such outing years ago, little James Lawrence had learned to swim. They'd got a picture of him, arms raised to a steeple there at the end of the dock, mad to dive, her son. He had collected rocks into the hundreds. His had been a small squiggly body with no respect for exhaustion, hunger or fear. And when Jessamine wrapped James Lawrence in a huge striped towel she thought he looked exactly like a twist of taffy magnified one hundred times in size. The nub of cloth against his perfect chubbiness . . . growing up to fight the Japanese.

"Hazen, shall we peek at the children swimming? Just for a minute?"

Hazen understood that Jessamine wanted him to leave the thoroughfare, up ahead detour a block and drive into the little neighborhood park where children splashed in a tiny swim pool, one of those cement crater affairs sunk into the ground. He drove into the park and coasted toward the pool. Pansies —a battalion of urchin-faced pansies—lined the curb in front of the pool and seemed to say Halt.

Jessamine clapped her hand to throat and twisted her beads. "Will you look at those little scoots!"

"Guppies swarming alive."

Jessamine looked and looked and swiveled her head far past the flowers, and when she looked straight ahead, into memory, Hazen understood. Pleasure bestowed, he swung back toward the main street. Jessamine had rolled down her window to hear the children better.

"Why don't you shut off the air now?" She stroked an invisible sky. "We're nearly home."

They moved back into traffic, crept several more blocks, then congestion let up and Hazen accelerated for a stretch. They crested the slope, bringing Hillcrest into view, and in that moment, riding high, buffeted by a sweet perfume of memory and possibility, Jessamine saw the building she now called home just as a stranger caught in traffic might see it: a three-story red brick structure with funny slab paneling between the windows. It was a building of a certain short-lived style whose red brick annoyed, though you wouldn't be able to say why the natural color of a brick would appear dated and tired. And a sign on the front lawn announced in black letters: HILLCREST RETIREMENT CENTER. Little light bulbs grew up through the grass for the purpose of distinguishing the sign after dark. Indeed, the entire lawn was lit up at night for no reason at all that Jessamine could think of. Her heart turned as she thought, We fall asleep as early as babies; folks traveling by after dark might mistake us for a nursing home.

Across the street on their left the cornfield, valiant behind spirea hedges, held sway. The glinty green there compelled Jessamine to see that land as if for the first time. She observed the field from upstairs in Hillcrest many times a day—it was a comfort and an attachment to the early farm days at Walnut Grove, a lucky and astonishing sight to find here in town, this patch; but now the sadness inherent in a view, in a good view, seized Jessamine. She had never sought to—and expected she never would—walk across the street, pass the bushes, kneel and touch the real good earth. A view. Except right this minute, this very minute, she had a mind to do that. Vacation:

breathe, stoop, touch. What else in the world was there to do of any consequence?

Hazen's turn signal was plinking mightily in Jessamine's mind, pointing and flashing the car toward Hillcrest. She looked this way and that. Field on left, plink. Hillcrest on right, plink. They were leaving the flow of vacationer traffic. They did not fit into it, after all; they did not make up a parade. What was she thinking? How futile even to buy the strawberries as if—Oh, it's just a ruse, she said. Of course Hillcrest provided desserts. Hillcrest provided and provided and provided.

Hillcrest's manager, Deborah, stood hands on hips inspecting the shrubs around the sign. How, how, how, have I come to live somewhere public and named? Jessamine asked herself. She had been tricked. Five years ago she had blotted out her sense of dignity for the sake of civility and ease, in order not to be a bother. There she was, an eighty-year-old widow, which some people had found alarming in itself. But in all her born days she had never thought old age would consist of regimentation, dormitory living, food on trays served to her by strangers. No! Fields and berries and infinite sky were in order. Walnut Grove had not forewarned. Walnut Grove had had no idea what the world would grow to be. Jessamine's beads were twisted to her throat as she declared herself too young for all of it.

"Hazen, go straight. Yes, Hazen. Drive me to California!"

But Hazen, having got all set for the turn with much squealing of the power steering—he had nearly overshot the drive—was swinging into it. Jessamine's cry jarred emergency reflexes: a jerk and tremble of hands. His steering wheel went left, then right on him. His hands leaped off the thing entirely to stroke the air, and he saw bright nonsense out the window: he was pointing straight at Hillcrest—no hands on the wheel—and the car was moving sideways. Like a sled. Like a sled hitting ice on the sledding hill, and you went keen with the raw cold and excitement and crazy zigzag, that's what he remembered of sledding. That steep, steep hill out

back and the free, fast sliding. You shouted, "Hey!" at the
bottom of that hill, and snow plowed into your nose and
packed your mittens. But he kept himself headed toward Hillcrest, he certainly managed that. And he could do without
Deborah coming forward in the lawn, swinging her arms the
way she did to get them all started singing at those dumb
monthly birthday parties. Huh-uh, Hazen told himself. He
would not do it. He would not sing.

All this turning racket: chewing moan of metal! Hazen
drove the noisiest car on earth, noisier than anything, than a
truck or a Model A, than anything Jessamine could remember
hearing, and you'd think this was a rutted lane he'd chosen
and—gracious!—why did Deborah's hair look like it had
caught fire? Jessamine held her beads. What was happening
to the sun, that bright vexed giant? Deborah fell into it,
and how could it be that James Lawrence—bless him—a
full-grown man, yet carrying that huge striped towel from
his youth, raced a healthy race, leaped through the sun,
thank goodness. It was a monster sun, a South Pacific
sun, the wartime Japanese sun, and James Lawrence came
signaling from the trench: rescue. What he could do was
yank her clean off this earth. Of course, Jessamine realized.
Heavenly Father, I'm ready. She waved, motioned James
Lawrence to her, closer, but no; he flapped the towel harder,
snapped it, shooed her away, menaced her with that towel.
Get back, Mama! He looked exactly like his father, too.
Get away from me! he screamed above an unholy Japanese
racket.

The car itself looked to be in pain, as well as painful to
touch, Deborah had thought idly, but later—she wasn't sure
if she should say this, or to whom—she positively remembered seeing an aura around it, a band of indescribable color
marking Hazen's car in some peculiar way. The sun had
ringed and captured that car. Depth of field was lost. As it
came over the hill Deborah had thought, in fact, that the car
hardly looked like a vehicle per se, more like arrowed light. It
pointed at Hillcrest, yes, and Jessamine's hand could be seen

fluttering at the open window. Deborah slapped a mosquito on her arm. "No!" she heard from the street. And next, who could say? Did Hazen have a heart attack? Lose the brakes? Attend to a bug bite? Next it was all a matter of split-second misjudgment and misfortune as the car behind splintered up against Hazen's monster sedan. No one could stop. Gravity and velocity have no sentiment; Deborah thought this as if reading from a tract. They pushed and piled and finally Hazen's car was scooted off the road, over the curb, up into the Hillcrest hedges, crashing into the floodlights where violets were sprouting in their shadow. A crunch of light bulbs popped color into the air.

Deborah ran into the foyer and dialed 911 at the desk phone. She tore outside again. Adrenaline gave her oarsman's arms. She would pull both Hazen and Jessamine from a flaming wreck if need be.

As Jessamine stepped gingerly from the car, Deborah bit her own hand so as not to scream. Blood was streaming. Matted, red, chunky; no, she couldn't look.

"Jessamine, oh my dear God, Jessamine." Deborah peeked between her fingers. "Sit down, Jessamine, be still. You're . . . you're bleeding." Agh! Do not throw up, she commanded herself: you are sixty and young.

Jessamine appeared to rub the blood back into her skin, and she actually picked loose a hunk of gleaming redness—

"Jessamine, stop!" Deborah screamed. She held her own head tight by the palms, held back some bursting horror.

The old woman stood statuesque. "We were shopping," she explained. She waved a wilted hand in front of her face.

Deborah came forward to assist and she did not mean to think, amid the horror of it all, *Fresh fruit;* but it got stronger as she drew nearer, this overwhelming fragrance. There must be some protection at work in the face of seeing the maimed. The mind insists you smell goodness, it that it? I work with the elderly—endure this shock—to strengthen belief? I am made to inhale the freshness of life when it seems most unbearable. God is a maniac!

Pinched to a sting, finally Deborah's nose smelled nothing.

Jessamine went down stiff as a board, but in sections, like some sort of folding lawn apparatus. First the knees hit ground, but Jessamine didn't know it and continued to look poised and perturbed. The knees gave way and she was plopped on a hip, sitting in the grass.

"Well, look at me. I'm sitting on the ground." She pulled free a handful of grass. She put it to her nose. Grass, Deborah knew, would be exactly what Jessamine smelled. Deborah went toward the car, where Hazen sat, too tall, hands on the wheel and mouth agape.

"Hazen," Jessamine continued, "I expect you read my mind." She was scattering grass overhead as if this were a parade. "Hazen, look at me sitting on the ground," she called, inclining toward his imminent chuckle.

C H A P T E R   1 9

*T*he VA hospital doesn't have babies! The idea seemed more fatal and sad to Carla than the sight of the seer-sucker-robed men drifting and wheeling through the halls, the old familiar nightmare. But you could believe that Alice did not see a thing. Brisk and sporting her thick white bandage, she could have been mistaken for an outpatient, once a young WAC in service to all these fighting men. She slapped along hallways, up the service stairs of bleak echoing concrete rather than wait for an elevator, and headed for the fourth-floor ward where every sneeze seemed too terrible, a war remnant, where each man was laid out in a tiny room, maybe his last room.

They found Hazen next to the nurses' station. He lay sleeping and was tube-rigged by nose and arm. Hazen Batten: an

old man out cold, broken in two at the hip, with whom Carla
had eaten one meal, attended a birthday party, and toughed
out the popcorn caper. And Alice had visited with Hazen only
twice. But to see Jessamine at his side, her one foot in white
sandaled slipper planted inches forward as if she would now
begin a violin concerto, bespoke a lifetime of regard. She
cupped Hazen's hand and crushed a yellow handkerchief to
her face. She sat very tall with no use for a chair back. "He's
sleeping. Let me tell you, he's fine."

Alice went to Hazen and vowed, "I know exactly what it's
like." She kissed his cheek and drew back. "The air is too
close," she said and butted quickly from the room. Carla and
Jessamine followed. Alice stood in the hallway, pretending to
adjust her hair.

"Allie, it's his hip." Jessamine spoke in the low voice she
always used to excuse a marginally successful relative who—
she would tell anyone as illumination—had suffered the
doomed beginning of premature birth.

"On a lesser man it would mean a fatality," she continued.
"Already he wants to come home. Imagine! Hazen has no
idea. He's never been in a hospital. Never." Jessamine's voice
had thinned to a trill despite her attempt at corraling it in the
low octaves: she had chinned her neck to this end. The bright
hankie flagged over her fingers, two of which were bandaged
due to a minuscule injury sustained in the accident. "I don't
know what to believe," she admitted.

"Let's go to the day room," Alice suggested.

They walked as if avoiding major cracks in the earth, Jessamine with just enough royalty in her step to clear from left
and right the seersuckered men.

The day room was empty save for a bristly-haired man
turning on the TV. He tightened his robe belt upon seeing
the women enter, and stood back. He had tuned in to a golf
tournament, but the picture was not the best. Legs and arms
and faces were a confetti of reds and blues. The man fiddled
with the dials.

"The picture won't get any better," Alice told him. "These

institutional things never do." She rummaged for a cigarette and absently lit it, her first cigarette in front of James's old-style-Methodist mother, ever. Carla flapped her arms: *Put it out!* Her mother whirled on Jessamine, who seemed not to notice, and Carla saw a definite wry smile cross Alice's face. *Pooh!* Alice mouthed back at her, and smoked.

"Allie, you don't own a color set, do you?" Jessamine spoke with gentle regret, hankie poised.

"I wouldn't want the news in color, and that's all I watch."

Alice's exhalation was flagrantly imperial. Since the yard sale two weeks ago she had been like this—on stage, given to pronouncing with more relish than ever. They were deep in August now. The *Register* was full of State Fair news, though it was winding down rapidly, and despite the lure of fair food —Carla admitted that corn dogs slathered in mustard sounded especially divine—she had chosen not to go. These were days of breath-sucking heat that muffled even the loudest cries and soaked your blouse against your back. (Early summer had cornered the rain.) Carla spent her time sitting indoors propped before the fan, her feet on the ottoman, staring at TV without a plan, knowing that the time to go home wasn't quite upon her, but not knowing why. She did want to see Brian, but her body had no intention of moving. From TV she learned that chickens were dying in Georgia. "But not in Iowa," Alice had proclaimed, watching the news with her. "And we're just as hot. *I'm* dying in my work clothes." "You could go bare-legged," Carla suggested as the weatherwoman warned against another day of one-hundred-degree heat, with humidity just as high. Alice snorted, "Honestly!" Since the yard sale Carla had felt her mother's quizzical eye on her often: when *would* she go home? And Carla couldn't say. By telephone she kept soothing at Brian's perplexity; she muttered that she was helping Alice adjust to spaciousness; and most recently she claimed, "I think we're going to look for a dog." She had counted Brian's diplomatic sighs: three. She had listened to her little-self who simply did not want to leave Wakonda yet. Now she sat on an orange plastic chair in the

VA's day room and was glad she had listened. She patted her grandmother's hand.

"Golf is pure catatonia," Alice declared with her cigarette in a loop-de-loop.

"But golf was James Lawrence's sport in the early days," Jessamine reminded all, including the man in the corner, who gave her a curt nod. A faint smile lifted and colored Jessamine's cheeks. Her fingers traced the hemline of dress sheathed over her knees. Everything was aqua today, from the satin earrings and the wooden-bead necklace to the tattersall dress, and the more distant the history, the greater the comfort, Carla knew; the stronger Jessamine's voice.

"I can't help hating golf," Alice said lustily. "I never figured out why he liked it. No sir, don't change channels." The obliging patient had come half out of his chair; again he tightened his belt. "I hate it, but let me watch. Look at the men. Oh, the women are worse. I do hate it." She flourished the cigarette.

"Now, Allie . . ."

"Grandma," Carla cut in, pressing her lips at Alice, who ignored the gag order, "Mother means that golf on television baffles her. Daddy would watch Sunday golf for hours."

"Drinking beer," Alice added.

"James Lawrence was professional material!" Jessamine's voice swooped fast as a hawk on its prey, then rose to a point too high for beer-drinking news, way up to one of the famous James Lawrence stories:

"He could have gone with a golf professional. The man came there to Minneola and wanted James Lawrence to tour. Yes, he did. But how could I let a seventeen-year-old go?"

"Knowing what I know now," Alice said, "I would have."

Jessamine turned her head slowly about the room, and when she spoke it was to history, to a gathering of Walnut Grove and Minneola luminaries. "I disliked his consuming interest, I suppose. He was so young to be there at the country club every day."

"The clapping gripes my soul." Alice wrung her one hand

at the TV while she put out her cigarette. "It's weak. The audience hates it, too."

The man in the corner jerked to his feet. "I'll turn it off, dammit."

Jessamine whirled. "My word."

"I'm the patient here. I'm stuck." Slippers patting across the floor did not do justice to the man's indignation. Right before exiting he turned up the TV volume.

"And it still sounds hushed, do you see?" Alice hooted. "Men could play golf right here in the halls and not disturb a soul. They should," she decided. "I wish I had brought James some golf clubs to play with. I wish we had done more for him."

"Mother, the expression is 'I'm going golfing,' not 'I'm going to *play* golf.' "

"Piffle. Whatever. These golfers are Southwesterners prone to skin cancer."

"I'm starving," Carla said.

"Of course you are, dear." Jessamine's voice curved and feathered to fit the occasion of Carla's hunger. "You need a snack. Go to the canteen."

Carla could feel her grandmother watching her retreat. At the slightest ruffling of hair or shifting of weight, and especially as you walked, Jessamine would be calculating family resemblances, real and expected, adding to the story.

"I believe red hair skips generations," Jessamine said, now that Carla was gone. "Allie, Carla's baby will be a redhead." She folded her hands. Oh, she was sure of it. Yes, and its newborn eyes would open to reveal the shocking brief Morrow blue. She prayed for a glimpse of this baby. She prayed for a strong heart. But what was Allie going on about?

". . . the mystery to me, Jessamine, was how did James become a golfer? Did it really suit him as a boy to dress in these ghastly plaids and pastels, and stand in the sun?" She pointed at the TV. "Will a boy do that?"

Oh, Allie, Allie. Look at dear Allie, on her feet now, always moving, such a busy little person. Jessamine had to smile, watching Allie swing her arms like a pendulum. Allie was the family soldier really, she knew.

"Why didn't he take it up again later, Jessamine? What stopped him from doing the one thing that made sense for him to do?"

"It's not as if people have a particular use, Allie. A man is not a rutabaga."

"I loved him." Alice flopped back into her chair.

Allie, Allie. Allie would have dismantled this Veterans' Hospital brick by brick if she had thought it would help James Lawrence, you could be sure. Allie still went about with that attitude fit for safecracking, due, in part of course, to the fact that she had grown herself a career.

Jessamine's plastic chair creaked as she leaned toward Allie. She wished her daughter-in-law to know that world history had proven her, Jessamine, a good mother, really the best of mothers. Childhood is the short season. And Jessamine thanked God she had given James Lawrence everything she could, during it. She had known from the start that lavishness and spoiling and the look of a jaunty cap would emerge as James Lawrence's salvation. Whatever else, she had determined that he would have—and so he did—the sustaining memory of youth.

"He had so very little in manhood, Allie."

"He had a family."

"The war changed him."

"We praised him for outdistancing war. I think we hurt him. He knew better."

Jessamine stood and fanned a hand over her bosom and felt the "onward" thrust of her hankie weaving her fingertips. In another time, James Lawrence might have lived as a rightful dandy, providing steady employment for a battery of shoeshine boys, on through to the end. He would have wished to do so, a gentle boy, her cloud-reading son. Of course she had known of his early mischief; she had found his teenage chemistry experiments (for firecrackers? for bootleg?) in the cellar and lived on through without comment. And his derring-do with cars. Well, the dears Allie and Carla came too late. They knew only the James Lawrence shattered into manhood, and all along hadn't she tried to tell them his childhood story, to protect them too?

The first sorrow of motherhood is a natural one: as the baby grows up, the mother will grow old; the mother will not be there to protect forever. She had wept bitterly in confronting this natural order, she loved the baby so. The worst shock came later. It was the certainty of natural order being ambushed: she would outlast her baby after all. She would bury him. These hospital halls, these very smells, had taken James Lawrence to them. Somewhere in this building—she did not wish to remember exactly where—James Lawrence had lain down for the end.

The TV was advertising razor blades. Alice rose to stand by Jessamine. They looked out the window to, unfortunately, another hospital tower. On TV the electric-shaver commercial switched to golfers trudging overhill, exiles intent on a flat, smooth destination, *the green*, Alice knew, and the announcer was muttering endless golf-prayer over the hike. Alice felt like an enthusiast with a metal detector, out on Sunday morning certain of bizarre big fortune. It must all be let out, everything must be said. Anything and everything must be said when checking for common ground. The helium property of words made her giddy with their release. One time she had gulped Carla's carbonated spring water and felt this way. At a time like this, a person might wish for her sachet-voodoo doll simply to give pause and perspective to the wacky and the new. Yet it seemed that a person could as easily do without it now; she could drop the game of dramatic intervention.

Jessamine's voice struck the still room pentacostally: "Allie, in front of Hillcrest, at the moment of impact I believed James Lawrence had come to deliver me to the Lord. I held death's hand out the window, but no, he ordered me back for a spell."

Jessamine's eyebrows went up toward her heaven, and it seemed to Alice that infinity would be exactly the shape of that brow. She would not venture to say that in times of high emotion all a person knows is what she has known. High emotion brings forth James.

". . . such a strong busy little boy. So stout. Yes, he was mischievous, I'll say. It was that red hair."

Jessamine's breathing had become audible, though it remained as even as a sleeper's, a part of the strangely tuneful air made up of TV golf, the exertions of a vast building apace with machines, and a person's own exhalations. Alice heard a jackhammer blamming in the distance, too.

Jessamine moved closer to the window facing the brick tower and positioned herself in the wide-legged stance that could support hours of family speculation. She stood like that, breathing the Morrow hymn. She stood through birdies and putts and trudgings, commercials and an interview with Jack Nicklaus. Jessamine stood through another one of Alice's heartily smoked cigarettes, staring straight ahead to brick.

" . . . and once," she said, surfacing from the long, long story that wrapped her mind, "I caught James Lawrence on a rooftop opening an umbrella, ready to jump. That child. I looked up to the Huffmans' rooftop and there he was." Jessamine looked up toward the tower's roof, so high as to be negligibly visible. " 'James Lawrence, an umbrella is not a parachute!' I cried. James Lawrence!" Jessamine cried out. She lowered her eyes somewhat and gazed at the bricks straight ahead. "James Lawrence." Her voice was toneless.

To be back in this hospital, with Hazen failing now, the strain was obviously too much. Jessamine had begun to quiver all over. Right this minute the past was ready to nab her, nab and sink her sure as an umbrella fall would have finished off her James Lawrence. Alice's mind raced to points of reference. But everything she could think of, all that she knew of Jessamine, hearkened back, was history. It was Jessamine's way, to have emphasized history, not the future, the un-known. Perish the thought. But Jessamine was bowed by her dream.

"Jessamine!" Alice felt her voice cold as a slap, full of bright new vexation. She grabbed Jessamine's arm and pumped it. "Jessamine Batten, listen to me. It's Alice here. Listen."

Jessamine's eyes jimmied around to gain depth and curve, the keenness of present.

"I have a new friend. A man. When I was in the hospital he visited."

"A man?" Jessamine stared slowly around the room, then at Alice.

"A man from work. He brought me a plant. Well, two plants," Alice ended quickly. Her bandage was terribly itchy, ready to come off. She reached for her bun. In Jessamine's old pictures she wore her hair in long wraps around the head. At what age and why and with what reservations and glee did she cut off her hair? Alice wondered. (Right at first, would a person's neck feel helpfully longer? Would annoying thoughts flee the lighter head?) But she would not ask after the past. She helped Jessamine back to her chair.

"He's a man friend. Someone I talk with."

Jessamine dabbed her hankie to forehead and turned slightly amazed round eyes on Alice.

"He's an unmarried friend, Jessamine."

"A gentleman friend." Now Jessamine was straining for-ward, her hands clasped around that hankie. Frank wonder showed in the color returning to her cheeks. Alice could shout out a disclaimer now, with Jessamine back in the day, but she chose to fortify herself with the memory of Jessamine's sly triumphant look as she had mentioned Phil Donahue's show. It was all on TV, wasn't it? TV felled all the taboos. The Hazens and the Jessamines watching side by side permitted them to fall. Tragedy among families, misalliances, great dis-cords, disasters that developed and played themselves out week by week (transvestite fathers!) were digested by the most staid citizens in the land. Jessamine, a bona fide TV monitor of mores, should be sparing in her alarm.

"I don't know what to call him," Alice confessed, shaking her head.

The way Jessamine had taken to smoothing and smoothing her hankie over her lap, a person might think she was reading fortune in the wrinkled yellow cotton. "Who is he, Allie?"

"Melvin Gifford."

"Gifford," Jessamine tested. "No, I don't know any Giffords."

"I'm sorry, Jessamine. This isn't really the time for all the details. Which are few, of course. Don't think the wrong thing. This is not terribly important."

Resuscitation of Jessamine had been the point, and beyond that Alice had no further confidences to impart. She felt bushed suddenly, and brittle, like a young thing full of nonsense.

"For shame, Allie. If a man visits you in a hospital room he's very important and don't say otherwise. Did I ever tell you how I met Hazen? Through a third party he got himself invited into my room. I had received a fruit basket from California. Now, it seems that Hazen has always despised figs . . . "

Jessamine's voice faded. They sat in a heavy hospital silence. Now and then Jessamine would tilt her chin, then relax it downward. Alice thought the golfers might have fainted, as the TV murmur had grown so dim. And Jessamine conducted an innocent suspense of silence. She was abroad in the very recent past, the Hazen-past, which was also the present, thus safe, however sad. And was Jessamine wondering about Mel Gifford's looks? His income? His religious affiliation? (Alice was wondering if Mel's name really was Melvin.) And how was it that aqua tattersall could look exactly like a judge's robe?

Many commercials, the main concern of which seemed to be public kissing, flashed by with Alice wishing Jessamine would notice them, please be moved to break this silence. And when Jessamine finally cleared her throat, Alice felt her calves stiffen. She thought, Thank goodness Carla has left. Now Jessamine will grant or deny the permission to date. For heaven's sake!

"You're blushing," Jessamine noted. She folded and refolded the hankie. A glint of necklace caught the fever in her eyes, the endless green of James's.

"There's no shame in having a friend, Allie. You must enjoy him. We assume, of course, that James Lawrence will be agitated by our carryings-on."

Jessamine leaned toward Alice, who was feeling extreme carbonation in the head. The proffered hand felt boneless-soft and warm, the gesture of common ground acknowledged. "We're guilty of denying the truth. My dear, James Lawrence is not with us. I see you flinch. He's truly gone and we know it. We dishonor him by calling him up to lend a hand, as it were, to watch us, lead us. Of course James Lawrence shouldn't have rescued me from the consequences of the car accident. I was somewhat to blame, Allie. I distracted Hazen. And I need to tend to him. That's the good sense of the Lord. But we've made James Lawrence officiate long after his time."

The older woman wept a moment into her hankie. It fluttered to the floor as she stood. She might have been at the helm of a ship, sighting land or whales, the sheer enormity of discovery radiated from her look to a distant horizon. "Of course I've known this, but I've been willfully ignorant just the same." She paused. It seemed to Alice that a store of gem-quality revelations would spill from her aqua-encrusted mother-in-law.

Jessamine dabbed her eyes and removed her compact. "We would *not* have him rest. We were afraid to let go. I see myself in you. Thank you, Allie. Bless you." Jessamine powdered herself with tiny whisking motions, frowned, but quickly adjusted her look.

"Take me to Hazen, Allie. And do, please, smoke your cigarettes whenever your cigarettes want to be smoked. I've supposed all along that you smoked; it shows in your quick call to duty, and your walk." Jessamine reached for Allie's arm and proceeded out the door. They left a feebly clapping TV audience behind. She set a smart pace and might have been a volunteer exercising the hospital patient Alice.

"Allie, you can't imagine what it's like to shop with a man. We're like explorers in the supermarket; folks shopping in pairs are so energetic, too. I've felt supreme among them. At first I wondered if Hazen and I should keep company together at all times or how exactly we should shop. Should I ask Hazen's opinion on purchases, just to be kind? How much should he choose, considering his lack of expertise?"

They walked down the hall unaffected by the men in seer-sucker parting around them.

"I've felt young and capable," Jessamine continued. "Re-marriage is wonderful. Why, your whole life history becomes invigorated by the new man. He *sees* the adventure."

They would part at Hazen's door. Alice would collect Carla from the canteen and the two of them would take the bus home. Deborah had promised to come from Hillcrest to get Jessamine whenever she was ready.

Jessamine went to Hazen. For a moment Alice stood and listened to the low murmuring within the room. And what she wanted to blurt into the air was the news of Mel Gifford. He's big—watch your antiques! she'd tell Jessamine. I've seen him shopping, yes, she would want to mention; and she would make a story of color and surprise and premonition out of having seen Mel buying a woman's gown. He's modern, she would like Jessamine to know. At least as modern as Hazen, but *not* so modern as to belong on a talk show. Thank goodness.

Hazen slept, and whatever the charts and the tubes regis-tered, Jessamine knew they meant *normal*, no need to ask further. She moved to the chair near his headboard, an unfor-tunate blond headboard. She laid her hand on Hazen's fore-head and imparted recovery wishes, an impression of clear, strong love unrelated to her quantity of scrapbooks or Hazen's rescuing her by way of marriage, private dining or shopping.

"If you can't drive or do anything of the sort, I love you still, Hazen." There. She wasn't so sure she could have known this fact in all its precise generosity even a short while ago. She wasn't so sure that back when Reverend Lyton married them (and where *was* the minister, due here earlier in the day?) the prospect of infinite car-riding hadn't been the superseding glory. Now she felt as if Hazen had driven her to California and back.

Despite her high-souled resolve, an aroma of gentle helplessness swathed the air around Hazen, and Jessamine sniffed it through the dabbings and powders. She removed Hazen's tortoiseshell comb from her pocketbook and raked little furrows across his head, at a downward slant, bringing the hair a bit lower at one side as Hazen would wish it to be. He slept in the deep sleep to which only forthright avowals would reach and stir him.

"Deborah served us oatmeal this morning. Salty old porridge in summer! But it's a cooler day," she told Hazen. "The very early morning was dewy, and guess! All the hydrangeas are blooming. You know that ridiculous little ninety-year-old woman they've just let in? She insisted on the poisonous properties of canned fruit. She caused such a stir they gave her an orange from the pantry while the rest of us ate pineapple ring."

Somewhere deep in his heart Hazen chuckled broadly.

Jessamine would not lie down alongside Hazen the way you hear so many old folks (and the not-so-old on TV shows) attempt in a hospital bed. The risk to his poor hip. Not to mention that even a private room could not shield a nurse's entrance. Jessamine sat very close to Hazen, and a terrible fatigue rent her alertness.

The evidence of recovery lay in his hands, Hazen's dear Hazen-hands, palms up on the sheet, determined, busy hands even in sleep. They positively twitched once. These hands would signal his awakening, as they did each morning. These hands made Hazen Hazen, were that which had introduced him to her, and extended the world. "Where to, Jess?" his hands seemed to ask. "What next, Jessamine?" With his eyes closed, uncertainty sloped away and trampolined itself off the pillow, onto a breeze jetting out the window. Jessamine released a long clear breath.

She cradled Hazen's one palm in her two. Years ago, why, ages ago, though she dared to tell no one at the time—back in the days of minstreling and traveling Jewish photographers— the gypsies came, too, selling scrap metal and fortunes. Out back of the barn a gypsy girl, older than Jessamine, had read her palm. Her foreigner's large teeth had clicked as she deciphered; and her hair seemed a giant crow flashing light and dark all at once; and fever had seized them both. The palm revealed head and heart as clear smooth parallel lines. And a long lifeline, the Mount of Venus plain. "No crazy love," the girl had read. Jessamine let her steal away with a skirtful of fresh eggs. Then everything eventually came true. Love. Tears. Travel. Sickness. Death tatted her long white life.

She traced Hazen's palm, the puffed peachy unread skin, lined and quavered and frayed like old cord ends, vales and highways splotched. There was webbing at the thumb's base. Every inch meant something to the life lived. And in that palm Jessamine fell into eternity.

She held the palm, raised her head to look through the wall and tracked the Morrows' lives, and as she did she sang a little tune:

> *"Some men plow the open plain, some men sail the brine*
> *But I'm in love with a pretty maid, for work I have no time.*
> *My truly, truly fair; truly, truly fair; how I love my truly fair.*
> *I've songs to sing her, trinkets to bring her, flowers for her golden*
> * hair.*

"It's one of your old favorites, too, Hazen. Don't worry, dear. We're here together and I can feel this moment stretching on. We're snug as bugs in a rug. Nothing will disturb us. This moment is big enough for every sort of occurrence to whisk around the sides. I wonder if Reverend Lyton knows the feel of such a moment.

"Boxed cakes, Hazen. China slippers. Look at me, Hazen. I'm laughing. Wasn't I silly? Sometimes I was downright pesky with you. And what does it have to do with eternity and love, with this very moment? Not a whit, Hazen. I am Mrs. Hazen Batten," she said firmly. "Come home with me, Hazen. Break what you will. You'll come home."

The idea of home opened out as a stretch of glorious purple shrubbed highway running end to end in Jessamine's mind. "I'll say," she said, startled by and drawn to the immensity and color.

CHAPTER 20

Alice had fixed three cheese sandwiches, two for Mel, on good Italian bread lined with Murphy lettuce, and tomatoes that old Mrs. Vedaducci had come selling door to door, the remains of which sat between the lawn chairs. Her forehead was free of its bandage, itchy and enjoying a fine air massage, and thank goodness for the breeze vacuuming insects to another province. Mel had the better lawn chair, but he managed to evince constant tiny squeaks from it which Alice, with her eyes closed, knew had to do with uncertainty. Let the senses be launched skyward, be calmed, she prayed. Let the fussing nanniness of oak leaves preen and instruct and settle the day.

"I wouldn't mind a radio," Alice said, as she reviewed her reasons for caution: Mel had seen her cry and lying prone in a hospital ghoulishly headgeared. He had known her to chase thieves. He had kissed her. All transpired over a shockingly short period of time, in this summer without rain.

"Your back yard is great," he said. "It's a very spinachy back yard."

"That's a wonderful way of seeing it. I keep watering." Alice relaxed. The breeze back-combed the embankment grass up toward Calvin's, paused, then ruffled it silvery again. Her marigolds bordering the house had really outdone themselves: they resembled a dwarf citrus grove.

"But what's with that spot?" Mel pointed to a rank weed patch near the alley.

"Carla's tetherball pole used to stand there. The ground got impossibly hard with the kids playing. We let it go."

"Tetherball. I can see her playing tetherball." Mel slapped his thigh. "Now she's an expectant mother happily going home. And before you know it she'll be thinking of tetherball all over again."

Alice lit a cigarette, as she was pleased to do on her own turf. She had seen Carla off just that morning, and Mel had wasted no time in inviting himself over. "Let's hope she doesn't deliver some wild wooly creature. I'll pack civilizing thoughts when I go over to help her." She meant to sound reproving, but pride insisted a lilt into her voice.

"I can think of advantages to being raised on the land," Mel said, but hurried to add, "They may decide to move, though. You never know the future."

Alice exhaled noisily. She admitted that she did not know the future. She did not know next year's top Craftique hit, nor had she ever known it. And from this admission, a revelation visited upon her one evening as she stood in the center of her newly spacious living room and looked out through the fan blades to see Londo's cousin moving into the little house downhill, she determined that presumption was nonsense. Live well now, or some such thing, was the more sensible guide. She had performed her favorite (only) stretch exercise facing the window. Then she had turned on the radio and waltzed.

As for Carla's baby, who would neither know nor care, Alice would try one of these nonsense quit-smoking programs and try not to call it nonsense even if they advised, as such group schemes were wont to do cultishly, "Never be without a package of red licorice. *Only* the red can save you." Of course she would not tell Carla, and if Carla were ever to see her drooling red licorice, let her daughter draw her own conclusions. The future mattered and the damnable sidekick to that admission, suspicious fear, rallied to buck at her heart. Might the future be whisked from her now that she cared? Mel was rummaging around in a satchel and didn't hear her mutter, "Pooh."

"Here's your own Meadow-in-a-Can. I'm ready to go to work, Alice."

She managed one smooth motion, coming upright in her lawn chair, and took the large can from Mel. "What a surprise!" The container was papered with flowers, every kind of flower, it seemed. She shook the can and heard the rattle of Girl Scout mixed nuts which Carla had sold during the tetherball years. Her foot crunched an acorn, one of the many acorns that lay on the ground in late August, scouting fall. A long cicada chorus started up from high in Calvin's trees, and then another from behind added a staccato beat. A summer serenade filled the sky, a celebration in rhythms and pitch.

"It's opera," Alice said, sweeping her hand overhead. "It's joy and gossip."

"What starts them?" Mel wondered. "What determines the tempo?"

"Honestly, how can this be the result of their legs—or is it wings?—rubbing together?" Alice held the can and they listened. The music swelled and filled the sky with the invisible light of the voice, held on with the great light strength that *is* summer, she thought, then the song died as quickly and cleanly as it had begun.

Legs. Alice envisioned a cartoon-style choreography, string and bow, little violin legs working themselves into a dither.

"A person wants certain mysteries to remain mysteries," she said.

"I agree. Let's plant flowers."

Hi-diddly-dee, then. Mel set off across the yard in his nimble way. Moments later Alice heard the dim yawning sound of a car trunk being opened and shut. He reappeared swinging shovels. "Let's make over that weedy square you've got. Next year at this time Carla can show her baby the garden she inspired."

"Well, yes," Alice said, not sure whether she felt perturbed or pleased that Mel had thought of this. But, after all, he was the one who had come to surprise and entertain her. Now he was producing work gloves and little colored spikes, string and packets of miscellany. He lowered himself to one knee and began marking off a square of unyielding old tetherball ground. His elbows dimpled, and his back sloped in the way that begged a child to leap upon it. Alice could touch him right between the shoulder blades without even stooping.

Mel handed her a pair of blue work gloves. For Pete's sake, who did he suppose had planted the marigolds and lilies and all of this in the first place? Who anchored the flamingo and tied up morning-glory strings? She had her own work gloves hanging from a peg. With a snort, she put on these new blue gloves however, and took up a shovel. It struck shallowly and skimmed the ground, barely rattling pebbles.

"Clay," Mel said, examining a hard-won shovelful. "Pure clay."

"I'll get the hose."

Presently she stood watering. Mel sorted through his trinkets.

"That's ingenious packaging," Alice said, noting the colorful and clearly marked Ziploc bags of seeds.

"They're an East Coast outfit," Mel said.

After softening the ground, they set to turning it up: rocks, worms, hunks of moist clayey earth. Like Mel, Alice would dig and pause, extract a chunk and then use her shovel edge to mash and crumble dirt. Watered, this earth smelled of permanent dark underside, cool exhilaration.

"Look at this." Mel had uncovered a miniature bottle like those a person sees in thrift-shop windows.

"Well!" Alice dug all the harder, sensing treasures.

After a while Mel took a handkerchief from his pocket and wiped his face. "We sure picked a hot one. Say, I hope your mother-in-law will keep inside and take it easy."

Alice paused on her shovel. Poor Hazen. The talk was of transferring him to a nursing home, if he recovered to that extent. In any case, it was understood that Hazen Batten would not be returning to Hillcrest. "Not soon," Jessamine had added, speaking in a low even voice on the phone. The outing Alice had wanted with Hazen would never come about. She had pictured the two of them standing in a downtown skywalk, enclosed and climate-controlled, watching over the bombshell Kresge's block, votaries of a more dignified downtown, but humoring each other as the business people hustled by: Hazen exclaiming that all three majestic theaters were demolished likewise in the last decade; his arm in Alice's, a fedora on his head.

She resumed digging. She was losing someone dear with whom she had dared to make a plan. From very early on with James she had learned not to make plans. She was startled by the vividness of the plan she'd made, if mainly in her head, with a kindred spirit whom this stubborn earth before her recalled, and she dug harder for his sake, telling herself that planting wildflowers on Iowa soil was exactly what Hazen would approve. She could cherish Hazen and plant a garden all at once. The scope, the magnitude of her progress made her shovel feel heavy when she realized this. Her shoulders ached. She dared not stop, though the sound of the shovel saying *do*, *do*, *do* as it struck ground maddened her with its singsong insistence on what her life was now. A person was glad, but worn out too.

"These accidents are easier to take when you believe there's a sense, a pattern, to life," Mel said.

"God spies from the petunia bed, if that's what you mean. Yes, I'm convinced." She was sweating and her forehead itched.

"Well, yes!"

She turned and smiled at Mel, knowing now that his resemblance to Humpty-Dumpty grew in direct proportion to his discomfort and attraction. Out came the joviality, up went the eyebrows and the volume. He bent to a particularly stubborn clod of dirt.

Alice would never have chosen to dig a flower patch so close to the alley. She was used to more or less flinging down seeds in the fertile spots James had cultivated years ago. A mounding of dirt around a twiggy stalk soon enough yielded up a hollyhock stand. She had never considered purpose when planting, nor tribute. Somehow Mel had connected the wild-flowers with her family and future. He had contrived to gather Hazen, Carla, the unborn, and even James to the celebration.

"You're a character," Alice said. "You are quite a person, Mel."

Mel stabbed his shovel into the ground and whirled on her, those big arms uselessly free and his flattop shining. "I've been philosophizing at my beans all these years. What do I know? What do I know about us? Not any more than you do." They both gasped. "I could sure go for a glass of ice water, Alice."

"Water, of course." Alice hurried to the house for glasses, for ice and cool cloths, for an ocean if she could find one. In the bathroom she splashed and dunked herself with water. And she would certainly brush her teeth. She opened the tidy medicine chest and gathered her new supplies. She brushed on mascara to alarming spikiness, wondering only briefly how you removed it. She recoated her lips and kissed a tissue perfectly. It *was* a bright shade. She considered taking the pins out of her hair, but modesty and habit checked her. She tried to fan the loose curl across her forehead, though her bruise, thank goodness, was only a slight discoloration now and need not be camouflaged. Anyone might assume she had been bitten by triplet mosquitoes, nothing more.

Alice went into her bedroom and sat on the bed. Her heart was shooting and jerking down like a popgun. Water was the time-honored request of the soybean farmer. He had come into her house many weeks ago simply asking for water. The cool walls gleamed and Alice loved the spacious feel of these bare walls, the grain of wood and knots in the pine such perfect hieroglyphics. Having space inside the house was a wondrous new concept, a relief. She had no reason to move. Wakonda was her home. She thanked the mucky little thieves for confirming this.

Out the back window she watched Mel digging. One foot pushed on the shovel as if he powered some great machine. Then he did a few chops handsomely. Tweaking his pantlegs up, he squatted now and began crumbling handfuls of dirt. He would be finding treasure. He was framed in the window perfectly, digging. There was no doubt about it, Alice conceded: she was on a date. A first date that had commenced in her back yard. Mel paused. He clamped his neck and then, no! As he came to standing he reached a drumstick arm behind and plucked at, sort of readjusted, the seat of his pants and began scratching along the seam. A person did not want to see this!

Alice quit the scene, her face burning. A person would make such a gesture like that only in private, of course. Mel would not have wished to perturb her in this way, to embarrass them. For heaven's sake, he did what needed doing, Alice argued with herself. After all, her body often itched, too. She tried to reason: this is minor, usual, human. We *do* itch! She scratched her forehead to prove it. But, in fact, Mel was strange all over again. Suspect. And a little bit weaker for having scratched his bottom. She was reminded that, really, each "episode" she had with him remained discrete, only minimally contingent on the one before, as there had been so few. They could not really be said to be gathering togetherness by the pound or the bushel. The relationship defied mathematics. Each meeting was separated from the others by vast impossibilities of time and forgetfulness and habit. She admitted to enjoying and forgetting Mel in the space of a day. Fixing cheese sandwiches for a visitor had startled her into sprinkling on parsley and cutting the sandwiches with an exactness that practically annoyed her, the habit of aloneness ran so deep.

When she looked outside again Mel had resumed working. His back was wide and readable. She supposed that little rude transgressions on the sly were the extent of most people's devilment. Imperfection is beauty, so hee-haw loudly and wear checked pants, by all means.

She sat on the bed and felt the chenille spread, rough and agitating in her hand. In the dark-wood room, darkened further by trees that grew close to the house, a waiting stillness enlivened the room. She wondered what it would be like to find Mel coming through the doorway smiling. Imagination skipped to find him lying belly up in his one-piece attendant's suit on her bed. He was wearing socks but no shoes because a person never wears shoes on the bed. She closed her eyes. It was terribly intimate, imagining his removing those shoes. Alice lay down on her usual side of the bed. Did Mel sleep with one hand protecting his heart? Did he snore or talk in his sleep? In the morning his flattopped hair would not even be mussed. That was a nugget of assurance. Mel would always look exactly like Mel.

Her one hand was hot and itchy, with the spread bunched in it still. The other rested heavily on her stomach, a rare instance in which a cotton blouse was an irritating weight. She passed the hand lightly up onto her breast and allowed a lingering wondering pressure.

An encore scream of cicadas bolted her off the bed so fearfully she slipped on a throw rug and had to catch herself on the dresser. What if Mel had been spying on her just now? But out the window, thank heaven, he continued shoveling away like a miner.

Alice brought a jug of ice water and a wet cloth which she slapped to Mel's forehead with the diffidence of flinging down bread crumbs. He rolled back on his heels and she felt him watching as she chucked a giant clod of dirt onto the surface. She kicked it with her heel. She pounded at it with the side of the shovel, causing a gong sound. "Aha, a hidden rock. Idiot thing."

She worked the handle back and forth and finally kicked loose the rock. She jammed her foot on the shovel. A person would seem adamant standing like that. "Just because Carla is gone don't think I want visitors—people—in my house. I'm sorry, Mel." She looked as far away from her house as possible, straight ahead to Londo's little hideaway shanty, away from Mel's silence.

"We're ready to plant," he boomed suddenly.

They lunged over plasticene-encased seeds, smaller plasticene wrappers than Alice had ever seen used in a Craftique assemblage. Save the earth, she said. Plant it wild. Hard, shiny seeds would assuage the spirit disturbed by a person's sudden digging. She and Mel would work and work, wear themselves out today, say "Whew!" as a vague hopeful goodbye.

"We can arrange by color or height or whatever you want," Mel told her.

"I want these flowers wild, just wild. And I don't care what Carla thinks, I'm getting more yard statues. Cascades of spirea and statues. We'll have a cartoon jungle out here. Let everyone think I'm a kook." She waved her arms. "Strangers beware of the kook."

Mel chuckled and dropped a row of seeds on the dirt. He smoothed them into place. "Speaking of being a kook, Alice, I've really got my soybean-processing plans in mind. I'm determined to offer something everyone likes—cupcakes or ice cream—along with my tofu, plain and herbed. Fresh and local, that's the key. Around here they think soy is exotica or pig food. I'm going to change that. How does Heartland Variety Soy strike you for a name?"

"It strikes me dead, Mel. That sounds like horse medicine, gruesomely healthy." Patting the ground, Alice became aware that her legs, parallel calves showing from beneath rolled-up printed pants, were white foreign plumpness on the turned-up dirt, but extraordinarily game.

"You want pizzazz, because the idea of beans is so boring," she stressed. "Go for magic. . . . Manchuria Miracles. Yes, something alliterative, intriguing. You'll want a bright chatty label. Oh, what was that liquid soap Carla used to swear by? The label was nothing but quips and stories. Dr. Bronner's. She even brushed her teeth with it." Alice snorted, remembering. "Your label will tell stories of that expedition to China. Stress the matching meridians."

"You've got it." Mel knuckled his head, and Alice refused, consciously and verily refused, to think he resembled an ape in doing so.

She picked up the Meadow-in-a-Can container. "See all the flowers, how the color catches your eye? You'll want a lacquered Chinese-red label."

"This is right up your alley. You're great, Alice."

She was experiencing the thrill of a good workday; she was Craftique-enthralled by the notion of a product. It would not hurt Smith at all to insert an ad for Mel's frosting mix or whatever in with a future mailing. A nationwide demographic sampling, free! Alice reached for a cigarette. She could feel the cool surface of her desk, and suddenly even Gloria's latest complaint had marketing possibilities. Her fat thirteen-year-old had taken to screaming "Meat is murder!" at the dinner table, imitating a rock star. ("She'll only eat brownies. I add walnuts," Gloria confessed lamely.) And there you are. Alice exhaled mightily. Fads rule the world, and who was to say that tofu might not enrapture the teens. Presented right, Mel Gifford could become an idol.

Alice hooted. "Good grief, I suddenly remember Carla wearing her awful Earth Shoes. She looked like a duck."

Mel was looking at her peculiarly.

"Chinese red is exactly what you want," she said. Mel should blink now, look away.

Surely he meant to hug her in his fierce good-natured office way, but it came on as a tackle. Alice's one leg stayed turned back, the other, charley-horsed, sent the foot jerking straight ahead. Mel was all-embracing, supporting her back with his hands, kissing firmly. Alice kissed back, her eyes flecked with spotted sunlight coming down between the leaves, her lids fluttering against light. She was oblivious to the upswing in the Wakonda-trapped breeze that just then brought Londo and blond Sheila forward to close a "shed" window that faced Alice's back yard. And Calvin, in need of fanning himself after showering, stepped toward his bathroom window, glad for a breeze, and gaped frankly at what he recognized as hope for the future.

"Manchuria Miracles," Alice said, straightening. "Yes."

Mel followed her back to the lawn chairs, which is where having been kissed seemed to dictate a person go. If his motives were to coax her out of the life she'd known, surely he wouldn't go to the bother of helping plant a wildflower garden. But if not that, then was his design purely sexual? She sank into the lawn chair and closed her eyes. She listened to the old friends, leaf and beetle voice, and wondered: how would she and Mel ever *proceed?* That is, if, in fact, they did get to the point of proceeding. Surely forthrightness banished coyness at their age. They could not avail themselves of such nonsense as crying, "What, me? This?" There must be a way, too, to behave this side of somberness. For instance, neither party should take too terribly much time removing a wristwatch.

Silence, always the comfort here, held Alice's head in a vise. "Zebras and giraffes. A family of duck statues, why not?" she called through pain and closed eyes.

After a stretch of silence she fluttered her eyes open. Mel had not relaxed. He sat forward watching her and now began that scooting motion with the hands, along his thighs, now cupping the knees as if for fortitude and then it was top to bottom all over again, the laborious hoeing gesture.

"Let's go to my place," he blurted. "That's what I've been trying to say all along. You just wouldn't have known it." He flipped a hand along the top of his hair. Alice should know how simple it would be. But her cheeks hurt from being friendly even if it was heartfelt.

"I'm bushed," she said.

"But we sort of panic when we stop doing things, Alice. We're both busy people. Come out to the car. I've got something to show you."

The long white car was, as always, deliriously white and inclined as if to suggest levitational qualities. Oil price fluctuations and tight parking were of no concern to Mel and this car.

"You'll have to sit on the driver's side a minute."

Alice sat behind the steering wheel, touching nothing, her back pressed to the seat while Mel went around the car and took the passenger seat. The steering wheel had an alarmingly willful nature; it thrust out from the dashboard on a dare, inches from knocking out a person's wind.

"How does it feel, Alice?"

Attending a drive-in movie was the only reason on earth to sit in a parked car. But a memory of brown-bag popcorn— James at the wheel, Carla in pajamas—was not the answer, not the impression Mel was seeking.

"Supreme," she said, as the car person would wish her to.

"Let me give you a driving lesson. With power steering and brakes it's a dream to drive this car."

"Ha!" Alice told the wheel.

Mel slid across the seat so that one arm reached around Alice's back and the other worked the wheel left and right. "Sure, we can start you out on the dusty roads by my place. It's easy with no traffic around. I can tell you haven't tried driving in years. Something kept you from it."

"I've never driven, really."

"Why not?"

"I've gotten to every place I've ever wanted without driving. I've been to California."

"But really, why not drive?"

"I'm a nondriver."

"Come on."

As Mel pressed closer his voice drifted into her ear and Alice tingled sleepily. She pointed her foot to the pedal. The toes just reached.

"The seat's adjustable, of course," Mel said.

Putting both hands on the steering wheel did seem to tame it a bit. Alice held on until sweat slicked her hands to the wheel, and still she held on. Yes, getting the thing in a person's hands was an entirely different story. She affected a traveling motion by bouncing a moment. Mel switched on the radio to something blasty, with thumps. She looked out every conceivable window, including the rearview mirror, which showed her hair frizzy. Her lipstick was terribly bright, she thought, and the mascara enhanced her air of alertness. At the final Kresge's sale she had scooped up every kind of nonsense.

"I'll drive us out to my place," Mel said. "Then you can decide."

They sat in the car and continued to look through the windshield to the riveting drama of a brown garage door. They watched without speaking.

"If we go west," Alice said finally, "we could stop at my mother-in-law's just for a minute."

Flying to Jessamine in Mel's long white car, announcing Mel's large heartiness in the now isolate vacuum of Jessamine's rooms, was what Alice felt she could offer her mother-in-law. The boldness of a new voice, pure and simple.

Alice tested the pedal. "It's a mystery to me how a driver stays in the lane." Honestly, from the passenger side a car looked dangerously misaligned on the road. Bus-riding granted a person a reasonable side view from which you policed no one, not even your fears.

"It's easy to stay in the lane," Mel said. "You'll see."

CHAPTER 21

*T*he Greyhound travels only as far east as Cedar Rapids. To take the craggy route northeast on up to Tillman, you transfer onto an old coach and meander for hours. After Center Point Carla had the bus to herself, traveling past fields of corn and beans and, now and then, alfalfa. Under a masked sun the greens were flat, and out at the horizon smoky. Somewhere beyond, the Mississippi was slugging and roiling its way south; if she were outside she'd catch the slightest whiff of porousness in the air. Summer was the season of Iowa's heart, the only season to remark, she thought, when you considered the state's business: a historical prerogative to feed the land.

Iowa is the most agriculturally shorn state in the union; it boasts the least wilderness, and only the extreme northeast corner grows true forestland. This Carla learned eventually, but as a child she was taught simply to chant, "Iowa is the breadbasket of the nation," along with the rest of the fourth-grade class once Mrs. Wilson had pulled the USA map down to cover the chalkboard. Iowa was one of the green states. The golden ones, Texas and California, had intrigued her with their rough and splendid histories; and the pink states such as North Dakota and Maine were places you might never go to. Mrs. Wilson, suddenly officious with a yardstick, would tap green Iowa and remind the class, "We're the center of the country. The heart. The breadbasket of the nation." And Carla would envision a good woven basket, corners of checked cloth petaled over its rim, a dizzying aroma of fresh-baked bread rising from its depths. Little Red Riding Hood with her basket, Iowa was cheerful, forthright and well-meaning.

Mrs. Wilson had built food reverence into the day, filling

shelves and bulletin boards with the wonders of grain, and somehow she had even presented the phenomenon of bread-growing-mold in a petri dish as evidence of Iowa's might. And as if to further explicate the character of the state, attention to food industry eclipsed cultural and historical concerns: class trips were diverted to dairy and hatchery. And after everyone was back in the schoolroom removing name tags, in possession of a pint of chocolate milk, Mrs. Wilson would conclude, "We feed the nation."

Iowa was not a vacation state, Carla conceded, watching the fields roll by. Her entire class might well have grown up to eat the rusty outer leaves of lettuce and arrange their dried beans schematically in fine glass jars.

The bus passed one white farmhouse after another, each posing a wide-hipped question. Window shades at half and quarter mast fought off the sun and turned low-lidded amaze-ment on anything that moved. In front of one house a man in bib overalls and a boy were leading a horse across the yard. A tire swing hung from the big maple.

As they drew near a small town the gravel road turned briefly to pavement. The bus slowed. At a creep it went down Main Street, passing a bar built in the flat-roofed frontier style, a Ben Franklin store and the newspaper office. The bus driver honked his horn in front of the café, and several hands waved. Then they were passing a residential stretch of ranch homes whose back yards were endless fields, deep canyon-lands of food, and the grain elevator rose in the distance.

Next came Oelwein, where Carla strained out the window to see evidence of the Amish, maybe a buggy load, their heavy black sheen of cloth, tailcoats whipping like grackles against a hot sky. It was a sleepy town in which she remembered once drinking lemonade on a patio roofed by corrugated marine-blue plastic, at the home of "a buddy from the service" whom James had abruptly taken her to visit. She was nine years old. The buddy was at work, though, and his wife served them lemonade. When the buddy came home he and James roared ecstatic greetings and then said little; in no time Carla and her father were driving back home. It was one of those mysteries of childhood remembered by the slant of sun shafting through blue plastic, a wilted Band-Aid coming off the knee and nowhere to throw it.

The bus left Oelwein, whose main street was forgotten in a swelter of low bird-busy sky. There was a sting in the air out there which Carla sensed but couldn't feel, riding the bus. The sky had flattened and pressed the clouds down to pancakes; they billowed only slightly fuller as the bus drove on toward the Mississippi and its wider sky. The metal slapping of pig feeders, faint inside the bus, would be clanging loudly around one farm, but a shady picnic was spread under the front trees anyway, the people inured to the ever-present sounds and smells of livestock. Next came some miles of undulating smooth-mown hayfields, baled into big shredded wheats.

"So what about you and Brian?" Alice had insisted, right before the taxi arrived to take Carla to the bus depot. They were standing in the front yard, Carla's suitcase and an extra box of "baby things" at the curb. Alice had fussed at her as if Carla were a child, as if she, Alice, were becoming a Jessamine suddenly: the way she kept touching Carla's hair and cheek, the wondering look. ("Did you get your toothbrush? Vitamins? The big shirt in the hamper?")

And yet Carla felt certain that Alice wanted her to be on her way, that an undefined but hectic anticipation had seized her mother.

"Snap beans and hand-cranked ice cream await me," she had assured Alice. Brian had promised these, as well as a carpentry surprise. She might very well find a cradle in the living room. When she thought of Brian she wondered what the nights would be, whether hope and habit and resolve would sail her on through faintheartedness to be her best self, or if that little cradle would break them. She passed over the image of Brian—his trudging, perplexed, industrious self—to his native willingness to be Brian. Therein, she loved him. She had packed hurriedly. "We'll be fine," she had

assured Alice, knowing it to be true deeply, in some un-
tried sense. "Just promise to come up when I'm due." "Carrying a chamber pot," Alice had retorted; "I won't use an
outhouse."

Carla had kissed her mother, and in the hug grasped the
knowledge that Alice would soon, very soon, find herself in
the arms of Mel Gifford. But Alice didn't know it. She didn't
know that her hug had an extra umph, that the fingers questioning over Carla's back were really seeking explanation,
were testing romance-wonderment. *It's your turn*, Carla had
thought, feeling much older than Alice. But it was a mother's
braille too, a claim on the body she'd borne, those fingers; a
mother's never-ending awe and timidity that caressed her
back.

"You're going to whoop it up, Mother," she had crowed,
harsh as biker-Mary, holding back tears. "See if you don't."
"Piffle," Alice answered, though she was lipsticked for Broadway.

And so Carla rode, talking to the baby of its bus adventure.
Cows! Green grass! Mallards on the pond! She felt the way
Grandma Morrow might have felt honeymooning: faith put
to gigantic uncertainty charges questions to the wind.

The sunkissed land was jeweled, just dripping rich, but
every day you read how it was losing topsoil by the ton, that
the farmers were broke, the weather a curse. How could the
fields look so lustrous if they were as fragile as the newspaper
claimed? These full fields of corn sassed the doomsayers.
They were winning, whatever the battle or the bad news. She
believed the goldilocks fields were absolutely winning.

Jessamine had receded to untouchable mystery as Hazen
worsened; she even refused visitors. ("My dear, get home to
your family now.") On the phone she had sounded sharp and
breathy and thrilled, distant as if she were calling from another town, reporting on a sports spectacular, wildly busy.
She would not stand for sympathetic inquiry. "Why, of
course I'm eating breakfast, lunch and dinner, Carla, and I
should hope you are eating heartily. A baby is due in Febru-

ary!" But the waggishness in her voice was new, and fervent
when she repeated the story of going to the VA chapel:
"Every sort of denomination is represented there on a rota-
tional basis, you understand. I had missed Methodist Tues-
day and thought a Lutheran service would do, but oh, my!
The display board announced only 'The end of your search
for a loving church.' I told myself to expect Universalists,
after all, that I would make do. I was already seated and
couldn't leave when they came on. Notice I say *they*, my dear.
Negro men with horns—trumpets, what have you—at the
VA chapel. They walked up the aisle and arranged themselves as if they were on a stage, five in all. I lowered my gaze
and prayed in the most ordinary way. I missed Hazen
through and through. I tried to pretend this was only TV.
But they began playing the horns, and immediately my head
was tipped back. Then my heart twirled round. These men
had the open faces of children and I couldn't look away. I had
never fathomed such music—horns answering a question that
I wouldn't have known to ask. Deep loud music. I thought of
James Lawrence and his big-band interests way back, but no,
that wasn't right. It was something I couldn't describe in
terms of hymn or melody. A deep surrendering joy. An exuberance that brought the one fellow right down the aisle
pointing his trumpet left and right. He played a slide trom-
bone, now that I recall. Yes, the leader played a slide trom-
bone. *I tapped my foot!* When they finished, that man raised
his horn over his head and declared, 'You've been hearing
gospel.' Gospel. No collection was taken and I believed them.
There has never been anything so riveting and true spoken at
the First's."

First Methodist Church, Carla had scrambled to understand.

The bus stopped out in the middle of nowhere at Todd's
Service Station, which had BUS STOP taped in the window
above a pyramid of oilcans. A woman carrying a plaid suitcase
came outside. The driver called, "Take a break," as if to a

load of people. The new woman settled quickly in the front
seat, and Carla followed the driver off the bus.

The gas pumps were the old lollipop kind that people photograph. Ancient 7-Up signs were shields attached high on
the stucco facade. Stacked rubber tires looked blue-black and
sent a ripe perfume into the air. Carla stepped around oil spots
and entered the gas station hungry.

The smell of the years contained here made her cough. She
tried to hold her breath. She retrieved bottled grape pop from
a rickety cooler and she considered the nickel peanut machine,
its little chute all scaly with shed shells, but went on to the
old wall-style candy-bar dispenser. Through the glassed front
she viewed candy bars resting face up in little berths. She
turned the knob, commencing a slow irregular sort of elevator
ride for the candy bars that would let her see the full range of
choice. The Clark bar, two Paydays, Neccos and Bit-O-
Honey rolled up and out of sight. Milk Duds, Butterfinger, 3
Musketeers were followed by Chuckles—those hard gumdrop
squares she had forgotten existed. Baby Ruth, Mars, many
blank slots followed. Dots. Then she was back to the Clark
bar. She dropped a quarter in and the Clark bar slipped from
its berth. She went outside.

She faced a cornfield that crowded right up to the gas station's back work area, and drank her soda. With the chugging
bus throwing its gassy fumes in another direction, she smelled
fresh country air. Here and there, geisers of crickets sprang
up from broken concrete, from among tufts of grass. Corn-
stalks grew way over her head. She stood amid the snapping
liveliness, the buzzing and growing and feeding of things,
feeling how electric the field was, how edgy and powerful. A
wall of heat issued from this cornfield. It was common knowledge that if a child got lost in such a golden field, air surveil-
lance offered the only chance of finding him.

During junior high, years after the visit with James to Oelwein, school officials decreed that Amish schoolchildren must
board school buses like everyone else and attend public high
school. It was a crime, a sin, educators said—*news to them*—

that these children were yanked from class after eighth grade
to work the farms. Suddenly you were hearing about the
Amish every day, how zippers were too modern for them;
they used plow horses instead of machines; they didn't have
electricity; their cheddar cheese was especially good. And
they must conform. Reading of the Amish, Carla had felt
secure in her heather outfit from Arnold's, knowing she would
not work a farm. She'd pitied the Amish kids and read the
paper as if she were quite adult, amused at times, or bored.
"How can it be religion?" officials asked each other in print.
But then one day there it was, spread across the front page of
the *Des Moines Register*, civilization's madness, a picture of
utter terror: Amish schoolchildren ran open-armed into a
cornfield, into hiding, death, it didn't matter what. They
were little ready-made crucifixions. These were the faces of
threshed wild things, and a school bus was bearing down
upon them. Government men chased after them with bull-
horns, their hair short and angry. The public went nuts in
their shame. "Let them be! They're set apart for a reason!"
the cry went up.

Carla calculated the field's breadth before her, the children's immense despair. If she could have learned from the
intensity of the photograph way back she might have grasped
an idea of how to grow up, that life is an exception to the idea
of itself. A rigorous imagination is required to preserve a hu-
mane heart over and above death and law and all other injustices.

The Clark bar was absolutely stale, as you'd expect it to be,
the grape pop delicious, a fitting drink by which to look back
on the gas station that was so solitary, dwarfed by the cornfield and lacking the customers from its heyday. The little
side-road outpost could just as easily contain all the old Morrow ways, all those starched years, along with its peanuts and
tire jacks. 7-Up signs and all, its beige inactivity reminded
Carla of the family's tiny misguided long-lived bravery.

She touched her abdomen and went on thinking how the
Morrows had become wildly unstuck. They'd had enough

tumult for a lifetime compressed into scant weeks. And it wasn't going to end, was the thing. She thanked her lucky stars that this was summertime, with the day long enough to hold you fast against its sky-blue pinks, tame you down with its equatorial sunsets. You got a chance to look around. If you recognized the wounds and the wonders, you'd be on your way. Dr. Hollingsworth would say so.

And Carla thought they would do it, keep on now. The Morrows weren't of that hysterical TV-mongering bent of people to whom each event is Armageddon. None of them would ever brag, "My specialist said . . ." They didn't make up trauma or whip frenzy from a day's minutiae. But romance and its vagaries—who was used to that? They'd had no experience in roller-coaster living, and yet here they'd been rolling and coastering like fanatic pros, blooming and drenched in whatever came their way. For the first time ever, her mother and grandmother had hurried through their good-byes. Everyone was onto a radical new plan.

Carla was looking at her ankles, slim and smooth beneath her cropped pants, when the bus driver whistled. She nodded as he ground out a cigarette with his heel. His shirt matched the sky.

Facing the field again, she felt its wall of heat and thought of the strength of the spirit, the way it slams you topsy-turvy onto your knees and will not be denied. You'll find the evidence everywhere once you're looking around, she was positive. Her life had been going on without her, but now that the heart's old tight territories were found to be just a mirage, she was catching up. She believed she could balance atop a great sequined circus ball and juggle too. She could ride this bus and imagine a future:

Her mother would take a lover; her grandmother was bound to be widowed again; and she stood in this field, a future mother in the thick of August feeling how momentum blazes through static and lights all the lamps. It was shimmering off the corn. And to keep up and catch at it, what she had been given was impossibly good, a new double-beating heart.

She was going to present this world to someone. That's about the best you could do. Her little-self yearned to split into the field already, go bold as a comet to glimpse and brighten the land. Fine, she heard herself say. Yes, we're supposed to keep watch. Good baby, let's spin with the earth.